SWINDLE in Sawtooth VALLEY

The Maxwell Family Saga (3)

A Novel by
CARL R. BRUSH
NEW VERSION

BOOKSIDE Press

Copyright © 2023 by Carl R. Brush

ISBN: 978-1-998784-99-8 (Paperback)

All rights reserved. No part of this publication may be reproduced, distributed, or transmitted in any form or by any means, including photocopying, recording, or other electronic or mechanical methods, without the prior written permission of the publisher, except in the case brief quotations embodied in critical reviews and other noncommercial uses permitted by copyright law.

The views expressed in this book are solely those of the author and do not necessarily reflect the views of the publisher, and the publisher hereby disclaims any responsibility for them.

BookSide Press
877-741-8091
www.booksidepress.com
orders@booksidepress.com

DEDICATION

To my wife, Susanne, for her loving support in this and in all things

Table of Contents

DEDICATION iii
ACKNOWLEDGEMENTS ix
One. 1
Two. 5
Three. 8
Four 11
Five. 17
Six 20
Seven. 23
Eight 26
Nine 29
Ten. 32
Eleven 35
Twelve 39
Thirteen 42
Fourteen 45
Fifteen 50
Sixteen 54
Seventeen 57
Eighteen 60
Nineteen 63
Twenty. 66
Twenty-One 69
Twenty-Two 70
Twenty-Three 74
Twenty-Four 76
Twenty-Five 79
Twenty-Six. 82
Twenty-Seven 84
Twenty-Eight 86
Twenty-Nine. 88
Thirty 90
Thirty-One. 92
Thirty-Two. 93
Thirty-Three 95
Thirty-Four 96
Thirty-Five. 100

Thirty-Six	102
Thirty-Seven	105
Thirty-Eight	108
Thirty-Nine	109
Forty	112
Forty-One	113
Forty-Two	115
Forty-Three	118
Forty-Three	120
Forty-Four	123
Forty-Five	127
Forty-Six	129
Forty-Seven	134
Forty-Eight	136
Forty-Nine	138
Fifty	141
Fifty-One	144
Fifty-Two	146
Fifty-Three	149
Fifty-Four	154
Fifty-Five	157
Fifty-Six	160
Fifty-Seven	162
Fifty-Eight	165
Fifty-Nine	167
Sixty	170
Sixty-One	173
Sixty-Two	177
Sixty-Three	180
Sixty-Four	187
Sixty-Five	189
Sixty-Six	192
Sixty-Seven	196
Sixty-Eight	199
Sixty-Nine	202
Seventy	205
Seventy-One	208
Seventy-Two	211
Seventy-Three	215
Seventy-Four	218

Seventy-Five	220
Seventy-Six	222
Seventy-Seven	224
Seventy-Eight	226
Seventy-Nine	230
Eighty	233
Eighty-One	237
Eighty-Two	241
Eighty-Three	245
Eighty-Four	248
Eighty-Five	250
Eighty-Six	252
Eighty-Seven	254
Eighty-Eight	260
Eighty-Nine	262
Ninety	266
Ninety-One	268
Ninety-Two	271
Ninety-Three	276
Ninety-Four	280
Ninety-Five	284
Ninety-Six	286
About The Author	292
Historical Figures In Swindle In Sawtooth Valley	293

ACKNOWLEDGEMENTS

Les Edgerton, Noir Master, Mentor, and friend, whose staunch backing and artistic nourishment has had as much to do with my novels as their author.

Dan Barth, for your general inspiration and for your the *Day After Hank Williams' Birthday*.

For the many teachers who helped foster my love for history and literature.

For my parents, who made sure I had plenty of exposure to outdoor life in Northern California and taught me how to make the most of it.

One

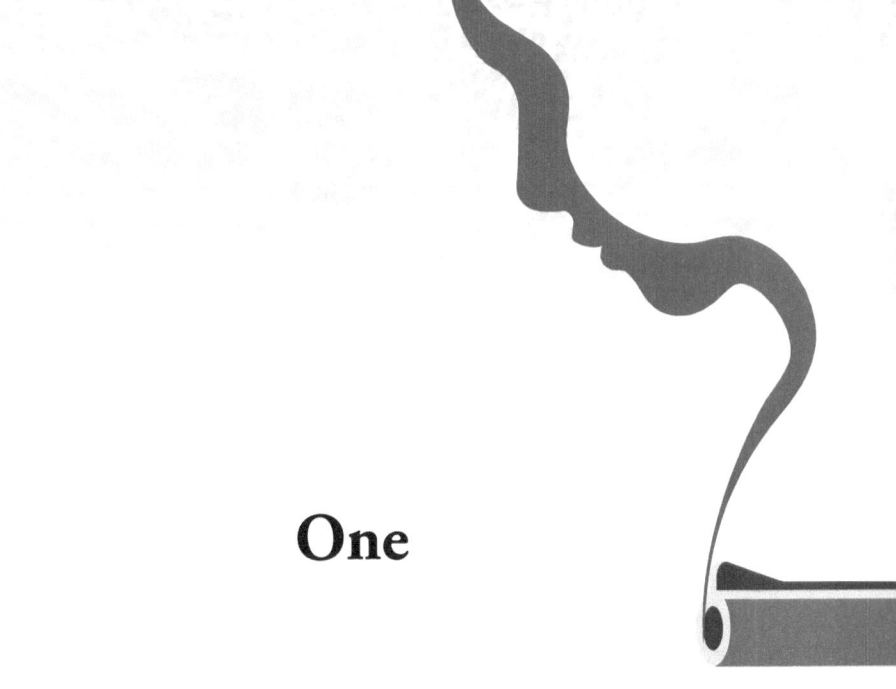

Theresa Many Clouds allowed herself to awake gradually. It was a luxury to which she'd become accustomed over the last few months. Quite a departure, she thought, from the crisis-filled existence she'd lived for the three years since she'd left the Wind River reservation in Wyoming. She slipped out of bed, leaving Andy to his rest. "Andy" being Andrew Maxwell, heir-apparent to the largest ranch for many miles around and her devoted lover. A rarity for him to slumber past dawn. A glance out the bedroom window, though, told her it wasn't really quite dawn. What had awakened her? Ah, yes.

It was Maggie's birthday. Her twelfth. A pulse of joy and, yes, pride thrilled through her. Another reminder that the delights and pleasures of present-day 1912 had replaced the horrors of the previous couple of years.

A person would search in vain for birth certificates or any other paperwork to prove she was Maggie's mother, or the mother of Maggie's younger brother, ten-year-old Willy. Their biological parents lay in solemn graves downslope from the house under an apple tree planted in their honor. No paperwork existed to acknowledge that parentage either. Their mother was a Shoshone woman named Swallow, felled by cholera years before. Their father was a white man, Miller Fitzpatrick, killed by Many Clouds' murdering uncle two years before. Though no one could truly fill that void, Many Clouds had taken on the role of mother in every imaginable sense over the last couple of years, a time filled with a volume of events that would overwhelm most any other two years of anyone's life.

Nausea washed through her, bile rising in her throat. She hurried out the front door and down the front steps just in time. Here she was in her nightgown, vomiting on the bare ground. Part of the house's new construction included, of all things, a flush toilet. But it would be loud, and she feared the noise she'd make getting to it and gagging as she'd just done. She scraped loose earth over the mess with a fallen stick. Like a dog covering its leavings, she thought. This was the third time in a week. If what she hoped came true, Maggie and Willy would before long have a sibling. It was the lot of all Indian females to assist at births from an early age, so she knew these were early signs and that the results were often disappointing. But the hope and joy she felt were as natural as pregnancy itself, and the thought of holding a smiling baby overwhelmed all other feelings.

The house, the family, would embrace not only Andy, herself, twelve-year-old Maggie and ten-year-old Willy, but an infant as well. The place would be crowded, but she knew the children well enough now to know they'd be overjoyed, not jealous, as she'd once feared they might be if her relationship with Andy progressed to this point. Still, she wasn't ready to share her suspicion with anyone yet. No sense in getting everyone's hopes up. She'd give it another while. These unexpected bouts of nausea might make it difficult to hide, though.

She hurried back inside to exchange her nightgown for a shift. It was chilly in the Northern California foothills as October waned, and the nippy air made her shiver a bit as she changed clothes. The chill, though, was a small price to pay for the luxury of having separate garments for sleeping and waking. She padded softly in moccasined feet from the bedroom through the parlor and back out the front door, across the narrow veranda that flanked the house on three sides. She counted it amazing that she and Andy and the children had agreed on so much as they remodeled and expanded the little cabin the children's father had constructed during their early childhood. The process and the result seemed emblematic of the harmonious life they were building together. They'd left the rudimentary pine walls of the original, kept the same look as they constructed four new rooms and a kitchen, and cut in several windows. The only conflict was over Andy's wish to paint the trim around the new windows. They'd finally compromised by trimming in white the windows that faced the road and leaving the others to weather in whatever manner nature decreed.

Many Clouds headed toward the shed that housed the family's two cows and their four horses—a mount each for Andy and Many Clouds and a wagon team for trips to town. It was past time to get Willy and Maggie horses of their own. She and Andy planned a trip to town to have Maggie pick out

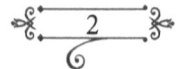

one for herself as a birthday gift. She scooped oats into the horses' manger, then grabbed a bucket and a stool and sat down to the milking.

It was comforting to lean against the Holstein's warm flank, surrounded by the pastel aroma of fresh hay and the darker smell of Swallow's hide. Even the rich odors of animal waste had their own appeal.

Many Clouds watched the milk bubble into the pail, its level rising with each jet. She loved the rich fragrance that rose from the white liquid, which was nearly viscous with cream. Maggie called this black and white cow Swallow, after the children's mother. The apple tree they'd planted in honor of Swallow and their father, Miller Fitzpatrick, was but a sapling, still too young to bear fruit, but it was nevertheless sacred to the children as well as to her and Andy.

Once she had finished with Swallow, Many Clouds carried the stool and an empty pail to Miller. As she worked on Miller, she heard a jingle of chains and creaking of planks that announced the approach of a wagon. Andy and Many Clouds' property bordered the road into Placerville and Sacramento beyond. Traffic from horses, wagons, and even the occasional automobile had increased in recent months as towns like Grass Valley and Nevada City to the north and east gained population.

She added the last few ounces of milk to Miller's pail and carried it outside the shed, preparatory to lugging it into the house. A wagon rounded the bend and came into view. It was not a freighter, but a buckboard, and except for the driver, it was empty. That was unusual, since the burgeoning communities had a great appetite for everything from foodstuff to construction equipment, and most of the passing wagons were overloaded.

The wagon's driver was dressed formally for a teamster. He wore Van Dyke whiskers, a black swallowtail coat, a bowler hat, and sported a blue and gold paisley cravat at his throat. His black and polished boots buckled just below his knees. He pulled over to the side of the road across from the house and stopped. He climbed down from the wagon seat and began inspecting the vehicle as if checking for some malfunction. He made Many Clouds uncomfortable even though he was not overtly hostile.

Andy appeared on the porch. "Good morning, my sweet," he said as he descended the steps and approached her. "Rising before the sun. You must be very nervous about this birthday." He opened his arms, and she stepped into them to receive the promised embrace.

"I want the cake to be absolutely perfect, Andy."

"And it is. They are, that is. Both of them."

Many Clouds had decided on a pastry feast. One cake for herself, Andy, and the children for breakfast, another for the larger family once Andy's mother and the family servant and friend, Ling Chu, arrived later in the day. "Didn't we prove it with yesterday's taste test?"

"But not the icing. I need to whip this cream. So, will you turn out the animals while I get into the kitchen?"

The kitchen. Many Clouds had lived so long cooking over open fires and heated rocks and the like that the idea of a kitchen as its own separate room was still strange to her, as was the notion of her own stove with its own oven. But she'd spent a few days at the Circle M ranch, Andy's ancestral home, a day's ride south and east through Placerville and the smaller community of Sawtooth Wells beyond. There, the family factotum, Ling Chu, had provided expert instruction, and Many Clouds had managed to translate that teaching into the fluffy concoction that rested on the pantry shelf. Pantry. Another strange notion.

Andy smiled and tightened his embrace. "You're liable to turn into a regular housewife before long."

"There's not much danger of that, my love. Not as long as I have to run to Ling Chu every time I bump up against a problem any respectable white girl was trained to solve from the cradle."

He stroked her hair. "Enough of that. I wouldn't trade your dark eyes and cheeks for the bluest, pinkest ones in Christendom."

She pushed away from him, smiling. She nodded toward the wagon. "That man makes me nervous."

"I'll get rid of him, but it will cost you a kiss."

She laughed. "More later. Away with you now. The children will be awake any minute."

"Here. Let me help with the pails."

"No. No. It is my chore. We agreed."

"You agreed. I gave in."

Many Clouds lifted both pails and headed out the door toward the little house. How long would it be okay for her to carry such a load? "Look to the cows, Andy. That is your chore." With a full bucket in each hand, she felt balanced and secure. Maggie's voice called to her from inside.

"I'm on my way, birthday girl," she called. "Please put some kindling in the stove."

Two

Andy whistled softly to himself as he led the cows out the shed door into the pasture. Whistling was a new habit for him, bubbling up, he supposed, from the happiness he felt since he and Many Clouds had joined their lives.

The grass in the little hillside field was all but gone this late in the year, so he forked some hay from the loft out into the field. The cows produced much more milk than their family could use each day, and neighbors would come by and take a share as they needed or wanted it. Many had warned Andy that it was a dangerous precedent to allow trespassers to wander in and out of his property at will. But he and Many Clouds had decided that the benefits of charity outweighed the risk of theft or lawsuits.

Both for privacy and security, Andy would have liked to move their residence farther back from the byway, but disturbing the graves of the children's parents was out of the question. He thought it possible to reroute the highway, and the Maxwell family had both the money and the influence to initiate the project, even though it was a major thoroughfare over land owned by the State of California. It would be a long process, however. The logical right of way was downhill toward the south, but that presented engineering difficulties and would require purchasing land from Southern Pacific, a corporation unwilling to surrender its holdings easily. The asking price proved exorbitant.

"I'll buy the land, Andy," his mother had said. "I want happiness for you and the children and Many Clouds. But I won't be robbed." So the whole idea was at stalemate for the time being.

Andy finished tossing hay to the cows and looked downslope toward the wagon, expecting that the rig would have traveled on by this time. But the driver had remounted and sat on the bench seat, leaning against the back with one leg cocked at a jaunty angle. He showed no inclination to put his team in motion. Andy waved at him, and to his surprise the man at the reins beckoned to him toward the gate.

"Hello, stranger," Andy said as he walked toward the road. "What can I do for you?"

"You that Maxwell fella?" The man spoke as if he had a permanent frog in his throat.

"Depends," Andy said.

"You're him, all right," the man said. "And this here belongs to you." He reached into his inside breast pocket, pulled out a thick brown envelope, and thrust it toward Andy.

Andy's family owned thousands of acres and had been involved in many land disputes. Plus, he had made a successful run for the state legislature, only to be denied his seat by a court injunction based on the fact that he was part Negro. He knew a process server when he encountered one.

He stepped back, raised his hands, and said, "Sorry, friend, but I'm not going to touch that. We have a lawyer in Placerville name of Barker. Everything legal goes to him and gets dealt with in its own time. I'd appreciate it if you'd just move along."

"Funny you should mention time, Maxwell. That's something I have plenty of." He pulled a cushion from under the seat and settled back, cocked his leg in what he obviously assumed to be a superior posture. "You got to come out of there some time. You and your squaw and your 'breed kids that ain't even yours or hers either one."

Andy bristled at the slur but checked himself. A confrontation at this point would set a bad example for the children and make Maggie's birthday memorable in a most regrettable way. He adopted as even a tone as he could.

"Well, now, I imagine you have a trove of such eloquent and original insults to offer, but I'm short on time so I'll bid you farewell. Perhaps we'll meet again on the front page."

After the brouhaha over his political appointment had died down, Andy had become a journalist, campaigning in print against racial injustice wherever he found it. He had the luxury of not needing to support himself with his journalistic efforts, so he placed his articles wherever he could, regardless of remuneration. In the process, his byline had become widely recognizable, if not prominent. He thought maybe this little confrontation had the promise of a marketable series, the dissemination of which might also provide a bit of a shield against clandestine retribution if the whole thing turned into an anti-Maxwell crusade.

The dandified teamster simply snickered, pulled out a book—Twain's *Innocents Abroad*, Andy was surprised to note—and made himself even more comfortable on the wide wagon seat. Andy decided to let the guy sit there, hoping he'd get tired and leave. He was undoubtedly working for someone with an imagined complaint against the Maxwells. Andy's mother, Carolyn Maxwell, and Ling Chu were scheduled to arrive in the afternoon for the birthday festivities. Perhaps their presence would be intimidating enough to send him packing.

He left the man to his own devices and headed back up to the house and to the little family celebration they'd planned before his mother arrived. Even with his back turned, though, Andy felt the shadow of the man's presence.

Three

Carolyn Maxwell took her time with her toilette. The Cary House was the only hotel in Placerville with en-suite facilities, including dressing tables complete with mirrors and electric lamps. She intended to take full advantage of all amenities considering that she was paying an exorbitant ten dollars a night. The price would be even higher had Ling Chu not insisted that he would be more comfortable staying in a boarding house in the small city's Chinatown at a dollar per night. The man had shared every travail, public and private, that had befallen the Maxwells for decades now. He had prepared virtually every meal, nursed both Carolyn and Andrew back to health after life-threatening injuries, and stood by the graveside for the burials of Andrew's natural father, the black man who had been the Circle M's foreman as well as Carolyn's lover. He'd been at the center of the conflict with Many Clouds' murderous uncle, Yellow Squirrel. He'd introduced the Maxwells to the glories of the industrial age by ferrying his beloved Model T Ford on its journey from Sacramento to the Circle M. In short, he was as much a part of the family as anyone in the universe. Still, he kept a measure of privacy and separation which had to be honored. At least he had allowed Carolyn to pay for his boarding house fees.

She managed at last to corral a fugitive curl and pin it to her chignon, trying to ignore the strands of gray sneaking into her dark tresses. The bun was not a tightly gathered schoolmarm affair, but a loose collection of braids and twists that she hoped gave the effect of casual elegance. Many Clouds had yet to venture into the world of adult coiffure, and Carolyn had no wish to upstage her. Nor did she wish to lower her standards too far. She could ride and shoot as well as any ranch hand, but when it came to celebrations, she insisted on a modicum of formality. She gave her coif a final pat and strolled to the window. It was a Saturday, and the streets were full of folks. Some busy, loaded with packages. Some sitting, loafing, spitting tobacco juice. Off in a nearby alley slept two Indians, no doubt anesthetized with alcohol.

The man in the paisley cravat leaning against the wall outside the milliners with one knee bent in a manner that projected a rather cavalier air looked a bit familiar, but, no, she didn't know him after all. In fact, she saw no one she knew. It was a bit disconcerting. Time was she'd have been able to pick out the faces of at least a dozen acquaintances in such a crowd. It was a measure of the increased population and her own tendency to isolate herself on the Circle M. She reflected that it was not a good idea for her to remain unfamiliar to the populace when so much depended on her reputation and visibility. Her father had been a natural politician, gaining energy from working crowds. She herself had been no slouch as a social butterfly, but the inclination had waned in recent years, and she had no impulse to become more outgoing.

She noted the variety of garb represented among many people jostling through the streets. What would Andrew wear today? He knew how to dress. He had moved among some elevated company during his brief political life. Governor Hiram Johnson had groomed him as a protégé in his run for the state assembly, then abandoned him when the news of his Negro father had evoked a court challenge against his taking the assembly seat he had won by a sizeable majority. She sighed and closed her eyes to remember Andrew's father, her beloved Shelby. She had no regrets about her clandestine affair with the Circle M foreman, but it pained her to know how much anguish it had caused her elder son.

Now, however, she supposed he would dress down to the level of his Arapaho mate. Mate, not wife. Still a sore spot for her, though she was in no position to lecture. She admonished herself for thinking in terms of high and low society. Since Andrew had begun his journalism crusade on behalf of a more egalitarian world, she had tried to adjust her thinking. But she was still a moneyed landowner, raised by a father with powerful connections, and neither her attitudes nor her circumstances would vanish automatically. Nor did she want them to. Gloomy thoughts for a joyous day. Let the sun shine. Her heart warmed to think of her brown grandchildren. Maggie, twelve years old, old enough to wear the dress she'd brought as a gift. She didn't want to suggest she quit wearing her customary deer-hide skirt and leggings, but if she was going to advance her station, to straddle two worlds—white and native—she needed to be able to wear more customary garb.

AHOOOGAW. AHOOOGAW.

She started at the sound of Ling Chu's New Model T Horn. He brought the vehicle to a dusty stop in front of the hotel. Several dozen pairs of eyes zeroed in on him. She giggled. He would probably bring the local militia down on their heads. She swooped her reticule from the bed and headed out.

Four

Maggie blew out every one of her twelve candles with plenty of breath left over. How uncomfortable she felt in her pink linen dress, with its broad ribbon belt and a bow in her hair to match. At least Carolyn had the good sense to let her keep her moccasins instead of insisting on something as frightening as Mary Janes.

"What was your wish, Maggie?" Willy asked.

"If I tell, it won't come true, silly boy," she smiled and wagged her finger at him.

"Well, you can at least tell me if I was part of it."

"Cannot. It has to be a secret, doesn't it, Andy?"

"That's what I was always told," Andy said. He stepped to the front window and moved the curtain aside. The wagon was gone. He didn't know if that was good or not. "Come now, Maggie. You can open one gift before grandma Carolyn arrives. Which one is it going to be?"

Maggie studied the three packages on the table.

"Hurry up, Maggie, or I'm going to take mine back," Willy said.

"Can't, silly. It's mine now."

"Not till you open it."

"You and your rules. Okay."

Maggie picked up the small soft package wrapped in tissue paper and bound with green yarn.

"You can tell it's from me 'cause green's my favorite color." Willy's voice was as excited as the grin on his face.

"Oh, really?" Maggie said. "I never would have known."

"Yes, you would—oh, you're kidding, aren't you, Maggie? Hurry and open it."

"Okay. Okay." A bundle of gaily colored ribbons spilled out on the table. Maggie caught her breath and brought a hand to her chest. "Willy?"

"I knew you would like a hair ribbon, but I just couldn't decide on a color so Many Clouds let me buy one for every day of the week. Of course, I know there are seven days in the week, but they only had four colors, so you have to wear the same color twice sometimes. Do you like them?"

"I've never had a gift more precious, Willy. Thank you." She hugged him and gave him a generous kiss on the cheek, which he wiped off, but not very hard. And he never stopped smiling. "Which one would you like me to wear first?"

"The green one, naturally."

Many Clouds helped Maggie gather her dark tresses, and they left Carolyn's bow in place, managing to arrange the bow of the green ribbon a few inches away from the pink one. It looked a bit unconventional but quite pretty. Everyone applauded and Maggie curtsied.

They each had a generous slice of the cake. As they were finishing up, Andy took one more look out of the curtains. A two-wheeled buggy zipped by, but the big wagon had not returned.

"Come outside everyone," Andy said. "Many Clouds and I have something to tell you."

They gathered under the apple tree next to graves of the children's parents.

"Join hands," Many Clouds said. "Andy and I need your help with an important decision, and we thought that Maggie's birthday would be a perfect time to ask you about it."

The children looked at one another then at the ground. Their feet shuffled. Andy noted the trepidation and hurried to alleviate it.

"Don't be scared. This is not bad news even though it's important. Many Clouds?"

"No, you, Andy."

"Okay. Many Clouds and I have decided we want to get married and—"

Many Clouds interrupted. "We would have done it a long time ago, but we didn't know what you'd think since we didn't want to dishonor your parents and you are more important than anything else to us and so we have waited until we thought maybe…" Her voice trailed off and her glance skipped from one child to the other.

"So how do you feel about the idea?" Andy said.

Maggie looked at Willy, who nodded.

"About time," Maggie said. "This is the very best birthday I've ever had." They shared another round of hugs.

"There is one more thing," Many Clouds said.

"More than that?" Willy said.

"You don't have to decide about this now," Andy said.

"About what?" Maggie said. "Why are you torturing us on my birthday?"

Many Clouds and Andy began talking together at once. Finally, Many Clouds took over.

"If you want, after we are married, we could adopt you."

"You would legally be our children," Andy said. He knew it wouldn't quite be true since the law wouldn't recognize his and Many Clouds' marriage, but they could still formalize the union in some way even if it wouldn't be legally so.

Many Clouds went on. "Of course, Swallow and Miller would still be your real mother and father too, but we… we would…"

Maggie and Willy cast confused glances at one another.

AHOOOGAW. AHOOOGAW.

Ling Chu's horn announced Carolyn Maxwell's arrival.

"Never mind," Andy said. "It's time for the party. But come close now." He motioned the children and Many Clouds into a huddle. "Can you keep a secret?" Maggie and Willy nodded and smiled. "Don't say anything about us getting married. We want to make the announcement ourselves. Okay?"

"Okay," Willy yelled. Andy put a finger to his lips. "Okay," Willy whispered.

"That's more like it," Andy said.

Ling Chu brought the automobile to a stop at the front gate, and the children rushed toward it, Many Clouds and Andy close behind. It was a splendid-looking machine, complete with plush front and back seats, brass-trimmed headlights and radiator.

Ling Chu assisted Carolyn as she climbed down, slapping small clouds from her duster coat.

"Brand new," Andy said to Ling Chu as they watched the children and women exchange greetings and hugs. "Did the old one break down?"

"No, no. But Miss Carolyn says this one much more pretty. I did not object."

Andy laughed. "I'm sure not." The children and Many Clouds rushed to Ling Chu while Andy stepped forward to greet his mother.

"Oh, Andy, aren't they precious? All three of them."

"No argument from me on that score, Mother. How are you?" he said as they stepped toward the house.

"Very fine, I'm glad to say. It does my heart good to see you so happy."

"And the Circle M? I worry about you trying to run it all alone."

"You could help with that if you'd come home." She held up her hand. "No. Pretend I didn't say that. I promised myself I wouldn't bring it up today."

Andy said, "Never mind. Many Clouds and I have some news that will take your mind off that entirely."

She stopped. "Andy, you don't mean —"

"No, no, no. Not that." He smiled. "But I guarantee it will warm your heart."

"Well get a move-on, then." She pulled him toward the house. "Double time, soldier."

* * *

Andy and Many Clouds made their announcement. They had planned to defer conversation about specifics till later. They hadn't decided on a wedding date but had speculated that sometime in mid-January might be auspicious. That was before Many Clouds had suspected her condition. Now, she thought, January might be cutting things a bit close, though she couldn't be sure. She thought the baby would not arrive till March or April, but how she might look in January bothered her. Willy's birthday, his eleventh, would come on the tenth. It would be fitting to start their new lives along with the new year. But Andy's mother intervened as usual and had insisted that it was Thanksgiving or bust. This time Many Clouds was in agreement. Only a little more than a month away. It was not only a time for unity and gratitude but also, according to Andy's cultural tradition, the day that the pilgrims and Indians had gotten together to create America.

Andy stood and pointed his finger at Carolyn. "Mother, that whole idea is a lie and an insult to me and to Many Clouds and to—"

"Thanksgiving sounds just fine," Many Clouds said. If she was truly pregnant, the sooner the better. She tugged on Andy's coat to sit him down.

"We'll have the ceremony at the Circle M, of course, and, oh, there's such a lot to do. The guest list. The decorations. The menu. Oh, and listen to me go on and I haven't even asked you two what sort of celebration you would like."

"Maggie," Andy said. "Ling Chu hasn't seen our new stables. Could you and Willy show him, please?"

The children out of the way, Andy took his mother's hands. "Mother, we were thinking of a small private ceremony. We've found a pastor who is willing to officiate. Surely you see the problem with such an extravaganza. Many Clouds and I can't be legally married in this or any other state. The whole thing will have to be strictly *ex officio*. We could be arrested for even trying this."

"No one is more aware of the miscegenation laws than I, Andy. That's perhaps the main reason your father and I hid our relationship from the world. Poor Shelby. How he fought the whole idea of our getting together, but in the end, we were both too much in love to deny what was happening between us."

"If you understand so well, why are you proposing this huge party?"

"We talked a lot, Shelby and I, about how to observe our relationship without running up against the law. We never got to it, but we thought the secret was to have a celebration within a celebration. We can advertise this event as a sort of coming out party. We could announce it as a reemergence of the Maxwells from two years of tribulations and seclusion. As a part of the event itself, we can set up a special table appropriately decorated. It will be a sort of silent tribute to you four as a family. The whole thing will be obvious without any announcement."

"Well?" she said after a pause. "What do you think?"

Many Clouds drew a breath. Andy cupped her cheeks in his hands and kissed her forehead.

Many Clouds said, "Pastor Selkirk could still perform a small ceremony away from the crowd," she said.

"Perhaps right here." Andy gestured toward the fireplace at the end of the room.

"Yes," Many Clouds said.

Though she and Andy had had many discussions about keeping the arrangements simple, Many Clouds privately anticipated that her future mother-in-law would be unable to contain herself. She was perhaps incapable of even trying. The Maxwells had once been a political and financial powerhouse in California politics, but two years of fighting a vendetta aimed at obliterating the family had depleted their energy, resources, and influence. Even amid the legal tangles surrounding the matrimony, Many Clouds knew Carolyn would see the wedding festivities as a way to begin reestablishing Maxwell prominence. The whole idea frightened her not just because of threats to their valued privacy but to their very safety. There were plenty of people who would see Andy and her not just as scofflaws but as apostates who deserved no less than bullets and torches. Even on the large Circle M, they would have been vulnerable. Here in their smaller home next to a public byway, they were dangerously exposed to attack.

***

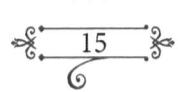

It was deep twilight, and the farewell hugs and kisses were in progress. Maggie's birthday party had not been forgotten even given the excitement of the pending nuptials.

"Married!" Carolyn exclaimed for the hundredth time. "What a wedding we're going to have, Many Clouds. We'll have to confer very soon. I won't do anything without your approval, but I will need your ideas."

Many Clouds smiled and kissed Carolyn's cheek. "Thank you," she said.

Carolyn said, "I'll do what I can to keep things corralled, but it won't be easy." She bent over to hug first Willy, then Maggie. "Such a big girl. I don't think even your new daddy—er, Andy—was this big at your age."

"Thank you for the wonderful gifts," Maggie said. "The dress, and just everything."

"I know you don't wear dresses as a rule. But now that you have an occasion… And don't forget that pony is waiting at the Circle M any time you want to come meet her. She needs a name." She turned to Many Clouds. "I'm sure you'll bring her soon."

Andy smiled and nodded. Carolyn had upstaged their own plans to present Maggie with a horse, but there was no way to object. They could have cared for the pony right here, of course, but it was typical of Carolyn to give such a generous present, then attach conditions that would satisfy her own desires. Most important of those conditions, more frequent visits from her son.

Ling Chu had walked to the Model T, and Andy watched him set about activating the acetylene generator so he could light the automobile's headlights. Andy knew he would have to purchase his own automobile soon, if only to feel as if he were part of the modern world, but he enjoyed the feel and smell of horses so much compared to the jouncing of the machine and the acidic odor of burning petrol, or the kerosene some of them used. He'd resisted so far. Nevertheless, he thought he might as well take the opportunity to observe Ling Chu at the task of lighting the headlamps. He was only halfway to the machine when Ling Chu stopped what he was doing and beckoned to Andy.

"What is it, Ling Chu?" he asked as he stepped to his side.

Ling Chu pointed. All four of the vehicle's tires were flat. In case there was any doubt about the cause, the wooden handle of a screwdriver projected from the sidewall of the front driver's side tire.

"Have one spare tire, but not four," Ling Chu said.

Andy looked up to where the women and children were still engaged in reluctant goodbyes.

"It seems our friend in the buckboard didn't simply vanish after all," he said. "And he wasn't just a process server."

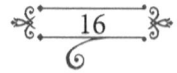

Five

"I'm glad you stopped by, Andy." Harry Barker had been the Maxwell family lawyer for some years. He and Andy stood in his second-floor Placerville office. "I was going to head out to your place in the next couple of days. We have to discuss this." He pulled a sheet of paper from out of a file drawer and slid it across the desk.

Andy needed only a glance to declare it ridiculous. A lawsuit against Many Clouds by a corporation named Western Explorations and Mining, an outfit he'd never heard of, to seize the acreage on which their house stood. "Many Clouds is not claiming ownership of our acreage," he said. We know she isn't eligible to own land. It belongs to the Maxwells, bought, paid for, titles and deeds duly recorded. You did it yourself. This belongs in the trash."

"Yes, and it will be easy to get it tossed out eventually, but once filed, it has to be answered. I've prepared the response. We will file this motion to dismiss, Judge Stevenson will grant it, and that should end the matter."

As Andy applied pen to paper, he said, "I'm afraid this will not end the matter at all, Harry. First of all, surely they know that it's the Maxwell family, not Many Clouds, who owns the land. There's more behind this, and we need some advice." He went on to describe the vandalism and the implied threat behind the man in the freight wagon.

Barker listened silently. Halfway through Andy's narrative he began nibbling on his lower lip, a gesture Andy had come to know as a signal of anxiety. Good. Barker was taking him seriously.

"Many Clouds and I are trying to build a family, Harry. We know what we're doing is against custom, and in some eyes even against the law. But we're hurting no one, so why can't they—whoever 'they' are—just let us be?" He laid the pen on the desktop, stood, marched to the window, and looked down on the bustling street below.

"You know the answer to that question, Andy. The real question is what to do about it?"

"Come here, Harry," Andy said. Barker walked to Andy's side. "You see there down the street, in front of Maynard's Dry Goods?"

"See what?" Harry said.

"The fellow with the Van Dyke whiskers and the paisley cravat. He's the one who was driving the wagon I just told you about. And there he is watching my every move. It had to be him who flattened Ling Chu's tires, or hired someone to do it."

"I see him, and I agree it's disturbing. But the question remains, what to do about it."

"I'm still wondering what he wants."

Barker sat in one of the two clients' chairs in front of the desk and gestured toward Andy to take the other. He leaned toward Andy, elbows on his knees. "You're a bright young man, Andy, and you've been through a lot. I have to repeat what I said a minute ago. You. Know. The. Answer."

He looked at Andy steadily. Andy leaned toward him as if ready to attack. "I know what you're driving at, Harry, but Southern Pacific can't be interested in our little five acres. The ground's so full of rocks it can't be farmed."

"They don't care about the farming, Andy."

"I know their game, Harry. They push up the freight prices till the farmer can't pay, then buy the land for a song or for a bankruptcy then take the crops for themselves. But we have no crops or any way to grow them. We've got nothing they could want."

"I'm about to take back what I said about you being bright. Right now, you're acting as dumb as a sack full of hammers."

Andy stood, angered by the insult. Then he slapped his head and turned in a circle. "Of course. The right of way."

"They could offer to buy it, but they know you won't sell. Besides, they've had a burr under their saddle about you ever since you gave them hell during your campaign. And you label them as villains in your column in that little paper every chance you get. You said it yourself, Andy. The whole area to the north and east is teeming, and a nice motorcar and truck route with roadside businesses to serve the travelers could bring in a nice hunk of change. You're a cork in one of their cash flow bottles."

Andy returned to the window. The paisley cravat man was gone. Andy thought back to when someone uprooted the first apple tree Miller Fitzpatrick and his wife had planted in front of the little cabin to which Andy had added rooms to house himself, Many Clouds, and the children. The uprooting was an anti-Indian act. Bad enough, but this was even more serious. Putting Many Clouds' name on the lawsuit was a spiteful reminder of how tenuous was the legal ground under his little family.

"Harry, I'd be grateful if you could find out who my shadow is. In the meantime, I'm going to ferry my brood to the Circle M and set up some protection at our place until we get a plan to deal with this."

"You should perhaps go to the sheriff. On your way out of town."

"Wilson Hilts? You know as well as I do that SP rigged the election for him."

"Nevertheless, it always pays to keep the law informed just so you can say you did if anyone accuses you of vigilantism. You've a bit of a reputation in that direction, you know."

"It irks me to think it, but you're right. Thanks, Harry." Andy hurried down the stairs and trotted the few doors to the sheriff's' office. A deputy, Heimholtz, a squat little man with a ragged Abe Lincoln beard, was on duty, which suited Andy just fine since he could leave Sheriff Hilts a note and not have to talk to him.

As he passed the town limits, something provoked fear in his gut. The lawsuit was annoying, but why would they stop at that? He fought down images of their little house burned to the ground and of Many Clouds and the children slaughtered. He kicked the sorrel into a canter and kicked himself for his naivety in thinking he'd constructed a safe and bucolic haven for his new family.

Six

Maggie and Willie couldn't attend the local public school, so Many Clouds was determined to superintend their education, using her mission school background as a foundation. Today was a day for calculations in the head with Many Clouds creating math problems for the children to solve as they strolled the property. Many Clouds believed it a handicap to always depend on paper and pencil. A black-robed Jesuit's knuckle-whacking discipline had ensured that both the arithmetic and grammar lessons stuck with her. She was glad for it and wanted the same literacy for Willy and Maggie. Maggie was up to triple numbers now, at least on paper, and Many Clouds wasn't sure where to take the lessons from here. She and Andy needed to seriously discuss next steps. She set the children to multiplying pine cones, then blue jays, then to inventing problems of their own. Willy even measured the distance between fence posts, and, with Maggie's help, calculated how many it would take to stretch a mile.

Many Clouds had no idea if the answer was correct since she didn't know the number of feet in a mile and guessed it as three thousand. They got the right answer for that guess, so as a reward, she took the picnic lunch she'd prepared, crossed the road, and headed down to the creek.

She was glad for a chance to sit down. Midday fatigue was foreign to her. Just one of many unfamiliar phenomena, probably, she'd experience as her condition progressed.

Willy chased a frog while Maggie and Many Clouds munched apples. Maggie said, "If we was adopted—"

"*Were* adopted," Many Clouds interrupted.

"Okay, *were*. Now I forgot, dag nab it. Oh, yeah, would we have to call you and Andy 'mom' and 'dad'?"

"Of course not. You could if you felt like it, but no one would make you do it."

"Would you like it if we did?"

"I don't feel I have a right to ask it of you. I did not give you birth. Your father and I are not yet man and wife. However, if someday you feel moved to honor me with the name, I would be gratified."

Maggie said nothing but took a small bite from her apple. Many Clouds felt uncomfortable. She supposed it was from Maggie's silence, but something caused her to turn and look back uphill toward the house. The man with the pointy beard had one foot on a boulder and arms crossed on the top of one thigh. He was staring down at her, casual but at the same time threatening. She stood and scooped up a rock, one large enough to do some damage, but small enough that she could hurl it a good distance.

"What do you want?" she called.

He just smiled and did not change position at all.

"Maggie, take Willy into the brush and wait," she said.

Once they were on their way, she strode uphill toward the man. He put both feet on the ground and folded his hands across his chest as she approached. His boots were polished, and she noticed how clean and trimmed his nails were. A silver pearl-handled six-shooter hung from his right hip. She stopped a good ten feet away from him, still clutching the stone. In place of the earlier buckboard, there was a two-wheeled buggy parked behind him.

"I asked you a question," she said.

"Who said I wanted anything? This is a public thoroughfare. I have a right to be here."

"You're frightening the children."

He glanced toward the willows that bordered the creek. "You've taught them to be wary of strangers, have you? A sound policy in most cases, but it will do them no good in this instance."

Many Clouds walked past the man and began unhitching the little mare that was harnessed to his buggy. She never turned her back, however, nor relinquished her grip on the stone.

"Whoa, now," he said. "You can't just purloin my transportation."

Many Clouds now had the reins free of the limb around which they were tied. She began walking the rig toward their house. "You said yourself this was a public thoroughfare. I just found this horse and buggy abandoned on the roadway and sheltered it while searching for the rightful owner."

"You can just stop right there, young lady."

He grabbed her arm. She swung the rock against his temple. He staggered. She swung again. He went down on his knees, stunned. She pulled his gun from its holster, threw open the gate on the weapon's cylinder, emptied the bullets, and threw them down the hill. She hurried back over to the buggy. It took only a short search to discover the rifle she suspected was there. She levered the shells out of the magazine and tossed them after the other ammunition, then threw the rifle in that direction as well.

"Come on, kids," she called. "Back to the cabin."

The man was climbing slowly to his feet, shaking his head. He was speaking in broken, half-coherent sentences. "Assault. Damn squaw. You wait."

Many Clouds grabbed the man's chin whiskers and turned his face toward hers. "Never again, mister," she said. "Never." She gave his beard a final tug and threw his head back. Then she marched back up the hill to the house. Her house. And Andy's house. And Maggie and Willy's. Theirs alone.

Seven

Andy covered the five miles from Placerville to the house in considerably less than an hour. He was relieved to find it standing and apparently unharmed. Once through the gate, he leaped from his horse and called out.

"Many Clouds, are you alright?"

She rushed out the front door, flew down the steps without touching one of them, and wrapped her arms around him, throwing him off balance nearly enough to send him to the ground.

"He was here, Andy. We can't let this go on. I came close to shooting him myself."

"Who was?" But he knew the answer.

Maggie and Willy appeared on the porch, crowded close to one another, as they had been virtually their entire lives.

"Never mind," Andy said. "You won't have to worry about him any longer. Let's take a walk, and you can tell me all about it. Maggie, Willy, why don't you come with us?"

They circled the house, headed up the hill to a rocky outcropping where they often sat and talked in the evening.

"You shoulda seen her," Willy exclaimed in the middle of her narrative. "Many Clouds whacked that rat so hard he couldn't get up."

"Willy," Many Clouds admonished him.

Maggie said, "Well it's true. Then she grabbed him by the whiskers and tossed him around like he was a rag doll."

Many Clouds laughed. "You always accuse Willy of exaggerating, but you sound just like him."

"My Lord," Andy said. "I leave for a few minutes, and look at the trouble you all get into."

They seated themselves on the rock and watched the sun beginning to slip down behind the peaks to the west.

"Anyway, it's clear you're no longer safe here," he declared.

Many Clouds nodded. "It feels a little like when my uncle was on the rampage, except now you're here, Andy, and I don't feel terrified as I did then."

"Yellow Squirrel was a lunatic murderer. I doubt these people are so savage, but they are still a threat. You'd best move to the Circle M for a while."

"You talk as if you wouldn't be coming with us," she said.

"You have to come, Andy," Maggie said.

Willy started to whimper, his chin trembling.

"I'll come till you get settled, but we can't leave the house and the animals alone for long."

"Zeke can take care of them."

"Zeke has to look after his livery stable. He only has time to look in once or maybe twice a day. Besides, it could be dangerous for him to be around here too much. Don't worry."

Many Clouds took his hand. "What's really happening here, Andy?" Andy looked at the children. "Don't tell me you want to protect them from bad news after everything they've suffered."

Andy chuckled. "That's laughable, isn't it? Well, here's what we're up against as far as I can tell at this point." He proceeded to tell them about his conversation with Harry Barker.

"So," Many Clouds said, "Southern Pacific wants our land and is willing to use any kind of force to get it."

"On paper, it's Western Explorations, but it could be Southern Pacific behind them. We just don't know for sure. Plus, they surely bear a grudge against me for what I said about them during the campaign."

Maggie said, "Well, they can't have this place."

"We live here," Willy said, "And so do mama and daddy."

"That's the spirit," Andy said. He leaned over and hugged each of them. "But we don't want you in danger." He waited for Many Clouds to agree with him, but she was silent, watching the sun disappear and the shadows lengthen. "Do we, Many Clouds?"

Many Clouds pulled the children to her with one arm and embraced Andy with the other. "We cannot flee to your mother every time there's trouble, Andy."

He started to object, then stopped. He'd seen those unwavering eyes and that steadfast pose before. The last time was when she'd argued for an honorable cremation ceremony for her most dishonorable uncle. The uncle who'd murdered not only her grandfather all those years ago but Maggie and Willy's father. The man who had nearly destroyed the Circle M and the Maxwell family. That same look was in the eyes of little Willy, who, when he was but six years old had picked up a pistol and fired a shot that had forced Yellow Squirrel to break cover and step into the open where Many Clouds finished him. Her own Uncle. Necessary, but she would carry the pain of it always. That was all past, though. For the present moment, Andy knew he'd lost the argument.

"If I live to be a thousand, I'm afraid I'll never be possessed of your wisdom or courage, my love." He kissed her lips and hugged her. He bent down and embraced each of the children. "We should fear nothing," he said. "They—whoever 'they are—they're the ones who should be afraid. And they should be shaking in their boots, right?"

They held hands and formed a circle. "Let's go inside."

They hurried downhill toward the house, but Many Clouds stopped them before they entered.

"We should talk out here so no one can sneak up on us."

"This is going to be fun," Willy said.

"Fun?" Andy laughed.

"It will be if we make it so," Many Clouds said.

"Then so will it be," Andy said.

Eight

Later, when the children were already settled for the night, Andy and Many Clouds stood in affectionate silence on the porch, gazing toward the road which was barely visible in the darkness. Many Clouds finally spoke. "You think this is a bad idea, don't you? To stay here instead of going to the Circle M?"

"Does it matter what I think? My head tells me it's the right decision. I just have to get used to it is all."

"What's the difference between having men guarding our property around the clock here and having the Circle M hands doing the same thing on the ranch?" she asked.

"No difference at all," he answered. "And we can probably trust Emmanuel and his friends more than the ranch hands. They are your people, these Indians. They think of you and the children as their own."

"Well, some of them do. There are still those who see me as a traitor to my race."

Before they exited the house, Many Clouds had watched Andy shift and fidget as he pretended to read *Twenty Thousand Leagues Under the Sea*. He said Verne's novel would take him as far away from whatever apprehensions assailed him as he could get. Many Clouds never understood his yearning for escape. She preferred to remain engaged and present in her world, even if that world occasionally took her into communion with her father and grandfather and other long-dead members of her family. They were as real to her as the moon in the sky, the children sleeping in their bedroom, or the beloved man reading in the chair. He'd lifted his eyes from the book to her. Then he rose, put a marker in the book and closed it. "Look Many Clouds, I can't imagine even the Indians who resent you would be likely to come against you with weapons. But I'll just take a quick stroll and check on things."

"Good idea. I'll go with you."

"No, no. It's too dangerous."

"I'll go with you anyway." She lifted two jackets from the coat rack near the door and handed one to him. "Come on." For the most part she welcomed Andy's proclivity to act as her protector, but he was becoming annoying. She had proved herself in combat many times, yet he acted as if she were a helpless maiden. There was always the baby to think about, but he didn't know about that. Even if he did, she would refuse to go into hiding from the world. He took the jacket she handed him, but hesitated as they were about to exit to the porch. She jumped toward him. "Boo," she said. He stepped back, startled. She laughed. Then he laughed as well.

"Let's get out of here," he said and pushed her toward the steps.

It was a half-moon, enough light to make out silhouettes and shadows, but not fully illuminate, say, a face. Her father, Standing Oak, would say it was perfect for attack, bad for defense. She wondered if she'd see Standing Oak again. He was unlikely to venture off the Wind River reservation any more. She was just as unlikely to visit it again. But he had taught her when she was but a child that in this light a person could creep along, indistinguishable from the many other shadows, but could still make out the target, whether man or animal. In this case, they were the target. However, the breeze was coming their way, and it carried no strange scent or sound. She felt comfortable, happy, at Andy's side. He began his tuneless whistling, which had become a comforting sound to her. Most of her life after leaving Wyoming had been lived in fear and anger. Peace had been a stranger to her. Now she had begun to feel what it was like.

"Are you happy, Andy?"

"With you, always."

It was a right answer but not an honest one. At least it didn't carry the truth she was looking for.

"Not just with me, but with yourself."

"I don't know what you mean."

"Of course, you do."

They were both silent for a time. Suddenly, a tall Indian man in overalls and a flat cap appeared at the gate near the road. Many Clouds froze. Andy stepped between her and the man. Then many Clouds moved him aside.

"Emmanuel," she said, "you scared me to death."

"You need help, so I am here."

"How did you know?" Andy said. "Never mind. I suppose I'll never quite understand how this works." Andy now remembered Emmanuel from his occasional trips to the house to pick up milk for his family. "I'm glad you're here, though. It will be comforting to have protection for Many Clouds and the children."

"I'll check around," Emmanuel said. "You need to be careful in this kind of light." He stepped through the gate and disappeared into the shadows.

They looked in the shed where the stock was bedded. The cows and the four horses seemed at peace. They turned back toward the house. Many Clouds recalled, as she often did, how it looked when it had just been a tiny cabin that Miller Fitzpatrick had built with his own hands. One room. A loft. A window too small for her to escape through the first time she'd awakened there, wounded and feverish. Now it had been transformed into a handsome cottage. Two bedrooms, kitchen, and—wonder of wonders—that flush toilet. Inexplicably, she sometimes missed the intimacy of the little crude building that now seemed little more than a shelter. But that lament didn't at all taint her love for this new home. Andy spoke as they headed away from the animals and back toward the house.

"I didn't want to say anything because it makes no sense. I know it's not logical, but I can't seem to get over the feeling that the Circle M is the only safe place in the world. Even when I think through all the horrors I've been through—that *we've* been through—at that ranch. I know there were times when the ranch offered no protection at all. I still have this notion that if we can only go there, we'll be safe from harm."

A shadow emerged from behind the house.

"Emmanuel?" Many Clouds said.

"Everything seems peaceful," he said.

"Thank you, Emmanuel," Andy said.

"I better take another look down by the road," he said and moved downhill.

Many Clouds turned Andy to face her. "Feelings have a logic of their own which the brain can't understand," she said. "Otherwise, we wouldn't be here together."

"Or anywhere else together," Andy said.

"But here we are. And I am more than glad for it."

"No more than I am, and well you know it." Andy embraced her.

She allowed Andy's apprehensions to pass through her heart like a cloud passing over the moon. A shadow one moment, gone the next. For tonight, they were here and safe. She felt his arms around her, enclosed his body in her own arms and let herself fill with the pleasure of the here and the now.

Nine

Corporate Thugs on the Loose
Special to *The Elevator* by Andrew Maxwell

 Readers of my past articles in The Elevator *are familiar with my history of conflicts with Southern Pacific. In their efforts to continue exploiting our small landowners by charging outrageous hauling rates to take the crops of honest, hardworking farmers to market, they opposed my assembly election campaign with a flood of dollars. I suspect as well that they were behind violent attacks on me and my family. Southern Pacific money undoubtedly instigated the court case that blocked me from taking office because of my race.*

 Now, apparently, they are back. My family and I have been harassed and threatened by someone seeking to drive us from our home. We have taken legal measures to block the attempt, but thinly-veiled threats continue. Our home has been spied upon and our children attacked.

 As before, I cannot prove Southern Pacific is behind these depredations. However, who else could it be? Judging from the nature of name-calling involved, it is clear that race as well as cash is part of the motivation behind this whole mess. If it is happening to us, it is surely happening to others. Just as Frank Norris describes in his superb novel The Octopus, *the tentacles of Southern Pacific reach out for us all. Be careful of their reach, especially if you happen to be black or Indian.*

***

A week went by with no incidents. Andy wanted to believe the crisis had passed, even though he knew better. Perhaps Harry Barker could figure out some way they could move against their opponents before they struck instead of merely reacting to the attacks.

Andy sat down in Barker's office amid a cacophony of construction noises—hammers, saws, workers yelling to one another.

"I apologize, Andy. That new hotel going up next door is a great sign of prosperity in our little burg, but it sure makes it hard to do business in the meantime."

"Fine with me." Andy scooted his chair close to Barker's. "I've gotten so I'm afraid to talk for fear of someone listening in."

"I've never seen you quite so spooked, Andy. Do you have any indication yet who these people are or what they might try?" Barker said.

"I have to believe it's Southern Pacific, but there's no proof, and everything they've done so far has been more of a threat than a direct move. Even the fisticuffs with Many Clouds would be laid on her in a white man's court. I need more. Any results from your inquiries about mister paisley cravat?"

"No one in Placerville seems to know anything about him. My clerk went down to Sacramento yesterday for a hearing on another case. He might uncover something."

"I understand how busy you are, Harry. I'm wondering if I should hire an investigator."

"Oooh. You need to be careful about that, Andy. There are a lot of guys running around claiming to be Allan Pinkerton himself who are either thugs or will take your fees and spend them in the saloons."

"Sure, but you must know someone."

"Well..."

"What's the matter, Harry? If it's the money..."

"No, no. It's just that the best man I know used to work for the governor, so I'm not sure you and he would match up."

"Worked for Hiram Johnson? What happened?"

"All I know are rumors. None of them good."

"Harry, if he's on the outs with Johnson, he's got to be the man for me." Andy had plenty to complain about when it came to the governor. In order to persuade Andy to run for the assembly in the Circle M district and assure the Republican party a solid majority should he be elected, Johnson had promised Andy a seat on the board of regents of the University of California. Andy's ultimate goal had been to persuade the regents to adopt a nondiscrimination policy for admittance in regards to race. In the end, after the lawsuit barred him from taking his seat, Johnson reneged on his promise to appoint Andy to the regents, so Andy lost out twice, and Johnson got to appoint his own man to the assembly anyway. "What's his name, and where do I find him?"

With the contact information in his hand, Andy hurried once more down the steps from Barker's office. He was entering the telegraph office when a man running out smacked into him. Both men stumbled backward, though neither fell.

"Sorry," they said in tandem.

"Wait a second," the man said. "You're Andrew Maxwell, are you not?"

"Uh, yes," Andy said apprehensively.

"Then you just saved me a trip. This here's for you." He stuffed a yellow envelope in Andy's hand. "Care to sign right here, please?"

A telegram from his mother.

GENTRY AT IT AGAIN. MUST TALK.

Hale Gentry owned a disreputable saloon on the outskirts of Sawtooth Wells, about five miles east of Placerville in the direction of the Circle M. He also operated a number of semilegal and illegal businesses in the area. He'd once fancied himself a suitor for Carolyn and had been Andy's opponent in the Assembly race, a tool of the corrupt democrats. So he was in the middle of all this, too. Andy might have known.

Ten

"You won't never understand—"

"Won't ever," Maggie corrected Willy. "'Won't never' is a double negative. Many Clouds just went over that the other day."

"You know what I mean," Willy said. "Why can't you just listen?"

"I'm listening. But you can't just always talk to everyone like you talk to me. We have to learn to speak so other people respect us."

"'Other people' is white people."

"Well, yes, mainly, but not them only."

"Who else do I have to worry about?"

"Any educated person, Willy. Can you just get on with what you wanted to say?"

"You make it too complicated. I quit." He took out his jackknife and started performing some of his favorite mumblety-peg tricks—off-the-knee flips and behind-the-back throws. He could put on quite a show with that knife. Maggie thought it was a shame they couldn't go to a regular school where he could really show off, but he'd learned a lot from the street boys while the adults were in town shopping. There were other times when he disappeared for a while, saying he was exploring in the woods. She suspected he trekked into town or maybe hitched a ride on a wagon to meet up with friends he'd made there. She feared for the kinds of people these new acquaintances might be.

"Can you teach me a couple of tricks?"

"Girls can't do these, Maggie."

"Who told you that?"

"Sammy says—"

"I don't know who Sammy is, but you listen to me, Willy Fitzpatrick. We've been running together since we was born—"

"'Were born,'" Willy said. "Plural subject, plural verb."

"Glad to hear you were listening, you maddening little rapscallion," she said, "but now listen to this. I've always been able to run, shoot, ride, and rope every bit as well as you or better, so why all of a sudden am I not even qualified to handle a jackknife?"

"'Cause boys and girls is—are—different" and—this is too complicated figuring out how to talk and who can do what. It ain't fair. And I know 'ain't' ain't correct but I don't give a damn."

Willy ran off into the trees, pocketing his knife as he went. Maggie felt bereft. She was losing her little brother, her lifelong companion. He'd been the only constant during all the losses they'd suffered. Now he was gone also, or might as well be. She trudged down the hill and sat on the front doorstep, tears burning her eyes. She didn't wail or sob. It wasn't her way to show her sadness or anger in that manner, but her cheeks were wet and salty, and her head and shoulders sagged.

Soon, Many Clouds sat beside her. "When I was your age, maybe a little younger, my brother went on a vision quest. It's a tradition for the males in our tribe and in many others to spend a time in the wilderness searching their spirit, their souls, to find their true name. I felt abandoned. Walking-in-the-sky and I had been very close, perhaps as close as you and Willy."

"What did you do?"

"What could I do? My father is a good man, but a fearsome one. I couldn't complain to him. My mother was dead. Our tribe had just gone through a time of horror and bloodshed, and to shed tears over a brother who had merely gone on a spirit quest and would return after a week or two would have not only shown horrible weakness, but would make me a burden to those around me. I bit my tongue and waited."

"What happened?"

"Just as I feared, he never returned. I somehow knew he wouldn't. I didn't want to admit it at first, but I knew even my love was not strong enough to hold him. He always thought the tribal customs held him back and that he could make something of himself outside the reservation. I suppose he became like many other Indians and found jobs here and there at various ranches. Or perhaps he became one of the many drunken natives you see passed out on doorsteps and alleyways. I look for him everywhere still. Wherever he is, I hope he's found that sense of freedom he was looking for."

Maggie said, "But Willy's not like that."

"Of course not. Willy will return. Your love—our love—is plenty strong to hold him to us even if he goes away for a time in heart or body. My story was merely to show I could understand the pain you feel at the way he's treating you right now. I don't expect it will help ease your hurt much, but at least you know you have company."

Maggie was silent for a few moments, then she stood. "I think I'd like to go down to the creek for a while."

"Good idea to be alone for a time. Of course, I need to come with you, but only to be near, not to intrude."

"What if something happens to Willy?"

"He won't allow us near him right now I don't think. No danger has threatened us from the uphill side of the cabin yet, so we have to hope that pattern will continue."

***

The man in the paisley cravat held his hand over Willy's mouth and growled, "Listen to me, kid. Stop kicking and punching. You can't get loose. Put your hands in your pockets and cross your ankles. That's it. Now just listen and you won't get hurt."

Willy went still. The man's hand stank of tobacco and tasted like a horse stall. He didn't like it, but he could stand it for right now. Till he could figure what to do about it.

"I'm not going to hurt you. All I want is for you to deliver a message. Nod if you understand." Willy did. "Tell Maxwell to quit talking to lawyers or there's going to be some bad things happening to Maggie and Many Clouds. You, too. You understand? Go ahead and nod like before if you do."

Willy nodded vigorously and whimpered to make it seem he was too afraid to fight. Meanwhile, he'd been taking advantage of the man's order to put his hands in his pockets. His right hand had unfolded the big blade of his jackknife, and his exaggerated nodding had loosened his captor's grip on his face. He opened his mouth and chomped hard on the man's ring finger. At the same time, he drew the knife and sent the blade flying into the man's instep. He was rewarded with enraged cries of pain and with the freedom to sprint into the trees.

"Don't forget what I said, you little son of a whore," the man called from behind him. "I will be back. And I won't be alone."

Willy didn't stop or slow down or yell back. But he heard the man, and his guts turned somersaults as he ran.

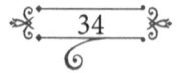

Eleven

Andy and Many Clouds sat on the porch, shoulder to shoulder, though not quite touching. Both looked straight ahead rather than at one another.

"I didn't want to even tell you about Willy's encounter, Andy," she said, "because I knew you'd say we should go to the Circle M. And now with this telegram…"

They were about to commence the same argument they'd seemingly settled only a few days earlier. But the settlement had been an illusion that now blew away like dandelion fluff in a windstorm.

"We can't pick up the house and animals and move them to the ranch. I wouldn't if we could."

"But Mother needs—"

"Hush." She put a finger to his lips and took his hand. "Kids," she called. "It's time for the evening milking."

Maggie and Willy emerged from inside the house. Willy said, "But we can't—"

"Yes, you can, Willy," she said. "You've helped out enough times that you don't need us. I'll be out to see how you're doing before too long."

"I—"

Many Clouds heard an uncharacteristic whimper in Willy's voice. His chin shivered a bit too.

"He won't come here, Willy. Don't be scared, now. Right, Andy?"

"She's right, Willy. Just do as Many Clouds asks. We'll be along."

The children reluctantly headed to the pasture to bring the cows to the shed. Andy whistled a bit of "My Wild Irish Rose," trying to lighten the atmosphere. Maggie took Willy's hand. Willy succumbed to her leadership. His defiance of her had dissolved in the cloud of fear that had surrounded them since the incident in the forest.

Many Clouds took both Andy's hands and forced him to look into her the eyes.

"No more music for now," she said. He stopped his whistling.

"I know you have to go when your mother calls for help. Even if it means leaving us behind."

Andy pulled her closer. "Please don't make it sound like I'm choosing her over you. She wouldn't send a telegram unless she was in real trouble."

"Or unless she wanted to see if you'd still jump up and run to her."

"That's unfair, Many Clouds. She's done a lot for us. We wouldn't even have this place if it weren't for her."

It was true enough, what Andy said, and Many Clouds knew she should be grateful. But she couldn't stifle her resentment. Carolyn Maxwell, she felt, had bound them to her with chains of kindness and obligation.

"Ah, I know that, Andy. And I appreciate it. But if we let these people drive us away, even temporarily, it will be forsaking her benevolence, won't it? Surely she wouldn't want that."

She knew she'd spoken a half-truth. Andy's mother would probably be quite happy if they rid themselves of this entire homestead and moved everyone under her protective and possessive wing to the big ranch. But the Circle M was not only fifteen miles from the graves of Maggie's and Willy's parents, it was that far from their independence, which this house represented. Andy had said as much himself. But now, under this threat, he seemed to prefer the risk of getting tied up in the maternal apron strings to that of getting attacked by the man in the paisley cravat.

"No, of course she wouldn't," Andy said. "But I wouldn't think of leaving you here unprotected. I'll tell you what. I'll have mother send a couple of Circle M hands to stand guard to add to Emmanuel and his men, Gus and Sylvester. Mike and Harry both fought in the Spanish-American war, so they should be able to keep you safe."

"They're probably good men, but I'd rather have our own people, yours and mine, than Circle M men."

"Rather than mother's people, you mean," he said.

Many Clouds swallowed. His tone hadn't been particularly harsh, but she knew how tender Andy was about the subject of his mother. Theirs was a complex relationship built on mutual emotional dependency and tied in with the murders of his younger brother and his father. Then there was Carolyn's need to control the people and events around her. Many Clouds didn't pretend to understand it all. She often felt like an intruder, so she did her best to tiptoe around it.

"Emmanuel fought in that war too. And he can recruit more friends. There's his friend Ezekiel. I've met him. Emmanuel says he's a true warrior."

"Emmanuel is a handyman, not a gunman."

"And Mike and Harry are simple ranch hands now, are they not?"

Andy stood. He stepped toward the fence and the road. Many Clouds thought he must feel as if the sands were shifting under his feet. It was a moment when Carolyn Maxwell and the Circle M no longer automatically held the solution to a crisis. She wanted to relent and save him the pain of seeming to choose between her and his mother. However, she felt she had to fight for their independence even if it hurt. She walked to his side.

"We must be able to stand on our own, Andy, at least to some extent, or we are not truly a family."

He took a deep breath. "We should arm the children."

Fear shot through her. She stepped back, hand to her mouth. "Andy."

"It's not so outrageous an idea. You're the one who taught them to shoot. If you hadn't, Willy wouldn't have taken that shot at Yellow Squirrel and saved us all."

Since the six-year-old Willy had ambushed her rampaging uncle, he'd never exhibited a desire to take up firearms again. But the spunk he'd shown recently when he'd thrown his knife into his captor's foot demonstrated that he still had the temperament to act if he needed to. She didn't know about Maggie, but the girl had plenty of gumption and had taken the same shooting instruction her brother had.

Andy continued. "I'll buy pistols more their size—derringers maybe. They can't lug around hogleg six shooters anyway. But neither you nor Gus and whoever else can watch them every minute. They should be able to protect themselves."

"Shouldn't a knife for Maggie be enough? And a new one for Willy? Something more than that jackknife?"

Even though everything Andy said about past conflicts was true, the idea of children with guns repelled her. "You know I still think they should know how to handle firearms, but to carry them all the time? Surely that's not necessary."

Andy placed gentle hands on her shoulders. "You're right, of course. Knives should be enough. Willy can teach Maggie how to use hers. Now, let's go see how the milking is going." He held out his hand. She took it. "You're trembling," he said.

"Yes," she said. And she pulled him toward the cowshed.

Twelve

Carolyn Maxwell prodded her gelding into a canter along the recently mended fence surrounding the Circle M's western pasture. Beyond the fence, the slope climbed sharply into the forest. Farther upslope she could see the trail that went through the forest and continued beyond Circle M land toward the main road into the small community of Sawtooth Wells, which shared its name with the valley at the foot of the peaks where the Circle M sat. The springs that supplied water for the Circle M and the rest of the valley welled up between the ranch and the rugged mountains that led to the peaks themselves.

Three. That's all the men it had taken, judging by the sign they'd left. They'd ridden to a high point on the trail, tethered their mounts, then climbed on foot down the slope to cut the barbed wire surrounding the pasture. The ugly thing was they hadn't come to steal cattle. Rustling would have been bad enough. Instead, they'd simply slaughtered a dozen cows. Cut their throats, stabbed them using big knives, probably swords or bayonets, then left them. Barking coyotes and a large committee of buzzards had led the Circle M hands to the kill.

More than a thousand pounds of beef left to rot. It wouldn't all go to waste. They would salt down what they could, share some with neighbors and with the itinerant Washoe Indians who lived nearby.

This was seemingly an act of random vandalism, but Carolyn knew better. It was a cowardly way of showing the Maxwells that enemies were lurking, that everyone connected with the Circle M should always be looking over their shoulders, never get comfortable. As if they needed reminders.

A week earlier, she'd been surprised returning home after her morning ride to Granite Spring uphill from the ranch yard to find a luxurious buggy parked in front of the ranch house. Sitting on the veranda and smoking a cheroot sat her old nemesis and unrequited suitor, Hale Gentry.

He had discarded his longtime costume of black leather vest and silver conchos in favor of an outfit more suited to a banker than the saloon owner and racketeer he was. The grey pinstriped suit and maroon silk cravat were perhaps a bid for respectability. Surely even he wasn't so obtuse as to think it would impress her. She pulled her thirty-thirty from its saddle scabbard and levered a shell into the firing chamber.

"You're trespassing, mister. Get off the property."

The man stood and smiled. His teeth shown unnaturally white as always. "I have something I need to tell you, Carolyn."

"Put it in writing and send it to my lawyer."

"I thought you deserved to hear it from me in person."

She turned the rifle toward the buggy and fired. A hole appeared in the padded upholstery. She knew the exit hole would be as ragged as the entry hole was neat. She jacked another bullet into the chamber.

"Whoa," Gentry said. "There was no need for that."

"Yes, there was. Now move before I stitch up the rest of that seat."

The threat sent him down the steps and into his buggy. "We've been through a lot together, Carolyn. I deserve better."

"Actually, you deserve worse. Much worse. Now skedaddle."

As she watched the buggy roll under the Circle M archway, Carolyn felt her insides churn. Life had settled down recently. Maggie's wonderful birthday party, though she wished it had been held here on the Circle M, had been a joy. Andy seemed to have found his place. He was settled with Many Clouds. He earned only a meager income from writing civil rights articles for Joseph Francis's Negro periodical, *The Elevator,* and other pieces for various newspapers and magazines. He worked as well for political campaigns championing progressive candidates. Even though California had become a women's suffrage state, attacks on the idea continued, and there was still no federal law in place assuring women the right to vote in national elections. Then there was the question of the progressive income tax. And so forth. Carolyn was happy to support him in his worthwhile work. After all, the ranch was his as much as hers, and he deserved both the income and the happiness that came with it. His choice of a squaw and two half-breed children violated the notion of a conventional family but so had her relationship with her Negro foreman. If it was loneliness that first carried her into Shelby's arms, it was a deep and abiding love that kept her there. Once in Shelby's embrace, she never missed or seldom even thought of the lawyer-husband who decided ranch life was not what he wanted after all and left on a business trip from which he never returned.

Years later, the revelation of that secret love and of Andy's mixed-race heritage had caused all the upheaval she'd feared it would and more besides. But now, on the other side of the fracas, it was a better world after all. Whatever Gentry had in mind, they were prepared to deal with it. She hurried up the steps into the house.

"Ling Chu," she called. The door to the kitchen opened, and Ling Chu entered. Outside his pillbox hat, Carolyn noticed gray hair had begun to lighten his temples. She'd noticed before but chose to ignore it every time, just as she did now. To acknowledge his aging would be to acknowledge her own. She chose to concentrate instead on that fact that he appeared as lithe as he had in his youth. As did she. A thought she immediately dismissed as vanity.

"Yes, Miss Carolyn," he said. "What you need?"

"I need you to fire up that Model T of yours and deliver a message to Marshal Halstad in Sawtooth Wells." She grabbed a piece of paper from a tablet on the huge coffee table in front of the outsized couch that characterized the size of everything in the house her father had constructed when he founded the ranch in 1864. Could it really have been over forty years now? Twenty since he'd been murdered? She pushed aside the morbid thoughts that would inevitably lead to self-indulgent immersion in past misfortunes and disasters. Ling Chu's face, all smiles now, cheered her mood. Old-fashioned as he was in every other way, he loved his machine passionately.

"Right away, Miss Carolyn." He rushed toward the front door.

"Hold on. Hold on. Hold on," she called. He turned back. "Don't forget the message."

"Oh, yes, sorry. Sorry." He snatched the paper and hurried out the door.

Carolyn smiled at his enthusiasm and smiled as well at the prospect of sitting down with her son to plot a strategy for dealing with this latest threat.

Thirteen

Harry Barker stared at the dollar bill lying on his desk. "What's that?" he said.

The blond man with a thin, prominent nose facing him smiled and leaned back in his chair. He was rather nattily dressed in a frock coat, dress shirt and string tie with a turquoise and silver slide. Closer examination, however, revealed that the shirt collar was too big and pulled into a wrinkled bunch by the tie. The coat was meant for a bigger man and hung awkwardly from his shoulders. "I pay you, means you're my lawyer and everything we talk about is confidential, right?"

"Mister Morelli—"

"Please, I'm just plain old 'Otis' to you and the rest of my friends."

"*Mister* Morelli," Barker said. "You seem to fancy yourself a pretty slick operator. However, I have not touched that money, let alone accepted it nor agreed to take you on as a client. Now, what brings you here?"

The man who called himself Otis winked. "Oh, I think you know the answer to that question."

"I have no idea what you're talking about, and I'm too busy to play guessing games." He gestured toward the piles of documents littering his desk. "Now get to it or get out."

"Ohhh. No need to get testy. I'm here about that squaw man up the road, of course."

Barker felt an impulse to pull out the .45 revolver he kept in his desk drawer but thought he might yet get some information out of this repulsive character. "You're referring to Mr. Maxwell, I presume."

"See, you do know what I'm talking about. No one here in Placerville or anywhere else for that matter wants to deal with an Indian lover. I'm the client you want."

It was Barker's turn to smile. "And why would I forsake the Maxwells, who have been my clients and friends for decades, in favor of someone I just met and don't trust?"

"Pick up that dollar, and I'll tell you."

This time, Barker yielded to impulse, pulled out the pistol, used it to push the dollar to the far edge of the desk, then pointed it directly at Morelli's forehead. "Out," he said quietly.

Morelli stood and put his hands up. "You're going to regret this, Barker. You and the squaw man both."

"And take the money," he said.

"The dollar is yours, Barker."

"Oh, no." He grabbed the bill and stuffed it into Morelli's shirt pocket. "Now, out," he repeated.

Morelli smiled and waved as he exited. His whole manner was smug. Barker suspected that the meeting had gone just as he wanted it to. He stood for quite a while, the pistol at his side, staring the door through which Morelli had just passed. For some reason this repulsive, ill-dressed, incompetent man had frightened him, and he'd left before Barker had obtained any information about how to contact him. Never mind. He or someone like him was sure to be back. He needed to be prepared and to warn the others. But warn them of what? That was the question he pondered as he stepped across the room and gazed out the window that overlooked Placerville's main street. Directly opposite his office stood the town's most popular saloon, the Hangtown. The bar's name paid homage to the original name of the town itself, when a huge live oak tree in town center became a favorite vigilante location for executing criminals for crimes real and imagined, or to settle personal scores. As the gold rush frontier became more civilized, certain city fathers became more interested in commerce than vengeance. Down came the tree (except for a huge stump and protruding branch scarred with the rope marks of dozens of executions) and the town henceforth went by the more respectable name of Placerville. The saloon and a few other renegade establishments preserved the old name, but the wild west flavor became decidedly diluted.

Morelli came in sight as he emerged from Barker's building and crossed the street toward the Hangtown. He entered the place with the purposeful stride of a man on his way to a business appointment rather than to meet someone for a convivial libation. Morelli, it appeared, was not working alone.

Fourteen

Andy was nursing a second bourbon and water at the Cary House bar in Placerville while he waited for Barker's investigator to show up. He wanted to get the meeting over so he could head on to the Circle M. Traffic in the bar was light, with only a half-dozen well-dressed patrons scattered among the tables. Two of them were respectable-looking women. Definitely outside the bounds of tradition for them to be there without male companions. These were challenging times for customary mores. Andy was the only patron who had chosen a barstool over a table. He was edgy, and he reasoned that if he needed a quick escape, it would take more time to untangle himself from a chair than to just jump off the stool.

He began to worry about his choice of a meeting place. He was well-known in the area, and he didn't know who might be involved in whatever plot was brewing against the Maxwells. He worried that Many Clouds' friends, Gus and Sylvester, and their friends, might not provide enough protection for his family. Maggie and Willy had shown themselves skillful at handling the hunting knives he'd supplied for them, and he had no doubt of their willingness to use them against attackers. Still, knives afforded little protection against guns. He had half a mind to turn back and leave his mother to cope with her situation on her own. She was certainly capable. She and Ling Chu and the ranch hands. He felt he had to go forward with this original plan for the time being, though.

A tall, slim man with broad shoulders, dressed like a simple cowhand—Levi's, boots, bandana, Stetson—entered and crossed to the bar. "Whisky, neat." he told the bartender. Andy estimated the newcomer was two or three inches taller than his own five eleven.

"Howdy," Andy said, trying to appear casual, as if he expected no meaningful reply. Instead of acknowledging Andy's remark, the man only gave a subtle shake of the head and mumbled into his glass just loud enough for Andy to hear.

"Don't turn around. Count to a hundred. I'll meet you outside."

He downed his shot, slapped a coin on the bar. "Thank you, sir," he said.

Andy sipped and counted. Finally, he dropped a bill on the bar and headed out the door. The boardwalk was deserted. Andy turned right and walked a few steps past the blue- and red-stained panes of the picture window that adorned the front of the hotel, keeping close to the building. A few feet past the hotel building, the walk dropped two steps to the earthen street. A right turn would take him into an alley between the hotel and an abandoned storefront, a left led across the main street toward a livery stable. Straight ahead lay a dark path that ended at the Catholic church, its steeple silhouetted against the moonlit sky. The alley was unknown, as was the walk toward the church. Crossing the street would leave him vulnerable to every window in sight as he stepped into the open space. He turned around and headed the other way, which would take him past the sheriff's office, a dry goods store, and a gunsmith's shop before he ran out of boardwalk again.

"Not that way." The voice came from the alley. The thought of entering the dark space between buildings was daunting. Andy hadn't felt such trepidation since Yellow Squirrel's murderous campaign had him looking for an assassin around every corner. He'd decided against wearing his .45 revolver around town. He loved the gun, and it had served him well, but it was bulky and heavy and seemed to presage or even provoke a gunfight even if none threatened. He didn't want to go unarmed, however, so he'd strapped on a shoulder holster in which he carried a Browning semi-automatic .32, a brand-new model that he hoped would provide all the protection he needed without being as obvious as the hogleg. He drew the weapon now and let it hang at his right side as he moved toward the voice. He stopped, back to the building and peeked around the corner.

"Not smart, friend. If I wanted to pop you, that little glance gave me enough of a target to splatter your brains all over the street. Now put up the pea shooter and walk my way."

Andy drew a breath, feeling foolish, and holstered his pistol. "Where are we going?" Andy asked as he joined the man.

"Right here. Name's Remy Dillinger." He extended his hand. Andy shook it. It was not calloused to match his attire. "Remy's short for Remington.

Remington Dillinger. My folks had a sense of humor if nothing else. You should call me Remy. I had a brother named Colt if you can believe that. He died as a youngster, though. Diphtheria. I still have a sister, name of Iris. No suggestion of firearms in that name, thank goodness. She lives in Iowa, though. Wants nothing to do with me, and I don't much blame her. If you knew more about me, you wouldn't either. My folks have been six feet under for more than twenty years back in Kansas. Cholera got them when the Blue River flooded one year."

After their encounter in the bar, Andy had expected a taciturn man who wanted to get down to business. The rush of words and personal information took him aback. He was glad, though, for the choice of a meeting place. He had no wish to make his dilemma more public than necessary.

"How much do you know about my situation?" Andy said.

"Harry said some folks seem to be after you and you ain't figured out who or why."

"And he told you about my family."

"You're a Maxwell is all he said. You have enough notoriety he didn't have to go into much detail."

"Okay, here's what I know and what I suspect." Andy sketched out the situation quickly. He felt hampered without pencil and paper, but Remy had not pulled out a notebook and had stopped Andy from employing his.

"I'll keep it here," he'd said, tapping his temple.

"Lotsa people involved for not knowing what's going on," he said after Andy finished.

"I may know more after I talk to mother," Andy said. "I'd like you to come along and meet her so she knows who you are and how you're involved."

"How I'm involved? Unless I forgot something, I ain't said I want to get involved at all. You said you got suspects. Who?"

"Number one is Southern Pacific, believe it or not," Andy said.

"You think the railroad is after you? Why in the world would you think that? The rail line runs through Placerville all right, but your place is off to the east of it and sure couldn't accommodate no train traffic."

"When I ran for the assembly last year, I was pretty tough on the railroads. Maybe they want some revenge. Maybe they have something else in mind. Maybe I'm just crazy. But someone's after me and my kids and my mother as well. That part's for sure. I need to find out who and why. That's what you'd be getting paid to find out."

"If it's the railroad, why wouldn't they just come in with money and offer to buy you out? No need for all the shenanigans."

"That's a good question. First of all, maybe they know we have no intention of selling but think they can bully us into it. Maybe it's not them after all. Maybe you can find out one way or another."

Dillinger chewed his lower lip. "Any other suspects?"

"A man named Hale Gentry. Owns a saloon outside of Sawtooth Wells a few miles from here. He runs a number of shady businesses out of that bar of his. He's a small-time ruffian and a longstanding enemy of us Maxwells. He'd love to make trouble for us. He's not one to go about a big project on his own, though, and is sure to be working for or at least with someone. He might be a good starting point if you can find out who's behind him."

Dillinger turned his back. Then he paced to the far end of the alley. Andy feared he was about to refuse his help.

"I don't have forever, Remy. Are you going to join us or do I look elsewhere?"

The challenge brought him back face-to-face with Andy.

"I'm going back and forth in my head about this, Maxwell. Lots of big-time players here if your suspicions bear out. On the other hand, they're so big time, it makes me wonder if it's some sort of fantasy you people cooked up. Delusions of grandeur and all. On the other hand, you all are used to operating with the hoi polloi. You got to understand. I've handled a lot of jobs, and mostly it means I normally got to be discreet and set up a smoke screen at the same time. But here there's not much discreet possible. Everyone is too upscale to be in the shadows, so there's a lot of risk. I'll be skylined most of the time."

"But you're used to operating with the hoi polloi as well, are you not? Barker mentioned a stint with governor Johnson."

"He told you about that?"

"Yes, though not in much detail."

"Let's just say it was brief and unfortunate. And, no, I don't normally operate in those circles."

"Back to my question."

"It's going to cost."

"Understood."

"And I mean upfront cash."

"You'll find it waiting at the Circle M. See you at supper there tomorrow."

"Okay. But don't look for me to come by the main road through Sawtooth Wells and all. I'll be taking the back way, and don't bother to direct me. I'll find it. If you got any trigger happy protectors running around, best to warn them I'm on my way or you may find yourself short a gunslinger or two."

Andy smiled. "We don't hire gunslingers, Remy. But I will make sure the cowhand patrols are alerted. You'll be dressed the same as now?"

Remington Dillinger nodded and strode to the end of the alley opposite the main street. Andy watched him go, wondering if he'd just hired a powder keg with a short fuse begging to be lit.

Fifteen

Many Clouds wanted to make sure both Maggie and Willy learned how to handle a team of horses, so she made Willy responsible for driving the team into town, planning for Maggie to handle the reins on the return trip. Both children were proud of the new hunting knives they wore in silver-trimmed leather sheaths around their waists. Now they looked forward to taking over the wagon reins. Looking and acting all grown up. Many Clouds was both proud and regretful.

The sojourn took about an hour, and Many Clouds had to admit it felt good to get away from the house for a while. She told herself over and over that Gus, Sylvester, Emmanuel, and now Ezekiel, could protect the house and that the family needed supplies they were going to purchase—flour, salt, beans, and the like. At such times, she found herself wishing for reservation life where such necessities were a tribal responsibility and there was no need for economic commerce. But she lived in the white man's world now, and it was no good hankering for the past.

She had Maggie hitch the horses in front of the dry goods store while she and Willy climbed down from the wagon. Automobiles passed them, one in each direction. They were noisy and smoky and stinking. Even though she'd urged Andy to buy one, she did not welcome them into her world. But here they came, unbidden, and doubtless the children would grow up with them, learn to drive them as well as they drove teams of horses. A bit unsettled with all these thoughts of a mysterious future, she ushered the children into the store, keeping an eye out for the paisley cravat man. It took only a few minutes to gather what they needed and place the lot on the front counter. They were about to step up to pay for their goods, when a man with a big belly and a bushy beard pushed in front of them.

"Excuse me, sir," Many Clouds said, "but I believe we were here first."

"White man goes before you, squaw," the counter man said. The man placed a brick of chewing tobacco and some change on the counter.

"Never will learn, will they, Jake?"

"Oh, I expect they will Clancy. I expect they will." He slid the coins into a drawer and gave a few smaller ones for change. The customer called Clancy pointed to the shiny brass and silver cash register on the counter.

"How come you don't use that, Jake? Looks pretty expensive."

"Soon as someone teaches me how to use the dang thing, I guess we'll go to it. But for right now, it's just decoration."

Clancy laughed. "New world's too much for me, too, Jake. Take care now." He headed toward the front door, leaving Many Clouds and the children as the only customers.

"Now, you want these items, do you?" Jake said.

"That's right, *Sir*," she said.

"Getting sassy won't help you none," he said as he added up the charges. When he told her the total, she said, "Put that on the Maxwell account, please."

He shook his head. "Need cash, lady."

"I don't have that much with me, and we have an account here."

"Ain't no Maxwell account here nor anywhere else in town I know of. I need cash or no goods walk out the door."

"Since when?"

"Been about a week now. All the owners got together and said Maxwell can't do business except by cash."

"Did they give a reason?"

He shrugged. "Don't need to far as I know. They just decided and I got to do what I'm told."

It was an old story for her, this pattern of rejection and discrimination. She and Andy had learned to work through and around it to a great extent, but there was no avoiding it completely. Pained and enraged, she dug out what cash she had, money she'd planned to use for treats for Maggie and Willy, and scattered the bills and coins on the counter. It was enough for flour and beans. She handed the flour sack to Willy and the beans to Maggie and started for the door.

"You need to neaten up this cash and put the other goods back where you found them," Jake said.

"You need to neaten up your manners," she said. "Come on, children. Let's go."

"Are you going to let him get away with that?" Maggie said as they exited the store.

"No, but I want to choose a better battleground than here and now."

She'd planned to stop by the bakery and the livery stable, but there was no use of that now. They tossed their bags into the wagon. Maggie unhitched the horses, climbed into the wagon and made to hand the reins to Many Clouds.

"Nope," Many Clouds said. "You're the driver now."

"Hey, why not me?" Willy said.

"You had your turn coming, my boy. Don't worry. There will be plenty more opportunities."

She admired the dexterity with which Maggie maneuvered the horses as they pulled away from the hitching post and turned for home. As they neared the edge of town, Maggie said, "Something feels funny, Many Clouds."

"What do you mean?"

"I don't know, exactly, but…" They had reached a downslope at the bottom of which was a sharp turn. Drivers had to rein in their horses to avoid wagons gathering too much speed and careening over the bank. Maggie tugged on the reins as she should have, but they suddenly hung dangling, useless, from her hands. The horses grew skittish as they sensed the wagon picking up speed and veering toward the bank. Many Clouds was prepared to gather up the children and jump before the whole situation became a crashing disaster. Maggie was faster.

Nimble as a circus performer, she leaped to the back of the lead horse and crawled on hands and knees toward its head.

"Maggie, no," Willy yelled.

"You'll be trampled to death," Many Clouds said simultaneously.

It would have been difficult enough if the reins had been cut off near the wagon and left at least a bit of length to grab on to. But whoever had done it had sliced them off near the bridles. Maggie had to scramble all the way to the lead horse's head to find enough leather to work with. By that time, the wagon's speed had picked up, and without guidance the horses were weaving from one side of the road to the other, the wagon rocking behind them.

"Whoa, Buster, whoa," Maggie yelled as she pulled on the frightened animal's bridle, steering him toward the bank on the lefthand side of the wagon. She knew if she could get Buster under control, his harness mate, Lily, would soon follow. She almost crashed the stallion into the bank, but she was able to slow him enough to turn back to the right and continue down the slope at a safe, if still frightening, pace. She finally steered him back toward the bank and brought him to a halt a few yards from the bottom of the hill.

Many Clouds leapt from the wagon, pulled Maggie down from Buster's neck, and embraced her, squeezing her so tight she elicited a squeal of protest. Willy stayed in the wagon, jumping up and down, yelling and applauding. "You oughta be in Barnum and Bailey," he said.

The three finally calmed, along with the equine team, and thought about how to proceed after their narrow escape.

"We have to walk all the way home?" Willy said.

"No," Many Clouds said. "There are still enough reins hanging from the harness rings to rig something to the bridles so we don't have to walk."

"Sure," Willy said. "A little half-hitch will do it."

"I'd do a bowline, if I were you," Maggie said.

"Maybe, if we have enough length," Willy said.

Many Clouds watched and listened as they argued and worked as a team at the same time. They finally settled on the half-hitch, and before long, the three were back in the wagon and headed home.

"They can't beat us no matter how hard they try, can they?" Willy said.

"No matter how hard they try," Maggie echoed.

"No matter how hard," Many Clouds said.

She hoped their house would still be standing when they arrived home. And she wished Andy would be there waiting instead of on his way to the Circle M.

Sixteen

Downtown Sawtooth Wells—"Sawtooth" after the three soaring peaks that stood at the south end of the little valley which was their namesake—sported a livery stable, the Jensen ladies' Family Café, Marshal Halstad's office, and the Methodist Church. Little else. Gentry's Saloon was not far beyond the area that might be construed as the city limits, though no such boundary was marked. Andy rode through without stopping. He was in such a hurry to get to the Circle M that he failed to take his usual delight in the pleasant five-mile ride up granite creek, past the farms and pastures sprinkled through the little valley. One of the farms belonged to his aunt Amelia and uncle Cooper Duprée, his father's sister and brother. His mother's affair with her Negro foreman had been a scandal, and there was residual disapproval even after the man had been gunned down, and Andy had proved himself a good citizen. Amelia and Cooper were the only black landowners in the valley, but they had earned marginal respect and acceptance by virtue of their own behavior and their connection to the Maxwells. Andy knew that by themselves, they presented no threat. Were others of their race to move in, tamped-down racist sentiments would likely come to the fore. But that was not the issue of the moment. He pushed aside the guilt he felt at not having visited them for a long while. He vowed to find an opportunity to call on them soon.

He finally reined in as he approached the archway spanning the little bridge into the Circle M yard. The archway bore an ax-hewn replica of the ranch's brand, carved into a single cedar log by his Grandfather Maxwell.

It had always been there. "Always" meaning his whole life, and he had a responsibility to make sure it would be there for Maggie and Willy. And it was not impossible that he and Many Clouds would have a child of their own to add to the mix. Once again, though, he reminded himself to concentrate on their current predicament.

Carolyn emerged from the house, Aunt Amelia and Cooper right behind her. So much for worrying about a visit. They all hurried across the porch, calling his name. He nudged his horse into a trot and met his mother at the bottom of the steps. They hugged and looked into one another's eyes. Her embrace seemed out of proportion in enthusiasm and duration for the small amount of time they'd been separated—just the few weeks since Maggie's birthday—but it had been quite a while since he'd visited the ranch. Finally, one of the ranch hands appeared and took the reins of his mount.

"I'll water him and rub him down, Andy," he said.

"Thanks, Mike. But I can do it if it's going to keep you from sentry duty."

"Oh, don't worry. We got three men covering."

"And you got the message about the new man, Remington?"

"We'll be looking out for him."

He then started to shake hands with Cooper, who stepped closer and turned the handshake into an embrace. He saved his last hug for Amelia, a woman he'd known for only a couple of years, but who seemed like she'd been in his life forever.

"Andy, Andy," she said. She cupped his face in her hands and planted a wet kiss on his cheek. "Every time you go away, I wonder if you'll ever come back." He turned to Carolyn. "You have things so under control, seems like there's no need for me at all."

She slapped his shoulder. "Ha. Ha. Let's go inside. I'll tell you how under control things are."

They stood in the kitchen, drinks in hand—bourbon for everyone but Amelia who chose lemonade as her beverage. She'd declared herself a teetotaler as a youth because she hated the taste of alcohol. The depredations she'd witnessed by drunks over the years had reinforced her attitude. She had migrated west with Cooper to join her brother, Shelby, the man she later learned was not only Carolyn's secret lover but, it turned out, Andy's father. Before they could complete their reunion properly, though, he was gunned down by the renegade Yellow Squirrel. Carolyn and Andy were the closest people to family either of them knew about, so they'd settled on a small farm in Sawtooth Valley.

Normally, the group would have gathered in the living room on the massive leather couch, a piece of furniture courtesy of patriarch Carter

Maxwell. However, with Ling Chu on his errand, Carolyn poured the drinks and they just stayed in the kitchen.

"Gentry came around in his new carriage," she said, "all shiny and bright."

"Are you speaking about the carriage or Gentry?"

"Both," she said with a chuckle. "He's adopted a banker's costume so he won't look so rough and ready, I guess. Not that he ever did."

"What did he have to say?"

"Just that he had something to tell me. I told him to write Barker about it then ran him off."

"Leaves us a little short of information, doesn't it?"

"Not necessarily. We'll see if he tells Barker anything important, or anything at all, or if he was just here to stir things up." Carolyn refreshed their drinks and now guided Andy toward the living room. When he was away, he always forgot how enormous the fireplace was. His grandfather Carter, the Maxwell and Circle M's founder and patriarch, had built it so a man could stand comfortably inside, even with his Stetson on. High on the wall, a few of the logs were superficially charred, the blackness varnished over. It was a purposeful reminder of the fire begun by Yellow Squirrel in his last assault on the Circle M, just before Willy ended his murderous campaign.

"We've been getting more trouble around our place, too, Mother. A man grabbed Willy the other day, might have abducted him if the boy hadn't stabbed him in the foot with his jackknife. Never let it be said that mumblety-peg is just a kids' game."

"Willy? Oh, my word. You're of course going to bring all three of them here for safekeeping."

"That means turning the Placerville property over to whoever's behind this. No, all three of them have weapons now. One of those new little Colt .25's for Many Clouds and knives for the kids. And we've hired guards. We're ready for an attack, if it comes."

Carolyn glanced at the floor. It was a moment Andy had been dreading, the moment when his mother knew they weren't depending on—dependent on—her support entirely. It was over in a flash. She finished her drink and stood. By unspoken mutual consent they strode out the front door and on to the veranda.

"First step," Andy said, "is to figure out who's masterminding all this and why."

Seventeen

The wagon horses lay in the meadow, Buster and Lily both, their throats cut and the earth around them stained dark with their blood. In their stalls lay what was left of the two milk cows, Swallow and Miller. The children leaned toward one another, but neither was sobbing. Unbelievable stoicism, Many Clouds thought, as she tried to imagine their feelings. Both parents gone, and now the animals who represented their spirits on earth slaughtered in front of them. They'd absorbed so much loss in their young lives. No tears. Not yet. But the pain had to be intense.

Many Clouds herself mourned the loss of the gentle animals. Gus Macy stood beside her, his rifle hanging at his side. "I'm sorry as can be, ma'am. I swear I was keeping a close watch, but I never saw nor heard nuthin'."

"Nor me, neither," echoed Sylvester Cunningham.

So two skilled and devoted sentinels hadn't been enough. Maggie realized the predators could just as easily have cut her throat as well as Willy's and Maggie's. Despite her brave words to Andy, she knew they weren't safe. Not yet.

Maggie rose and wrapped her arms around Many Clouds' waist. "Maybe we had better go stay with Grandma Carolyn for a while, Many Clouds." And it was a temptation. In fact, it had been her first impulse. But no. Not yet.

"Sylvester, do you still have friends among the Miwok outside of town?"

"Sure. My uncle and I hit the beaches together when Admiral Dewey landed us in Cuba. Fought shoulder to shoulder at San Juan Hill, too. Saw

Teddy in person, even though he didn't have as much to do with the battle that day as people think. Me and Antonio—"

"I'll listen to your war stories over a campfire sometime, Sylvester. For right now, I'd like you to go down and tell your folks that we have some meat right here free for the butchering. It'll just spoil if they don't take it. Tell a few of them—ones skilled in arms and trustworthy like your uncle—that we need extra guards around here. You and Gus are doing well, but there's only two of you."

Gus hung his head and kicked his toe hard into the dust. He obviously felt responsible.

"Gus," she said. He lifted his eyes.

"Ma'am?"

"You do that often?"

"Do what, ma'am?"

"Blame yourself for things you can't possibly control."

"Not generally no. It just seems like I hired on to do a job and didn't get her done."

"I want to sit down with you and Emmanuel and develop a new plan, Gus, but if you don't think you're up to it, I'll find someone else."

Gus squared his shoulders and looked her straight in the eye, though he had to tip his head downward to do it. "No, no. Don't fire me. Let's just us figure this out."

"Sylvester," she called to her other watchman, who was halfway to the gate. "Wait a moment." She hurried down to him and spoke in a low voice. "We both know that we Indians hear things other folks don't. Whites speak to each other like we aren't there because they don't think we're any more human than their furniture or their livestock."

"Mmm." He nodded.

"Andy's been talking to lawyers and lawmen about who's bedeviling us. I'm thinking that the Miwok could get twice the information in half the time."

Sylvester nodded and winked. "Good thinking," he said. "For a squaw."

Many Clouds smiled. "Watch your mouth or you'll end up with those cows." He laughed. "Out of here now."

When she returned to the corpses, Willy had joined his sister, both of them staring down at the remains. "What're we gonna do for milk without Swallow and Miller?"

"All the neighbors who have been getting free milk from us will probably help us out. If not, well, we'll cope somehow. What we most need to do is figure out who's after us, and I've put Sylvester on that job. And Andy and

Grandma Carolyn are working on it from their end. In the meantime, we've got other stock to take care of."

"I'll give the riding horses their oats," Maggie said.

"I'll lug some water for them and the goats," Willy said.

Even in the middle of danger, children or adults, we crave whatever's normal, Many Clouds thought. She started to go inside to commence some morning chores but thought better of leaving the children out here, even with Gus keeping watch. Instead, she grabbed a broom from off the porch rail and began sweeping. She had just gathered a pile dust at the top of the steps when a familiar buggy came in sight. The sight jolted her and she froze, the broom still a good foot from making contact with the porch.

The hawk-faced man with the paisley cravat was handling the reins. He didn't stop, but looked uphill toward her, smiled, and tipped his hat. Many Clouds came close to stepping inside to grab her .25 from the dining room table but restrained herself. The wagon didn't stop and soon disappeared around the uphill curve. Had Willy and Maggie seen him? They were still absorbed in their chores, so apparently not. Many Clouds drew her broom back and shouted an angry curse, an Arapaho word that was perhaps the worst name possible. In English it meant something like "ghost" or "skeleton", but she couldn't think of an accurate translation. Just as well. Let it stand on its own. She swung the broom and blasted the pile of dirt into the air. Its turmoil matched her own sense of isolation. A woman raised in one world and compelled to live in another.

Eighteen

"So I figure this," Remington Dillinger was saying. He was sitting at the head of the dining room table, with Carolyn, Andy, and Marshal Halstad, chief lawman of Sawtooth Wells, as his audience. "Hells, bells, what's this?" He coughed, his voice went hoarse, and he pointed his fork at the rice dish Ling Chu spooned on to his plate.

"Kung Pao chicken," Ling Chu said. "You like?"

Remy was guzzling water, emptied his glass and poured more from the pitcher.

"I grow the peppers myself. Good as anything you find in China."

"I'm sure they are," Remy said. "But I'm wondering if you got anything a little less potent?"

Carolyn smiled. "Ling, perhaps Mister Dillinger would like a few pot stickers and some won ton soup."

"Yes, Miss Carolyn," he said, an incipient grin on his face.

Halstad said, "That stuff's pretty good once you get used to it, but I had pretty much the same reaction you did first time." He smiled broadly, his grey mustache lifting at the corners.

"Why the hell didn't someone warn me?" Remy actually seemed a little angry.

"It's a touch of initiation," Andy said. "We went easy on you by not asking you to use chopsticks. That can get pretty comical. We've seen men throw down their napkins, storm out, and never darken our door again. We know we don't want to work with them after that anyhow."

"It remains to be seen whether I want to work with you myself, you know."

"Understood," Andy said, "but you didn't come all this way to tell us you're turning us down. Now, what is it you said you were figuring?"

Remy forked himself a pot sticker. "Now that's better. One of the best damned things I've ever tasted actually. You grow all this stuff also?"

"Even the pigs," Ling Chu said.

"Well hats off, and I'll take some of that wine, Miss Carolyn, if you've a mind to give me some now I've passed the first test." While Carolyn poured, Remington went on. "Andy, your guess about Southern Pacific seems to have some merit."

"But why would they fiddle around like this?" Carolyn said. "They've got enough money to buy whatever they want. Wouldn't they try that first?"

"Word is you're among those strange people who would rather have your land and freedom than money. And next step is that SP would starve you out by raising their shipping rates to the point where it cost more to send your crops or animals to market than it did to raise them. But that tactic is usually so they can control the markets by buying land at bargain rates then raising the products themselves and shipping on their own cars for no fees."

"And they've tried that here, but it doesn't pay with Sawtooth Valley," Carolyn said. "The cattle can travel on their own four legs and because we're off the rail line; we have to transport everything to market in Placerville on our own dime, and there's not enough agriculture happening around here to make a spur line profitable for the railroads."

"But Auburn is another story, way I hear it," Remy said.

"How so?" Carolyn said. "Auburn's thirty miles north of Placerville, and there's already a mainline heading east out of there to Chicago and the other big population centers."

"Wait a minute," Andy said. "What about toward Echo Summit and the south shore of Lake Tahoe?"

"Bingo," Remington said. "This soup. I've never tasted anything like this. How about another helping, Ling?" While Ling Chu ladled another bowlful, Remington went on. "You've seen the traffic increase along the road in front of that little cabin of yours."

Andy bridled at the notion that the two-bedroom house he and Many Clouds had built could be called a cabin. It was small, sure, but still… "Yes, they've been hauling a lot of materials up there in the last few months."

"The population's moving that way, Andy. The road could shoot right past the lake and into Nevada, then turn south and east past all the states and cities that were bypassed when the first transcontinental was built."

Carolyn said, "And you're suggesting that Andy and Many Clouds' house is in the way?"

"Have you heard anything like that?" Andy said.

"Not exactly, no. It's fifty-percent conjecture and fifty-percent gossip, but I'm going with it as a working theory. Plus, they're the only people I know with enough muscle to be hassling both Sawtooth Wells and Placerville at the same time. Think of the money it takes to payroll all the people they've got going after you."

"I used to be just a little country marshal before I got tangled up with you folks," Halstad said.

"And you'd expire out of boredom without us, Sheriff," Carolyn said. She placed a hand on his forearm. "Admit it, Michael."

"Pass that Kung Pao stuff again, Remington, will you? Since you're not using it," Halstad said.

The conversation turned to lighter themes for a time, then Remington stood. "Time to head out," he said.

"You're welcome to stay the night, Remy," Carolyn said. "We have more than enough room."

He shook his head. "I prefer to keep moving. Less of a target that way. Thanks for the hospitality. Compliments to the chef. See you all soon."

And he was out the door into the moonless night.

Nineteen

Many Clouds brought the children, Emmanuel, Gus, Sylvester, and Ezekiel together at the boulder uphill from the house.

"I've decided we're too vulnerable the way things are," she said. "We have to go to the Circle M after all, and we'll go on foot instead of the route we usually take. We'll be less of a target that way. Gus and Sylvester, please take the animals we have left to safe places. Don't tell me where, and try to make sure no one follows you when you leave."

"No," Maggie said.

"It won't be for long, kids, and it's for their own safety. And yours. Now please help me on this. It's hard enough without having to fight you."

"Do you really think—"

She interrupted Willy. "Yes, I do, or I wouldn't be doing this."

Emmanuel knelt beside Willy. "If anyone understands how savage these people can be, it's you, son. We can beat them if we're smart. And this is one smart move Many Clouds is proposing. Please hear her out."

Willy turned in a circle and growled again. "All I have to do is teach her a couple of more knife tricks and won't no one dare—"

"And no one will dare," Many Clouds corrected him. "Except they will dare, and they'll have more powerful weapons than even your new knives. Better to keep ourselves away from combat. Until we get this figured out, I think we'd be safer if we didn't stay in the house at all. Let's make moving targets of ourselves. We'll stay on the go, won't camp more than two nights in one place."

"We'll be vagabonds, won't we?" Maggie said.

"Where in the world did you learn that word?" Many Clouds said.

"It was in that *Oliver Twist* book Andy gave us. Mr. Fang called it of Oliver. He made it sound like a curse word."

"So, yes," Many Clouds said. "Vagabonds. But vagabond is only a description, not a curse. And for us, it's only temporary. Till we get more information and can talk to Andy."

"When will that be?"

"I don't have a time yet," she said. She wished she could give a better answer. She handed an envelope to Emmanuel.

"Please have someone deliver this to the Circle M so Andy and the others will know what we're up to. I'm afraid to send a telegram. The wrong people in Placerville are liable to read it."

Emmanuel took the message. "I'll make sure it gets there, but why don't you move to the village? They would protect you."

"Ah, it is a tempting idea. But if they attack you because of us… I can't get over the thought of that terrible fire in the Miwok village when Yellow Squirrel was after me. The infant who burned…"

"That would have happened even if you weren't there."

"Perhaps. But if it happened because I was there, and with Maggie and Willy… Even the idea makes me shake."

In one way, the fire three years earlier had been a blessing because it had brought her to Maggie and Willy and Miller Fitzpatrick, their father. She'd been traipsing through the hills on her way back to her tribal home in Wyoming when she was attacked by an itinerant preacher and his sidekick, hungry for any stray female they could find. Naked and hungry, she'd wound up in the Miwok village where Emmanuel and his men came from. The village had been swarmed on that night by an anti-Indian mob whipped into a frenzy by the same preacher who attacked her earlier. The horde burned the village and a sizable section of forest and brush land beyond it, and Many Clouds had been lucky to escape alive. Wounded, burned, and faint from thirst, she'd managed to crawl some distance to a dry creek bed where Willy and Maggie found her. It was bad enough imagining that she might not escape if it happened again, but much, much worse was the idea of what might happen to the children.

Ezekiel spoke up. "I will come along with you, Many Clouds."

"No," she said. "That's too many people, Ezekiel. It will be harder to conceal ourselves."

"Okay," he said, "but I'm an expert tracker. I could shadow you on your back trail, keep constant watch and check in with you time to time. With just you and the young 'uns it'll be harder to keep around-the-clock awake."

Many Clouds was silent. Everyone watched her.

"When you're this quiet it means you're going to do it, so why not let's just get going?" Willy said.

She smiled. "You know me too well, child. All right. Ezekiel, we'll be heading east and north, keeping to the north side of the road. We're packed up and ready to go. You can catch up, can't you?"

"It won't take me long to gather a few things. I'll find you."

"Excellent. And thank you, Emmanuel, for keeping the house safe. Gus and Sylvester, same to you."

"Our people must stay together and strong or we are lost," he said. "As well you know, Many Clouds, your first lookout needs to be for these kids."

She'd already prepared rucksacks, one for each of them, including Willy. His contained only a bedroll with a canteen attached. To Maggie she allotted only a loaf of bread, a brick of cheese, her bedroll, and the canteen. She herself carried the major portion of the few rations they had. She let Maggie take the lead while she brought up the rear. They headed up the hillside away from the house, the shed, the pasture, the graves of Maggie's and Willy's parents. Away from the apple tree, still small, but now considerably bigger than the sapling they had planted beside the graves. It should bear fruit the following year. Many Clouds didn't, somehow couldn't, look back.

Twenty

Remington Dillinger reclined on the leather sofa in the living room of the Circle M. His arm was bandaged, and Ling Chu was in the process of inserting the last of the dozen or so acupuncture needles that sprouted from his head and arm.

Ling Chu said, "Miss Carolyn, please move pillow under his knees. Yes. Much better."

Andy paced in front of the fireplace. "They were threatening. Now they're shooting. It's an escalation."

"How's the pain, Remy?" Carolyn asked.

"Don't know if it's the needles or the whisky, but it's calmed down considerable, Ma'am."

Carolyn laughed. Ling Chu smiled even though he had argued against the whisky. Ling Chu, she thought, was developing a sense of humor in his old age. No, he wasn't that old. Though she didn't know how old he was, she'd always speculated they were the same age, and she wasn't ready to call herself an old woman by a long shot.

Andy said, "I was thinking I need to get out in the morning and see if I can find some tracks of whoever ambushed you, but on second thought I don't think it'll do much good. The tracks will just get lost once he gets to the main road."

"I'll go with you," Remy declared.

"Mr. Remy, you must not ride tomorrow," Ling said. "Day after okay, but not tomorrow."

"Doctor's orders," Carolyn said, gesturing toward Ling Chu.

"And this is one doctor you'd better not cross," Andy said.

"Thanks for the help. All of you. But that bullet didn't hit nothing but meat, so it's not going to keep me out of the saddle."

Ling Chu flushed and raised his arms, but Carolyn raised her hand to stay him.

"At least let us keep you from any hard riding and from taking unnecessary chances. We'll take a leisurely tour of the ranch. I'm sure you'll agree you'll be more help to us and everyone else if you know more about the history and lay of the land around here. Am I right?"

Remy started to raise himself to object, then fell back with a groan. He sighed. "All right. But second day I'm back on the road to earn my money."

***

Not long after sunrise, Carolyn and Remy, his arm in a sling but with no needles visible, dismounted and sat side by side on the boulder that gave Granite Spring its name. The sun warmed the rocky base of the three huge Sawtooth Peaks to the west.

The icy water pooled clear below them, so clear a person could see small pebbles many feet below the surface. It was a two-mile ride from the Circle M yard to the spring, and their vantage point gave them a view of the place as clear as if they'd been hawks cruising for prey.

"Looks like an architect's drawing," Remy said. "If it wasn't for the horses kicking up dust in yonder corral, it wouldn't look real."

"That's what I like most about it," Carolyn said. "The order. Dad wanted to make sure the Circle M didn't just sprawl all higgledy-piggledy like most ranches. He was a planner."

"What's that pile of sawdust, though?"

"We usually keep that cleaned up, but things have been busy. We have our own small sawmill. There was no lumberyard in the beginning. This was pretty much wilderness."

"So your old man built his own mill. Nicely done, but how's all this going to help now?"

Carolyn was beginning to get irritated. She loved every aspect of the Circle M, loved explaining its history, but she was coming to the part she hated to admit. "Dad located the ranch in an ideal spot to match his vision. Springs at the base of the peaks generate Granite creek, which waters the whole valley. But..." Her voice caught in her throat.

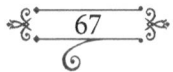

"But it's also an ideal spot for an ambush," Remy said. "You can sit up here in the rocks or up in the trees and shoot wherever and whoever you want."

"And that's happened more than once," she said. She remembered holding the bloody head of Andy's father in her lap. She recalled the pain of the bullet that had passed through her own side and nearly killed her. And those were just the first incidents that sprang to mind. "We have patrols on the fences and trails, but we can't surround the place with an army."

"No self-respecting army officer would choose this. It's pretty much indefensible."

"He was thinking about ranching, not military strategy. But we can't pick up the whole place and move, so we must do what we can. In the meantime, we have to stop the attack before it even gets here, which is where you come in."

"Well, I haven't done much good at all so far. Didn't expect shooting so early in the game."

"It may not be as early in the game as we thought."

"Let's ride back downhill and approach from the east. We'll talk more on the way."

Carolyn welcomed the companionship and the opportunity to share ideas. However, she wished it were Andy at her side instead of Remy. She feared that Andy would not stop at trying to track the ambusher but would be so concerned about Many Clouds that he'd keep riding north, figuring she herself would be safe with Remington. Why couldn't she accept that her son was approaching thirty years old, an adult, making adult decisions that might not include her? She'd made such choices of her own when she'd gone off to school instead of staying home to take over the Circle M as her father had wished her to. It had happened again when Andy's younger brother, Julian, had been stabbed to death, and Andy had gone off to Wyoming looking for justice. Finally, he'd moved in with Many Clouds and the children, choosing a life with them in that small cabin over one with her in his capacious ancestral home. Illogical though it was, she felt forsaken. Once again, she and the Circle M were in someone's sights, and she had to defend it alone.

Twenty-One

Andy felt like a traitor, and his stomach was tight with guilt. He'd found the vantage point the shooter had used to fire on Remy, a knoll near Shingle Lake just off the trail about halfway between the ranch and the main road. What's more, the right rear shoe of the sniper's horse had lost the hook off its right rear heel caulk, making it easy to track. He'd followed it all the way to the main road, had determined that the rider had turned left toward Placerville rather than right toward Sawtooth Wells. However, the deep dust and heavy traffic on the main road defeated his tracking efforts. Sawtooth Wells was closer, so he inquired at the livery stable, asking after animals sporting such an anomaly with no luck. He wasn't going to catch up with this guy today. The sun was low in the west, and every minute that passed, he grew more worried about his little family in Placerville. He suddenly knew that's where he was headed rather than back to the Circle M. Was he deserting his mother for Many Clouds? He couldn't look at it that way. Mother had Remy. Many Clouds had him and her Miwok friends. A lot of protection, granted, but he felt he belonged there, not here. He rented an extra horse for night riding, sent his mother a telegram, and headed for Many Clouds and the children. His woman, his children, his property. Their children. Their property.

Twenty-Two

It was nearing noon, and Remington was becoming impossible to contain.

"I need to earn my keep and stop whoever's after you Maxwells, and I can't do it sitting around here. I should be out talking to people, looking up deeds and records and the like."

"Okay, okay," Carolyn said. "After lunch you're free to go. Just stay out of the way of those stray bullets."

"Only thing stray about that bullet was it hit me in the arm instead of between the eyes." He imitated a gunshot, pointed to the middle of his forehead and snapped his head back.

Carolyn laughed. Remington had been a chore to take care of, but his lighthearted humor was refreshing. "Well, don't take any unnecessary chances. We'll need you upright for the duration."

"Now that's one order I'll be happy to comply with, ma'am."

Ling Chu had laid out a spread of sandwiches and cold tea on the veranda. Carolyn had in mind that they would chat and plan while they ate, but Remington wolfed his food and gulped his beverage and leaped to his feet.

"I'm off," he said. "I'll be back in touch when I can." So Remington was leaving, and Andy hadn't yet returned.

"Keep an eye out for Andy, will you? I'm starting to worry that the same sniper that got you might be after him as well."

"It's faster to go by way of town than the back trail, but you make a strong argument for changing my plan. Adios." He leapt off the veranda, then stopped, obviously listening to something.

"What is it?" Carolyn said. Then she heard it, too. The chuggety clank of an approaching automobile. Presently Ling Chu joined them.

"Big car. Big engine," he said.

The sound of an internal combustion engine had ceased to be the novelty it once was on the Circle M, especially since Ling Chu had pioneered its use a couple of years earlier. But it was still unusual enough to get people's attention. The eyes of all hands were riveted on the archway, and before long their vigilance was rewarded with the sight of a sleek, silvery, six-seater touring Oldsmobile. Its top was down, and it kicked up enough dust for a half-dozen galloping horses. It sailed into the yard and slewed to a stop just short of Remington, who refused to move as the machine roared toward him.

"So much for curbing your reckless behavior, Remy," Carolyn remarked.

They descended the steps when the automobile stopped and watched the driver alight and open a rear door for a pinstripe-coated man with a plump mustache, primly waxed at each end.

He marched up to Carolyn and declared himself to be at her service with a click of heels and a quick bow of his head.

"William Sproule, is it not?" Carolyn said. "You left out that detail."

"Detail?"

"Your name."

"Oh, dear," he chuckled. "My apologies. The ride has been a rough one, and the heat ferocious at for this elevation and so late in the year."

What would he have done, Carolyn thought, on horseback with the heat and dust a good deal heartier than they were on a fall day such as today? She stood silent as Sproule went on. "May I present my associates, Mr. Craven Moss— " he gestured toward a plump man in overalls and a denim work shirt, who remained seated in the rear seat. "Mr. Moss is a mechanic. I find it prudent to have one such available on these journeys. This Oldsmobile is as dependable a machine as any on the road, but it wouldn't do to be marooned in the hinterlands without help." Moss made no movement of greeting. "And this," Sproule said, "is Mr. Otis Morelli, who is doubling as chauffeur and accountant today." Morelli, deep-set eyes peering past a thin nose, tipped his chin in silent hello.

"And, in turn," Carolyn said, "I'd like to introduce Mr. Remington Dillinger, Mr. Sproule. Mr. Sproule, Remy, is the president of the Southern Pacific Railway."

"We have evolved beyond that name, Mrs. Maxwell. We are the Southern Pacific Transportation Company now, and our reach extends well beyond the rails. We—"

Carolyn interrupted. "Yes, yes. How soon one forgets. You monopolized the ferry traffic on San Francisco Bay, and you now own practically every freight wagon in the state in addition to the railroad." William Sproule smiled and squared his shoulders in pride. Carolyn did not share the smile.

"To what do I owe the pleasure?" she said.

"Well, if we could sit up on your handsome veranda, I have some observations to share with you."

"I'm comfortable here, if it's all right with you," she said. This time she smiled, but Sproule did not.

"If you prefer, of course. You own property outside the town of Placerville."

"True."

"Southern Pacific would like to purchase it."

Carolyn and Remington shared a glance. Here came the offer they'd speculated about earlier. Maybe Sproule figured the intimidation efforts had weakened their resistance.

"Is that so?"

"Yes, and at a very handsome price."

"I'm sorry, Mr. Sproule, but there are two obstacles to such a bargain. First of all, my son, Andrew, shares the ownership of the property, as I'm sure you're aware. Second of all, I feel confident in speaking for him when I say that it is not for sale."

"Once he hears the price, I feel sure he'll change his mind."

"Not as sure as I am that he will not."

Sproule stepped toward her. "There are other considerations than money, of course. We understand that your son and his… mate are in a rather vulnerable position."

Remington stepped between the cravat man, Craven, and Sproule. "Vulnerable? Care to explain that?"

Sproule sidled away from Remy and toward the man he'd introduced as Otis Morelli. He said, "Well, the house is next to a public thoroughfare, easily accessible to various undesirable elements. And there are children at risk."

"At risk of what?" Remington said.

"We're getting off track here," he said. "I haven't had the chance to present our full offer. In addition to the money, we know there is the sensitive question of exhumation."

"You're not much for subtlety, are you, William Sproule?" Carolyn said.

Morelli stepped forward. "We are aware that the children's father and mother are buried near the cabin."

"House," Remington said.

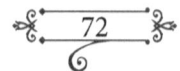

"Yes," Morelli continued. "Even though the children's mother was an Indian, their father was white, it would be disrespectful to ignore them. We would as gently as possible relocate them to a place of your choosing. Perhaps in that small graveyard you maintain here on the ranch."

Carolyn quivered with rage as she advanced on Sproule. It felt like an invasion of privacy that he would even know of their private family burial plot, let alone speak of it. "Does this man speak for you and all of Southern Pacific?"

Sproule glanced at Morelli, then looked Carolyn in the eye. "Yes, of course."

"Only from a perch of corporate arrogance could you even mention such a thing. And let me assure you that we are fully aware of what you call our 'vulnerabilities.' You've tried to soften us up with everything from intimidation to gunfire, then you come here with this obscene proposal."

"Gunfire?" Sproule seemed genuinely puzzled.

Remington said, "This bandage ain't on my arm for a shaving nick."

She had to give Sproule credit for a quick recovery. "Southern Pacific would not be responsible for such outrages. We are a business corporation."

Carolyn had remained in a face-off with Sproule. Remington stepped between them.

"Probably want to back off, partner," he said.

"And head out," Carolyn said.

"I hate to leave you with the mistaken impression that—"

"—no 'mistaken' about it, Mr. Sproule." Carolyn's tone was arctic-cold. "We had our suspicions, but you've confirmed them all." She wished for Andy at her side.

They watched the three men pile into the machine and drive away. Sproule slammed his hand on the door, obviously angry.

Ling Chu joined them as the car drove out of the yard. "Don't know, but one thing very good."

"What's that, Ling?"

"That Oldsmobile have electric starter. No Crank." He smiled and threw Carolyn a glance.

Carolyn pretended she hadn't noticed the smile, but she knew what he'd be asking for next.

Twenty-Three

"I can't go no further, Many Clouds," Maggie said. She shucked her rucksack and dropped it in the dust.

"Me neither." Willy followed his sister's lead with his own rucksack.

"*Any* further," Many Clouds said. "But never mind that. It's getting dark, and even though we haven't come as far as I wanted, we'd better stop."

"Where's Ezekiel?" Willy asked.

"I'm sure he'll be along presently," Many Clouds said. "See that little flat downslope from us? That should be big enough to spread our beds. It'll be a dry camp, but nothing we haven't done before, so let's get to it while we can still see a little."

In truth, Ezekiel's absence had her worried. He was an expert woodsman and under normal circumstances, he would have caught up with them hours earlier. She could imagine only three possibilities. He had met with an accident, had met with foul play, or had abandoned them. Or, she thought as they made their skitter way downhill to the campsite, perhaps some unknowable circumstance had delayed him for a period of time. He would appear the next day. She decided that was the most optimistic alternative and fastened on it for the time being.

They laid their bedrolls on the bare ground, there being no evergreen boughs or other padding in the vicinity. They also decided against a fire, settling on water and pemmican for supper. Their supply of neither would last long, but if someone other than Ezekiel was tracking them and intending harm it would be best to make themselves hard to find for as long as they could.

"Tomorrow, we will reach the Yuba River," Many Clouds said. "From there, we will find water and more cover and food—fish and squirrels if nothing else."

"Then what?" Maggie said.

"I'm thinking that once our message gets to the Circle M, Andy will come find us with reinforcements."

"What if he doesn't?" Willy said.

"We'll go back south and circle back over Yuba pass till we get to the Circle M. But I'm sure he'll find us. Our plan is in the note I sent. For now, we sleep. Without rest, we'll all soon wear out, and all the plans in the world will get us nowhere. Willy, you take the first watch. Two hours."

"Hooray. I can use the railroad watch Andy gave me for Christmas."

"Exactly what I had in mind. I'll take the second. Maggie, you take the third. Then it's back to Willy till the sun appears."

As she lay down, all the anxieties about Ezekiel returned. The whole idea of sleep seemed as distant as the farthest star. But to her surprise, Willy had to wake her from a sound slumber to take her lookout shift. Maybe their little trio was better prepared than she thought.

Twenty-Four

Harry Barker hadn't yet opened his office when Andy arrived not long after sunrise, so he proceeded to the lawyer's house. It was an unpretentious two-story clapboard affair with a tin roof and a tangle of dried sweet peas curling around the four-by-four pillars that supported the roof over the small porch. Despite its unkempt appearance, the paint was in good shape and the place appeared to be well taken care of. Barker answered Andy's knock promptly, knotting his string tie, a small drop of egg yolk on his chin.

"You can't leave yet, Harry," called a female voice from within the house.

"I'm in a hurry, sweetheart," he answered.

A blonde-haired bundle in pink chiffon flew into the room and wrapped her arms around Barker's waist. "Not before you kiss me goodbye, Mr. Barker."

"Marilyn, not in front of company."

Marilyn paid no attention but stood on her tiptoes and planted a long smooch on Barker's plump lips. Barker reacted by drawing back at first but before long hugged his wife back and answered her kiss fervently. Andy felt he should have been embarrassed, but instead he enjoyed the man's romantic moment, not as a voyeur, but just because he was glad for him. Though he had never thought about it before, he realized Barker had always seemed a bit of a stuffed shirt, and it was both gratifying and entertaining to see him enjoying himself.

Once the kiss was finally concluded, Barker straightened himself, took his wife's head in his hands, and whispered a farewell.

"Bye, Harry Berry. I'll have those loose boards on the back porch replaced and painted and dinner ready when you get back."

He smiled, blew her a kiss, and joined Andy on the front porch.

"What in the world brings you here at this hour, Andy? Are both those horses yours?"

"Your wife does carpentry and cooks too?" Andy said.

"Being married to Marilyn is like being married to a handyman and a chef all in one. If it weren't for her… but never mind that. Let's talk while we walk, Andy."

By the time Andy finished explaining the situation, they had arrived at the livery stable, which was on the way to Barker's office.

"Shot? Remington was shot? Was there a man named Morelli involved?"

Andy didn't recognize the name. "I don't know who pulled the trigger, but you can bet that Southern Pacific paid him. Why don't you go on to your office, Harry? I've got to get a fresh mount then head out to the house."

"I'll wait right out here," Barker said. "I'm not letting you out of my sight."

It was a puzzling remark, Andy thought, but he was too anxious to get his horse exchanged to pursue it. The second he emerged from the stable with a spry young paint in tow, Barker stepped close to him and told him about the visit from Morelli as they walked toward his office.

"You pulled a gun on him?" Andy said. "I didn't know you kept one in your desk."

"First time in twenty years I've had it out. I didn't know if it would even fire. Believe me, I've oiled it and tried it out a couple of times since."

"What do you think he wanted?"

"Pretty obvious, I think. He wanted to see if he could drive a wedge between me and the Maxwells, maybe even to the point of hiring me away from you. Failing that, he wanted to make sure I understood you and I both were under a threat."

"He never said that, did he?"

"Nope, but the implication was pretty clear. So, when you told me Remington turned up wounded, I thought it was all of a piece with that visit from Morelli."

"Damnation," Andy said. "Have you heard anything about Many Clouds and the children?"

Barker shook his head. "Not a thing. However, you should know that your accounts have been cancelled all over town. Order is out that it's cash only for a Maxwell or anyone connected with them. Many Clouds ran into some trouble with it a couple of days ago. Get on out there, Andy, but be extra careful." He clapped a hand on Andy's shoulder. "I never imagined… well, I thought all the Maxwell misfortune had finally settled down."

"Apparently not," Andy said. "I'll get over and talk to Meyer Sturges at the bank as soon as I can. He's either behind all this account-canceling business or knows who is and why. First, though, I have to get on out to the house." He leaped into the saddle. He started to calculate how long since he'd had a wink of sleep, but he gave it up as an unprofitable exercise. As he emerged from the telegraph office, where he'd wired a new article to *The Elevator* as well as a message to the Circle M, he noticed an Indian leaning against a hitching rail rolling a cigarette. The man looked uncommonly sober compared to the drunks that commonly slouched in the alleyways and doorstops around town. Andy nodded to him. The man lit the cigarette without responding. Or maybe he hadn't seen him. But the encounter was so brief and seemingly insignificant that it fled Andy's mind almost immediately. He was seeing danger at every turn whether it was there or not. He hurried toward his anticipated reunion with Many Clouds and the children.

Corporate Gangsters Resort to Firearms
Special to *The Elevator* by Andrew Maxwell

My previous column outlined the depredations of Corporations like Southern Pacific in their unrelenting attacks on local businesses and landowners. I wish I could report that their activities have diminished. Instead, they have not only redoubled their efforts at intimidation, but have escalated the situation into a shooting war. A private investigator looking into recent assaults on honest landowners in Sawtooth Valley was fired upon and wounded. Luckily, his injuries were relatively minor, and he has vowed to continue his investigations. We hope that what he and others discover will help bring the schemes of these scoundrels to an end and deliver just deserts to the perpetrators.

In the meantime, I send this message to the malefactors: We will not rest. You will not prevail. Justice always finds a way, and it will crush your perfidy in the end.

Twenty-Five

It was around noon when the rattler hit Willy in the leg. It was a powerful strike that pierced his boot top. Maggie pulled out her derringer, dispatched the creature, and tossed the carcass far into the brush. Nevertheless, the damage to Willy was done. He was not one for tears, but they flowed now.

"I'm scared. Am I going to die? I don't want to."

"No, darling, no dying. Just sit down here on this log. Willy, can you get that knife out of its sheath? And, Maggie, get the matches out of the rucksack."

Many Clouds pulled the boot off and inspected the leg. The bite mark appeared just below the calf muscle, and there was evidence of only one fang. The other somehow didn't make it all the way through the boot leather or perhaps had been broken off earlier in the creature's life. At any rate, she hoped one fang meant less venom. There was almost no blood, but Many Clouds hadn't expected any. Snake bites didn't bleed much, deadly though they were.

She untied the rawhide sash from around her waist and cinched it tightly around Willy's leg, just below the knee, between the bite and the heart. Then she picked up Willy's knife, directed Maggie to light a match, then passed the blade through the flame several times. After that, she gave Willy a stick to bite on while she made a small incision at the point of the bite.

Willy was whimpering but trying hard not to cry out.

"Brave boy," Many Clouds said. "Now I'm going to try and get rid of some of the poison. I promise this part won't hurt."

She sucked and drew blood, then spit it out. She repeated the process several times, hoping it would draw off the worst of the poison. Soon the puncture and all the skin around it was almost white. She didn't know whether this would cure or even help. Both her reason and her knowledge of her ancestors' treatments for bites dictated that the poison didn't pool just around the injection point but would get into the bloodstream, and she didn't know what to do once that happened. All she could do was try to prevent it. Her people sometimes used a sweat lodge as part of the treatment, but that wasn't possible here.

"Is that going to make him better?" Maggie said.

Many Clouds knew the most important thing she could do for the moment was to project calm and confidence, even if it meant lying.

"We're just going to rest here for a while, kids, so Willy's heart doesn't pump that venom through his system too fast. With only one fang to work with, that critter couldn't do as much harm as he wanted to, so we'll just take a breather till you feel a bit better, Willy. I'm sure you'll be okay before too long."

Willy nodded with faint conviction.

There was no real clearing, so they spread their blankets on the trail single file.

"It's a long way down to that creek, Maggie," Many Clouds said. "Think you can make it down there and fill up our canteens for us?"

"Sure, I can. I'm not the one got snake bit. Be back directly."

She gathered the canteens, then sidestepped down the steep hillside with all the agility of a deer in flight. It was a good hundred yards to the bottom of the little canyon and the creek looked to be no more than a dribble at this time of year, before the winter rains started. But the shallow pools should yield enough to keep them going for a while.

Many Clouds turned her attention to Willy, who was lying on his blanket holding his injured leg. His eyes were wet, and beads of sweat clustered on his forehead. "It hurts, Many Clouds, and I feel kind of sickish."

"I've done all I can for now. Just hold tight and go on being brave and we'll be just fine before you know it." Willy snuggled closer, and Many Clouds started murmuring the prayer they'd had to say every day at the missionary camp. She said it only occasionally, but now for some reason she needed it. "Our Father, who art in heaven…" Willy shivered, leaned over the side of the blanket, and threw up his breakfast.

Many Clouds wiped his mouth with a bandana, reflecting on her own recent bouts with nausea as she did so. "Maggie will be back with water any time now." How she was supposed to give courage to these children when she was so terrified herself, she didn't know. Where was Ezekiel? Where was Andy? She hated being dependent, but right now she felt like she'd reached the bottom of her bucket of courage. She needed to find a way to fill it up again for the sake of this shivering boy in her arms and the sake of the little sister—Many Clouds was somehow sure the new baby would be a girl. "Amen," she whispered.

Twenty-Six

The rider galloped into the Circle M ranch yard, pulled back on the reins, and left his horse dancing in a circle while he leaped to the ground.

"Telegram for Mrs. Maxwell," he bellowed, his mouth opening like a megaphone through his thick black beard. He waved a yellow envelope in his upraised hand.

"Right here, Billy," Carolyn said from the veranda. "As you can plainly see. Are you ever going to quit playing like you were in the circus or something?"

"Job's too important for acting ordinary, ma'am." He handed her the telegram and pulled a notebook from the satchel at his side. "Sign here if you please." Signature gathered, Billy Avila leapt on his horse and sped toward his next station as if he were one of the old Pony Express riders. Ling Chu was on the porch to watch him go.

"Something from Mr. Andy?" he said.

Carolyn mounted the steps while tearing into the envelope. "He's gone to Placerville." The news jabbed her heart, but at least he was safe. She could understand the logic, since he probably figured Remington and the ranch hands were here, while Many Clouds and the children had comparatively little protection. But Remington was gone. Spread out like this, the family couldn't communicate. If Many Clouds had been here… but then there was that damned house to protect. That precious house she had paid for. Of course, it was Andy's money too, she reminded herself.

"We could go there, too," Ling Chu said. "Drive car. All be together. Better for us."

"You've gone mad, Ling Chu. We can't leave the ranch unprotected. All the animals and buildings, and there's so much to tend to. Feeding, repairs, maintenance. The weather's going to turn any time."

"Cowboys can fix fences without you. They ride like now. Two, three, together with rifles."

"And who feeds them? You don't want a stranger in your kitchen."

"Bunkhouse have kitchen, and Mr. Cory cooks chuckwagon on roundup. One week, even two, everything be fine."

Carolyn remembered how much damage Yellow Squirrel had done in a mere twenty-four hours when he set fire to the house. And he was just one man, and they'd all been here along with extra guards. What could the Southern Pacific men do when everyone was absent?

"I'll think about it, Ling. It's worth considering, even though it frightens me beyond measure."

"We could drive there very fast and drive everywhere around there also."

"I suppose you think it would save time if we bought a new car with an electric starter so we didn't have to waste time with the crank."

"You smart woman. Someone say they sell these in Placerville now."

"'Maybe' on the idea of a sojourn to Auburn, Ling. But 'no' on the new car."

"Even smart women sometime not so smart. Have much work to do," Ling said as he hurried inside, his step coming as close to an angry stomp as he was able.

Twenty-Seven

Midnight, and Willy couldn't stop vomiting, even though there had been nothing left for him to throw up for some hours. Skunk cabbage was a good remedy, she knew, but it had to be boiled and fed as a liquid. In any case there was none in the vicinity, so she was out of ideas. Even if his stomach calmed immediately, Many Clouds was afraid that he would be too weak to continue. Waiting and hoping was obviously not a good strategy. They needed help. Ordinarily the place to find it was back at the house they had just fled, yet possible danger awaited there now. Never mind. Conditions and distances were too uncertain to go forward. At least there were some of her people at the house.

By dawn, Willy seemed some better. At least his stomach had quit its convulsions. However, he could barely sit up enough to sip some water, then he fell back asleep. Many Clouds had to do what she'd feared doing.

"Maggie, you see what a fix your brother is in. I'm going to ask you to do something no twelve-year-old should have to do."

"I can make it," Maggie said.

"Make what?"

"Make it back to the house and bring some help."

"Well, aren't you the smart one?"

"Seems obvious that's the only way out of this if we're going to save Willy."

"I guess it is. I thought a long time trying to find another way, but I kept coming back to it like a mule plodding his circle at a mill. So listen carefully. It's important to be mindful. Speed is important, but if you try to go so fast you fall off a cliff, it's not going to help. Watch your step. Second, keep an eye out for whoever's trying to do us harm. I wish I knew the exact who or why of it, but trust no one you don't know. I hope to goodness you run into Ezekiel or Andy on the way, but if not, just explain everything to Emmanuel and lead him back here. I'll carry Willy as far as I can, but with him on my back, you'll be much faster."

She gave Maggie the last of the brick of cheese she'd brought. Then she hugged her tight, whispered a good luck, and watched her trot back in the direction from which they'd come until she disappeared around a bend in the trail.

She rigged a carrier for Willy out of her shawl and her own rucksack, shedding herself of all rations except the canteen. She began her own trek toward the house, her heart filled with a mixture of fear and determination.

Twenty-Eight

When Andy arrived at the house, he was dismayed to find it empty. No one was in sight. What had happened? He emerged after searching the inside, jumped off the porch and started to circle the cabin, pistol drawn, eyes darting back and forth between the ground where he was looking for signs of someone lurking or approaching. He was almost finished circling the building, his back to front gate, when Emmanuel challenged him.

"Stop where you are, mister, raise your hands, and explain yourself."

Andy obeyed the command to raise his hands. "It's Andy, Emmanuel. Don't shoot."

"Andy. Where have you been?"

Andy ran to Emmanuel. "Where are Many Clouds and the children?"

"They are on the run. Things got too dangerous around here. I'm guarding the house."

"You're alone?"

"For right now. I was supposed to have help, but they disappeared. More will come."

"Disappeared? Why for God's sake?"

Emmanuel hesitated, drew a deep breath, then invited Andy to sit on the front steps with him. "Not every Indian is happy with Many Clouds, Andy."

"I know there's been opposition from both races about our getting together, but surely that wouldn't get so intense they'd let her come to harm. And the children."

"That is what I thought as well. I had men I trusted, some I wasn't that sure of, but no one I thought would desert. Yet right now, I am alone."

"Where did Many Clouds go?"

"North and east. That's all she would say."

"I guess she didn't trust folks to keep a secret."

"It turned out she was right to be suspicious," Emmanuel said. "Ezekiel went with her, though, so she's got some protection."

Andy had to give no thought at all to his next move. The house didn't matter. He had to find his family.

"Keep guard here, Emmanuel, the best you can. Be careful. There's already been some shooting." He told him about Remington. "I don't want you to be the next victim."

Twenty-Nine

Maggie's legs ached, and she was gasping, but she wouldn't stop running except for brief breath-catching pauses. She kept picturing Willy, weaker than a newborn puppy. She didn't know how far she was from the house. Several times she'd seen surroundings that appeared familiar, but their familiarity had turned out to be an illusion. She leaned uphill against a boulder, afraid if she sat down, she wouldn't get up. Suddenly Ezekiel appeared beside her.

"Ezekiel." She was almost sobbing she was so relieved. "Willy's been snake-bit. He's bad off. We got to get him to a doctor."

"You know no doctor—"

"I know no white doctor's going to treat him, so we need a shaman or someone who knows how to deal with rattler bites. Where have you been, anyways?"

"I was… delayed," he said. "You go on back to Many Clouds and Willy. I'll follow with someone who can help your brother. You'll kill yourself trying to run all this way."

She knew Ezekiel only slightly. He'd never been close to the family the way Emmanuel was. She suddenly didn't trust him. Something about the hesitation in his answer about the delay seemed false. She couldn't have explained it, but she had to obey her instincts. She dodged around him and kept running. He reached for her and got a brief, light grip on her shoulder, but his hand slid off before he could stop her. She heard him behind her, thought of how much longer his stride was than hers. The landscape was flat at that point, so it was a sprint she was bound to lose.

There was a downslope to the left and a cluster of boulders. She dashed for that, leaped from rock to rock, then slipped and slid over dead leaves downhill. At one point, she had to grab a tree trunk to brake her downhill momentum and risked a glance upward. Ezekiel stood watching. She thought he was smiling, but from the distance, she couldn't be sure. The main thing was he wasn't following. Before long, she reached the creek. All she had to do now was follow it to the house. It was a longer way than the trail, but it seemed Ezekiel wasn't interested in catching her. Someone might give her trouble at the house, but she had her knife, and if she was thwarted there, she knew the way to the Miwok village outside of Placerville. One way or another she would get Willy help.

Thirty

On foot, leading his horse, Andy trotted up the path that led in the direction Emmanuel described. He mounted and rode over the stretches where it was possible. Once he met up with Many Clouds, he figured, they could lift Willy to the horse and make better time. He wished there were an automobile at the house. They could motor into town and get some help. From whom? Maybe Barker had an idea. He was afoot when he rounded a sharp turn and nearly ran smack into Ezekiel, who was sitting quietly on a rock.

"Andy," he said.

"What are you doing here, Ezekiel? I thought you were with Many Clouds and the kids."

"I was, but a rattlesnake bit Willy, and I left him with Many Clouds and Maggie while I came for help."

"Snakebite? How long ago? How is he? Why are you just sitting here?"

"I was just stopping for a quick breather."

Ezekiel's reply rang false, but there was no time for an argument. "Go get help, then. I'm going to find the others. Meet you at the house."

Andy jogged up the trail and around a curve. He soon lost sight of Ezekiel and shortly came to a wide spot where he could mount up. He nudged his horse into a trot, the fastest pace he could risk.

He wasn't in the habit of prayer, had no particular religious convictions. His only exposure had been to a couple of revival tent meetings his mother had dragged him to because she thought he should at least be exposed.

They'd disgusted him. The obvious demagoguery from the pulpit and the exploitation of the miserable creatures who dragged themselves down the aisles to receive the phony blessings and prayers put him off any thought of joining an organized religion.

Now, though, he caught himself engaging in something that seemed a lot like prayer. So be it, he thought. I wish, I hope, I, yes, *pray* my people are safe. He nearly broke into tears when he saw them at last. They were a couple of hundred yards away, but a few moments after he spotted them, he lost sight of them behind another rise. Many Clouds was almost staggering under the bundle on her back, a bundle he judged to be Willy.

The trail, a deer path, really, was too narrow on the precarious hillside to mount up. He jogged as fast as he dared, reminding himself that none of his efforts were worth anything if he got hurt as well.

At last, he spotted her again. He called as he approached. Many Clouds stopped, waved, then came on. And so they hurried slowly toward each other, and Andy's heart filled with hope. But was he too late to help Willy? He'd soon find out.

Thirty-One

Many Clouds stumbled, caught herself before she struck the ground, then kept going. She sensed Andy was close, coming nearer by the minute even though she couldn't see him at that instant. She had nothing but instinct to suggest his presence, but she was convinced he was near. Even so, she couldn't stop and wait for him. Every second of delay might be the one that meant it was too late for Willy.

"Many Clouds."

She heard Andy's shout, but her vision had turned hazy, and she couldn't see him. The trail now looked like a painting that had been smudged and smeared. She felt she was underwater, unable to tell whether she was diving or rising. If she kept hold of Willy, he would fall with her, if she was indeed falling, and she couldn't have him sharing her fate. She lifted the bundle that was the precious child and set it aside all at the same time she felt herself spiraling away from him. She heard Andy's voice again, or thought she did. She couldn't be sure. For a few moments she continued unsure of anything, then darkness wrapped her in a blanket of forget.

Thirty-Two

Maggie lay on her belly, alternately gasping and drinking deeply from the creek below their house. Her thirst quenched, she leaped back on her feet and headed uphill. She had expected Emmanuel or one of the other Indians to be on guard, but the place looked deserted. She felt bewildered and terrified. Where could she get help for her little brother now? Running all the way to the native village was too time-consuming. She could wait here. Maybe whoever was watching the place was away for only a few minutes. Maybe if she headed back in the direction she'd come, she could at least help Many Clouds carry Willy. Everything she could think of seemed desperate and doomed.

"Help us," she yelled. "My brother's hurt."

Silence.

"Help."

Silence.

Then she felt a hand on her shoulder.

"It's all right, Maggie. We can take care of this together."

She looked up. Ezekiel was smiling, but not in a way that comforted her in the slightest.

"I thought you were going for help, Ezekiel."

"And so I was, but I had a slight interruption. Come with me, now, and we'll complete what I started." He held out his hand and stepped in the direction of town.

"You go," Maggie said. "I'll wait here."

"It's best you follow," Ezekiel said. He grabbed her wrist and pulled.

"No." Maggie yelled now and pulled back. "I'm not going with you." She twisted and yanked till it hurt, but Ezekiel was too strong. "Help," she yelled. "Emmanuel. Anyone." She suddenly tasted horse sweat and manure as Ezekiel stuffed a dirty bandanna in her mouth.

"It truly is best you come with me," he said. He scooped her up, flailing and kicking, and headed uphill toward the thicker timber. "This is only the first of many lessons you and your mongrel brother have to learn." She continued to scream into her stinking rag, even though she knew well it would do no good. No better than the knife she'd been unable to reach.

Thirty-Three

Andy retrieved the precious bundle that was Willy, then managed to help the woozy Many Clouds into the saddle. The boy was alive, but unconscious, and his heart was racing. Andy had developed in his mind a plan to get help for him but stopped short when he neared the house. Emmanuel and some other Indians were supposed to be guarding the house, but it looked deserted. Mindful that he might be stepping into a trap, he decided that he had to risk it for the sake of the helpless child in his arms.

"Hang on to the horse, Many Clouds. He'll take you to the house. Can you do that?" She managed a weak nod. "I can get Willy to help faster if I go ahead on foot." How he could leave Many Clouds behind he didn't know, but he had to. He hugged Willy to him. How much did he weigh? Sixty pounds? Seventy? It didn't matter. He trotted over the gritty trail toward, he hoped, help.

Thirty-Four

Many Clouds began to emerge from her semi-stupor into full consciousness as her mount approached the house. The closer they came, the safer she felt. She had a hard time recalling exactly why she had tried to run with the children. Danger, yes, but from what and whom? Details stayed hazy, but she knew that they were under attack from numerous directions, some known, some unknown. Poor Willy's encounter with the snake proved that running away would not solve the problems.

A lone figure jogged toward her and took hold of the reins. "I've got you now, my love," Andy said.

"Willy?"

"Emmanuel knows a healer who lives close by. He thinks he'll be okay now that he's made it this far. Right now, we have to take care of you and Maggie."

A bolt of fear lanced through her. "Maggie's not at the house?" She suddenly snapped into full consciousness, as if someone had dumped a bucket of cold water on her.

"Ezekiel said he'd left her with you."

"Ezekiel? I haven't seen him at all. What happened to Maggie, Andy?"

"Lots of unanswered questions, Many Clouds. Let's get you inside and start figuring things out."

***

Many Clouds sat on the sofa, a glass of water in her hand. Emmanuel sat next to her, his head wrapped in a white bandage, spotted with a small patch of blood in the back. A faint odor of mildew and unwashed bodies wafted through the room. Many Clouds entertained a vagrant thought of all the housework awaiting, then dismissed the concern as comically trivial. Andy was pouring water for Emmanuel from a pitcher.

"I wish I had something a bit stronger for you, my friend. Your head must be aching something fierce."

"It is a minor concern, Andy," Emmanuel said. "Poor Willy in the bedroom there is much more important. But there is nothing more to do for him until Walks-On-Rocks gets here."

Many Clouds said, "Do you truly have no idea who struck you, Emmanuel?"

"None at all. One minute there were three of us guarding the house. The next I knew I was alone. I began circling the place, trying to figure out what happened to my companions. Then the blow. After that, nothing."

"Well, they searched the house pretty thoroughly," Andy said. "What they expected to find, I can only guess. I do know that someone is interested in this land, and if I'd been foolish enough to keep the deed in my desk, they might have it now."

"Emmanuel," someone called from the yard outside. "Emmanuel, come see." Strangely, the voice came from behind the house.

Emmanuel pushed himself up from the sofa, fending off Many Clouds' offer of a helping hand. "Walks-On-Rocks," he said. "She is out back."

"But why there?" Andy had risen to his feet.

Emmanuel didn't answer but walked with a fairly steady step through the kitchen toward the back door. Andy started to follow, but Many Clouds stopped him with a word. "Let him," she said.

"But Willy…"

"Believe me, Andy," she said.

Andy stood by the couch, a hand on Many Clouds' shoulder. She clasped his hand. They listened to the murmur of the voices outside, then stepped in unison toward the kitchen when the door opened.

The slender, wizened woman was dressed in an elaborate caftan-like gown bejeweled with turquoise, silver, polished antler fragments, and a number of other adornments. Her dark hair, streaked with silver, draped her shoulders and hung below her waist. She carried a large, fringed, leather bag, and she spoke in a native dialect that neither Andy nor Many Clouds understood.

"This way," Emmanuel said and led her to the bedroom. He started to follow her into the room, but she stayed him with her hand. She stepped into the room and closed the door.

"No." Many Clouds said. She moved toward where the woman had disappeared. Emmanuel took her by the shoulders.

"She says she came in from the back because it is dangerous for her to be here. There is a faction opposed to you. She does not know why."

"Opposed to us enough to attack a healer?" Andy said.

"Perhaps not her, but people she helps."

"How do we know that she doesn't belong to that faction herself?" Many Clouds tried to move toward the bedroom again. "What are you doing to Willy?" she called. Again, Emmanuel restrained her.

"Many Clouds, she has taken a blood oath to harm no one, besides which she is a person who seeks to do only good on this earth."

"Does she know anything about Maggie?" Andy said.

"Later," Emmanuel answered.

Many Clouds knew that healers among her own Arapaho people took similar oaths and spent years of deprivation and apprenticeship before they dared to treat anyone. She relaxed and put Emmanuel's hands aside, but she still paced, her own hands at her temples, chanting as she walked.

Andy made a move to comfort her, but something warned him that he would not be welcome, so he backed off, stood with Emmanuel, both men's eyes on the bedroom door. Fumes, odors, and singing began to flow from beneath and through the door.

How long? None of them could have told. And though there were a number of watches and clocks available, no one thought to check. The whole ethos seemed to mitigate against measured time.

Before long, Andy could not bear the wait. "I'll head upstream and look for Maggie."

"It's a good idea, Andy," Many Clouds said. "I was so woozy I could have ridden right by her." A quick hug and Andy was gone.

When Walks-on-Rocks finally emerged, the forest shadows had begun to point decidedly east as the sun dipped toward the western coast a hundred miles or so distant. Many Clouds had grown increasingly distraught. Only Emmanuel's restraining words and arms had kept her from barging through the bedroom door.

"What's happening?" she called.

But the healer didn't answer. Instead, she headed straight for the back door, motioning to Emmanuel to follow. Clearly excluded from their conversation, Many Clouds went immediately into Willy's room.

The boy was no longer breathing in the shallow and spasmodic way he had been. Instead, his respirations were comfortable and regular. The air was thick with camphor and sage and fennel. Black oak leaves were sprinkled on his bed, and the healer had applied a paste of some sort to his forehead and hands. Perhaps elsewhere as well. Many Clouds knelt beside the bed just as Andy reentered the cabin.

"In here," Many Clouds called, clasping the boy's hand in her own. "Any luck?" she asked as he took up a position on the other side of the bed. He shook his head. He laid a hand on the boy's chest. "His pulse is strong," she said, "and he no longer breathes as if every breath will be his last."

"We must take care, of course, but it's possible the crisis is past for the poor little guy."

"Yes," Many Clouds said. "But Maggie?"

AHOOOGAW. AHOOOGAW.

It was the sound of the horn on Ling Chu's brand-new yellow model T. "And it sounds as if we'll have company, like it or not," Andy said. "Let's hope they're ready to help."

Thirty-Five

The small house was suddenly brimming with people and activity. Emmanuel, much to his discomfort, was forced into announcing Walks-on-Rocks' prognosis to the whole assembled group. He cradled a small pouch in his hands and held it before him.

"Willy will need a paste of this powder rubbed on his chest and throat and forehead day and night, and some of it should be burned in this—he held up a small cup fashioned from deer horn—at his bedside each evening."

"Like incense," Ling Chu interjected. "Very good idea."

"None of your needles, now," Carolyn said. "Everyone in the family knows and respects your medical powers. But we'll let the Native healer do her work here."

"I know when to step forward and when to step back," Ling Chu said. "Boy doing fine."

There was a knock on the door. It turned out to be Remington. Everyone had to shift position to make room for the big man. "Sorry to intrude on the party," he said. "It took me a while to track you all down, and I've got some important news."

"Sorry to put you off, Remy," Andy said, "but our daughter's missing. She came to get some help for her little brother in there and hasn't been seen since."

"So they've taken to grabbing kids now," Remington said. "Can't say I'm surprised, exactly. But you're right, Andy, we've got to find her—what's her name?"

"Maggie," Many Clouds said.

"I had an auntie named Margaret," Remington said. "Loved that woman to death, but never mind. Maggie gets our full attention till we find her. Tell me what you know, then I found a few things that might help."

"How—?" Andy began.

"I'm an investigator. That's why you hired me. But you first. Go."

Andy and Many Clouds explained recent events briefly, then it was Remington's turn.

"First thing you got to know is, they got Barker."

"My lawyer?" Andy said. "What do you mean 'got' him? How? Why?"

"Plugged him in the heart, right inside his office. The place was torn apart. Sheriff, name of Hilts, thinks he walked in on them judging by the fact that they found him near the door, not at his desk."

"It's best not to trust anything Hilts says," Andy said.

"They searched this house, too," Many Clouds added. She stepped closer to Andy. "What's happening, Andy?"

Andy took her hand. "Let's see what else Remy's come up with."

"Biggest thing is, I don't think any more that Southern Pacific is behind this. Least they aren't the only ones."

"Who else?" Andy asked.

"Someone who shoots lawyers and kidnaps children," Remy said. "Southern Pacific, all the money they've got, doesn't need to resort to those kinds of primitive tactics. I remember how angry that Sproule fellow was that we thought SP shot me. I think he might have been sincere."

"If not them, who?" Andy asked, shaking his head.

"That's the question. Point is we've got to start casting a wider net here, and when we figure out who we've caught in the net, we'll find our girl."

Many Clouds spoke next. "We should start searching in every direction, but unlike what I thought before, we should trust nothing that comes from the Indians."

Carolyn Maxwell took a turn. "Well, I can get some people moving right now."

Then Remington. "Now we're cooking. Carolyn, you gather some troops. Andy and Many Clouds and I will figure out who and what to focus on."

"And I will make sure the automobile is ready to go any minute you need to go," Ling Chu said.

And thus did the search for Maggie Fitzpatrick begin in earnest.

Thirty-Six

"Why the hell did you bring her back here?"

Maggie couldn't identify the voice in the next room.

The loud anger faded, but she could still identify Ezekiel's voice. She scrunched herself as small as she could next to the door, straining to hear. She could catch only an occasional word, but she could tell they were talking about what to do with her.

It had been morning when Ezekiel gagged her and tied her to the horse, flopped over the saddle as if she were a sack of oats. The ropes had rubbed her ankles and wrists raw. Ezekiel refused to stop or untie her for any reason, so she'd wet herself. For a self-possessed girl who prided herself on keeping clean even in the dust and mud of farm life, this was a humiliation tantamount to stripping her naked and parading her through town like a prize goat.

Sunlight was dimming fast when they arrived at last at whatever this place was. Ezekiel had been a poor monitor of her state, so was mad as a wet cat without a fish when he saw she'd managed to rub her blindfold off. Not that the maneuver had done her any good. She saw mostly the ground under her horse and recognized nothing. He was probably mad at himself, mostly, but that didn't stop him from taking it out on her. Her legs bore the red welts of his fury. She wished she could figure out why he hated her so much.

Right now, though, it was Ezekiel, unseen in the next room, who was on the receiving end of someone else's anger. He was in the process of justifying bringing her to this house.

"… didn't have no place else to keep her up there… looking for whoever shot that lawyer… Miwok village tossed around."

The angry voice raised again. "So you bring her right here to Placerville, where half the people know who she is and where she came from. Did you stop by the sheriff's office to let him in on the situation? That way we could just go straight to jail and forget about all this running around."

So she was in Placerville. If she could escape this room, she had lots of places to go. She could hide behind the Hangtown Saloon till dark, then make her way home. Ezekiel hadn't bothered to tie her when he locked her in here. That didn't seem to be much help, though, as near as she could tell. The room she was in was a bit bigger than a jail cell, but it didn't appear to be much easier to escape from. The wallboards were stout pine, and there were only a couple of small windows mounted high up. Nearly to the ceiling. Her tree-climbing skills wouldn't do her much good on a flat wall.

She surmised that the room had once been a smokehouse, or at least part of one. The danger of fire made it illogical to attach a smokehouse to a building, so maybe it had started as a shed which had been expanded and integrated into a larger building. The greasy smells lingered, and the walls were oily and stained. Furthermore, the structure was sealed tight to keep as little smoke as possible from leaking out. Half of a fifty-gallon drum with charcoal residue sat in the middle of the floor. Above were crossbeams to which ropes and hooks had probably been attached to hold butchered hams and haunches. She thought one of those hooks would be a welcome tool at the moment, but except for the drum, the structure was bare. Just a few saddle blankets tossed on the dirt floor for her bed and a tin bucket for her slops.

She circled the walls twice but found only one small knothole. She poked a toe in that and raised herself a couple of feet, but with nothing she could reach or grab on to, she was forced to slide back down to the floor, which gave her the notion of exploring for loose floorboards. Maybe even a trap door. She systematically covered every inch, poking and prodding and checking for wide cracks that might signal a place to pry or lift.

All the while Ezekiel and the other man argued her fate. It was all repetition of the first words they'd spoken. Finally, they finished just as she concluded that neither wall nor floor offered a way out.

Maybe if she yelled. But several cries for help yielded nothing. Either the walls were thick or they were isolated in the hills or fields. She turned back to attempting to analyze her way into an escape.

What was even harder than discovering a way out of the shed was figuring out what they wanted from her. It certainly had to do with all the fear and intrigue that had been hanging over the family for the last month or so. But what? How?

Something about the way the second man spoke suggested that he was white, not Indian. There were plenty of Indians who spoke white English, though, so that impression didn't mean much. Besides, she couldn't see how it helped her one way or another.

"Okay, we'll take her there then," the white-sounding voice said. "Get out of here now, and hide yourself till dark. I'll take care of the rest."

Shortly after, someone began fumbling with the door. Removing a padlock?

"Step away from the door, Maggie," a female voice said. "It's time to bring you lunch and empty the bucket." She hesitated, but having no escape plan, she obeyed. The door opened only wide enough to admit one person, and that person was a diminutive Indian woman dressed in a plain muslin tent of a dress. She carried an empty bucket and a small pail containing a few pieces of meat and fruit. She kept her gaze on the floor while she set down the lunch pail. She picked up the bucket Maggie had been using and replaced it with the clean one. She turned and exited the room without a word or a glance.

The sound of whatever they were using for a lock followed. The sounds she heard were not particularly metallic, so she guessed it was a wooden bar that was blocking the door. Might be. So what?

She walked around the shed once more, pushing against the boards, looking up and down, again trying to find a crack of light or a loose joint or any other sign of weakness. Nothing.

She tried calling for help again but evoked no more response than before. Finally, she carried the saddle blankets to a corner, bundled them into a cushion, and sat down to wait. She'd never been good at waiting, but she could figure no other option. Perhaps if she waited long enough and quietly enough, an idea would float its way into her mind or something would happen to change the situation in her favor. She certainly hadn't intended to take a nap, but before long, it seemed that was the way she was headed. She decided to let it happen.

Thirty-Seven

Many Clouds and Carolyn Maxwell sat on the small veranda of Andy's and Many Clouds' house. Emmanuel and his shotgun stood watch near a great oak short way down the hill. Another sentinel was guarding the rear of the house. Andy and Remy had headed into town, Ling Chu driving, to investigate lawyer Barker's death and glean whatever else they could about the conspiracy.

Presently, Willy appeared at the front door.

"Many Clouds? Why are you here, Grandma Carolyn?"

Carolyn had objected mightily to the idea that she was old enough to have children running around calling her Grandma, but her protests didn't last long. She came to first endure, then to welcome Willy's and Maggie's endearment. Now she rushed to the wan boy who was tottering his way into the sunlight. She picked him up and sat with him in her lap.

"You've been very sick, little man. Did you know that?"

Many Clouds leaned over and placed a hand on Willy's arm. "We're very glad to see you up and around, Willy. How are you feeling?"

"Okay, I guess. We're home, aren't we? Weren't we walking to get away from here? Where's Maggie?"

Many Clouds felt her heart shudder, reliving the fear of trying to save the boy. Then joy replaced the fear seeing him recovered. "It gives me the shivers to explain all this, Willy, but you're going to find out some time. You got a snake bite."

"A rattler got me? How come I don't remember?"

"It was a rattler, yes. His fangs went right through your boot."

Carolyn intervened. "You probably don't remember because the poison was so strong it blocked the experience."

Afraid again of being dominated by this powerful mother-in-law of hers, Many Clouds picked up the narrative before Carolyn could continue. "And we decided to bring you back here where we could get some proper treatment instead of going farther into the wilderness."

She stood and extended her arms. "And look at you. Up and walking. You're going to be fine."

Willy started to move from Carolyn's lap, but she pulled him closer. "Not yet, Willy. We'll have to take small steps before you're ready to run around at full strength."

Many Clouds let her arms drop. Her lips tightened, and she sat back down, trying to push aside her anger and frustration at Carolyn's possessiveness and insistence on dominating this situation as she did every other in which Many Clouds had a part.

"Where's Maggie?" Willy asked again.

Carolyn picked him up and placed him on Many Clouds' lap. Then she did something astonishing. "Many Clouds will explain about Maggie, Willy. She's her mother after all." She turned to Many Clouds. "All in all, I don't see there's much more I can do here. As soon as Ling comes back, we're going to head to the Circle M. I think I'm more needed there."

She leaned down and kissed the top of Willy's head. "I know I'm sometimes a trial for you, Many Clouds. Believe me, I try not to be." She placed a gentle kiss on her cheek.

The sound of Ling's automobile drifted toward them. Carolyn turned and walked downhill to meet him. Many Clouds smiled. She welcomed every act of tenderness from Carolyn, but she still didn't quite trust it. She supposed she could do more herself, though exactly what she didn't know. For the moment, though, it was Willy who needed her attention.

"We don't know exactly where Maggie is right now," she said.

"Did she get hurt, too?"

"We don't think so." As she went on to explain in the gentlest terms she could imagine what they knew about Maggie's disappearance, she fought to keep the tears and sobs of fear that threatened to overcome her narrative. Willy needed her strength, not her anxiety, and that, she determined, is what she would give him.

"We've got to go find her." Willy squirmed to get down.

"We need to stay here in case Maggie comes back. Besides, we're helping guard the house. Come on, let's say hello to Emmanuel."

"Okay."

She moved Willy off her lap and grabbed his hand as they headed down the steps and toward the big oak. She spoke in a low voice. "Emmanuel is one of the few people outside the family we know we can trust right now, so don't get into conversations with people you don't know, and most especially don't go anywhere with anyone you don't absolutely know you can trust."

"Okay."

She stopped, knelt, and looked him in the eyes. "Willy, I can't tell you how important this is. Some of the humans we are dealing with are more poisonous than the snake that bit you."

"Like Yellow Squirrel."

"Yes," she whispered. "But this time we will stop whoever is plotting against us before he can do nearly the harm that my uncle did."

"Promise?"

"Yes." Ah, Many Clouds, she thought. This is a vow you have no power to keep. And to a child. When will you stop trying to turn wishes into certainties by merely saying the word?

Thirty-Eight

Maggie awoke from her fitful nap filled with new determination to escape. Supper came. Some kind of mush with hunks of what Maggie figured were the remnants of crust that had formed while it sat untended for who knew how long. They certainly weren't meat. A male arm in a denimed sleeve with a heavily haired hand had shoved it through a partially open door. She wondered what had happened to her Indian woman caretaker from earlier. She heard the clunk of the bolt sliding home right after the door closed and the sound of the man's heavy footsteps faded. After that, only silence answered her questions about where she was or what they intended to do to her.

Hungry to the point of feeling weak and a bit sick, she managed a few spoonsful of the pasty muck but soon gave up on it. Finally, in an attempt to get warm, she hugged herself and began walking the perimeter of her prison. She'd already explored the room so thoroughly she expected to find nothing new, especially in the dark, but movement felt better than lying on the hard floor. For variety, she changed movements each time she circled the room. Once running, once skipping, once with eyes on the floor, once with them lifted to the rafters, hoping for an inspiration that she began to fear would never come.

Thirty-Nine

Many Clouds thought perhaps she'd recovered from the intense fatigue that accompanied her pregnancy. Her bouts of vomiting had stopped while she carried Willy toward home, but they resumed once she'd rested. So far, she'd managed to conceal them. However, she felt unmoored, a sloop with no anchor and a damaged rudder. Outwardly, she thought, she moved around normally, but inwardly, she felt unable to find direction or purpose. Willy had improved markedly in the twenty-four hours since he'd awakened. He'd be back to full strength before long. But her heart had not yet emptied of the fear for him it carried during his illness, and she was afraid to let him out of her sight. She was like a child, fearful that if her mother went into the next room, she would never see her again.

And now Maggie. Where? How? Why? One child restored should be enough to repair her sense of purpose. But it turned out that *should* didn't mean much. If anything, it made for more guilt and anxiety.

She'd lived so many years of wandering and violence and uncertainty. Father and uncle both beyond reach. Her father, Standing Oak, in Wyoming on the Wind River reservation, old and feeble and still refusing to leave. Yellow Squirrel dead at Willy's hand while acting like his own version of an avenging angel.

Even all the Maxwell money had not shielded them from confusion and bloodshed. But amid it all, she and Andy had cobbled together this little family. She and he and the two children Yellow Squirrel had rendered fatherless. They were hers now. Andy, the children, this house. No more aimless wandering and hiding.

Except now, Maggie was gone. At least with Yellow Squirrel they knew who he was and knew his purpose. This latest was as mysterious as the turns of the earth or the movement of the tides. A twelve-year-old girl. Her own twelve-year-old, as certainly hers as if she'd been born of her own body.

Suddenly, she realized she didn't know where Willy was. She called, ran through the house, calling the while. Out on the veranda, and there he was under the oak with Emmanuel. Mumblety-peg. She felt a little dizzy. Why? This was not an event to faint over. In fact, she had never fainted. She was not that kind. Then she remembered that who she was was changing.

She called Willy to her, sat down on the step. Willy left Emmanuel reluctantly, allowed her a hug. Not so long ago, he was hungry for these embraces.

"Please don't go outside without telling me, Willy."

"Okay."

"I just wanted to tell you that. You can go on back to Emmanuel now."

He scampered away. The extraordinary fright over Willy's absence. The dizziness. She felt sure enough of her pregnancy now that she could share the news with Andy. In the meantime, she reminded herself, she was still the woman of action she'd always been. Andy and Carolyn could investigate Barker's death, but Maggie was somewhere and in trouble, and Many Clouds wasn't doing her any good sitting here.

She turned, hugging her belly, walked to the kitchen and pumped a dipper of water into a glass. Her reflection in the water shifted with the ripples. The water had a fresh, revitalizing scent she'd never noticed before. She breathed again and drained the glass. It had seemed a good idea for her to remain here on watch, but her way was to confront fear, not hide away. She saw no need to give that up, pregnancy or not. She pushed aside the anxiety that counseled her that Willy could be taken any second. She listened instead to the reason that assured her Willy would be fine in Emmanuel's care.

She hurried outside to Emmanuel. "I don't suppose you've heard anything else about Ezekiel."

Emmanuel shook his head. "Not yet."

"Nor Gus or Sylvester either?"

"Vanished, it seems."

"It's obvious Ezekiel's in this up to his neck and afraid to show himself. The other two, I can't imagine."

"Perhaps I should go, talk to some of my people," he said.

"No, Emmanuel. We need someone strong and trustworthy to stay with the house and with Willy. We already know what comes of trusting people with other agendas. Not only that, but I can't stand to sit here doing nothing any longer, not knowing about Maggie. There's another man who could be part of this, and I don't think Andy's thought of him. I need to go to town and warn Andy and Carolyn. I shouldn't be long."

Emmanuel stood, placed a hand on Willy's shoulder, and stepped toward her. She led the remaining horse into the yard, glad Andy had thought to rent extra saddle horses. She slipped a bridle over the big bay's head, named Horace after the Roman poet. Andy had taken the other horse, Virgil, to town earlier. Many Clouds decided to forego a saddle both because of the extra weight and because she thought it would enhance the warrior attitude she would need for the task at hand.

"You should not leave, Many Clouds. I am afraid for you. It will be dark soon."

"I'll be careful. I'm armed, and I can shoot, and I'm Indian. We don't get captured easily." She smiled.

"No, not easily. But it's not impossible either. Take great care."

"Of course." She smiled. If Emmanuel knew of her condition, he would object to the skies. She could use a nap. Not a feeling she was used to, but there was no time now. She said to Willy, "I will see you soon, little man. Be good. No more snakes."

Willy had his new knife in his hand. He executed a triple flip and stuck the blade perfectly in the earth. "Any snake comes after me's got that waiting for him."

Emmanuel and Many Clouds joined in laughter.

"You've already proved that, haven't you? I thought Emmanuel was the protector here, but now I see it's the other way around. Goodbye for now." This time Willy accepted her hug and actually waved as she rode out of sight.

Forty

Despite the discouraging results, Maggie didn't give up. She continued her little round-and-round of the room in ten-circle increments with rest breaks and calls for help in between. Ten circles. Rest. Yell. Ten more. Rest. Yell. It wasn't till she had completed her hundredth circle that she focused on the rafters. Every other rest period she'd spent sitting. This time she'd flopped on her back, eyes upward. She'd tried climbing the walls but had ignored the supports, which she calculated crossed the building at about twice her height even with her arm outstretched. If she could make it to the rafters somehow, she'd be able to make it to the windows. She couldn't tell whether the windows were fixed or moveable. Better if they were moveable, but even if they were fixed, she could break them. She also didn't know whether they were elevated as far above the ground outside as above the floor of the room. She did know, however, that she stood no chance of escape as things stood. If there was a rope, she could climb it. It had been one of the games she and Willy played often. There was no rope, but the idea of it gave her a notion that provided more energy than she'd felt since Ezekiel had bound her to that horse. It was an idea that required daylight, though. She'd had trouble sleeping before. Now she was sure she'd get not a wink.

Forty-One

Andy met Remington at the foot of the stairs leading up to Harry Barker's office. They'd decided to dig into Barker's files in the search for some clue to Maggie's disappearance. Maybe something tied to his murder was also tied to Maggie's kidnapping. The sounds of building construction were as loud as ever, though the smell of fresh-sawn pine helped sweeten the atmosphere. The two men talked as they ascended the stairs.

"You find out anything, Remy?"

"I been up and down this county, Andy," Remington had to nearly shout to get past the noise of the hammering. "I never found a place where folks are so close-mouthed. Seems they're scared enough that they don't want to commit to whether the sun's up or down. You live here. You think that's normal?"

Remington's question was valid, but Andy didn't want to have the discussion at this moment and out here on the street. The "normal" he was talking about varied a great deal according to who was talking to whom about what. Remington was a stranger who would inspire little trust among the locals at first contact. However, he was supposedly skilled at extracting information no matter the circumstances. Andy was beginning to think it had been a mistake to hire him. He suggested they go on up to the office where conversation might be more possible.

Halfway up the stairs, Remington stopped and put out an arm to block Andy.

"You smell anything?" he said.

"Smoke," Andy said. "Let's go."

The door stood open. A knee-deep pile of papers was ablaze in the center of the floor. A straight-back chair had been broken to pieces and used for kindling on top of the fire. The two men stomped on the flames and scattered the paper and before long the fire was reduced to harmless embers.

"Wonder what was in there. Maybe nothing. Maybe the key to everything. It will take a while to go through it." He walked over to a window that opened on an alley. "Look here." Andy pulled up a rope that had been hanging from the window. "The guy had an escape route all set up."

Remy toed the ashes, hands on hips. "If I was you, Andy, I'd be wondering if hiring me was a waste."

This, also, was a discussion he didn't want to have. He wanted only to get to the heart of the violence. "If you take off now, Remy, who's going to help me sift through this mess? You say you didn't find out anything."

"Oh, I didn't come up with zero. I never do that. But it was damned little compared to what I hoped for."

"Well, maybe between the two of us, then."

"I can tell you this, Andy, there's more going on here than folks growing vegetables and cattle and hay. And that Marshal Halstad guy in Sawtooth Wells is useless as tits on a boar pig when it comes to stopping it."

"Halstad's a good man, Remy. You won't get anywhere with me by attacking him."

"I didn't mean to say he's anything but a good man. Just that this thing, whatever it is, is bigger than him or any one man. And this Sheriff Hilts here in Placerville? I interrupted a poker game when I went to his office yesterday. So he's either useless or corrupt or both."

Andy nodded. "But there is something?"

"There's a name that keeps coming up. Whenever I get a sniff of it or even mention it, that's when the information spigot shuts off."

Loud voices erupted in the street outside Barker's office, drawing both men to the windows. They looked down on a most remarkable sight. An unclothed young girl streaked past the office and disappeared behind the Hangtown Saloon.

Remington tipped his hat back and shook his head. "Andy, this case is full of more things I never expected nor can't explain than all my others combined. Wait. Where you going?" Andy was halfway down the stairs and running toward the street by the time Remington finished his comment.

Forty-Two

Just when she had given up and drifted toward an exhausted sleep, Maggie's efforts finally paid off in the glimmer of an idea. She began executing her plan at the earliest kiss of dawn. First it was off with her shirt, then her pants. She fashioned them into a sort of rope and swung them overhead. The device almost reached the rafters, but did not loop over them, and she had no way of attaching them—neither nail nor hook—so she must find a way to lengthen her improvised rope. All she had left was her shift and her drawers. She laid out her "rope," then lay down to figure how much length her underwear might add to her improvised device. Not a sure thing, but maybe.

She was not used to being fully naked, not even inside a house. In fact, her nudity occurred only in the brief period when it came her turn for the weekly bath, and she had to drop the towel as she sank into the water. Then Many Clouds would hold the towel to screen her when she stepped out. But she decided modesty couldn't stand in the way of her escape. Off came the shift and drawers. She knotted them to the other garments quickly, glancing hither and yon, though she knew no one was there to spy. In truth, she was in a way spying on herself, unaccustomed as she was to looking at her own body.

She shoved all such random thoughts to the back of her mind and focused on the main job. Once all the fabrics were in essence transformed into a single tool, she gathered it up, twirled it over her head and threw it at the nearest rafter. It slapped the board, but dropped back down to the floor. Once more she sent her improvised line sailing. This time, she let the whole thing go instead of holding on to the closest end. The result was disastrous. Now it was draped over the rafter with both ends hanging down but both too high to reach.

What now? She'd been excited about transforming herself from victim to victorious. Now she was more vulnerable than ever and in the most embarrassing way possible. She sat in a corner, knees up and arms hugging them to her. A bit of light presented itself at the small windows, which appeared much smaller given her failure to reach them in time to help her situation.

Whoever delivered her meals would be approaching soon. The Indian woman had apparently returned, but she didn't show herself now. She would poke a meager portion through a door opened but a crack, then withdraw. The room's greasy smell oppressed her. Maggie trembled, though it wasn't really cold.

Suppose whoever brought breakfast decided to enter all the way instead of just leaving a plate? Perhaps they'd decided to move her somewhere and would tie her up again to do it. Or worse, maybe they'd decided she was too dangerous or too bothersome to live. They could take her to the big river, the Sacramento, not so far away, and drop her right in, hands and feet tied, and all that would be left of her would be a small splash as she sank into the current. Or there was always slavery. There were plenty of ranches and farms, she'd heard, who would welcome a pair of working hands at no cost save a few meals. Or sex slavery, which Many Clouds had explained to her and which terrified her. She couldn't quite figure out how it worked, but she knew well enough that it involved a violent attack on her nether regions, something she thought would be far worse than death itself.

Light came streaming through the windows now. The smoky, lardlike smell strengthened as the temperature rose. Her captors would be here any moment. Of a sudden, desperation inspired her, and she scampered across room taking a leap toward the roped garments one more time as she went. Still too high.

She took up a post behind the door to wait for whoever opened the door. Despite all her work, she had no clear plan now. She crouched low, eyes closed in an effort to focus all her energy on the task before her. Footsteps. A distant voice.

"You'd better have her out of here before noon. She's a wild one, and there are too many people around."

"Don't worry." The footsteps grew louder. A man's voice called, "Okay you little cur. Eat hearty." The arm—the denimed one, with the thickly haired hand—entered the room holding a cracked plate, which held a hard-boiled egg and a slice of bread. Just as the hand set the plate on the floor, at the moment when she thought the man attached to it might be most off balance, she yanked the door inward. The man stumbled in, off-balance.

"Hey, what the hell?" he yelled.

Maggie grabbed the collar of his shirt, braced her foot against the door jamb and yanked hard. While her antagonist concentrated on saving himself from falling, she dashed past him, through the door and into the hallway, bare feet slapping against rough boards. She had a momentary fear of splinters, followed quickly by how comical a thought that was compared to the other dangers she faced. A shout followed her. She opened the door at the end of the hall, hoping for an escape. Inside, a blond-haired man in a frock coat sat at a desk examining an account book, a pen in his hand.

"What the hell?"

She slammed the door and turned toward another to her left. This one led outside to a long stairway to the ground. She knew the room in which she'd been imprisoned was on this side of the building and thought how far she'd have had to drop—two or three stories—to reach the ground from the windows she'd planned to use as an escape route. Still, she preferred that route to the one she'd been forced to choose. Once at the bottom of the steps, she found herself alone, afraid, and naked as Eve, running for her life down the main street of Placerville.

Forty-Three

No one in a big city would have used the word "crowd" for what Many Clouds saw on main street as she entered the town. But ten people constituted a crowd in this small community, and they were all clustered around the entrance to the Hangtown Saloon.

By the time Many Clouds got to the door, too many were trying to squeeze through the door to allow any newcomer through. Somehow, Many Clouds knew the commotion had to do with her family, and she was in too much of a hurry to bother with courtesy. She grabbed the collar of a smallish man in a checkered shirt and yanked hard.

"What the hell?" he called as he stumbled backwards.

She circled in front of him, used both hands to shove a very fat man aside and squeezed past him into the bar itself. There, tables and chairs and people made for an obstacle path even more formidable than the one she'd just negotiated. Two big-shouldered men in overalls blocked her way now. Her shoving got her nowhere with them, so she knelt and punched hard at the back of the knees of one of them. His knees buckled obligingly, and though he didn't go down, he staggered enough to allow her to slip past.

"Hey, you goddamn squaw" was the slur that followed her as she made her way to the bar's storeroom. Nothing she couldn't let slide off her like water off a duck in these circumstances.

What she found among the hanging bottles and barrels was Maggie, wrapped in a saddle blanket. A woman in a long skirt, a merry widow, and prodigious makeup knelt at her side, stroking her hair.

"It's all right, love. You're safe now darling," the lady cooed.

Many Clouds dropped to her knees and nearly bowled over her daughter in her eagerness to embrace her.

"Maggie, my Maggie, where have you been? Did they hurt you? Let me look at you." She pulled back, put her at arm's length to get a better view, then hugged her close again. "No, I can't stand to be apart long enough to even look at you. Isn't that awful?"

The woman laughed. "I guess you're her mother? Must be quite a story how she got in a fix like this."

"Quite a story, yes," Many Clouds said. "Thank you for your kindness. Oh, dear I don't even know your name."

"Sadie. Just glad little Maggie here is safe."

Then a welcome and familiar voice said, "Maggie, Many Clouds, are you all right? What happened?"

"Well," Sadie said, "I guess it's time for a family reunion and time for me to say 'so long.'"

"Thank you again," Many Clouds called as they watched Sadie disappear into the crowd.

"Come on," Andy said. "Let's get out of here. You're a brave girl, Maggie, but the Hangtown Saloon is no place for you."

Maggie, who had been silent and paralyzed during the whole exchange, finally spoke up. "It's not such a bad place when there's people like Sadie around."

"Very true, dear," Andy said. "But we're getting out of here anyhow."

Forty-Three

They hurried to the dry goods store a few doors down the street and managed to find a shirt and a pair of overalls that would serve as a wardrobe till they got back to the house.

"You know we can't charge your account, Mr. Maxwell," the clerk said.

"No one said anything about charging," Andy said as he waved a bill in the clerk's face. "However, when this is over, this place will be on a list of establishments that will never see another penny of Maxwell money. And the change you just gave me is twenty cents short."

"Sorry, I don't have enough small change right now."

"Then I don't have enough cash to pay you," Andy said. He snatched back the bill. "Come find me when you have my change."

Then it was on to the livery stable, where Andy rented a large surrey to convey Many Clouds, Maggie, and himself to their house. He tied the recently rented horses, Virgil and Horace, behind. They would make quite a convoy, he figured. He asked Remy to finish the interrupted search of Barker's office. He wanted to help, but the family had to come first. Neither of the men expected to find that the murderers had left anything behind, but they wanted to explore every possibility.

Despite the fact that the surrey had a bank of three seats fitted with cushioned backs and closed-in side panels, Many Clouds, Maggie, and Andy all rode on the front seat, as close to one another as they could get. Andy whistled "A Bicycle Built for Two" and "The Band Played On." Then he taught them the one verse he could remember of "When You and I Were Young,

Maggie." They sang it together while Maggie wrapped her arms around Many Clouds as if she were five years old instead of twelve. None of them could wait to reach the safety and privacy of their little house. Privacy, however, was not what awaited them. Ling Chu's new automobile was parked out front.

Many Clouds was heartily dismayed. She'd already decided she couldn't wait any longer to tell Andy about her pregnancy and that this evening should provide a perfect opportunity. Now, with Carolyn here and Ling Chu besides, she despaired of a secluded moment to deliver the news, let alone savor it as it deserved. That was her first reaction. Her next was a determination she had made many times in the past—not to let Carolyn Maxwell run her life.

Andy had scarcely brought the rig to a halt before Willy hopped aboard, yelling Maggie's name, grabbing her shoulders and shaking her like a rag doll.

"I bet you been taking care of some bad guys all right. You better tell me right now or I swear I'll never teach you another knife throw."

"You're shaking the life out of me, you idiot. Let go now." She pushed him away, but he was not in the least penitent. "Come on, Maggie, tell me. Okay. Okay. We'll wait till the grownups are gone and you can tell me the juicy parts. I'll bet there's plenty."

Andy intervened, lifting Willy down to the ground. "There will be plenty of time for all that, Willy. Your sister's been through a lot, though, and she needs a bit of a rest before she starts telling her story."

"When we find out, we're gonna knock a few heads together, Andy, right? No one gets away with treating my little sister like this without they answer for it, and answer big." No one reminded him that Maggie was his big sister, not his little one. He swung his fists and bounced around like a prize fighter in the ring. Ling Chu had walked down from the house in the meantime. He walked up to Willy, grabbed both his wrists, then released his grip and stepped back.

"Hey, what did you do? I can't barely feel my hands."

"Breathe deep now."

Willy did so, and his hands began moving normally.

"Too much energy bad as too little, young man. Remember."

Emmanuel appeared and took the reins from Andy. Ling Chu in turn took them from Emmanuel.

"I will stable the animals," he said. "Emmanuel, better you stay on guard. The rest go inside. Food and drink there and much to talk about."

Many Clouds, Andy, and the children started up the slope toward the house. Of a sudden, Carolyn Maxwell stepped out on the porch, resplendent in a rawhide skirt and linen blouse, her hair tied up in a red ribbon.

"Well, well, at last. I didn't know when you'd arrive, but I knew you would be starving, so Ling Chu and I have taken care of everything. Come in, sit down, and tell me all."

She spoke in a kindly tone, and her face was adorned with a sincere smile. She was doing her best, and Many Clouds felt she should appreciate her efforts. Nevertheless, she wished herself and her family back in Wyoming among her Arapaho people. She wondered if she would ever feel she belonged here.

Forty-Four

Late afternoon the day after Maggie's escape. Carolyn and Ling Chu were gone. They'd insisted on driving up for a party to celebrate Maggie's return, but they'd left immediately afterward. Maggie and Willy were sound asleep. Many Clouds and Andy sat on the porch enjoying the aftermath of what Many Clouds had to admit had been a very successful gathering despite the fact that Carolyn had managed it all. For the moment, they enjoyed the silence after all the noisy bustle that had accompanied the little party and Maggie's recounting of her capture and escape. It had been all Many Clouds could do to leap to the girl's side and wrap her in a protective embrace with every turn the story took. However, Maggie seemed to gather more courage as she spoke, feeding perhaps off the attention the group paid to her every word. She even spoke more with pride than embarrassment about her nude dash for freedom down Placerville's main street.

Twelve years old and such horrors already. It was a wonder she didn't just curl up in any corner she could find. But she obviously wasn't made that way. What would have destroyed a weaker person appeared to have made her stronger yet. She was a marvel.

Emmanuel slept in the stable, which he preferred to the pallet they'd offered in the living room. Two trusted Circle M hands, one in front, one in back, guarded the property. It was a peaceful scene, and Many Clouds thought the opportunity had arrived after all to share the secret she'd been harboring for what seemed like forever, though it had really not been so long. She took a few moments to gather her thoughts and words, then said, "Andy, there's something I have to tell you."

He drew back and regarded her. "Oh, and what would that be?" He looked a bit apprehensive.

"Oh, I don't mean to scare you. It's nothing bad, but it is important."

A clatter of hoofbeats sounded from the roadway, accompanied by shouts of "Andy. Andy. News."

The Circle M hand raised his rifle. "Whoa, there. Rein in and up with the hands."

Remy complied. "Andy, would you tell this fool to put down that gun?"

"He's no fool, Remy. He's trying to keep us safe. So barging in like that is going to get you what you got. Mike, he's a friend. You can let him pass. Thanks for staying alert."

"Sure thing, Mr. Maxwell. I remember him now."

Remy was leading his mount into the yard and shook hands with the man Andy had called Mike. "Sorry. It was pretty foolish of me to rush in like that knowing how touchy everything is around here."

Many Clouds suffered a wave of disappointment, but she went inside, found another chair for Remy, and the three of them sat down.

"What's this news, Remy?" she asked.

He waved a sheaf of papers around. "Well, Andy, you remember after we put out the fire, I was just about to tell you a name when that poor girl came running down the street without a stitch on her?"

"Her name is Maggie, Remy, our daughter." He took Many Clouds' hand. "And she's—thank goodness—inside sound asleep."

"Maggie? Oh, yeah, like my aunt Margaret. How could I forget even though I've been busier than a one-armed paper hanger? I'm sorry you won't get to taste Aunt Margaret's biscuits. Sorry for anyone who won't be able to. Anyhow about Maggie, I knew she'd be all right the minute you took off after her. But here's the thing I've been trying to tell you if you'd let me get a word in. Hale Gentry's the guy everyone seems to be intimidated by. You know him?"

"Know him?" Many Clouds said. "He's been an enemy of the Maxwells since forever. He ran against Andy in the last assembly election and lost and never got over it."

"And before that, he fancied himself in line for my mother's hand and half the Circle M by marriage. But he's nothing but a saloon owner and small-time gangster. Don't tell me he's in the middle of all this."

"Not so small time. I found this taped under one of Barker's file drawers. Could be your lawyer surprised the crooks and paid for it with his life."

Many Clouds said, "So you think this is what they were looking for?"

"Had to be," Remy said. He held the papers out, unsure whether to hand them to Many Clouds or to Andy. Andy nodded toward Many Clouds. "Read it over, Many Clouds."

She was a little surprised but gratified at being given a pivotal role in this kind of transaction. She took it as another indication of the growing maturity of the relationship between herself and Andy. However, as she leafed through the packet, she wasn't sure what she was looking at.

"It's obviously a contract," she said, "and it's between Gentry and some company. Wait a minute. The corporation is Western Explorations, Incorporated, Howard Weitzel, president. It says Gentry is to render certain services in return for compensation as enumerated. What services? What compensation? It doesn't say."

"Oh, it most certainly does, Many Clouds," Remy said. "Look in the margins."

She turned the pages sideways, and there it was, cleverly masked by the decorative border. She handed the packet to Andy. "Just look at this."

"'The undersigned is hereby authorized to take whatever measures necessary to induce the parties in question to sell or surrender the described plots of land.' Why this gives Gentry the authorization to coerce us into giving up our place however he can. He was behind Maggie's kidnapping. His was the other voice she heard. I'll bet he was also the man in the office she saw while she was escaping."

"And the ransom he was going to demand was giving up our home," Many Clouds said. "Our very home."

"There are lots of questions this paper doesn't answer, though, Remy," Andy said. "First of all, why would they put something criminal like this on paper?"

"Who is this man Weitzel? Have you ever heard of this company?" Many Clouds asked. "And what do they want with our property? And what are these other plots of land this paper talks about?"

"One thing," Andy said, "it looks like it confirms that Southern Pacific may not have had anything to do with these shenanigans."

"Unless they own Western Explorations," Remy said.

"That's quite possible, Remy," Andy said. "But despite what I said earlier, I somehow don't think so. The SP approach is generally much more direct. Offering outrageous prices for whatever they want or perhaps making the thoroughfare impassable so no one else can use it. No, I think the offer they made my mother earlier was the beginning, middle, and end of their ploy."

It was Many Clouds' turn next. "So we need to find out more about this Western Explorations company."

"That's my next step," Remy said. "And at last, I have something to sink my teeth into. I'm sick of wandering around in the fog."

"Maybe you'd like to catch some shuteye and breakfast here before you launch into that project," Many Clouds suggested.

"Nope." Remy was quite definite. "I'm headed back to Barker's office. I found that." He pointed to the contract. "Might be something more hidden beneath a floorboard or something. You keep those safe, now, you two. Not to mention yourselves."

Many Clouds opened her arms and embraced Remy. "You are an angel."

"If I'm that, I'm in a pretty good disguise, I'd say."

Many Clouds released him so he and Andy could shake hands. "And to think I was doubting you," he said.

"You had good reason, Andy. I was doubting myself."

"Well, we can give those doubts up for good. See you soon, and thank you."

They watched Remy walk his mount through the front gate, climb aboard, and head back to town.

"Well, I'd better hide this away," Andy said as he held up the secret contract.

Many Clouds took the papers from his hand and laid them on a chair. "Before you do that, you might recall our friend interrupted me just as I was about to say something."

"Oh, yes. Yes. What was it?"

She reached up, cradled his face between her hands, and told him. For a moment she was afraid his whoop would wake the children. Then she didn't care whether it did or not, and it was too late anyway because Willy and Maggie had already hurried to join them, both looking both curious and a little frightened. Many Clouds noted their anxiety and knelt to tell them the news. It wasn't long before a virtual river of joy flowed through the yard and down the hillside from the house Andy and Many Clouds had built together.

Forty-Five

It was noon the next day when Remington Dillinger returned to the scene of what had become a considerably cheerier household. Many Clouds insisted that they get back to some semblance of a normal routine. It was obviously impossible to recreate the conditions that had prevailed before the appearance of the mysterious man in the paisley scarf and the subsequent frightening events, all of which seemed to pale before the revelation of Many Clouds' pregnancy. But some sort of calm seemed essential. Thus, Willy and Maggie, amid considerable grumbling, were mucking out the stable while Andy tried to get some of the neglected and damaged tack back into shape. Many Clouds concentrated on the house, which had undergone some unwelcome rearrangement during the visit from her future mother-in-law.

Emmanuel was back on duty, but he was solo since it had been deemed unnecessary to have more than one guard during the daylight hours for the time being, especially when so many had proved untrustworthy. Many Clouds prepared sandwiches, and the family convened on the porch to hear what Remy might have discovered. In the recent past, Willy and Maggie would have been sent to play, but they had now become as integrally involved with the people and events as all the adults, so they'd been accorded a seat at the table.

"So, Remy," Andy said, "what did you find out?"

Remy had a mouthful of baloney and bread, so Many Clouds filled the silence.

"Don't tell me it took you only overnight to find out about this Howard Weitzel and Western Explorations?"

"Who are they?" Willy asked.

Remy held up a hand, swallowed, and gulped down some lemonade. "Hey, hey, hey. We all know I'm terrific, but I'm only one person and I haven't learned to do simultaneous voices yet, so please let's slow down a bit."

That drew a laugh, which allowed the big man to redirect the focus. "Willy and Maggie, Western Exploration and Howard Weitzel seem to be behind some of the skullduggery that's been going on around here lately."

"Skull what?" Willy asked.

"Where you break the law and kidnap people, dummy," Maggie said. "Now just hush."

"You're free to ask questions, though, kids," Andy commented. "We want you to understand what's happening."

Willy cast a gloating smile at Maggie. It seemed those two were back to normal, though how it had happened so soon was a mystery to Many Clouds.

Forty-Six

Ling Chu and Carolyn were halfway to the Circle M from Sawtooth Wells when Carolyn decided she'd like to learn how to drive the automobile. She knew getting Ling Chu's permission would be a struggle, not because the machine was so complicated—though it probably was—but because Ling Chu viewed the car as his. Even though her money had purchased it, it had been his idea. First came the rather primitive Model-T two-seater, which she had resisted because of the smell and the noise. Ling Chu's arguments about convenience and speed were somewhat convincing, and she'd come close to relenting. But, she reasoned, even if the claims were true, where would they drive it? The roads and trails for miles around them were built for horses and wagons, far too rough and rutted and narrow to accommodate anything like the Tin Lizzie. Finally Ling Chu's insistence along with her affection and respect for the man had won the day. And they'd stepped up from the Tin Lizzy to this touring car, this sleek yellow chariot, and they traveled over roads which had been widened and graveled to accommodate them. Bridges had even been constructed over several of the fords whose flooding would have rendered them impassable only a couple of years earlier. It was time for her to step into the modern world along with her automobiles and these new roads. She leaned forward and tapped Ling Chu on the shoulder. He turned.

"Yes, Miss Carolyn?" He had to yell to be heard.

"Please stop," she yelled back.

It was somewhat quieter when the engine was idling instead of operating at full throttle. She moved to the front passenger seat, which she could tell by the way he listed slightly to the left, made Ling Chu uncomfortable. She felt uncomfortable as well. They'd always kept their relationship professional, even when cataclysmic events such as her bullet wound that he'd doctored with his acupuncture skills three years earlier, brought them to some version of intimacy. Now, they were seated side by side. He stared straight ahead as he spoke.

"Something a problem? Something forgot?"

"No, Ling. There are no new problems. But I have a request to make of you."

"Of course, Miss Carolyn. You know I do whatever you want."

"You may change your mind about that. I want to learn how to drive this automobile."

For a long moment, Ling Chu sat as frozen as a stone statue. Was he considering how to make this happen, or was he considering how he could get out of it? Finally, she got the answer she expected.

"Such a thing, it is not possible Miss Carolyn."

"Not possible? Can you explain why?"

"No. Cannot explain."

"Cannot explain? What's the problem?"

"One more hour we be home to Circle M." He reached for the lever to the left of the driver's seat and slid his foot to the drive pedal. Carolyn laid a hand on his arm.

"No, Ling. Please. Let me."

Neither of them moved or spoke for a time. Ling Chu finally broke the silence. "So sorry, Miss Carolyn. Woman cannot drive big machine."

Carolyn had been ready to counter a slew of arguments from Ling Chu, but she hadn't anticipated this one, and it both amazed and angered her. Her first impulse was to stand up and put her hands on her hips, but that being impossible in the constricted space, she simply sat up straight and crossed her arms. She remained in that posture, speechless for a moment, then pointed at Ling.

"Ling, have you ever seen a horse I couldn't ride as well as any man on the Circle M?" He didn't answer, but she thought he might have slumped a bit. "You've seen me shoot pistols and rifles aplenty. Is there any man on the place that could outdo me?"

"Maybe perhaps one."

She was about to ask who, but then realized he was talking about Shelby McNeal, her murdered lover. Though his death was nearly four years in the past now, the thought of him still stabbed her heart. Ling had now crossed a line. He had stepped away from the employer-employee distance that had helped keep their relationship stable for decades and into personal territory. It was unfair and hurtful of him to bring Shelby into the conversation, and she wondered for a moment what had driven Ling into this uncharacteristic combative mode. Then she did something uncharacteristic herself. In a flash of self-examination, she understood that it was she who had precipitated the whole thing. She'd forced Ling into a corner. It was neither in his character nor in his culture to deal with sensitive matters so directly.

Ling Chu sat like a thunderhead, dark and bloated with resentment. How much, Carolyn wondered, did she really want to sit behind that wheel? From a practical point of view, she could imagine emergencies in which she was the only person available to drive. In such a situation, people could conceivably die for lack of a driver, and the idea that she would be the helpless one frightened and infuriated her. At the moment, though, she had to admit her frustration was beside the point. For the stoic Ling Chu to display his feelings so obviously signaled a deep bruise to his pride. She certainly didn't want that. For another, if she turned him hostile, she might lose his goodwill, not to mention the chance for driving instruction. She didn't want to lose either one.

"It's fine, Ling." She settled into her passenger seat, sitting up front, though, instead of behind Ling. "I shouldn't have been so pushy about this. Let's just get on home. You driving, of course."

After a brief hesitation, Ling put the car in motion. Beside the road, Granite Creek winked occasionally in the dim moonlight. The smell of fresh-cut hay rose from the adjoining fields. In a short while, they climbed the hill overlooking the Circle M yard. House, barn and other outbuildings were but dark silhouettes. A shadow moved from the veranda down the steps to the yard. Ling Chu braked.

"Who that?"

Carolyn reached behind her and retrieved the deer rifle she always kept in a scabbard next to the seat. "Hello the house," she called as she levered a round into the chamber.

A red dot flared on the veranda, then settled back to a steady glow. Soon a shadow separated from the deeper shadow of the house, then disappeared a moment later. The cigar, if that's what it was, remained in place. A trick? Were there two intruders or one?

"Owl Feather," came the reply in the voice of Amelia Duprée. Owl Feather was Many Clouds' grandfather, and to call his name was their signal that all was well on their end. The code had been Ling Chu's idea and might have saved them trouble or even lives if they'd instituted it a year or two earlier. However, Ling Chu's shrewdness was proving itself now. She looked at Ling Chu and smiled. His demeanor remained serious, though, and he motioned her to go on. Carolyn realized she couldn't relax yet. There was another step, a counter word remaining. In addition, the burning cigarette was not part of the protocol.

"Standing Oak," Carolyn said. This last was the name of Many Clouds' father, and combined with "Owl Feather" constituted the all-clear signal. Ling Chu had reasoned that the initial password could have been uttered under duress. If Carolyn had said "Yellow Squirrel," those at the house would know she was being held against her will and could then act accordingly. What they heard this time was an exhalation behind them. They straightened up and turned in unison.

"I'm happy as a bullfrog in warm mud you didn't say 'Yellow Squirrel.'" It was Andy's Uncle Cooper. "All the shooting trouble we been having around here done wore me down."

"Cooper," Carolyn said, "You nearly frightened us silly skulking around in the dark like that. Now climb in here and let's go on home."

"Scare me to my death," Ling Chu said.

Cooper stepped on to the running board and said, "Tally ho, Ling Chu, tally-ho."

As they descended the hill toward the Circle M yard, Carolyn said, "Cooper, what was the idea of the cigar business on the porch?"

"One cigar plus one shadow means there might be two people on the porch. Amelia was the shadow, naturally. Me sneaking up behind the car, it's almost like you got three guards working."

Carolyn was aghast. "You used Amelia as a decoy?"

"It was her idea, and you saw she was in and out of sight in the blink of an eye."

"I don't care whose idea it was. Putting her in danger like that is just not right."

"Very smart, Cooper," Ling Chu said. "I, you, and Amelia are thinking a good way."

By the time they reached the ranch yard, Amelia had a lantern alight on the veranda and one inside. They chugged over the Granite Creek bridge and crossed under the arch. Amelia, her soft features lifted in an ecstatic grin was on them almost before Ling Chu could bring the automobile to a stop. In such moments, Carolyn knew, her freckles would jump into relief, but it was too dark to see that happen in the moment. After the initial greetings,

Carolyn said, "That cigar was a clever variation on the code, Amelia. Cooper says it was your idea?"

"Clever might be one word for it, but there's one part I'll never do again. How that man can stand to puff on those nasty things is beyond me. Way beyond."

"Still, anyone shooting would have aimed at the cigar, not you. And it was your idea."

"Next time, it'll be me sneaking up on the car while you sit down here like it was Sunday afternoon sucking on your stinking weed."

"How you going to climb up the hill in those skirts, girl?"

"I been climbing hills since skirts got invented and with milk pails in my hands and babies in my arms, too, and you know it, so don't go throwing that one at me."

"The point is," Carolyn said, "we're all safe for the moment, so let's get on inside for some refreshment."

"I drive car to shed and come in," Ling Chu said.

It meant something that Ling Chu was willing to allow Carolyn to assume hostess duties and prepare comestibles while he turned his attention to the car. He climbed in and started driving while Cooper held the door open for the women to enter the house. They had barely closed the door behind them, when the sound of a yell and a shout came from the yard.

AHHH OOOGA. AHHH OOGA. Sounded the car horn.

Ling was in trouble.

Forty-Seven

"It's Hale Gentry, then?" Many Clouds asked. "He's behind all this?"

"Looks like it," Remington said.

"Not by himself," Andy said. "He's mean enough, but not smart enough or rich enough to engineer this on his own." The three of them—Remington, Andy, and Many Clouds—sat in the dark on the veranda as they talked, occasionally passing a pitcher of lemonade. "He has to be working for someone, and our best guess at this point is this mining company. We should find out why they're after our land."

"That won't be easy, but it's what you hired me for."

"It was indeed, Remy, but I'd like to suggest a different tack. There's little chance of getting hold of any documents from the companies themselves, but coming at things from a different direction might work."

"No guns, Andy, please, if you can help it," Many Clouds said. She restrained an impulse to place a protective hand on her belly, where her thoughts were most focused.

"Should be no firearms involved, my love. I met a lot of people during my campaign for the assembly. Many of them I can still call friends, or at least 'friendlies', people who were quite upset when governor Johnson refused to appoint me even though I got the most votes."

"I thought he couldn't appoint you," Remington said, "after the court barred you from taking office because of your race."

"He could have, though. It might have meant an appeal, and it might not have won, but he chose to tuck his tail between his legs and go off whimpering into the willows. Not only that—"

"Andy, don't," Many Clouds said. They'd agreed that whenever Andy got wound up about the election, as he tended to do too often, Many Clouds had permission to cut him short. She was determined to hold him to it, to try live into the future instead of in the mire of past regrets.

"All right. All right. The point is, I believe that with a combination of sweet talk and the occasional bribe, I can find what I need in the public records of mining claims filed and in the not-so-public assay reports."

"The sweet talk's right up my alley," Remington said. "I know just where to start."

"I'll be glad for you to point me in the right direction, Remy, but I think you should stay on guard here. I believe I'll be able to gather all the ammunition we need in a couple of days."

"Andy, you know I'm no good at cooling my heels. Besides, I think this Gentry fellow needs to know that he can't get away with the kind of thing he did to Maggie."

"We're fine, Emmanuel and I," Many Clouds declared. "And Maggie and Willy are the best lookouts. Both of them can climb trees and jump from branch to branch like squirrels."

"Mmmm, I don't know," Andy said. "I don't like the idea of leaving you so unprotected again."

"You're not listening, Andy," Many Clouds placed a hand on his arm. "Everyone wants to help. Needs to help. None of us wants to sit idle. Not even the kids. Especially not them."

"But…"

"Shhh," Many Clouds said. "It's settled. You get the documents you need. Remy will torment Gentry in as many ways as possible. The rest of us will make sure nothing bad happens here."

Andy stood. It was obvious he was about to proffer more objections. Many Clouds placed two fingers gently on his lips. "One by one, we are weak. Together, we are a force." She kissed him, not something she did in public. No more huddling down waiting for you to save us, Andy."

"Have I ever failed you?" He placed a hand on her belly. "Either of you?"

She smiled and covered his hand with her own. "You are a remarkable man, my love. But you are human."

"I most certainly am," he said as he pulled her against him. "I'm as human as can be."

Forty-Eight

The shot was still echoing when Carolyn screamed, "Ling. Are you all right? Answer me."

"To the floor, all of you," Cooper yelled.

He dived onto the veranda before he was even finished speaking, crawling on knees and elbows to the railing.

"Ling," Carolyn called.

"Hush now," Amelia whispered. "You don't want him to give himself away." She continued her whispering. "Cooper, where are you?"

Silence.

Amelia signaled to Carolyn to go left, while she went to the right. They were crawling just as Cooper had been earlier. Cooper himself was no longer in sight. Carolyn understood that Amelia wanted to flank their attacker and hoped that somehow Cooper could reach Ling. None of them anticipated what happened next.

First came the crash, then the sound of a man calling to God in a most uncivil way, then the sight of Ling's precious automobile bursting through the wall of its garage and into the ranch yard. To Carolyn it appeared more like a prehistoric monster with bulging eyes and misshapen black hooves than the gleaming machine Ling so prized. Even more outlandish was the sight of Ling himself standing behind the driver's seat laying into the man at the wheel with the starting crank kept handy for emergencies in case the electric starter failed. With each blow, Ling bellowed in Chinese, presumably profanities, in a roaring voice no one on the Circle M had heard him use before. Behind him appeared the shadow of another man who doubled his fist and clubbed Ling twice on the side of the head, but his blows didn't slow Ling at all.

A rifle shot cleaved the night air followed by Cooper's commanding, "Hold it right there, mister."

Ling's failure to yield followed by Cooper's order was apparently more than enough to discourage the second attacker, who leapt from the car and ran uphill from the Circle M yard and disappeared into the darkness.

By this time, the ruckus had drawn two cowhands from the bunkhouse. "Sam, Ezra," Cooper called. "After that guy. It's dark and he's got a head start, but do what you can."

Meanwhile, Carolyn ran to the car, yelling Ling's name as she went. By the time she arrived, Ling had fallen back into the seat behind the driver's and was holding his left arm with his right hand. She glanced at the man in the driver's seat, determined that he was bleeding and semi-conscious, opened the car's back door, and stepped up to sit beside Ling Chu.

"Your arm, Ling, what's the matter?"

"Broke maybe I think. Hurt like hell."

"We'll take care of it," Amelia said.

Carolyn spoke next. "Cooper, can you take care of Ezekiel? Amelia and I will help Ling into the house."

"Ezekiel?" Cooper said.

"The driver," Carolyn replied. "He's the one who kidnapped Maggie." She stepped down and yelled into the face of the groggy and bleeding man. "You are a beast, Ezekiel. You will pay for trying to steal that poor little girl, and Cooper here is just your first stop on the road to hell." Ezekiel's eyes were still glassy. His only reply was a grunt. "Well said," she continued. "In the meantime, please accept this sign of my regard." She drew her fist back and slugged the man in the mouth. Her hand stung, and the blow jolted her from palm to shoulder. But the pain felt somehow wonderful.

Forty-Nine

Andy took the train to Sacramento and headed straight to the public records office to explore the history and status of the Western Exploration Company. His days as a history student at the University of California had given him the research skills for unearthing arcane facts in dusty tomes, and he began his search with gusto. As the hours wore on, his gusto became tainted with frustration. He discovered that Howard Wietzel was indeed the head of Western Exploration, but that was only one of many titles he carried. Andy had wondered how a man with such obvious power and influence could operate in their community without becoming known. The answer was that he was not himself operating in their community at all. Western Exploration was but one of the companies owned by United Mining and Refining, which was based in New York City, and of which Weitzel was a vice president. One of five. He recalled one professor's admonition that even finding a negative was a positive. It meant that you could move on to more productive endeavors that might produce a payoff. "Negative is positive" he chanted to himself as he traveled farther and farther down the dry and dust-covered stacks.

  The musty smell of these parchment pages, so long shelved, so seldom opened, began to tell on him. A small ache settled in behind his forehead and his lower back. He pictured Maggie as she'd huddled in the blankets in which the bar girl Sadie had wrapped her after the abduction. Shivering and terrified. He pictured Willy, weak and nearly delirious as he clawed his way to recovery from the snake bite. He pictured Many Clouds. He imagined the life they had planned with one another. He ignored his pains and pulled another register from the shelves. Even the whistling which usually cheered him a bit didn't help.

As a distant and hands-off vice president, was Weitzel giving orders as specific and detailed as that of directing Maggie's abduction? It seemed unlikely. Andy had anticipated he'd find a villain, someone who had been giving orders and payoffs to Hale Gentry. From the documents in Barker's office, it seemed Weitzel could be that person. But how and why would he concoct and direct such a scheme from a New York office? Even if he were making executive decisions, it seemed unlikely that he'd put his stamp on such details. He would need someone on site. Might that someone be Gentry after all? Weitzel might not have had the opportunity to evaluate his men properly, and from three thousand miles away, Gentry might have seemed like a good bet.

Andy wondered if Weitzel still thought so. Wondered if Weitzel even knew what Gentry was up to. Or perhaps Gentry wasn't his man on the scene. Perhaps Gentry was taking orders from someone else entirely. Andy combed through registers and deeds and every imaginable transaction until the clerk told him for the third time that the office was closing.

"Just a few more minutes," Andy said. The clerk shook his head and rattled his keys. A day wasted, it seemed. He tried to hang on to his "negative is positive" motto, but it was difficult since a day's hard work left him with little more than he had when he started.

His train back to Placerville didn't leave for more than an hour. Andy was at loose ends. Free of the stultifying atmosphere in the public records office, he wandered along the banks of the Sacramento River, enjoying the smell of fresh, cool water as the muddy current swept through the channel. He felt unreasonably disheartened by the underlayment of vegetative rot that hovered below the river's crisp air. He felt like a target of nature's normal processes. Idiotic, he knew, but he couldn't shake the disappointment.

Barges and riverboats crowded the piers. Stevedores loaded and unloaded cargo from the trucks and wagons that waited in turn or drew away on their journeys to factories and merchants in the metropolis that California's capital was becoming. He knew that the wagons would disappear before long, that trucks and autos were the dray horses of the future. Maggie and Willy would grow up with them, become as familiar with the sight and sound of them as horses had been for Andy.

He found a seat on a driftwood log and watched the uprooted trees, the scraps of lumber and tin and other human detritus the river was delivering from upstream to unknown destinations below. He hoped the flowing waters might provide some insight, some inspiration, that would show him what Weitzel or his people might want from him, from the Maxwells, that would drive them to such crimes.

A nearby steam whistle pulled him from his cogitations. No enlightenment from the river. Might as well try reading tea leaves. Discouraged by his failure, he rose from his seat and walked toward the train station. Perhaps the click clack of steel on steel would deliver an answer. If not, he still had an arrow or two left in his quiver.

Fifty

By dawn, the group gathered in the ranch house living room once the ruckus was more or less under control. Paradoxically under the circumstances, Carolyn renewed her appreciation of her father's vision in constructing this massive, gabled near-mansion with its spacious rooms and oversize fireplaces. True, it was a residence, but its stately lines gave it the aspect of a sort of frontier palace. It seemed an entirely appropriate setting for Marshal Halstad's interrogation of Ezekiel.

The prisoner lay back on the couch, his hands and feet securely bound and his head swathed in improvised bandages. The cowhands, Ezra and Sam, who had chased Ling Chu's other assailant until they lost him among the trees uphill from the ranch yard, stood sentry behind the couch. The two guards were brothers, and looked it, both swarthy and broad-shouldered. Sunlight bathed the room in a cheery light that belied the ugliness of the occasion. Ling Chu's arm was splinted and supported by a sling, ironically constructed from the same worn bed sheet that had provided Ezekiel's bandages.

"The sooner you give us some answers, the sooner we can get you some medical attention," Halstad said.

Cooper, Amelia, Carolyn, and Ling Chu inclined forward, ready for Ezekiel's reply. He didn't acknowledge the marshal, didn't even bother with a denial. Just lay stoic as a log.

Carolyn interjected, "This has been going on for more than an hour, Michael. We need to get Ling Chu to a doctor and to see what's going on with Andy. How about if we just toss this creature in the smokehouse till he's ready to talk?"

Halstad shook his head. "As a man, I'd love nothing better, Carolyn. As a marshal, though, this session here is about as irregular as I'm prepared to go. Let's leave him trussed up, chain him to a buckboard, and transport him to my little hoosegow in Sawtooth Wells proper. Maybe the rough ride will shake the truth out of him."

"I'd rather drag him behind the wagon, but I suppose there are niceties we have to observe," she said.

"Shame, ain't it?" Cooper said.

"Come on, you all." Amelia placed a calming hand on her husband's shoulder. "The less bloodshed the better, don't you think?"

"Wife of mine, you saved a lot of lives with that attitude."

Amelia looked at Carolyn. "He's not really as savage as he sounds, you know."

"I do know. Only when it counts, eh, Cooper? And then we're all grateful."

Cooper acknowledged the praise with a small nod of his chin, then set off for the front door. "I'll round up the mules and ready the buckboard. Ezra and Sam, you two bring the prisoner to the barn. We'll leave from there."

"Wait," Ling Chu called. "What about my car?"

Everyone froze for a moment, traded questioning looks. Carolyn broke the impasse. "You know I'm going to miss it, Ling, but it will have to wait. We have to get it all the way to Placerville somehow to find someone who knows how to repair it, then probably wait for parts. Right now, Andy and his family are the priority."

"Better to use car than horses. It will take only a short time to tie automobile behind buckboard now. Livery stable in Sawtooth Wells can hook up team and take to Placerville while we see Andy and Many Clouds."

Once again, the members of the group traded looks. Cooper jumped in this time.

"I don't care much for those noisy, greasy things, but they're a fact of modern life, and Ling's right that it won't take much time to hook it up. But I won't take it any farther than Sawtooth Wells. We've got to get to Placerville quick as we can. Now let's get moving."

It was an odd caravan—Carolyn driving a mule-drawn buckboard, Ling sitting beside her. In the wagon bed sat Ezekiel chained to an improvised two-by-four cross which Cooper had nailed to the frame of the buckboard. He was flanked by Sam and Ezra, Winchesters at ready. Marshal Halstad rode astride a paint horse, his rifle out of its saddle scabbard and its stock resting on his thigh. Bringing up the rear was the bent and twisted carcass of Ling's precious model T. As they passed under the Circle M arch, crossed Granite Creek, and headed up the hill Carolyn looked back toward the ranch yard, corrals and outbuildings, and at Cooper and Amelia, who were now charged with keeping the ranch safe in her absence and who together waved their farewells.

"What are we doing, Ling? We've got Ezekiel, but unless we can get him to talk about who's behind all this, what good is he?"

"It's very good, Miss Carolyn. Let us get to Sawtooth Wells. You will see."

"Well, you've saved the show before, Ling. Now would be a great time to do it again."

"Ouch, Miss Carolyn. Not such big bumps. Arm hurts."

"Okay, okay. Can't afford to injure our savior more than he's hurt already, can I?"

"No, Miss Carolyn. Can't afford that."

Carolyn turned toward her longtime friend and invaluable employee. Only someone who knew him as well as she did would have been able to tell from a certain lift in the corners of his eyes that he was smiling, which started her smiling as well. She slapped the reins and urged the mules out of their preferred torpid pace. "Onward, team," she called. "Onward."

The animals increased their speed to a near-trot, which she knew might be a little rough on Ling, but with so many threats looming, there was no time to assume the pace of a Sunday drive.

"Go, mule," called Ling. "We go fast."

Soon, Ling and Carolyn were laughing together as the buckboard jolted down the road toward Sawtooth Wells.

Fifty-One

Andy had gone to the Placer County seat in Auburn, thirty miles north of Placerville. He was searching for documentation he hadn't been able to find in Sacramento, something with the name of the person behind all the scheming. He'd left Many Clouds and the children behind after urging them to stay close to the house. With Andy gone from the house on this errand, they were all of them without focus or purpose. It was hard to maintain a sense of urgent danger when no threats had appeared for a while. The most discontented was Remington, who had grudgingly agreed to serve another day of sentry duty, but whose heart was clearly not in the job. He raced his horse up and down the road, doing the kind of tricks you'd see at a rodeo—mounting and dismounting while the animal was in motion, riding standing up instead of sitting down, twirling loops of rope for his mount to run through. He'd just started teaching Willy and Maggie to mount a moving horse bareback when Maggie took a spill in the dust and dirtied the pants and shirt Many Clouds had just laundered. As soon as she determined that Maggie was unhurt, Many Clouds was at first irritated to see her hard scrubbing work undone, then realized it was just the inspiration she'd needed.

"Maggie, Willy, we're changing clothes and going to town."

"Sawtooth Wells?" Maggie asked.

"No, Placerville. I have an idea that what Andy's looking for is there in Placerville."

Remy spoke up. "You know I don't like this being tied down more than anyone, but Andy was pretty clear about staying close to the house."

"I've been stewing over a vague idea, and watching you just now finally made it clear to me. I hate going against Andy but now that I have this notion, I have to act on it, and we have no time to waste. I'll explain on the way. Get into the house, children. Quickly now, and do what I say. Remy, after I've laid things out, please follow at a distance. Emmanuel, take a step into the woods uphill and keep watch from there. We'll stop by your village on the way and send you an extra man or two for reinforcements."

It was the Maxwell standard procedure to get spruced up to a fair-thee-well before heading toward town. Many Clouds and Andy both wanted to combat the notion that Indians were generally poor, dirty, and tattered. Now, however, she made sure they were both dressed in frayed and faded overalls, clothes they wore only when cleaning the stables.

"Willy, you're going to have to leave your grandfather's pocket watch behind," she said.

"But I've got it in my pocket. No one can see."

"I can see a bulge. It looks suspicious. To the manger with it." Andy had built a chamber at the foot of one of the poles holding up the stable. He figured a nondescript hiding place was more secure than something obvious, like a safe. Willy climbed down from the wagon, hating to surrender perhaps his most precious belonging, second only to his sheath knife. Regrettable, but it had to be. Many Clouds secreted her pistol in the same cubby. It was one thing to use it for defense of home and hearth, but to be caught with it in town would turn her automatically into a criminal.

"Now go to the pump and muddy yourselves head to toe. And hide the knives as best you can."

Finally, she was satisfied that the trio who climbed into the buckboard was as sorry and filthy a group as one could imagine. She smiled to think what Carolyn Maxwell would say if she could see them. She did carry a buckskin bag at her waist in which she secreted a knife of her own, some lengths of rawhide, and a few pieces of pemmican. Nothing that would appear dangerous to a law officer or even a hostile captor, but which might prove useful in a tight situation. They pulled the buckboard close to the creek, and while Maggie and Willy had a great time splattering it with mud, Remy expressed his bewilderment.

"They're going to think you're poor, dirty, and shiftless redskins," he said.

"And that," Many Clouds said, "is exactly what I want them to think. That's good enough, children. Now jump in and let's go."

Fifty-Two

Ezekiel was safely ensconced in the Sawtooth Wells jail, and Marshal Halstad sent a telegram to the County Sheriff in Auburn to come get him. They took Ling Chu to Dr. Forbes, the only physician for miles around. He was an old-fashioned country doctor with minimal formal training—"No Harvard diplomas on the Forbes wall," he often boasted—and he often remarked how proud he was of his ability to cure without all the academic mumbo jumbo. Carolyn knew they could count on him to give Ling Chu effective, if basic, treatment. She most respected Forbes because he knew his limitations. In an office whose shelves were loaded with saws and knives and glass-stoppered brown bottles, its air redolent with odors of alcohol and ether, he helped Ling Chu lie down on a white-sheeted table. Carolyn knew Ling Chu's arm was well within the doctor's abilities, so she left him there for Forbes to do his job.

By the time she returned, he had set the humerus, fashioned a cast with meticulous care, and done it all in record time. Carolyn had intended to consign her wounded friend to the care of Marshal Halstad, but Ling Chu objected, declaring that he should be beside her.

"Many bad men. Four eyes better than two."

"But your arm. You should be resting."

He waggled his fingers, peeking out from the end of the cast, which still emitted the odor of wet plaster. They were swollen but still operable. "I can pull trigger. You heard doctor say good for me to keep arm moving. Not so?"

"I should have known better than to think I could leave you behind."

"Okay, we walk, talk, plan now."

"Wait a minute, mister. You are still the patient. And—small miracle—the livery stable had an automobile to rent. A gentleman from San Francisco traded it for a wagon, team, and quarter horse. He said he guessed he wasn't ready for the mechanical age after all. It looks as if you'll be forced into teaching me how to drive."

Ling registered his objections, but it was a gesture only. In short order, they were putting along toward Placerville in a two-seater Model T with a rumble seat. Carolyn had endured the lectures and warnings that Ling Chu delivered as they got on their way. He was particularly adamant that she be careful when she turned the crank lest the engine backfire, sending the crank into a jerk and a spin that could inflict on her a broken arm to match his own. And, indeed, the backfire happened, but she avoided injury by heeding his cautions, tucking her thumb under and jumping back in time to avoid the whirling iron. After that, she tamped down her impatience with his extended instructions.

Once underway, Ling Chu asked, "We should go to check on Andy and Many Clouds, yes?"

"No time. I left a note at the livery stable explaining what happened at the Circle M. I'm sure that Many Clouds and Emmanuel have things well in hand. No, we're headed for a certain saloon on the outskirts of town."

"Mr. Hale Gentry? Not sure that is a good idea, Miss Carolyn."

"I'm not sure either, Ling Chu, but I've had enough of sitting around waiting for the next attack, haven't you? And you know me well enough to know I do have a plan."

Ling Chu didn't answer immediately. His silence frustrated Carolyn, but she didn't press him, knowing that his answer would come only in his own time. Two cowboys passed them, heading in the opposite direction. Carolyn exchanged waves with the men automatically, ignoring their curious looks at the sight of a woman at the wheel of a car. Her real concentration focused on what Ling Chu might say about her idea of confronting Hale Gentry. It wasn't long before he broke his silence.

"What is your idea, Miss Carolyn?"

"He will be surprised to see me. I will insist on talking to him in his office and confront him, using what I know and pretending to know far more than I do. All the while I will pace around the office, looking for incriminating evidence of some sort. Even if I find nothing, it should shake him up to see me snooping. He will send a message to someone. I will follow whoever takes the message and hope it goes to the person we're looking for."

"You follow alone? You will be seen."

"I have a slouch hat and a pair of trousers. He won't suspect it is me. However, now that there are two of us, I have an even better idea."

"I think now, yes. We need surprise for Mr. Gentry, but no hat or trousers I think."

"You think my showing up like this should be enough of a surprise?"

"No, not that either."

Carolyn started to object, but Ling Chu held up his hand to stop her. He winced, having inadvertently used his injured arm, but it didn't stop him from continuing.

"Listen please. We should do something more like this."

It took them nearly the rest of the way to Gentry's saloon to formulate their ideas, but by the time they approached the clapboard building tucked away among the spruce and eastern hemlocks, they knew what they were going to do.

Fifty-Three

Many Clouds left the buckboard in a brushy arroyo on the outskirts of Placerville. The children squatted near the entrance to the Hangtown Saloon.

Many Clouds had trepidations about leaving the children alone but made sure they had exit plans and a designated meeting place should they get separated. Her original thought had been to have Remy stay inside the saloon trying to gather information as he sipped whisky. But he said he'd become too well-known, and once they'd safely arrived, he took off for Auburn, hoping to encounter Andy.

The children were to remain outside the saloon unless that seemed dangerous. If that happened, they would return to the wagon. If worse came to worse, they could even make their way back home. In the meantime, they were to use their pleading eyes and open palms to look like beggars while keeping their ears and eyes open for any information about people and plans that might help put an end to the depredations they'd been suffering.

Many Clouds figured the most likely place for her to gather information was city hall and that her best cover was as a cleaning lady. It was customary for cleaners to work at night, so she didn't figure to run into the regular staff, and she had a cover story all ready for others who might question her. Armed with a broom and a dustpan, she trudged to the back door of the modest stone building that housed the city offices. Soon she was sweeping her way down the hall till she was in front of the mayor's office. The brass engraving above the door read *Mayor James George*. She knew most white people wouldn't be able to tell the difference between a Mexican and an Indian, so she affected a Spanish accent as she walked up to the counter, putting a nervous smile on her face.

"Excuse, please."

A stout blond woman in a puff-sleeved yellow dress looked up sharply from a document she'd been examining. "Whatever it is, spic, I don't have time for it." The name plate on her desk read "Ada Morgan."

"*Lo siento*, not understanding," Many Clouds answered. "*Mi prima*—is cuzno in English, yes? She say find Señora Morgan. Need place for *basura*."

"What's *basura*?"

Many Clouds held up her dust pan and dusting cloth.

The woman rose from her desk and virtually stomped toward Many Clouds.

"We're not a place to dump garbage. And what are you doing here anyway? Cleaning doesn't start till after sundown, and then it's up to Josefina and her people."

"*Sí*, Josefina. She sick. *Soy* Maria Elena. *La prima*. Must come day, not night."

"You little, worthless people don't seem to know the meaning of a regular schedule, do you? You'll find a wastebasket in the mayor's office through that door. Don't put a single paper out of place on his desk, though. He'll know it, and I'll be the one to get scolded."

Many Clouds just smiled and nodded. "Thanking you. *Gracias*." She moved around the counter with small, timid steps, smiling and nodding the while. Once she was inside, she peeked to make sure the other woman had returned to her desk, then started moving the broom back and forth on the floor while at the same time scanning the papers on the tidy desktop. The mayor was organized and kept little beyond an inkwell and pen in sight. Just a few letters ready to sign, none of them pertinent to her situation as near as she could tell. She lifted the wastebasket a few inches off the floor, then dropped it to create the illusion she was actually cleaning.

"Quiet in there. I'm trying to work."

"*Lo siento, señora.*"

"And I ain't no *señora*. You see a ring on my finger?"

"No, *disculpe*."

Many Clouds was on hands and knees now, delving through desk drawers which held folders looking for anything to do with Western Explorations or Hale Gentry, but she was finding nothing. What had seemed like a promising idea was turning into a foolish enterprise. She could afford no more time. Indeed, as she rose to her feet, her nemesis clomped into the office.

"What do you think you're doing down there, spic?"

"*Encontré estos, señorita.*" She held up a few tiny scraps of paper she had harbored for just such an emergency.

"In there." She pointed at the waste paper basket. "Then get out of here. The office can gather a few more grains of dust till Josefina gets back."

Many Clouds tried to appear on the verge of tears and to insert a bit of a whine in her voice as she held out her hand. "*Pero, señorita*, a little *dinero*, please. *Para los niños.*"

"Are you kidding? For fifteen minutes of no work at all? Now, scoot before I call the sheriff."

And scoot she did, out the door into the hallway, carrying her broom before her in case she needed something resembling a weapon. She'd hoped to leave the building with a feeling of victory. Instead, she headed toward the front door, mired in defeat. Then two things happened in quick succession.

First, the door to the office across the hall opened, and a clean-shaven young man in a frock coat and bowler hat emerged. It was easy to tell that the office was no bigger than a large closet and that the man who was leaving had been its only occupant. He had just pulled a key ring from his pocket and made to lock the door when a female voice, dripping with false sweetness, called from the hallway that intersected the one Many Clouds occupied.

"Oh, Prentice. Prentice, are you there?"

"Gloria? Do you need some help?"

"If you would," Gloria said in a simpering tone.

Prentice hurried in the direction of the voice, neglecting to lock his office door. Many Clouds slipped into the office. The desk was a smaller version of the mayor's. She had no idea what she might find, but perhaps, just perhaps, her mission wouldn't be a complete failure. She worried about Maggie and Willy, but a few more minutes shouldn't hurt. Before she could close the door behind her, a huge voice worthy of a big top announcer sounded from the direction of the front door. She opened the door a crack to glimpse its owner.

Striding down the hall came a large and florid man with ginger hair and flourishing sideburns. His boots were tipped with pointed toes encased in shiny steel. Two steps behind him followed a carbon copy of the man except much smaller. The big man bellowed as they walked. "The mayor better be here even if the sheriff's hiding out somewhere."

"Perhaps if we'd made an appointment, Mr. Russell."

"You know better than that, Miles. Jacob Russell doesn't make appointments. He demands service when he wants it, and this whole business has gone on way too long."

Presently, the pair disappeared into the office Many Clouds had just left. The front door opened once again, admitting a lady in a dress that resembled a cloud of pink organza ruffles and a hat that rode like a clipper ship on a wave of Gibson Girl curls. As the newcomer floated down the hall, loud voices erupted from the mayor's office.

"Tomorrow? I didn't come all the way from San Francisco to see him tomorrow. I shouldn't even have to show my face here at all, but I'm here today and I'll see Mayor James today."

Many Clouds couldn't make out the reply, delivered in the commanding baritone of the woman she'd wrongly called *señora,* but there was no mistaking the retort, delivered just as the organza woman entered the office.

The man called Jacob Russell softened his tone and lowered his volume the instant the lady entered. "Oh, good afternoon, Miss Dove. Delighted to see you."

Stephanie Dove's Bunkhouse was one of the best-known brothels for miles around, and she and Hale Gentry were rumored to be in partnership, though neither of them acknowledged it.

Ada Morgan—It was difficult for Many Clouds to connect the word *señorita* with her, given her matronly appearance and deep voice—spoke next. "Oh, you two know each other? Mr. Russell is one of your best customers, no doubt, Miss Dove."

Russell either didn't catch Ada Morgan's insult or chose to ignore it. "I do like to chat with my old school chum when I'm in the neighborhood, don't I, Stephanie? Nothing wrong with that."

"The pleasure is all mine, Jacob. To what does our fair city owe your visit?"

"Apparently the entire officialdom of this *fair city* has decided to take a holiday on the occasion of my visit. Quite the coincidence. But I will not be thwarted. Forgive my abrupt departure, my dear, but I must be off to our fair state's capital post haste. Farewell. And farewell to you as well, Madam Morgan."

"It's 'miss' not 'madam.' Mr. Russell, and I'd thank you not to forget it."

"I apologize. I meant no offense, did I, Miles?"

"No, sir, of course not."

"Of course not. He knows me well, so you can take his word. When I want to give offense, it will be more than obvious, won't it, Miles?"

"Absolutely, sir."

While the conversation—if it could be called that—proceeded, Many Clouds had been frantically searching the office for folders in the "w" end of the cabinet drawers. She walked her fingers, looking for something labeled

"Western Exploration" or some similar designation. Nothing. Next, she tried for "Powell." Again, nothing. Then "Gentry." Yes.

It was a thick file, more than she could carry in her satchel. Perhaps just a few pieces of the most important. Here. Contracts. Eight or ten of them. The outside voices ceased and Russell's clomping footsteps faded. She had no time to even scan these documents, but surely, they contained something of value, and she dare not take any more time. Prentice would return any second. She folded the papers into a neat bundle, intending to carefully tuck them into the beaded deerskin satchel at her waist, but felt the pressure of time. Instead, she dumped them in a wastepaper basket and placed a piece of crumpled paper on top of them. Then the doorknob turned.

Fifty-Four

Carolyn and Ling Chu figured the patronage at Gentry's saloon should be sparse at this time of the afternoon. Gentry's new touring car was parked outside. Good. They wanted him there. They parked their own car nearly touching Gentry's rear bumper. Ling Chu hunched his shoulders and lowered his head. A submissive pose that should enable him to escape the notice of casual observers. He sidled along the side of the building toward the back door. Carolyn strode boldly up the steps and through the batwing doors. She fancied herself as David bearding the lion in his den. Not that Gentry was much of a lion. More of a jackal, and a mangy one at that.

"You can't go in there, lady." The call came from the small sallow-faced bartender, who pulled a sawed-off shotgun from under the bar as he spoke. Even at the quick pace with which she crossed toward the office Carolyn had time to note that the sawdust on the floor hadn't been swept and freshened for at least two days. She paid no attention to the bartender's orders and reached for the doorknob, then stopped. Two men were arguing inside, and both voices were familiar. One of them was Gentry's, but she was astonished to recognize Remy's as well. Had he been working with Gentry all along, spying on them while he was pretending to work for them?

"You're going to let me do this my own way, Gentry, or you can get someone else."

"I'm paying you to do what I say, Dillinger."

"*You're* paying me? Hogwash. You're small change. I'm going to your boss, the man with the money."

"Good luck finding him. I don't know where he is myself."

"Which only goes to show how unimportant you are to his operation."

She reached for the doorknob, but the bartender stepped in front of her, his shotgun held at port arms. The smell of gun oil suggested it was a weapon that saw careful maintenance. The man's body suggested that he was less careful about his own hygiene. And of course, there was the aura of liquor surrounding him. "I said no admittance, lady."

She heard footsteps approaching the door from the other side, stepped aside so that she would be out of the sight line of whoever was about to emerge, and emerge is just what Remy did. Vigorously. The bartender stumbled out of the way as Remy pushed through. The Maneuver not only screened Carolyn from Remy's sight but gave her an opening into Gentry's office. Into the breach she charged.

"Why, Mr. Gentry. I am so glad you are in residence, so to speak. I have matters to discuss that must be broached face to face. You'll excuse me if I sit even though you're standing."

Carolyn perched on one of the two bentwood chairs in front of Gentry's rather elegant walnut desk, an obvious signal to visitors that they were of lesser status than he. She noticed also that he had sawn off a half-inch or so of the chairs' front legs, an old trick to make them less comfortable and thus shorten the visitor's stay.

"Now," she said.

Gentry started to sit in his own leather padded chair but decided to remain standing.

"I'm busy, Carolyn." She shot him a look. "It's Mrs. Maxwell, then, if you insist. Please state your business." She caught a whiff of his ubiquitous cologne, a strange mixture with an astringent sweetness to it. She'd known him a long time, but the odor was new. Carolyn considered herself broadminded, but men wearing such perfumes always struck her as sissified, especially on a man who had once had aspirations to court her and become head man at the Circle M. She had gotten over her anger at his effrontery, her emotions toward him having softened to ironic amusement. But something about this cologne reawakened those atavistic impulses. She tamped them down and returned to the matters at hand. Given their mutual antagonism, there would be no pretense of cordiality. Things were working out perfectly so far.

"You can calm yourself, Mr. Gentry, I am not here to castigate you for your crimes, as you probably assume."

"Crimes, Mrs. Maxwell? I have done—"

"Even Maggie's kidnapping. I can't prove a single significant violation against you, so just to allay any fears you might have about that area of your aberrant behavior."

"Aberrant behavior." He smiled, a grin that was closer to a sneer. "You may leave immediately."

"Soon, soon. You own stock in a company called Western Explorations. Don't try to deny it."

"I don't deny it. I—"

"Fine. Now we're getting somewhere. I'm serving notice that any further assaults on me, my family, or my property are attributable to that company and by extension to you. So you will cease and desist or you can expect further visits from me and mine." She stood. "Clear?"

Gentry smiled in that infuriating white-toothed way meant to hide his villainy behind a mask of friendly good cheer. "Since I am guiltless, I will fear no more attacks, though I always welcome time spent with you, Carolyn."

So he was back to his presumptuous first names again. Not so her. "The next time you see me, *Mr. Gentry,* my mood is not likely to be so convivial."

Carolyn strode out of the saloon having accomplished what she'd set out to do, and she trusted that Ling Chu had managed his part as well. But Remy? A complication she not only had not planned on, but which frightened her as well.

She and Ling had planned to meet at the car, but he wasn't there. She paced a circle around the machine then she saw what she hoped for. An "X" chalked on the bumper. "*Xingfú*" was the Chinese word for "happiness." Ling had found something and was investigating on his own. Had he been in trouble, the signal would have been "J" for Jiùmìng or "help." She rubbed out the chalk even though there was little chance anyone would decipher what it meant. Well, without Ling, she was on her own now, but she knew her next step. She had to reach Andy and Many Clouds and warn them about Remy.

Fifty-Five

Many Clouds had managed to grasp her broom and pretend to be sweeping Prentice's office when he entered. The dapper young man, however, had not fully bought into her masquerade. Now, she found herself in the office she had just pretended to clean on her hands and knees. They'd seated her in a large leather wheeled chair and surrounded her—Jacob Russell, the man called Prentice, and the baritone *señorita*. The lady in organza and Russell's toady Miles stood in the background. Not only had her mission failed, but she'd left Maggie and Willy in danger. Although she knew them capable of heading back to the house as she'd directed, she also knew they would not follow her instructions. Their first impulse would be to rescue her. She had to get away, but she was outnumbered, and force wouldn't work. She tried to make herself as small and unthreatening as possible, the next thing to invisible, as she responded to their accusing questions.

"*Señores*," she paused "*y señorita*. I want only *un poco dinero* for *mi familia*. *Mis niños*, my children, they are hungry."

The *señorita* snorted. Russell waved her into silence.

"*Señorita*, you appear to me to be Indian even though you speak Spanish. Am I right?"

Many Clouds nodded.

"What is your tribe?"

She wondered whether she should answer truthfully but saw no advantage to lying. "Arapaho, though *mi padre*, my father, was Mexican."

"Arapaho, eh? Have you heard of John Chivington?"

Many Clouds tried to arrange her features into a look of puzzlement and shook her head. Every Arapaho knew the story of how that particular soldier had led his men to commit the atrocities at what became known as the Sand Creek Massacre. Not a single Arapaho warrior had been killed in the battle because the only ones in the sleeping village had been women and children. "Nits make lice" was Chivington's infamous comment when he ordered that even infants, even the unborn, were not to be spared.

"It was a long time ago, *señorita*, but he was a military man who believed that all Indians, even the very young should be eliminated for the good of the country. There are many who still believe that, not only about Indians but about Mexicans as well. Now, neither I nor any right-minded citizen wishes to see children starve, especially when their parents are trying to make an honest living. However, many among us are not as right-minded as I am. Miles, a dollar, please."

"A whole dollar, sir? Are you sure?"

Russell spoke with a sharp edge to his tone. "Do I appear uncertain, Miles?"

"No, sir. Of course, sir." He dug into a pouch and handed his boss a coin.

"Take this, *señorita,* and go with God."

Many Clouds fought the impulse to leap from her chair and dash out of the building. Instead, she drew back in an attitude of fright and uncertainty.

"Oh, *señor*, it is so much."

"Take it and go. We are busy here."

She took the coin and shuffled toward the door. She passed into the hallway and moved toward Prentice's office. As she crossed the threshold from the office, she heard Russell say, "Fun to watch them grovel for a pittance, isn't it, Miles?" She didn't make it quite to Prentice's office before he called to her. "Where are you going?"

She pointed toward his office door. "My broom, *Señor?*"

Prentice started to object, but Russell overrode him. "Yes, yes. Whatever you need, just move along."

Once inside Prentice's office, she picked up her broom, then retrieved the documents from the wastebasket where she'd tossed them just before Prentice had discovered her. Into her pouch they went, and she took herself out of the office and out of the building as quickly as her shuffle would carry her. Once in the street, she breathed deeply without pausing a step. She was grateful to have escaped, but suspicious that she had eluded capture too easily. The generous tip and her release over the objections of the others? What Russell's design might be, she could only guess. Perhaps she had succeeded in her mission after all in ways which would be revealed only later. For right now, though, her concern had to be Maggie and Willy. They were no longer outside the saloon doors. She hadn't expected them to be. They'd be no doubt waiting at the wagon. Once she crossed the street, she stepped into an alley and looked behind her. She was not surprised to see Miles standing at the door of City Hall, looking in all directions. She stepped from behind the tree, making sure he spotted her before she headed for the wagon. She hoped she looked like just another dirty Indian on her way to nowhere important. She hoped that he would consider her not worth following. If he did, she had an idea for another surprise.

Fifty-Six

Andy was excited as he approached home in the waning light of dusk. Not only did he believe he'd discovered the reason behind the myriad violent incidents that had plagued them recently, but he'd finally gone beyond talking about an automobile and actually bought one. The word about canceling the Maxwell accounts had not reached as far as Auburn.

He was anxious to show it off, and he missed Many Clouds. He'd thought his affection was already beyond measure, but now that she was pregnant it seemed to have doubled. He was sure the sound of the engine would bring the household down the slope to the front gate, but only Emmanuel awaited when he braked to a halt. He was glad to be free of the noise and petroleum smells of his vehicle, but foreboding rose in his stomach over the absence of his family.

"Where is everyone?" He jumped down from the car. He felt cheated of his moment of triumph in displaying the machine and sharing his new information.

"They went into town," Emmanuel said as he handed Andy the note Many Clouds had left. "They should have returned by now, though."

Andy's fists clenched with anxiety at the thought of waiting in the dark for his family, or worse, having to search the area with no more notion of where to begin than that they had gone to Placerville.

"Was Remy with them?"

"He took off toward Auburn to try intercepting you." Andy turned and kicked the tire. If he hadn't taken the extra couple of hours to buy the car, he might have met Remy. On the other hand, what was the use of making plans if no one followed them? His people were spread all over the map, each of them ignorant of the other's location or plans. Each of them vulnerable and isolated when they needed to be united and mutually protective. In a few moments he'd gone from feeling the ebullience of a general on the brink of victory to the consternation of a lone warrior, beleaguered and besieged. He took a deep breath, trying to still himself and savor the tang of the pines, the mellow aroma of the oaks that surrounded them. Emmanuel gestured upslope and moved toward the veranda. Andy followed.

"What do you think, Emmanuel?"

Emmanuel said nothing for a time, simply arranged chairs, sat down and gestured for Andy to do the same.

"I think we stay here. Evil spirits thrive on chaos. Our best weapon now is stillness."

"That may take more patience than I have."

"But it also takes courage, which you possess in abundance."

Andy stood and paced the veranda. Evening shadows had nearly embraced the few acres of their simple homestead. The place was home to him now, as much as the Circle M where he'd grown up. More. He'd been born into the Circle M family, but this family he and Many Clouds had created, and her pregnancy heralded a new generation, a modern new world of inclusion and peace instead of separation and violence. His first impulse was almost always to hurl himself into action, but now, despite his anxiety and misgivings, he saw the wisdom of Emmanuel's words. So, yes, stillness made sense, at least for the moment.

"I'll make us some coffee," he said. He arose and went toward the kitchen as darkness descended.

Fifty-Seven

Many Clouds didn't find Maggie and Willy at the wagon. At least they weren't making themselves obvious. She called for them in loud whispers, then walked in a large circle through the brush. Maybe they didn't trust that she was alone, were waiting for reassurance before they showed themselves. She got no response, though, and the shadows were deepening. She examined the surrounding landscape, looking for signs of a scuffle that would probably have taken place if the children had been seized. Nothing. Where was Remy? She should have listened to Andy and stayed put at the house. Yet, she thought there must be something in the documents she'd purloined that would at least shed light on the plot against them, if not a way to confound it altogether.

All well and good, but with Remy and the children at large, it was difficult to know what her next move should be. Miles could still be following her, and she might be inviting his attack if she stayed put. She couldn't see him at the moment, but she had a feeling he was near. Her emotions were in turmoil. She felt one minute as if she could challenge all enemies, then the next minute she thought she'd been a fool and was headed for certain defeat. She'd never suffered such emotional contradictions. *Is it you, my little one, making me feel this way?*

She climbed onto the wagon seat. Returning to the house seemed to admit defeat, or near-defeat, in the errand she'd embarked upon so bravely. But it was the only thing that made sense at the moment. At the very least Emmanuel would be there to help. Perhaps, best of all, Andy might have returned. She started to turn the wagon around, then decided that she might spot something important if she took a short detour through town. The horses needed watering, which she could take care of in the nearby creek, but it gave her a believable errand to stop at the trough near the town well where she might overhear something useful. It had grown dark enough that she wouldn't be recognized.

The new electric lights that adorned the picture window on the Hangtown Saloon sparkled in the early evening gloom. The daytime crowd of women, children and their baskets of vegetables and dry goods was well on its way to being replaced by cowhands and hardcases looking for an evening of liquor and loud laughter. An acerbic odor of alcohol overlay such daytime smells as soap and honest sweat.

She did see Miles, but he looked completely innocent, sitting on a bench in front of a gunsmith shop and chatting amiably with someone who was a stranger to her. He made no gesture of recognition. She saw no sign of the children, and she had no inkling of where to look. She suddenly felt terribly lonely and vulnerable. An involuntary sob rose in her throat. Onward, then, to her own house, which had become the font of security. She turned the team toward home.

Traffic thinned to almost nothing at the town's edge. She passed the point where the wagon had been parked, climbed down with the notion of checking to see if the children had somehow made it back here after all. The sound of a female voice lifted her spirits, and she was about to call out when a male voice brought her up short.

"Just a while. Maybe a month," the man said. Though he spoke so softly he nearly whispered, there was no mistaking the voice of Jacob Russell.

"We've waited so long already, Jakey."

"I know, Marilyn, honey, I know. But there's no help for it. You took the first step, the big one. We'll soon be in clover together forever after. Now another hug." Silence. "And a kiss." Another moment. "And just keep the feel of those with you till next time."

"When will that be?"

"Hard to predict exactly, but not long. I'll let you know. Now you go first. I'll wait a few minutes and leave in the other direction like always."

"I do so hate to let you go."

"And I you, sweet one. But away with you, now."

Many Clouds huddled in the wagon bed, hoping neither Russell nor his female companion would head toward her. If either of them did, she thought, let it be the woman. Russell would recognize her in an instant with results she was sure would be certainly unpleasant, perhaps dangerous. But suddenly, she decided she was tired of cowering. She slapped the reins and put the team in motion. Indeed, a blond woman in a pink bonnet, corkscrew curls bouncing at her cheeks, emerged from the brush before the wagon wheels had taken their first revolution. She was a bit startled to find the wagon in her path, but Many Clouds pretended to concentrate on her driving and not to notice.

Who this woman was and what she and Russell had been up to she knew not, but she had no desire to get involved in the man's romantic affairs. She gave the reins another slap, glad to have Virgil and Horace pick up their pace on cue.

Fifty-Eight

When Carolyn saw the Model-T parked in front of Andy's and Many Clouds' house, she braked their machine at a distance, unsure how to proceed. For a moment, she had thought the automobile might be the repaired version of the one that had been wrecked at the Circle M, but she instantly realized that time and distance made that impossible.

"What do you think, Ling?"

"They see us for sure, but maybe I sneak now. Go uphill around back like at Gentry's. You go in."

It was the very plan she'd been thinking of. The other thought she had was to head on past, proceed according to what they saw as they went, then double back if something seemed suspicious. However, their headlights were too weak to show them much.

"Good luck to both of us."

The place looked deserted as she drew near. No lights from inside. No movement in the yard or around the stock shed and storage shed. The apple tree beside the graves of Maggie's and Willy's parents seemed the lone guardians standing sentinel over whatever life the house supported.

"Hello, the house," she called. She waited for a few moments, then made to call a second time, but before she could make a sound, she heard "Mother?" from some place nearby.

"Andy?" she said. "Why are you hiding like this?"

"Are you all right?" he said. "Are you driving? Is Ling with you?"

"Can you please help your mother inside so we can discuss all this in a civilized manner?"

There was a moment of silence, then the car rocked with the weight of a new occupant. "I had to make sure," Andy said, "that you weren't being held at gunpoint or that there wasn't some such threat afoot." He sat beside her and grasped her hand. "I'm glad beyond words to see you and to see that you're safe. Emmanuel," he called. "All is well. You can come out now."

"Hello, Miss Carolyn," Emmanuel called from the porch. "I too am happy for your safe arrival."

"Now that we've gotten all that out of the way, I'd be obliged to have some refreshment. Ling and I have had a long drive and an exhausting adventure."

"Ling?" Andy said. "Where is he?"

"You aren't the only one exercising extra caution, my son. Ling," she called. "All is well, thank heavens. Meet us inside."

"Right away, Miss Carolyn," came a voice in the distance.

"From the looks of things," she said, "we have a great deal to tell one another. Let's get started."

"Not till I get there," called still another voice, this one from downhill near the creek.

"Remy," Carolyn said, her voice low. "We've got to be careful, Andy."

"Why on earth?"

"Just take my word for it." The investigator's lanky shape emerged from the shadows. "And follow my lead when we start talking." She turned from Andy. "Why, Remington. What a nice surprise. Please join us." She poked Andy in the ribs.

"Yes," Andy said. "As mom said, we definitely have a lot to tell one another."

"So," Remy continued, "let's get started."

He fairly trotted through the gate toward the house. Andy and Carolyn shared a look. Carolyn took Andy's arm, and they all headed upslope together.

Fifty-Nine

They burst on horseback from a stand of roadside manzanita. They both wore masks, bandanas folded in triangles across the lower half of their faces. It wasn't much of a disguise, though. Many Clouds recognized Miles by the steel toes on his pointed boots. Either he was dim-witted or didn't care if she knew who he was. Or perhaps he wanted her to know. If so, then why the mask? Miles grabbed the bridle bits to stay the horses while his partner boarded the wagon. Neither man spoke a word at first.

"What are you looking for? Maybe I can help," she said.

Miles chuckled. The other man rifled the lunch basket and the blanket she had planned to use for a picnic if everything went as she'd hoped. So far nothing had. He rifled the rucksack with the dress-up clothes inside, ripping them as he went. They tore into the satchel she'd used to hide the papers she'd stolen. Those papers she'd now secreted in her leggings. They were so intent on searching the wagon they missed her furtive transfer of the knife from beneath her skirt to her hand.

They knocked fists against every board and climbed underneath, looking for secret panels, she guessed. They'd be disappointed. She hoped they'd be satisfied with searching the wagon, but once they'd come up dry there, Miles turned his attention to her.

"Stand up, sweetheart," he said to her.

She shook her head, leaned forward as if cowering and gripped the knife's wooden handle. Pine. Absorbent. Less slippery than metal, even if bloodied. The blade was seven inches of honed steel. Both she and Andy had grown up with the attitude that knives were to be respected and cared for, both in the kitchen and on the trail.

"I said stand up, squaw." The man gripped her shoulder. She twisted and sliced.

"Goddamn," he yelled and grabbed his right hand with his left, trying to understand what had just happened. Many Clouds leaped from the wagon seat on to the back of Virgil, the horse on the left. From there, she jumped straight at Miles, who was still tending the bridles. She swung the knife as she sailed through the air, seeking to disable or even kill him if she needed to, then to appropriate the animal for herself.

He was quicker than she anticipated, though, and grabbed her wrist before the blade made contact. He pulled and jerked and used her momentum to throw her in the dust. The impact knocked the breath out of her, and she lost the knife. She heard the click of a single action revolver and managed to recruit enough energy to roll off the road and into the brush. The bullet went wild, and she curled up in the dark trying to catch her breath.

"Grover. You okay?"

"Hell, no, I ain't. Dirty redskin fixed up my hand something fierce."

"Well throw your bandanna around it, and we'll get you to a doc soon as we finish this job."

"What the hell you mean? I'm finished now."

"Not till I say so." Apparently, Miles was meek only to his boss. Away from Jacob Russell, he turned into a bully himself. "Now get those axes off the saddles and let's do it."

"What about the horses? I could use them on my place."

"Boss says take care of everything, and that's what we're going to do. You can pull the trigger, though, if you want."

"Aw, I hate to ruin good horseflesh for nothing."

"You going to keep whining, or you going to do what I say?"

"I'm gonna… Aw, hell."

Two gunshots followed, then the pounding and splintering as the wagon was reduced to kindling. The wagon could be replaced. Horace and Virgil, too, she supposed, but the rate at which their livestock was being slaughtered was both dispiriting and infuriating. Many Clouds suppressed a sob. This time, she nearly strangled on it.

She crept farther into the brush. After a while it seemed that both men mounted up and rode off. When the hoofbeats receded, there were no more sounds, but she stayed put anyhow. One of them might remain behind and wait for her to come out. Or they might send a confederate. The worst part was that, although plenty of people would be glad to ride to her rescue, no one knew where she was. Any more than she knew where her children were. Surely daylight would bring clarity. In the meantime, she was as comfortable as she was going to get here in her refuge amid a clump of willows. Exhausted though she was, sleep seemed impossible. Finally, though, weariness left her with no choice but to succumb.

Sixty

Maggie and Willy smelled the blood long before they stumbled across the bodies of the horses and wreckage of the wagon. A pungent odor that had become familiar to them in the course of the exigencies of farm life—birth, death, accidents. They had dodged behind an uphill boulder as Miles and his henchman trotted past, one of many instances on this journey where they hid to avoid people traveling the public roadway. They recognized Miles by his voice even in the dark. They had remained at their posts outside the Hangtown Saloon until the two men in the silver-tipped boots parked their gleaming automobile across the street.

They started toward City Hall, but the bigger of the two said, "Long drive, Miles. I'm thirsty. How about you?"

"I wouldn't say no to a libation, sir."

"Okay, then. Thirsty work, but someone has to do it, since we can't seem to find someone can do it for us, eh?"

"Yes, sir, Mr. Russell," the one called Miles said as they approached the saloon entrance. "Out of the way, urchin," he said to Willy, drawing back his foot as if to kick him. Willy stood, but he didn't run. "Oh, feisty, are you? I'll teach you to behave like a proper redskin." He swung his steel pointed toe in Willy's direction, but Willy sidestepped the kick easily and moved his hand to his hip, ready to brush aside his shirt and draw his sheath knife if Miles kicked again. It was against Many Clouds' orders to use the knife only if absolutely necessary, but he didn't see why he should put up with the abuse.

"Don't waste your energy, Miles. We have more important matters to get to."

"Yes, sir," Miles said. But he took a threatening stutter-step toward Willy, who crouched, ready to go on the attack.

"It's not worth it, Willy," Maggie whispered, moving her lips as little as possible.

Willy shot Miles a defiant glance, turned his back, and spat in the dust of the boardwalk.

"You little pissant," Miles said.

"Leave it, Miles. Whiskey awaits."

"Okay, Mr. Russell, but I hate to see these swine get away with defying white people."

"Whiskey, Miles. Come on."

As the two men entered the bar, a pair of grimy, ragged men struggled from the sidewalk bench and staggered toward the youngsters. Maggie looked around for Remy but saw him nowhere.

"Come on, Willy. Time's up."

"But what about Remy?"

She said nothing else but grabbed his arm and threaded a path between wagons and motor vehicles toward City Hall across the way.

They scuttled through halls, opened closed doors, hid in closets looking for Many Clouds but didn't find her. Afraid to spend more time alone in these intimidating official surroundings, they fled toward the front door, but Maggie suddenly pulled up short and steered Willy into a space underneath a staircase. She held a "keep quiet" finger in front of her lips.

"Okay, Ada," came a man's voice. "It's not that important. I'll come back tomorrow."

"Sorry I couldn't help you, Mr. Gentry."

"*De nada*, as the peons say."

That little witticism elicited a chuckle from the stern Miss Morgan. Hale Gentry passed within three feet of them as he donned his hat and headed out the front door.

"What's going on, Maggie?" Willy asked.

"That's his voice. The man who was giving the orders in the room next to where they locked me up."

Maggie and Willy fled without discovering a trace of Many Clouds. After searching every where they dared without encountering either her or Remy, they decided to follow Many Clouds' instructions and return to the wagon. Except the wagon was gone. They'd have to hoof it.

As they trudged along, Maggie at first blamed Willy for their plight but knew underneath that was unjust, so she said nothing about it. It looked as if all they'd gotten for their efforts was a long walk and perhaps the wrath of worried adults who would have no idea where they were.

Then, at a point when they judged themselves to be halfway home, they found trouble aplenty. The scene was a horror. The horses' corpses, the wreckage of the wagon. Why? Willy threw himself prone, wrapped his arms around Virgil's neck and howled in rage. Maggie wanted to join him, but fear of what might wait in the shadows overwhelmed her grief. She tugged at Willy's arm.

"Let's get out of here."

"But Virgil and Horace."

"There's nothing we can do now, and who knows who's waiting out there? Come on."

Willy was still sobbing when they scrambled into the dense chaparral. They had to feel their way through the darkness, blundering into branches and stumbling over rocks. Before long, Maggie stopped altogether and hugged her brother to her.

"We're making too much noise, Willy. We should just stop right here till daylight."

"But there's no place to sit or lie down or anything."

Willy was right. Pebbles, small boulders, jabbing twigs and branches.

"Maybe we can go over here," he said. Willy took her hand and led her through a tunnel in the greenery that only he or perhaps a squirrel would be able to find. They ended up in a small dry creek bed. It was a bit rocky, but by bending some willow branches and stripping the leaves from sucker shoots of a black cottonwood, they created a tolerable emergency resting place.

"Good job, Willy," Maggie said. "Now all we've got to do is lie down and wait for Mr. Sun to find us. How about a bit of a nap?"

"Not me," Willy said. "I've got to stay awake in case they come back."

"You've done such a great job with this hiding place, I don't think we have anything to worry about as long as we stay quiet."

"Well, you go ahead and take a nap, Maggie. I'll make sure we stay safe."

"You're very brave, Willy. I'm lucky to have you to look after me."

"Don't worry about a thing. I'll see you in the morning."

Maggie smiled, tucked an elbow under her head, and lay down. Sleep wouldn't come, but presently, she heard Willy's deep breathing as he dropped off. They weren't in the habit of saying prayers, but she did so tonight, asking that they all would be safe in the morning, and it wasn't long before she followed her brother into the nether world.

Sixty-One

It was the fox that awoke Many Clouds just as the eastern sky was pinking with dawn. The animal skittered and sniffed, trying to decipher who she was and to solve the mystery of what she was doing in here prone in the underbrush where humans seldom ventured. She rose slowly to her elbow. The fox was a close cousin of the trickster coyote, so one had to beware in his presence, but the kit fox was also associated with the Creator. Powerful medicine. This was no kit fox, but a red fox, its coat resplendent to meet approaching winter. Nevertheless, she felt she could accept her greeting as a good omen. How she knew the animal was female—a vixen—she couldn't have explained, but it seemed somehow obvious.

"Greetings to you, sister." She spoke softly, both to observe the moment with reverence and out of caution against lurking enemies. "May sun and moon pour blessings on you and your children."

The fox yipped, jumped back, approached a couple of steps, yipped once more and bolted into the underbrush. An auspicious beginning, Many Clouds thought, to this day of discovery and decision.

She rose to her hands and knees, tried to see through the willow leaves and branches, to remember which way the road lay. It didn't take her long to orient herself and begin crawling in the direction of the road. She had no sense of whether the wagon and the murdered horses were ahead of her or behind her. She hoped she wouldn't have to see them again. They were ominous presences in the dark, the idea of seeing them in full light shuddered her. She gave a small yip, an echo of the fox's farewell, and began moving toward the road. She felt she was almost there even though she couldn't yet see it, when a loud rustling sounded a few yards away.

"Shush," someone whispered.

She'd been afraid Miles would leave a sentinel, and it seemed she'd been right. She froze. Silence. She couldn't stay here all day. She had to get to the house. Perhaps if she followed the fox. The road paralleled an arroyo, which eventually met the stream that flowed past the house. Perhaps that's what the fox had been doing here. Showing her a safe way home. She turned in the direction in which the fox had fled. She could see that the willows gave way to a stand of manzanita that seemed impenetrable. But she didn't have to crawl far before she found that there was a sketchy trail, and it was surprisingly easy to follow. She made it nearly to the manzanita when she heard another rustling of leaves and branches. This one followed by a loud crash.

A loud whisper. "You're impossible."

"I have to go."

"Be quiet about it."

What Maggie and Willy were doing here, she couldn't imagine, but her heart lifted to hear their bickering.

"Hey, children. It's me."

"Many Clouds?" Willy said. "How in the hell?"

"Quit cussing, Willy."

"I will if I want. Sorry, Many Clouds."

"Just stay put and keep quiet. I will come to you."

Their reunion was brief, but joyous, and Many Clouds led them down the fox trail to the bottom of the dry arroyo where they found rocks large enough to allow them to sit and talk. Faint smells of spring and summer still lingered in the autumn dust. The pungent waves of cedar and fir would have to wait for the watery heavens to wash them down to earth.

Many Clouds felt almost giddy with triumph despite their situation. The horses dead. The wagon destroyed. All that, and they'd learned nothing of value about the forces arrayed against them. She should have stayed at the house as Andy had ordered. And where was Andy now? She missed him more intensely than she thought possible. Once it was a yearning for his nearness that filled her when he was gone. Now the yearning had become a need, a feeling that without him, she wasn't whole. And he felt the same about her. They'd never said so. She just knew it. As intense as the feeling was, though, Maggie and Willy had to take priority.

"I've been imagining the most horrible things ever since I looked out the window and saw you were no longer at the saloon, and then you weren't waiting at the wagon either. What happened to Remy? He was supposed to be watching out for you."

"Well, what happened to you?" Willy said. "We went to the wagon, and it was gone."

"And Remy just disappeared," Willy said. "We never really saw him after you dropped us off."

Many Clouds reached out and grasped both children's hands. "You must have been terrified. Nothing seems to have gone the way I planned and hoped. But no help for it now. We have to go on from here. Tell you what. Let's each of us tell what happened and what we learned. But quickly. We have to get back home and share it all with the others. Maybe between all of us we'll have the whole mystery solved."

"Only thing we learned is that Miles guy is dangerous as a mad dog, and he hates Indians. If it wasn't for his boss holding him back, he'd have tried to kick us all the way to Sacramento. I had this, though"—he pulled out his knife—"so he wouldn't have got away with it."

Many Clouds said, "He's the one who ordered Horatio and Virgil shot, too. We owe him a great deal, and we will pay in full when the time comes. In the meantime, did anything useful drop in your laps while you were sitting out there?"

Maggie said, "A lot of disgusting noises and horrible smells and bad language."

Willy picked up where Maggie left off. "One guy was so full of cusswords I don't know if he knows any other kind. He was mad, too." He affected a gravely voice as he growled in imitation, "I knew the gold was gone, then they told me there was a lot of that black gold we dug back in Wales. But I ain't seen so much as a pebble of the stuff. That one smelled worse than any pig in any sty I been around."

"Black gold?" Many Clouds said. "I wonder what he was talking about. Did he say anything else?"

They both shook their heads.

Willy said, "We both run around—"

"*Ran* around," Many Clouds said.

"Rin ran run. What does it matter? I was peeking in windows and everything and still didn't see you or Remy or anyone. I was getting scared."

"So," Maggie said, "after Willy did that, we kind of scouted around some alleys and behind buildings and corrals with no luck. By that time, it was getting pretty dark, so we headed back to the wagon, but it was gone. So we decided to do what you said and make it back home as best we could."

"Then we saw Miles and that other fella riding back toward town, and the guy with Miles was cussing up a blue streak about his hand. Between him and those saloon guys I sure did learn some words tonight, Many Clouds."

She'd been worried about the physical harm that might come to her children but now began to wonder about what all this kind of talk might do to their minds.

"Well, forget those words if you can, and certainly don't go using them."

"What about you, Many Clouds?"

"I don't know yet. I had some close calls. I did get a good look at Miles and his boss. He's named Jacob Russell, and he's very worked up because things aren't going according to his plan so he came all the way from San Francisco to stir things up. I still don't know what the plan is, though. I think he might be the big man behind all this, but I really couldn't tell. And he's got a girlfriend he doesn't want anyone to know about. I don't know if that means anything or not. I did manage to get hold of some papers I think might be valuable." She patted her satchel. The papers had proved too cumbersome to carry very far in her leggings. "I'm anxious for Andy to get a look at them, but for the moment, I'm just glad we're all three safe. Now, let's get back home before something else happens."

As they were rising to their feet, Willy said, "Maybe we should all split up and take different ways home to confuse them."

"Willy," Many Clouds said, "how old are you?"

"You know, Many Clouds."

"Yes, I do. So I know that a ten-year-old should remember what happened the last time we all went in different directions."

"That was your idea," he answered.

"And I could have gotten us all killed. I'm hoping we all learned something from that mistake. Back on the road now."

"Wait a minute," Maggie said. "The road is this way."

"Not that road. We're going Miss Fox's way. Hands and knees now, and follow me."

Sixty-Two

It was dawn, barely light enough to make out branches and leaves instead of just vague shapes of the surrounding trees. Remy and Emmanuel were face to face on the veranda.

"I thought Many Clouds was taking care of those kids," Remy said, offering his excuse for the dozenth time.

"I heard her tell you to watch them but to hang back so you wouldn't be recognized," Emmanuel said.

Remy stepped toward Emmanuel till he was virtually nose-to-nose with him. "Are you saying I deliberately abandoned them?"

Carolyn stepped in. "Let's stop repeating this conversation. It isn't going to find them."

Remy continued. "It must have just got dark on them before they could get back here. They should be home any minute now that the sun's up."

"Just like you said they'd be home last night," Andy said.

"Look, if you don't want me here, just say the word and I'll be gone."

"Maybe that's the best idea," Andy retorted.

Carolyn chimed in again. "No one's going anywhere till we put this family back together."

"Breakfast ready." Working with one arm, Ling Chu had cobbled together a minor feast of eggs and bacon and some tomatoes Many Clouds and Maggie had canned. The seating was a bit crowded at the small kitchen table, but everyone made do.

"For my part," Remy said. "I think everything leads back to Hale Gentry. If we shut down that saloon, we'd get to the bottom of everything."

"Maybe so," Carolyn said, "but until Many Clouds gets back, we aren't doing anything so drastic. It might start some sort of avalanche that would destroy everyone and everything in its path."

"Mother, can we have a word?" With a nod of his head Andy motioned toward the front door. Once they were on the porch, he said, "Are you sure this isn't the time to confront Remy about what you saw at Gentry's saloon yesterday?"

"Patience, Andy. The longer he thinks we're ignorant of that little meeting, the more likely he is to let something slip."

"If you say so. But I don't like the looks of those thunderheads in the west, and the wind's picking up. If the kids get caught in a storm, they might never make it back on their own." Andy had a vivid image of Many Clouds' mother, her body blue and drained, when they found her after a Nevada flash flood had pulled her from their grasp. The thought of finding Many Clouds in such a condition clenched his stomach. "What if Emmanuel goes on a bit of a scouting expedition with a couple of his sidekicks? With all of us clustered around here, we don't need the extra security."

"Now that's a good thought, Andrew. And Ling Chu can be an extra pair of eyes hanging around the wagon, pretending to fix something."

"I can't wait to show you all what I found at Auburn and hear what everyone else has come up with."

"All in good time. But we can't discuss it yet. If Remy finds out something he can use against us, none of that might do us any good."

"Yes, yes, but it's so damned frustrating just sitting around here. If we haven't heard anything by midday, I say we organize a full-scale search party."

"With Emmanuel out there—"

"He's not enough. We have to blanket every inch of the whole five miles between here and Placerville. Every cabin, every wagon every—"

"Okay, okay. Point taken. Let's just hope we don't have to make that decision."

A minor whirlwind of oak leaves spun through the yard. The temperature seemed to have dropped several degrees in the last hour. Another image, this one of the improvised graveside service he and Many Clouds had performed in the Nevada wilderness so many years ago. Rocks heaped on a shallow depression they'd managed to wrest from the stony desert with some biblical words from him and an Arapaho chant from her. He shoved the picture from his mind and hiked back to the house to… to what? Wait. Maybe he could lure Remy into a conversation in which he revealed something. It was worth a try. He picked up his pace and hurried to where Remy stood on the porch, apparently staring into the distance, watching the rain begin to descend.

"How would you suggest we start searching, Remy?" Andy said. "And where?"

The atmosphere in the cabin matched the cold and wind of the weather outside.

"I've been thinking on it a bit, Andy, but we can't keep thinking. Got to act. Know what I mean?"

"Again, Remy, are you going to talk, or do you have something to suggest?"

"We need to go back to Placerville, to that Hangtown Saloon, and work out from there. It's the last place anyone saw them, far as we know."

The rain was picking up. Thunder and lightning began. He hoped Many Clouds and the children were sheltered. Even if the storm wasn't heavy enough to cause flash floods, the summer dust would turn to mud before long. It was no good searching till the storm passed or at least let up.

Andy hoped that by continuing to ask questions instead of committing to anything specific, he'd get Remy to inadvertently reveal himself. This little tidbit about where Maggie and Willy might be could be a start. A blend of action and inquiry seemed like a perfect combination.

"Andy. Everyone," Remy called. "Come on out here. There's some things I have to say to all of you."

Sixty-Three

Many Clouds grabbed Willy's shirt collar and pulled him back. In dry times, they'd be within sight of the house, but the downpour screened their view. Nevertheless, Willy had been about to rush forward, assuming they were safe at last. But when Many Clouds saw the knot of people on the veranda, she thought caution was the better choice.

"Hush," she said. "Let's stay put and stay quiet until we know what's going on."

"But we're getting soaked," Maggie said.

"Better soaked than killed," Willy said.

"Hush that kind of talk, Willy," Many Clouds said. "It's probably all right. Let's just make sure."

"But I can tell that's Mrs. Maxwell," Maggie said. "And Ling Chu."

"Quiet," Willy whispered.

"Look at all those cars," Maggie said.

"Just two," Willy said aloud. Maggie put her hand over his mouth. He shoved it away with his tongue.

"Don't do that, Willy."

"Same to you."

"Leave it alone, kids. And to heck with the rain. I see someone else I can't wait to talk to." Many Clouds abandoned her whisper and charged forward. She yelled as she approached the house. "Remington Dillinger. I want a word with you."

Maggie and Willy trailed close behind her. Despite Many Clouds' stormy approach, there was no quelling the enthusiasm that the children's safe return provoked.

What had been a huddle suddenly dissolved into a line of people along the porch railing. Andy broke from the group, leaped the railing and dashed to Many Clouds.

"Hello, Andy." They embraced, and she pulled back, giggling. "Look at both of us muddy as pigs at feeding time."

"A small price to pay," Andy said. He hugged her once more.

"But now," she said, returning to her hostile manner, "I've got business with your so-called investigator."

Shortly, she was on the porch and headed with the momentum of a runaway horse straight to Dillinger, whose face she reached up and slapped so hard it sounded like a pistol shot. Dillinger stumbled back a step, astonished, put out a hand to protect himself in case Many Clouds took another shot at him, which she did, but this time with the other hand. He'd neglected to protect that side, and a second shot reverberated through the yard. Everyone was so flabbergasted by her uncharacteristic behavior that no one made a move or uttered a word to stop her.

"I ought to rip your liver out for leaving my children at the mercy of those rabid wolves."

It was only an illusion that she was face to face with Dillinger, since she was several inches shorter. However, her rage seemed to have increased her stature to the point where she actually seemed as tall or even taller than her adversary. Thunder pealed and lightning flashed.

By this point Remy had managed to grab both her wrists, and she was twisting and struggling for her freedom. She did manage to kick one of his ankles, but her soft moccasins made the connection ineffective. By this time, Andy had reached the porch and dived between the two.

"Hands off, Dillinger." He chopped at the taller man's wrists and kicked him in the stomach. "Now back away." He didn't bother to check whether Remy obeyed, assuming there were plenty of others to step in if he didn't. His main concern was Many Clouds, whom he folded in a protective embrace.

"Tell me, love. Tell me. Let's do this together," he said in a voice he meant to be low and calming. Many Clouds, however, was in no mood to be calmed, though she did stay by Andy's side rather than returning to the attack. Her gaze never left Dillinger.

"You were supposed to watch the children, but you were nowhere in sight. They've witnessed the most brutal and ugly things. Lucky to be alive themselves. And all because you weren't where you were supposed to be. Promised to be."

Remy held up his arms as if in surrender. "I had an errand to run. I thought it would only take a minute. It seemed like no harm would come to them on a public boardwalk with everyone watching."

"And this errand?" Andy said.

"Wait a minute. I think I know," Many Clouds declared. "In fact, I'm sure. Andy, we've been looking at all these big corporations, but the criminal we've been looking for is right under our noses." She turned back to Remy. "Your errand was to report to your boss, who is none other than Hale Gentry."

By the way his eyes widened and the way his shoulders twitched, she knew she'd hit her mark.

"No outsider could have whisked Maggie away and hidden her right in the middle of Placerville," Many Clouds declared. "It had to be someone local. Gentry fits the description perfectly, and it would take a good half hour on a fast horse each way to get to Sawtooth Wells and Gentry's place not to mention whatever time it took to take care of your business."

"Many betrayals," Carolyn said. "Ezekiel—"

"Ezekiel," Many Clouds said, "is a weak-minded fool who thinks he's the last hope of the Arapaho people. Anyone who knows that can play him like a fiddle at a square dance. You, on the other hand—" she turned back to Remy now—"are a shapeshifter, like deer lady. Beautiful and romantic one minute then turns into a beast who tears her lover to pieces."

By this time, Remy was backed against the railing, surrounded by Emmanuel, Ling Chu, the children, Andy, and of course, Many Clouds. Thunder crashed once more, followed by a cloudburst. No one paid attention. The drama on the veranda proved more captivating.

Andy's eyes were wide with amazement, and there was an incipient smile on his lips. "I've never seen you like this, my love."

"Maybe I have a bit of Yellow Squirrel in me after all," she said. Remy surprised them all with his next declaration.

"Every word you said is justified, Many Clouds. I should never have left those kids."

"So you could go off and meet Hale Gentry. What I want to know is why?" Carolyn demanded.

Willy spoke up next. "Maggie's got something to say. Tell them, Maggie."

"Hale Gentry is the one who kidnapped me."

"Didn't you say it was Ezekiel?" Many Clouds asked.

"Yeah, but Gentry was giving the orders. I didn't know it till I saw and heard him when Willy and me were at City Hall."

"Willy and I," Many Clouds corrected her.

"Sorry. Anyway, he was the one talking to Ezekiel in the next room when I was prisoner. I'll never forget that voice."

Everyone turned from Maggie back to Remy. Carolyn said, "Any other juicy pieces of information we've got to share before we hear from the main perpetrator here?"

"All right, all right," Remy said. "I admit I came here under false pretenses, and the longer it went on, well, I was trapped in my own lie."

Many Clouds wished she had a weapon, then was glad she didn't. She would have used it on this pretender who had endangered her children and all the rest of them.

Typical of early season tempests, the downpour soon dwindled to a sprinkle, the thunder stopped, and dark clouds parted to admit slices of blue sky.

"Who are you really working for, mister investigator? It sure isn't us," she said.

"Can we all sit down?" Remy asked. "It's kind of awkward standing around like this."

Andy made a move toward a chair, but Many Clouds folded her arms and said, "I'm comfortable right here." She figured the more ill at ease Remy was, the better. Andy moved back toward the embattled investigator.

So, just who *are* you working for, Mr. Dillinger?" Many Clouds asked. She inched a bit closer to her antagonist, who in response appeared to push back against the railing.

"All right. All right. It started out, I was a Pinkerton operative."

"Pinkerton?" Carolyn exclaimed. "Pardon my French, but what the hell does Pinkerton want with us?"

"They didn't really. They were originally hired by Amadeo Giannini."

"The man who owns the Bank of Italy in San Francisco?" Andy said. "Just when I thought we were figuring things out, they get even more mysterious. Keep talking, Remy."

"Well, you know he and the Wells Fargo company between the two of them almost refinanced rebuilding San Francisco after the '06 earthquake, so The Bank of Italy is a pretty big outfit. But Giannini is a maniac for details, so when Western Explorations started running big hunks of cash through his bank into Sturges' bank in Placerville and other banks as well. He wanted to know why. He found out they had an agent who'd been looking at a lot of real estate around here. Buying some, but nowhere near enough to justify the amount of money they were processing. He hired Pinkerton to find out what was going on, and I was the man they put on the job."

Many Clouds pointed a finger in Remy's face. Her threat appeared more menacing because it nearly touched him, but not quite. "So when Andy was looking for an investigator, you just happened to be right there. What a happy coincidence."

Remy was about to reply when Andy jumped in. "But it was our lawyer, Barker, who introduced us. How does he fit into this?"

Remy held his hands out in a gesture of helplessness. "I don't know. And I'm completely baffled about who shot him or why. As for Gentry, he's in deep in whatever is going on, but I don't exactly know what or how. He pretends he's the big man, but he's nowhere near smart enough to be handling whatever is going on. I think I have him convinced I'm on his side, but he's suspicious."

Many Clouds turned in a circle and crowded closer to Andy. "In other words, your fabled investigator knows about as much as we do. I don't trust him any more than I trust Gentry, Andy."

Remy stepped away from the railing. "I don't blame you for what you're thinking, Many Clouds. I can say that whatever they want, it has to do with mining and minerals, and your land is sitting on top of something very valuable."

"Why don't they just make us an offer?" Many Clouds asked.

"That I can answer," Remy said. "They know Southern Pacific made you an offer which you turned down. Your attachment to your little plot here and the reasons for it are well-known. The children's parents' graves and all the rest. With the Maxwell fortune behind you, you'd be able to resist any offer they made. They were hoping to intimidate you into selling out."

Andy stepped in. "That fits right into what I found in Auburn. Deeds to modest plots of land bought by individuals with not much money. Rufus Murphy, for example. You remember him, Mother."

"A worthless layabout living in a tumbledown cabin outside of Sawtooth Wells."

"Correct. He now owns fifty acres just north of where we stand. Where did he get the money for that? And I've got a whole list of names of people just like him."

"So," Many Clouds went on. "Add up a few of those holdings like Rufus Murphy's and you have a pretty large hunk of land. It still doesn't tell us why, though, does it?"

Ling Chu made his first contribution to the conversation. "Who shoot you, Mr. Remy? Why they wreck my automobile? No one explain that or who kill Mr. Barker. I don't know. Let us sit on steps. My legs tired standing."

Soon they were all gathered as if for a family portrait. Andy said, "We should hire a photographer." The remark drew a few muted chuckles, but no one seemed in the mood for humor.

The scene reminded Many Clouds not of a photographic session but of a war council the likes of which she had witnessed often on the reservation. She had never been able to participate, of course, but she had watched and listened from high in a tree when she was a little girl and from behind the same tree when she was older. Quaking inside, but bewildered and angered by the wandering discussion, she decided to take on the role of council chief. She stood at the bottom of the steps and raised both arms to quiet the group. She scooped up a small stick from the ground beside her.

"We do not have a proper talking stick, so this will do. Each person who has information or opinion about what we know or what we do not will take the stick and speak. When we've all finished, we'll decide what to do next."

As each person spoke, the information organized itself in Many Clouds' mind as clearly as if it had been charted on a slate. Hale Gentry, they all agreed, was the force behind Maggie's kidnapping. Western Explorations or someone connected with the company had been buying up land for reasons unknown and was after Andy's and Many Clouds' house. They wanted it badly enough to send the man in the paisley scarf to intimidate them and perhaps to fire on Remy and to kill Attorney Barker. They had ransacked Barker's office, perhaps in search of the deed to the property. Picturing the chart she'd been constructing in her mind, Many Clouds organized the disparate pieces of information the discussion had produced. Just as important were the questions left to be answered.

Andy said, "What about that visit from the Southern Pacific people? And who wrecked Ling Chu's automobile and why?"

"Why would they destroy the wagon and kill Horatio and Virgil?" Maggie asked. There was a sob in her voice as she spoke.

"Why does Western Explorations want all this land?" Carolyn asked.

Many Clouds realized to her discouragement that the number of blank spaces outnumbered the filled ones by a great deal, but she forged on, determined not to succumb to the confusion.

"Well, now that we are clear on the questions, let's figure out how to answer them. Remy, maybe if you continue to work with Gentry, you can find out more."

"I'm sure I can," he said.

"And Andy, you do you have any other places to look for evidence?"

"I thought I'd try the bank next. If they were using the Bank of Italy, why not our local one?"

"I have an idea as well," Carolyn said, "but Ling Chu and I should handle it on our own. The fewer people who know the better."

"I guess that leaves Many Clouds and me to guard the cabin and children," Andy said. "The closer to them the better for me, but it seems like we should be doing more."

"And we will," declared Many Clouds. "First, though, I'd like a private word with my fiancé if there's no objection." Everyone smiled and nodded. She took Andy's arm and led him a few steps away from the others. "There's something else I don't want to tell everyone, Andy. It didn't seem so important at the time, but now I'm beginning to wonder." She recounted what she and the children had heard between Jacob Russell and the woman he called "Marilyn."

"Marilyn?" Andy stepped back, a look of astonishment on his face. "That's the name of Harry Barker's wife—our murdered lawyer. What did she look like?" When Many Clouds finished her description, Andy said, "That's her, all right. And Russell said, 'You did the most important part'?" Many Clouds nodded. "Well that opens up a horde of new possibilities, doesn't it? I agree we should keep it to ourselves for the time being."

"Yes," she said, giving Andy's arm another squeeze. She stepped back and raised her voice for all to hear. "Now, let's you and I and Maggie and Willy climb in your car, Andy, and head on to Sawtooth Wells. Once we change clothes, and wash up a bit, that is. Maggie and Willy and I can keep watch on Gentry's place while you come back to the bank at Placerville."

"I don't think it's a good idea to separate again, my love."

"It's not my first choice either. But we won't do anything without you. You can come back to find us once you're finished at the bank. We'll be together most of the time. Emmanuel, you said you have some friends coming to help with guard duty?"

"That's right, Many Clouds. They should be here soon."

"If you and your people stay out of sight, maybe whoever is after us will think we've all left and try something. Don't take any chances though. You know what happens to Indians in a white man's court." Suddenly the world seemed brighter to Many Clouds. There was a sun in her plans to match the one that had emerged from the storm clouds. They were no longer stuck in the murky, cave-like darkness they'd been living in for weeks.

"Why are we standing around?" she called. "We've all of us got work to do."

Sixty-Four

It was a squeeze to get all four of them into Andy's Model T. Andy told them he'd ordered a bigger model but that this was the largest available on such short notice. Maggie and Many Clouds took up the passenger seat, and Willy sat on Andy's lap while he drove. Many Clouds was excited beyond all reason. She thought she had no right to feel optimistic after all the calamities that had befallen them and how little they'd learned about who and what was behind all of it. Still, she was in charge. Before she'd taken up the talking stick, everyone had been in a swirl of confusion. Now they had direction and purpose.

There was still plenty to learn and risks to take, but sitting and waiting to see what Hale Gentry or some figure in a paisley scarf would do to them next had been both frustrating and nonproductive. And there was the information she'd kept to herself till just now.

"Stop, Andy," she said.

"Right here in the middle of the road?"

"No, silly man. Can you drive into the shadow of that grove of firs?"

While he was maneuvering the car into a bit of seclusion, she handed her deerskin pouch to Maggie.

"Pass these papers over to Andy, will you Maggie?"

"Sure," Maggie said as she gathered the sheaf of papers Many Clouds had smuggled out of the room across the hall from the mayor's office.

"What can I do?" Willy said.

"Take the papers from your sister and hand them to me one by one, Willy," Andy said.

"My grandfather, Owl Feather," Many Clouds said, "always told my father and uncle to keep some warriors in reserve. My father listened. He is still alive on the Wind River reservation. Yellow Squirrel never saw the sense.

He preferred to commit every brave to the battle immediately. You know his fate. These are the warriors I've kept in reserve.

"I still don't know what to think about Remy, so I thought it better not to reveal everything to him yet," she said as Andy perused the first page of the packet.

"Owl Feather was a wise man," Andy said. "The world would be better if there were more like him."

Many Clouds kept to herself the remark that sprang to mind. Arapaho and Shoshone were confined to a parcel of land too small to support either tribe. All her grandfather's wisdom and courage had held no more power than a handful of water against the prairie fire of white civilization.

"Those were in the desk of a man who works near the mayor's office," she went on. "They look important. I know what the word 'assay' means but I couldn't make head nor tails of the rest."

"'Important' doesn't begin to cover it, my love. I suspect this is one of the biggest pieces of the puzzle we've been trying to put together. Look here." He held the document so that all four of them could see. "These are symbols for elements the assayer found in whatever samples were brought to his office. This 'Au' stands for gold. 'Ag' is for silver."

"You mean they found gold and silver?" Willy asked.

"Yes," Andy answered. "But not enough to get anyone excited, I don't think. There's an awful lot of something else, though. Look at this."

"C" Maggie said. "What's that stand for?"

"Carbon," Andy said. "And Western Exploration is on the trail of a major deposit of it."

"Carbon?" Many Clouds said. "What is that good for?"

"You may not have heard of 'carbon' as a valuable item, my family. But I think you'll understand how important it is when I refer to its more common name. Western Exploration is tracking down major deposits of coal."

"Maybe that's what the guy at the saloon meant about black gold," Willy said.

They all looked at Willy as if he was a rock that had suddenly begun to speak.

"And you're just telling us now?" Many Clouds said.

"Well, hell, I didn't know," Willy said.

"And what did I tell you about leaving all those saloon words behind?" Many Clouds laughed and hugged him. "Watch yourself, mister." She kissed him on the forehead. He wiped off the kiss, but he smiled the whole time.

"Change of plans," Many Clouds said. "We have a stop to make in Placerville before we go to Sawtooth Wells."

Sixty-Five

Carolyn and Ling Chu parked in a secluded grove behind the Sawtooth Wells livery stable. They'd approached the town via a little-used lane that Southern Pacific had intended to use as a construction staging area for a spur line they never built. Carolyn knew she could trust the stable owner, Clyde McPhail, to keep to himself the enterprise she was planning. He'd owned the stable only a couple of years, having bought it after the long-time owner, old man Gilligan, died, but she'd helped him buy the small ranch he sold to buy the stable, deeming himself nearing an age where farm work would be beyond his strength and stamina. He'd demolished a couple of stalls and constructed a small bedroom and kitchen for himself. It was here that Carolyn and Ling Chu met Marshal Halstad, Amelia, and Cooper.

"How's the arm?" Halstad asked Ling Chu.

"Pain not so bad now. Be well soon."

"Hell of a thing. How about the car?" Cooper asked.

"Watch your cursing," Amelia admonished him.

"Car hurt worse than me," Ling Chu shook his head.

Carolyn said, "Parts have been ordered from Sacramento. It will be a while. But let's get down to business." She summarized the various situations. "Remington Dillinger is supposedly working on Hale Gentry, but even if I fully trusted him, which I don't, he's only one man."

The marshal spoke. "Well said, Carolyn. What you're talking about is full-time surveillance of the man. Even with all of us, that's a tall order, especially since he knows every one of us on sight."

"Very tall order indeed," Cooper said.

"I'm sure she knows that, husband. Let her finish, why don't you?"

"Thanks, Amelia. Here's what I think. We should forget about spying on Gentry for the moment for all the reasons the marshal just outlined. We stand a better chance of picking up information in Placerville. The Hangtown Saloon is a juicy place for meetings and gossip and a good cover for Gentry's cohorts to meet without attracting attention or suspicion. With what Andy's learned, Ling and I can make another stab at uncovering what's behind this land grab."

"It is a chance for me," Ling Chu smiled. "Many Chinese here. Come, go. Dig, wash. Riding donkey, pulling carts to deliver laundry. No one pay attention. Can't tell one of us from the other one."

"In the meantime," Carolyn said, "I can do some shopping. They may have canceled our credit, but Maxwell cash is still good everywhere, and I have plenty. I've been meaning to buy a couple of hats, maybe some boots. You'd be surprised what people let go of when their guard's down in a place like a haberdashery."

Cooper leaped to his feet. "Damnation if that shouldn't work."

Amelia slapped his arm. "How many times I got to tell you watch your mouth?"

"A few more, I guess." He sat down and put his arm around her shoulders. She pushed him away, but she was smiling at him while she did it.

Cooper went on. "But I don't know what we're supposed to do. Ain't no way you and me can hang out and stay anonymous."

Amelia said, "You can just park yourself in that cornfield of ours right next to the road. No one can see you hunkered down there, and anybody going from Sawtooth Wells toward the Circle M got to pass right by."

Halstad was the next to stand. "Sounds to me like we're in business," he said. "I can follow up on anything that comes through my office, which is plenty most days. Careful not to go out of here all at once, now, and leave a note with Clyde any time we have information we want to pass along."

"Wait a second," Carolyn said. She stretched out both arms. "Let's join hands." The gesture was so uncharacteristic of this often-aloof matriarch that everyone hesitated an instant. "Well come on," she said. In a moment, they had made a circle, Amelia grasping Ling Chu's elbow in lieu of his incapacitated hand. "I feel like we should be doing a war whoop, but this is a secret mission, so make it a whisper."

So with a hushed yell, Carolyn's little army crept off separately and silently to battle.

At It Again
Special to *The Elevator* by Andrew Maxwell

Although the primary mission of The Elevator *is to promote the well-being of the Negro in America, we are from time to time reminded that the fortunes of our race are inextricably entwined with those of all poor people. It has come to our attention that some person or persons in our area has begun purchasing distressed properties from farmers who are elderly and unable to devote their full energies to their lands and others who have simply grown too weary of that difficult life to continue tending their land. The various properties are being purchased by companies rather than individuals, which leads us to suspect that the land is marked not for agriculture but for some other nefarious purpose. We have so far been unable to discover who is behind the land grab, since each purchase was made by a different "company." Whatever is happening here, you can be sure that it is not to the benefit of the small landowner. You can also be sure that* The Elevator *will continue to investigate and will work with authorities to foil whatever plot is afoot. Look to future issues of our periodical for more news of this latest depredation.*

Sixty-Six

Many Clouds led the way into the city hall with Andy, Maggie, and Willy following. She felt like a different woman from the one who had skulked so furtively among these offices just a short time ago. She'd exchanged her deerskin dress and leggings for a modest calico dress with a lavender print. She plaited her hair into a single braid that hung down her back, secured by one of Maggie's birthday ribbons. A yellow one. Maggie used green ribbons intertwined in her pigtails. Getting her into her own calico dress—pink was her color—had proved a struggle, but she had finally relented. Even Willy had taken a step toward respectability with his hair combed and linen shirt cleaned, though not ironed. She felt the outfits were a kind of armor, signaling that she was in charge and confident.

"That's the office where I got the assay reports, Andy," she said as they passed Prentice's office. "The name on the door, Prentice, is his first name, I think, but I don't know what he does here exactly."

In any case, she wasn't here for Prentice. She led her contingent straight to the office of the mayor. The woman who acted as the mayor's guard dog sat proudly and defiantly behind the name plate on her desk.

"Good morning, Miss Morgan," Many Clouds proclaimed as the entered the mayor's outer office.

Ada Morgan looked up from a document she'd been perusing then screwed up her face in puzzlement.

"Yes? And who might you be? You and the rest of your little tribe here?"

Andy began pushing forward, but Many Clouds extended her hand, gently holding him back. This was her ground, at least for the moment.

"Why, *señorita,* you don't recognize me after the happy times we spent together?"

"Wait a minute. You're that redskin that was in here yesterday cleaning the office or pretending to. I checked, and there is no Maria Elena on our janitorial crew. Who are you anyway?"

"If you paid attention to the 'little worthless people' here, as you called them, you would know the names of the workers, and I never would have gotten into the mayor's office. We'll be going in now."

She beckoned to Andy and the children, and the group stepped toward the office door.

"Hey, I have to announce you first."

"Too late," Many Clouds said as she opened the heavy oak door, ornately carved with figures of eagles and elk, its fittings of gleaming brass.

Mayor James George was in residence, his gleaming bald pate fringed by a halo of shoulder-length white hair. He held a steel-nibbed pen in his right hand while he reached for a piece of paper with the left. He froze in mid-motion when Many Clouds entered.

"Over there, children." She gestured toward two leather-upholstered chairs standing against the wall.

"What's this?" George said. Ada Morgan entered right behind them.

"I'm sorry, Mr. Mayor, but they shoved right past me."

"It's all right, Ada." He laid down his pen and stood. "I know this gentleman, though I have never met his—How shall I say?—paramour, nor the half-breed urchins." He nodded to Ada, who slipped out, closing the door behind her.

Many Clouds noticed several scraps of paper on the floor near his chair. She herself wouldn't be responsible for those today, or ever.

"Would you like to introduce us, Mr. Maxwell?" George James's politician's smile shone bright and false as he spoke.

"You remember Mr. James, don't you, sweetheart?" Andy said.

"Of course. He supported your opponent Hale Gentry in your campaign for the state assembly."

"A campaign you lost, of course," the mayor said. "But let's not dwell on the past."

"A campaign I won, then had the office denied me by a certain Governor Johnson's broken promises. But, yes, let that go. This is my fiancée, Many Clouds, and our two children, Maggie and Willy. Stand up, kids, and shake hands with Mayor James."

Many Clouds and the children stepped forward and offered their hands to the mayor, who shook each hand in turn with obvious distaste. A frown replaced the fake smile with which he had greeted them.

"Now," the mayor said, "I suppose there's a purpose to this little invasion." He didn't offer them a seat, and the children chose to squeeze close to Many Clouds rather than return to their chairs.

"Yes, indeed, Mr. Mayor," Many Clouds said. "We ran across some assay reports that we found very puzzling. And since you work hard to keep yourself knowledgeable about whatever goes on in your jurisdiction, we thought you might be able to clear up a few matters."

"Well, after that rather clumsy attempt to butter me up, how can I refuse you anything? Now, these assay reports. They wouldn't be the same ones stolen from Prentice Sailor's office across the hall by a woman whose description is remarkably close to your own, Miss Clouds. Is that what I should call you?"

Many Clouds ignored his questions. "The assay reports are only part of the picture, Mr. Mayor. Andy, why don't you describe what you found in Auburn?"

"It's like this, Mr. James. It seems that there are parcels of land up and down the area here being purchased by individuals with little or no money to their names. We thought you might be able to shed some light on how this is possible."

"That does sound rather odd, Mr. Maxwell. But I have not heard anything about it."

"You don't think it suspicious?"

"Just because something is odd doesn't mean it is illegal."

"Of course not," Many Clouds said. "We just wanted to alert you and ask you to get back in touch should you learn anything. You see, our family has been threatened, and we have reason to believe all these things are somehow connected."

"Well, if it is impinging on your personal safety, I can see how it causes concern, but I can't see how it concerns me. Now, if there is nothing else, I have other tasks at hand." He gestured toward the pile of paper he had been addressing when they entered.

"Thank you for your time, sir," she said. She held out her hand. He deigned to shake it one more time.

"I add my own thanks to hers," Andy said as he extended his own hand. "Maggie, Willy."

The children were as reluctant to touch the mayor's hand as he was to grasp theirs, but they all made it through the charade and left the office.

"Thank you, *Señorita* Morgan," Many Clouds said as she passed. "Best wishes."

Ada Morgan grunted and looked fire at them as she observed their exit.

On the city hall steps, Many Clouds leaned against the wall, closed her eyes, and let out her breath, which she hadn't realized she'd been holding.

"Andy, I was scared to death."

"It didn't show, Many Clouds. You can be on my negotiating team any time."

"But did it do any good?"

"We'll have to wait and see, but now everyone knows that we know something. They don't know what, and they don't know how much. So maybe this little meeting of ours might force them into the open at last."

"Maybe," she said. "So let's go back to the original idea. You drop the kids and me off at Gentry's and come back and find out what you can at the bank. We'll meet there around sundown." The idea of separating from Andy at a moment like this was hurtful and fearful. Never in the time they'd been together had she felt so full of affection for him, felt as if she wanted to be with him every minute. Frightening though it was, it still felt wonderful that together they were at last moving forward, instigating events instead of merely waiting for someone else to make a move.

They embraced one another, and the family headed toward the automobile. Many Clouds stopped and pulled Andy toward her again.

"You're coming back safe. Promise?"

"A vow so strong Hercules couldn't break it, my love." He cupped her chin in his palm and kissed her full on the lips, tenderly and for a long time.

She smiled, pushed him away and trotted toward Maggie and Willy, who seemed to be staring at something high and far away.

Sixty-Seven

Hale Gentry's saloon sat a hundred yards or so off the main road in a grove of mixed evergreens. The idea was to allow his clandestine activities to be carried out in seclusion. However, it also provided plenty of cover for surveillance, which Many Clouds hoped would enable them to keep watch without being discovered. They had exchanged their meet-the-mayor togs for their customary roam-the-woods clothes, though Maggie had prevailed on Andy and Many Clouds to allow her to keep the ribbons in her hair. Could it be, Many Clouds wondered, if she was changing from a frontier brat into a young woman with yearnings toward fashion? Surely not yet. Andy stopped a good distance from the small lane that led from the main road to the doorway.

"The problem is," Andy said as they climbed out of the car, "we never yet have seen him do anything illegal. He could be passing out orders to any of the lieutenants that stop by and we'd never know the difference."

"We've never been able to monitor him like we will now. With Willy, Maggie, and me watching all the time, we're sure to spot something."

"Whatever you do, be careful. Safety takes priority over everything else. Especially now." His smiling gaze moved from her eyes to her midsection then back up.

Many Clouds cupped her belly. "I won't forget. Can't." She remembered her morning bout with nausea, a constant companion these days. She kissed her fingertips and placed them on his lips. "I love you, Andy. I love us."

"I feel the same way, of course." He smiled at Maggie and Willy, who seemed to be watching distant clouds. "So let's keep us all safe."

"I wish I knew what your mother and Ling Chu and Remington were doing."

"Let's concentrate on what we're doing. We can't control mother."

"No matter how hard we may try," Many Clouds said with a chuckle. One more hug and Many Clouds disembarked with the children.

Andy called after them, "I'll do my best at the bank and meet you back here when I'm finished. God willing, we'll all have something to tell one another."

***

Ling Chu entered the Hangtown Saloon with a broom for a prop. He started in a back corner, swishing the broom here and there over the floor without much effect on the sawdust residue while he watched and listened. Carolyn had continued on to the livery stable to arrange for fresh horses.

Remington was there in the saloon all right, just as he'd promised, and he was drinking with Jacob Russell instead of with Hale Gentry. Still, that could be very good. They could learn a lot from the talkative redhead, even if he wasn't directly involved in their situation, as long as Remington used whatever he learned to their advantage and not against them. Ling poked Remington with his broom. The tall man turned and looked down on him.

"Watch it, there, partner."

"So sorry, mister sir. Chinaman not careful. Only one arm, see?" He waggled the sling-encased broken limb and lifted his chin so that Remington could look at him squarely. He saw no sign of recognition.

"Quite all right. No harm done." He turned to Russell. "Hire cheap help, you get what you pay for. Am I right?"

"Quite right," Russell responded. "My round, Remy. Then duty calls, I'm afraid."

"Now that you mention it, I'm neglecting business myself," Remy said. He asked the barkeep for a pencil and paper, wrote a note quickly, then called Ling Chu. "You, Chinaman, take this to your boss. Bring back an answer quick as you can."

Ling Chu saw the note was addressed to Carolyn. How had Remy known where she was? Maybe he didn't but guessed that Ling Chu would know. Clever man.

"Going, sir. Yes. Chop quick."

"And here." He handed Ling Chu a nickel.

"Thanking you. Yes, sir."

He hurried out the door without stopping to read the note. Its contents would be revealed soon enough.

Sixty-Eight

Many Clouds had a new problem. Three men had arrived and entered the saloon not long after they'd begun their surveillance. They came at intervals of a few minutes and did not appear to be together. Peter Simple was an unskilled farmer whose place boasted a healthy crop of weeds and a sickly looking stand of wheat. He favored brightly checkered shirts that would made spotting him easy as finding a crow amidst a flock of snow geese if they decided to follow him. Grazer Pendleton, slim and spry and in his seventies, hitched his donkey cart, filled with freshly split wood, to a stump outside the front door. He spit out a massive chaw of tobacco before he ascended the steps to the saloon entrance. Digby Morrison in faded overalls and a battered straw hat was the last of the trio. He walked with a pronounced limp. She didn't know the man or how he'd come by his infirmity, but it didn't appear to slow him down as he hurried his way into the saloon.

No one else was in sight, so Many Clouds tossed three small stones into the bushes as a signal to Maggie and Willy that it was time for a conference. They climbed down from their stations in the trees.

"I'm pretty sure those last three men are together somehow. It's too much of a coincidence that they all came pretty much at once," she told them. "They may come out together or one by one. If they stay together, we'll follow together. If not, I want you two to follow the guy in the checkered shirt."

She figured it would be easiest and safest for the children to keep track of Peter Simple as he left Gentry's saloon. Not only did his vivid shirt speak loudly of his presence, but he moved at the slow, steady pace of a man accustomed to following a plow, looking neither right nor left as if hypnotized by the rear end of his mule.

"Willy, you stay on the east side of the road, Maggie on the west. Just watch where he goes and what he does. Don't try to challenge him on your own. I'll follow one of the others. We can meet back here at sundown and decide what to do next. No later than sundown, now. Andy and I should both be here by then. At least one of us for sure."

"What if you're not?" Willy said.

It was a circumstance Many Clouds didn't want to entertain. "It makes me nervous to leave you on your own at all, but if worse comes to worst, let's plan to meet at the house again."

"The Circle M is closer," Maggie said.

It was true. Going by way of the main road, Placerville was five miles away, then their house was another five. The Circle M was only five miles in the other direction. But Many Clouds resisted the notion that it was her mother-in-law's house rather than her own that offered the safest haven. Her discomfort with Carolyn Maxwell right now verged on hostility. Perhaps her pregnancy had intensified her nesting instinct.

"Wouldn't you rather be in your own beds tonight?" Maggie and Willy looked at each other, then back at her and replied to her question with brief nods. "Besides, you brag all the time about how you know every shortcut in these hills between here and Lake Tahoe, so I'm sure you can get home as fast as you can get to the Circle M." Willy started to say something, but she cut him off. "It won't be necessary anyhow. Andy and I will both be here. Just make sure you are and that you just observe. Don't try anything heroic." She reached toward them, and the three joined hands. She hoped they would take her cautionary words to heart, though she feared they would forge ahead into dangerous territory if the opportunity arose. She planned to follow her own advice, carried no firearms for fear they could be wrested from her and used against either her or the children. However, she did strap her sheath knife, retrieved from the wagon wreckage, to her hip, concealed beneath her skirt. "Okay, now we wait."

As it turned out, they had to wait only a few minutes before Checkers, as they'd dubbed Peter Simple, emerged and began plodding toward the west end of town. If he continued in that direction, the road would take him ultimately to Placerville. She was willing to bet his errand for Gentry would take him off the main road in short order. Away he went, the children close behind. She longed to go with them. It would feel secure to have the children on either side of the man and herself bringing up the rear. They would have him virtually surrounded. But they needed to follow all the men they could, which meant both she and the children were on their own.

Before long, Pendleton the woodcutter came out and unhitched his donkey. She had to admire the craftsmanship of his outfit. He had lashed a bucksaw to one side of the wagon and a double-bitted axe to the other. A splitting wedge and a small sledge nested in a small box near the driver's bench. He reached in his shirt pocket and pulled out a plug of tobacco, bit off a fresh chaw, and climbed aboard his conveyance. He headed in the opposite direction of Checkers, toward Sawtooth Peaks and the Circle M. She gave him a bit of a head start, then shuffled on to the road, bent over a walking stick to conceal her youth and vigor, hoping she could keep up with donkey and cart on foot.

Ling Chu leaned his broom against the back wall outside the saloon and met Carolyn on the sidewalk across the street from the livery stable. She glanced at the note, which Ling Chu had not read, and crumpled it in her fist, eyes blazing.

"Tell Remy to stick with Russell. I'll get the wagon and you and I will go on to Gentry's place."

She turned on her heel and fairly ran back toward the livery stable. He picked up the note and read it as he hurried toward the Saloon. *Russell met G. plot moving.* Ling Chu didn't like the situation. Too many things unknown.

"Better to make Gentry come to us than return to his business," he said as Carolyn cranked the automobile into life.

"How, when he stays in that saloon like it's a bandit's roost?"

Ling Chu remained silent for a while, then had to admit he had no good answer to the question. "Still not good to go where he is most strong."

"I've known him for a long time, Ling Chu, and so have you. When has he ever been anything more substantial than a flash of white teeth and a handshake?"

"Rattler have big teeth. Still dangerous."

"I'm betting his venom is weak and his fangs are all for show."

"I'm hoping you are the one who is right, Miss Carolyn."

"We will soon find out, won't we?" She released the brake and propelled the car forward. "Just a few more miles."

Sixty-Nine

Grazer Pendleton set off in his cart at a fairly brisk pace, leaving periodic streams of coffee-colored expectorant as he went. Many Clouds feared he'd outdistance her in no time. Maybe she'd chosen the wrong man to follow, should have waited for the man in the slouch hat to emerge. Quickly as he moved, however, the fact that he made a number of stops enabled Many Clouds to keep up with him. The midday weariness that had plagued her lately crept into her limbs, but she persevered. He called at three different farms, leaving a document of some sort at each place. The documents brought grins to the faces of each of the recipients. She couldn't read the contents, but it wasn't hard to guess that the paperwork involved the land titles that Andy had discovered in Auburn. She'd been right in thinking that the project was picking up steam.

Many Clouds trudged the dusty road beside Granite Creek, innocently sparkling its way from its headwaters at Sawtooth Springs to the grounds of the Circle M itself. She began to wonder if perhaps the next stop would entail a meeting with someone with greater fortunes than these small farmers. Before he reached the end of this five-mile stretch of road and entered the yard of the Circle M, he would pass the farm that Amelia and Cooper, Andy's aunt and uncle owned. The land had passed to them from Andy's murdered natural father.

The spectacular natural beauty of this mountain valley belied its bloody past. The three giant peaks, their timbered flanks pierced by spear-like points of granite at their summits, had suggested the name of the valley. They stood like brooding guardians that should ward off such evil. However, they could just as easily be seen as harbingers of the wickedness that had laid waste to so many. Surely, they would act as nurturing parents as she and Andy built their family. And surely this strange man, the woodcutter with his axes and saws, could not implicate the Maxwells in this plot, whatever it was.

However, after his third stop, Pendleton took off at such a pace that he soon disappeared over a rise. It seemed she would learn no more from him today. She was disappointed, but there was no help for it. It would soon be time to rendezvous with Maggie and Willy. She laid down her walking stick, knelt on the creek bank and scooped a few handfuls of water, startling a pair of floating mallards who took off amid a chorus of quacks and flapping wings. She mentally apologized for disturbing them, inhaled the cool freshness of the stream, rinsed road dust and perspiration from her face and drank. Thankful for the nourishment of body and spirit, she rose and continued on her way—back toward Gentry's saloon and the rendezvous with Maggie and Willy.

It wasn't long before hoofbeats fractured the bucolic silence. She peeked over her shoulder. An approaching dust cloud announced the return of the donkey cart. She shrank down, seeking to make herself less noticeable. Then came the shout.

"Squaw. Hey, you, squaw, I'm talking to you."

She continued on, hoping Pendleton would tire of the game and just go on his way. Indians were not an uncommon sight in the area. The villages of the Washoe Rancheria a few miles east in the direction of Lake Tahoe provided labor to the kinds of farms Pendleton had visited this morning. However, Grazer Pendleton was not about to treat her as anonymous and inconsequential. He continued to shout as he slowed and pulled the cart beside her. She tightened her grip on her walking stick with one hand, surreptitiously laid a hand on her knife handle with the other and kept walking. Then he turned his donkey and cart broadside, blocking her way.

"Told you to stop, injun. What are you doing followin' me?"

He was leaning over the side of the cart, close enough to her that a spray of his rancid spittle befouled her skirt. He reached toward her, grabbed at her arm, catching a handful of her sleeve. Instinctively, Many Clouds turned sideways, grasped the walking stick in both hands, and swung. Her blow connected solidly with Pendleton's temple, and he tumbled from the cart to the dusty road.

She heard herself gasp, afraid she had finished him for good. She hadn't planned the attack, and it had happened so fast, she'd had no time to think through her actions or their consequences. She had no idea why she'd used her stick rather than her knife. Despite all the ugly and bloody episodes with

Yellow Squirrel, she'd never had to kill anyone, and she'd vowed to avoid doing so forever after. Now, though, her heart and breath stopped cold… Her heart and breath stopped cold as she stared at Pendleton, lying face down in the road. She knelt at his side and turned him over. He was still breathing. She glanced quickly around her. Apparently, no one had seen the encounter.

What next? Her first thought was to load him in the cart and hide him somewhere. But where? Besides, that he was too heavy to lift, and he was liable to wake up any minute. She checked once more to assure herself he was still breathing, then climbed into the cart herself and set the donkey into motion. She'd leave it in the brush somewhere and disappear. As for her victim, maybe he hadn't seen her face, or maybe he wouldn't be able to tell one Indian from another even if he had. Best to leave him prone in the road. He'd wake up eventually, then let him make his own way back to Gentry's or wherever else he might be going.

It was all she could think to do. Perhaps it was these situations that turned ordinary people into murderers. She hadn't killed the man, but she could have. And even if she had killed him, would that make her a murderer? He had assaulted her, after all. Still, the idea that her baby, not to mention Willy and Maggie, would have a killer for a mother was disheartening. She knew she wasn't thinking straight, but she also suspected that she'd carry the guilt of this encounter into the future. For how long? Never mind. Her most important errand for now was to find Maggie and Willy.

Seventy

Once again, Carolyn and Ling Chu parked virtually touching the rear bumper of Hale Gentry's touring car. Once again, Carolyn leapt down from the driver's seat. This time, however, Ling Chu was at her side when they entered instead of sneaking around back. The lone customer in the place occupied a barstool, his ample rear spilling off the seat. The barkeep polished a glass with a dirty towel. The place smelled worse than it had on her first visit. Janitorial matters had been neglected. Stale beer was the primary odor, but the spittoons needed washing, and something on the floor stuck to the sole of the shoe as one walked across it. How liquor could turn tacky seemed somewhat mysterious, but didn't merit consideration at the moment.

This time the bartender didn't try to stop them as they marched into Gentry's office, which they found empty. Undaunted, they headed through the back door to a small porch overlooking the back yard of the place. The main feature of the view from the porch were the overflowing barrels of refuse placed in no particular order over the twenty or thirty square yards of dirt enclosed by a four-foot-tall fence of rusty wire. Gentry was chewing on an unlit cigar, pacing and in deep conversation with a man in overalls and a straw hat. Carolyn recognized the man, though she couldn't recall from where. His name was Morse or Mason or something like that. More memorable than his name was the limp that characterized his step.

"Diggie," Ling Chu said, apparently noting the quizzical look on Carolyn's face. "Name Diggie Morris."

That still didn't sound quite right to Carolyn, but for current purposes, it would be close enough. Gentry stopped pacing and turned toward the sound of their voices.

"Hello, Mr. Gentry," she said. "You know Ling Chu, of course." Ling Chu bowed from the waist, hands inside his sleeves in his most obeisant Chinese manner.

"Twice in the space of a week, Carolyn." Gentry said. "To what do I owe the honor?" Carolyn noted that he continued to call her by her first name and that he neither bothered to tip his hat or even gesture toward the brim in an imitation of gentlemanly behavior. Sure signs of his agitation.

"Are we to be treated to the gift of this gentleman's name?" she said.

"Mr. Morrison, meet Carolyn Maxwell," Gentry said. "What is it you want now, Carolyn?"

"I want the names of the current and prospective deedholders to Western Exploration and mining company land in Placer County."

"And what makes you think I have that information? Moreover, what makes you think you would be entitled to it if I did?"

"Either Ling Chu or I will be back tomorrow. We will expect to have the names in our possession by sundown." She turned on her heel and headed back the way they had come. Gentry's voice followed them inside.

"You can expect whatever you like, Carolyn. I wouldn't tell you if I knew."

As they descended the steps, a cowhand rode up on horseback and tied his mount to the hitching post. He was entering the bar when Carolyn had an idea. She appropriated the lariat, a standard tool most cowboys carried with them everywhere, and tied Gentry's rear bumper to their front one.

"What you doing?" Ling Chu asked.

"Just having a little fun," she said. She stepped over to Gentry's machine and made sure the brake was released. Then she put their own car into reverse. In short order, Hale Gentry's touring car sat in the middle of the road.

She untied the rope and replaced it on the cowboy's saddle, then they drove away in the direction of Sawtooth Wells proper. It was in one sense a harmless prank, but Carolyn hoped it would send a signal to Gentry that he couldn't feel secure even in his little fortress of a saloon. Anything they could do to sow unrest and confusion might force him into mistakes borne of anger or even panic.

A short distance from Gentry's place and around a bend in the road a small lane veered to the right. It was overgrown with nettles and milkweed as tall as the car's roof, and the roadway's tracks were nearly obliterated by neglect and misuse. A thick-trunked bay laurel tree flanked the road, and Carolyn pulled the car behind it. The aroma of the laurel's leaves suffused the air, a peaceful odor that somehow underscored the danger that surrounded them. A diligent searcher might spot them, but they'd be unlikely to catch the attention of a casual passerby.

"We'll wait here," Carolyn said. "Now what are you doing, Ling?"

"Leaves good to cook and heal," he said as he stripped a small branch of its greenery.

"You are a great cook, but sometimes you are infuriating."

Ling stuffed a handful of bay leaves into a pouch at his belt. He ignored Carolyn's remark. "Bet you Gentry come along quick."

They both heard cursing followed by the clatter and sputtering of an automobile. They shared a smile.

"You are a prophet, Ling. Here's the man now. Looks as if we might have flushed our prey from his nest."

The auto sped past, canvas top down, dust billowing around it. Gentry drove. One henchman sat in the passenger seat, another in the back. Both sported rifles. They were so focused on the road ahead that they missed any chance they might have had of seeing the Maxwell automobile on its overgrown roadway.

Carolyn put the car in gear and took off in pursuit of Gentry. "Let's see where he leads us."

Seventy-One

Many Clouds hadn't gone far before she heard following hoofbeats once again. With sinking heart, she tried to urge the donkey to move faster, but it was a useless endeavor. She knew neither the walking stick nor her knife was enough weapon for the situation she feared was about to transpire. Her reluctance to use deadly force was dissolving. She knew she would and could do what was necessary to save and protect the precious lives around her and within her no matter the odds.

Was this what her savage uncle Yellow Squirrel had felt on his murderous rampages, that he was the savior and protector of his family? Of his entire people? She hated the notion. No, if she had to kill it would be necessity, not vengeance that impelled her. Mothers would go to extraordinary lengths for their offspring, and she'd shared counsel with other women about the power of the maternal instinct. Her earlier guilty thoughts suddenly seemed ridiculous, only the manifestations of fear that colored her determination. Now that she herself was the instrument of this natural force, she felt empowered beyond measure. She was unstoppable, not only in the moment but for the future of herself, her child, and for Willy and Maggie as well. She handled the donkey's reins with one hand and drew the knife with the other. The handle of Pendleton's axe lay within reach. Though lashed to the sideboard, a quick slice of the knife would free it. She tightened her grip on the reins. Whatever happened, she was ready.

"Many Clouds, dammit, hold up."

Cooper. Friend. Family. She'd known his and Amelia's farm was near, but it never occurred to her that he would become her salvation. It was enough to evoke images of the creator she'd been told of at the mission school, images she'd rejected long ago and seldom recalled except in the vague way one recalls inconsequential memories. She hauled back on the reins, and Cooper caught up to her. He wasn't floating on a cloud of glory the way the preachers had described, but he did ride a stout bay gelding, and after she described her situation, he quickly devised a plan to fix it.

"I saw you brain that guy back there, so I know something about what's going on. A few of us have been hiding out here and there looking for trouble. I thought I drew the short straw when they sent me off to this cornfield. Never expected any action just sitting in them rows of husks and ears, but it looks like I hit the jackpot. Who is this guy driving the cart anyhow?"

"He's one of Gentry's men. Maybe you can help me get him out of sight before he talks me into a cell."

"Oh, I took care that he's out of sight, and he isn't going to be telling anyone anything for a while. Let's hide this cart as well, then we can have a little chat with the man. Might be he knows enough to lift the curtain on everything."

"He might know, but will he tell?"

"Oh, I got a way of asking questions that makes people pretty anxious to give up their secrets."

***

With Grazer Pendleton safely bound to a chair, which was tied in turn to a sturdy post in Cooper and Amelia's tack room, Cooper was ready for a session of serious ask and answer. Many Clouds was anxious to learn what Pendleton had to say, but Maggie and Willy were on her mind. They might already be waiting for her outside Gentry's Saloon.

"Why didn't you say so, girl?" Amelia asked. She'd come out to meet them as they rode into the yard. "I got no desire to watch Cooper do what he has in mind for this man, and them children can't be left to fend for themselves. We'll take Cooper's riding horse and the plow mare and bring everyone back here."

"Don't forget to stop by the livery stable and tell what happened. Might be some more news waiting for us there anyhow," Cooper said.

"The livery stable?" Many Clouds said. "What is happening there?"

"Amelia can catch you up on things while you're on your way to meet Willy and Maggie. In the meantime, I'll be working with Mr. Woodcutter here. Good chance I'll be right behind you with some fresh information. Get on now."

When Cooper arrived, Many Clouds had pushed aside her anger at the men who had put them in such danger. Now, though, rage flooded through her once more, choking her. If Carolyn hadn't taken Ling Chu and gone off on her own, leaving Many Clouds and Andy in the dark about her intentions or location, they might be in a much better position. As it was, they didn't know what forces were coming at them or from what direction. Many Clouds had tried to keep their efforts focused and to maintain communication. But Carolyn's activities had not only made it impossible to bring their efforts to bear on a central target but made everyone more vulnerable to whatever Gentry and his ilk cooked up. On the other hand, whatever they'd done had stationed Cooper in the cornfield to rescue her. Still, that seemed more like an accident than a plan.

She swallowed, once more forcing her anger down. She wished there were time to hear the full story right now. Amelia knew everything, though, and she was plenty smart. Between the two of them, surely, they'd be able to weave their efforts into some kind of coherent whole. They sprinted toward the small shed and corral at the rear of the barn where their horses waited. If all went well, Pendleton would be spilling some magical beans before long. They needed to be ready to plant them.

Seventy-Two

Andy stormed out of the bank and charged toward his car. He needed to calm down. Meyer Sturges, the bank president, had yielded no information about Western Explorations and had, most surprisingly, refused to exert leverage over the storekeepers who were withholding credit from his family. He claimed that the merchants themselves had made the decision on their own and that he had no way of forcing them to change their minds. Even Andy's threat to pull Circle M deposits from his bank had drawn no more than a shrug. "There's a sentiment abroad that the Maxwells have had their own way in this valley long enough."

"And there's a sentiment abroad that the Maxwells have done business with this bank long enough." Andy stood and dusted his hands to signify that he and Sturges were done. He turned and hurried toward the door. Sturges called after him.

"And Andy."

"Yes?"

"If you're thinking about coming after me in print, rest assured that no publication outside that nigger rag, *The Elevator,* will touch the story. They'd be mighty sorry if they did."

Andy tried to maintain the anger in his looks, but the remark about *The Elevator* had been a shock. That paper was a leading Negro voice in the bay area. Its publisher, Joseph Francis, with an assist from the writer Ambrose Bierce, had given Andy his start in journalism. The widely respected Negro freelance reporter, Delilah Beasley, whose byline regularly graced the pages of every paper from the *San Francisco Examiner* to the *Oakland Tribune* had encouraged and mentored him as his career began to blossom. Mostly due to the small black population in the bay area, *The Elevator* had always struggled and might have gone under had it not been for the infusion of Maxwell funding Andy provided from time to time. Sturges's threat suggested violence. Whatever happened to Andy and his family, he had no wish to bring harm to his friends and supporters. Andy turned and stepped toward the banker's desk.

"Would you care to elaborate on that threat, sir?"

Sturges made a reflexive move toward standing to face Andy but sat back in his plush cowhide chair instead. He smiled. "Threat? Not from me, Mr. Maxwell. I'm a banker, not a gunslinger."

"Glad to hear it. I'd hate to have to change my opinion of a man who's depended so heavily on my family's business for so long." He turned and headed toward the door once again. He thought he'd had the last word, but Sturges wasn't quite finished.

"Nothing lasts forever, Andy." He shoved a yellow copy of telegram across the desk. ON MY WAY TO FORECLOSE STOP BE READY STOP W.

"What's this about?"

"A bright man like you should be able to figure it out, Andy." Andy reached for the telegram, but Sturges quickly retrieved it. "Nope. That's all you get." He tucked the telegram into his vest pocket. "Now, I suppose you have other business to take care of."

"Yes, as a matter of fact. Since our credit is no longer acceptable in these parts, I'm going to need some cash."

"Certainly. How much would you like to withdraw?"

"I think ten thousand dollars would suffice."

Sturges's visage switched suddenly from smug authority to surprise, then anger. "Preposterous." He practically choked on the word.

"We do have that much in our account. More, in fact," Andy said. "We just shipped out a major sale of cattle."

"Well, even so, we don't keep that much cash on hand, and our rules wouldn't allow me to authorize such a large withdrawal even it if we did."

"You're telling me this bank is out of money? I'm sure the good people of Placerville will be eager to hear about that." He turned and started toward the door.

"No, no," Sturges hurried from behind his desk and laid a hand on Andy's shoulder. "Everyone will be in here in no time demanding their money. We'll be ruined."

"Yes, I've heard that runs on banks can be difficult to survive. It would be a pity to see it happen to this bank. Come to think of it, it would be rough on the whole town, and you'd probably be blamed, wouldn't you?"

"That wouldn't be fair."

"Ah, but the world is full of injustice, Mr. Sturges."

They stared at one another for a time. Sturges was the one to drop his eyes. "Give me a few minutes," he mumbled.

Andy paced the office, even sat for a time in Sturges's large chair. It was too soft for his taste, and he decided that if he ever had a temptation to go into banking he'd recall this moment, ride a horse into the mountains till the feeling passed. It was a good forty-five minutes before Sturges reappeared. He carried a canvas bag that listed him to the right until he finally managed to heave it onto the desk. "Why the weight?" Andy asked.

"Gold is heavy," the banker answered.

Using gold instead of more portable paper currency was a way of delivering on Andy's request while still thumbing his nose at him. Andy opened the bag and saw that there were a few bundles of paper currency mixed in with the golden eagles coins. He had no time to pressure Sturges into coming up with bank notes. He supposed he should be grateful there were no bricks of bullion.

"I'll need a receipt, of course," the banker said.

"Fine," Andy said. He grabbed two pieces of paper and a pen from the inkwell on Sturges's desk, scribbled a pair of notes, and signed them. He slid the papers back toward Sturges. "And your signature as well on both copies, please."

Sturges glanced at what Andy had written and stiffened. "What's this?"

"Quite plain, isn't it? The ten thousand amount will be confirmed by an independent count, which I don't have time to conduct right now. Paper, I could manage, but weighing the gold, no."

"But the count has been executed by my most skillful and trusted employees."

"Too bad I wasn't there to watch. We wouldn't have to go through this."

"Mr. Maxwell, every business transaction requires some trust. How do I know you won't take some of what's in that bag and try to claim our count was short?"

"As you said, every business transaction requires some trust. Now, I have pressing business, as I'm sure you do. Just sign and we can both get on with our separate obligations."

Sturges signed. Andy retrieved his copy of the note and grabbed the money bag, trying hard to appear undaunted by its considerable weight, and stormed out of the office.

Andy's mind was awhirl as he hefted the satchel into his car, keeping a surreptitious watch in all directions. He was intent on getting back to Sawtooth Wells and his family as well as guarding his vulnerable wealth. He tried to glean conclusions from his conversation with the banker. Whatever was going on here, Western Explorations was behind it. Was "Western" what the *W* on the telegram stood for? He lined up his adversaries in his mind like ducks in a carnival shooting gallery. Sturges, Gentry, Mayor James, whoever had killed Harry Barker. Quite a bunch. He couldn't wait to get them all out in the open.

Seventy-Three

"Maybe we should just start for home," Willy said.

"Many Clouds said she and Andy would meet us at sundown, Willy. It's not time yet."

"How much darker you want it to get?"

"Look at the road in front of the saloon. There are still shadows."

"Barely. I'm tired of getting left out of everything all the time."

"Hush."

Maggie's loud whisper sounded so urgent that Willy obeyed immediately. They scrambled over an embankment, taking cover behind the trunk of an ancient spruce, hugging the ground as they heard approaching footsteps.

"Wasn't nothing but kids playing."

The words came in a growling voice Maggie didn't recognize. Gentry had posted guards since they'd been there that morning, a complication they hadn't expected.

"Yeah, sure. That girl was just a kid and look how much trouble she caused the other day."

Maggie felt a quick surge of pride. They were afraid of her.

"Well I ain't gonna risk another cussing out from Gentry. Maybe even getting fired." The other man's voice was a similar growl, as if they were dogs from the same kennel. "He'd never hire me again. Pay's too good and the jobs he gives us are too easy to just walk away."

"All right. All right. You go left, I'll go right and we'll meet out front."

"And then inside for a beer?"

"Sure. To celebrate a job well done."

The footsteps retreated. Maggie and Willy stayed put for a count of fifty, then Willy crawled to the top of the rise and peered out. The gloom had settled around them by now, but they could neither see nor hear anyone close by.

"Let's go," Willy said. "Something must have happened or Many Clouds would have been here by now."

Maggie was beginning to come around to Willy's point of view. It was a good five miles to the Circle M, but the road was good, and there was plenty of cover along Granite Creek in case they needed to hide. Many Clouds had often counseled Maggie on how important it was to take the initiative, not depend on others to make her decisions for her. She'd said the same to Willy, but had told Maggie privately, apart from her brother, that it would be particularly difficult for her to follow the advice. She was a woman and an Indian. Even though she was half white, the world would see her as Indian. There would be obstacles and expectations placed in her path that even Willy would not have to face. Many Clouds had done more than lecture. She'd shown her courage many times. The way she'd gone into city hall and stirred things up was just the latest example. Many Clouds wasn't physically here at the moment, but her spirit and teaching dwelt in the hearts of both Willy and Maggie. That spirit was urging them on.

"All right, Willy, let's go," she said. They rose, then dashed to the rear of the saloon. Backs to the clapboard wall, they sidled toward the front. Maggie kept watch as they moved forward. Willy watched the rear. Maggie was amazed that she felt almost no fear. There was instead joy in taking action and there was a feeling of control as well. They reached a point where they had to cross the clearing in front of the saloon entrance. There was virtually no cover between where they hid and the road that led in one direction toward Placerville, then home, and in the other direction toward the Circle M. She thought of hiding the paper they had lifted from the man they called Checkers. He'd delivered several of them to various farm houses before settling down in the shade of a huge windthrow to nap. Willy had sneaked up and extracted the paper from Checker's back pocket while he slept. Maggie was proud of her brother and of herself. They were a team. The paper looked like a deed. Though she didn't know if it had any value, at least they wouldn't report back empty-handed.

Now, she wondered if they should risk the paper falling into the hands of the enemy—that's how she'd come to think of Gentry and his henchmen—if they should be captured. Perhaps they should hide it somewhere for safekeeping and return for it later. No. She wanted to present it to Andy and

Many Clouds. If worse came to worse, she'd memorized the wording at the top of the document, and they'd tear it up if they got in trouble. Safety was a scant hundred yards away.

They were about to dash for it when a group of five men, dusty from field work, laughing, boisterous and loud, strode up the walk, climbed the steps, and entered the saloon. Willy and Maggie waited a count of a hundred, then broke from their hiding place.

Halfway to the road, another laborer appeared in front of them making his own way to the saloon. Willy, intent on getting to the road, ran smack into him, taking him back a couple of steps. He wasn't a big man, but the bear hug he gave Willy immobilized him.

"Watch where you're going, kid."

"Let me go," Willy grunted.

The man was so intent on Willy that he was unaware of Maggie, who ran up behind him and tipped his hat forward. Not only did the falling hat blind him for a moment, but he automatically threw both hands up to keep it from falling. Willy came free, and he and Maggie made it to a copse of willows on the far side of the road from the saloon.

"That was close," Willy said, smiling.

"No gloating," Maggie replied. "You and me—"

"You and I," Willy interrupted.

"That's not important right now," Maggie retorted.

"You're just mad cause I caught you," Willy wore a broad smile as he spoke.

"Okay, okay. The point is, something's happened or Many Clouds and Andy would be here to meet us. Time for us to take all those shortcuts we've been bragging about and get back home lickety-split."

"So let's quit arguing and get started," Willy said. "Hey, wait up." Maggie had taken off at a sprint. Willy was soon close behind her.

Seventy-Four

All the business with the woodcutter had taken too much time. Even though Amelia and Many Clouds kept their two horses at a quick pace, they were a good two miles from Gentry's saloon when dark fell. Andy and the children would be wondering what happened. Would they wait or come searching? Or would they head for home to wait for her?

Unable to contain her anxiety, Many Clouds kicked her mount into a lope. She left Amelia, who was riding the plow horse, well behind. No matter. The older woman would catch up presently.

A chill breeze sprang up from the darkness, and the aromas of hay and clover in the open fields began to fade before the odors of horseflesh, manure, and petroleum that announced the approaching settlement of Sawtooth Wells. She steered her mount off the road and behind the same patch of willows opposite the saloon where she and the children had arranged to meet. Willy and Maggie were not there. It was likely they'd gone on home, and she was glad they'd made an alternative plan in case their rendezvous went awry, but they were dealing with men who were cruel and devious and had shown no propensity for mercy even with children. And where was Andy?

She dismounted and called softly. "Maggie. Willy. Are you here?" Nothing. Then came the puttering of an automobile. Was it Gentry? She hadn't looked to see if his touring car was parked in its usual place alongside the saloon. She hitched the bay horse to a branch and peeked out. What she saw evoked a smile and a rush of joy. Andy. She suppressed an urge to forgo caution and run to meet him as he stopped just short of the path leading to the saloon. Instead, she waited till he had exited the car, then she stepped into the roadway, and waved.

"Andy. Andy. Over here," she called in a loud whisper.

He was at her side and in her arms in an instant. They maintained their embrace even as they shuffled aside to conceal themselves behind the willows. Andy had left the car running, lights on. When they pulled back to look one another in the eyes, they saw a very tall man weaving down the path from saloon to road. From behind the building stepped a slim woman in a ruffled dress with a low neckline. From her straight black hair and high cheekbones, she appeared to be Indian. She took the man's arm.

"Need some help, stranger?" she said. "This pathway's kind of hard to see in the dark."

They couldn't hear the mumbled reply, but he slung an arm around her shoulders and they headed toward town.

"Let's not do this anymore, Many Clouds."

She felt a stab of anxiety. "Do what?"

"Keep going off in different directions."

She smiled and kissed him. "Agreed. Did you find out anything?"

"Nothing good. What about you?"

"I'm not sure. A lot happened, but I don't know if we're better off or not." She started to recount the afternoon's events when Amelia rode up.

"Aunt Amelia? What's going on?" Andy asked.

Amelia paid no attention to Andy for the moment. "The kids aren't here?"

"Not a sign of them," Many Clouds said. "My best guess is that they got tired of waiting and headed for home, which was our plan if we missed one another."

"Unless they got waylaid," Andy said.

"Don't even think that, Andy. Let's tie the horses to the bumper and head out."

"By the way," Amelia said. "Hello, Andy. Nice to almost see you here in the dark."

"You, too, Aunt Amelia." He gave her a perfunctory hug, and they headed toward the car.

"Did I ever tell you how much I hate this smelly thing?" she said.

"More than once," he said, "but it's the fastest way, so no complaining." He stepped toward the driver's seat, then he stopped suddenly. "Wait. Shouldn't we leave someone here to keep watch?"

Many Clouds had to swallow hard to keep from yelling. "Andrew Maxwell, what did we say about splitting up?"

"All right. All right. Sorry I said anything. Jump in and let's go."

Seventy-Five

"Where is everyone, Emmanuel?" Ling Chu asked. It was a relief to be free of the clatter and chugging of the car. Here at the house, the twilight air was rich with the odors of animal sweat and the spicy pines that surrounded the little house.

"Andy was to drop Many Clouds and the children in Sawtooth Wells, then come back to Placerville to talk to someone at the bank," Emmanuel said.

Carolyn stomped her foot. "And none of us knew where the other was. My fault. I thought if they knew I was going after Gentry they'd try to stop me or maybe come along, and it would put us all in more danger. Supposedly, the older you get the smarter. Doesn't seem to be working that way for me, does it, Ling Chu?"

Ling Chu and Emmanuel shared a look. Neither of them spoke.

"All right, you don't have to say anything. What do you think we should do now? I'm ready to listen."

"It's good sometimes just to wait," Emmanuel said. He settled into a chair on the porch. "I'll take another turn around the hillside in a few minutes."

"Waiting. Sitting still. Ling Chu often advises the same. I seem to fail over and over."

"But action is you, Miss Carolyn," Ling Chu said.

"Nobody better," agreed Emmanuel.

"It's kind of you both to say so, but wrongly played, it can make a mess of things. Never mind. The best action I can think of now is to feed ourselves so we'll be ready for the action whenever the waiting is over. Let's go see if we can rustle ourselves some grub, as the cowhands say."

Carolyn hated being wrong. It made her feel guilty. She'd often mused that if she were religious, it would feel like this to commit some extraordinary sin or another. Given that comparison, she figured she'd just done her confession. No penance came immediately to mind. Maybe she'd plan something for later. Or maybe it wasn't necessary. There was only so much a body could do at once.

Seventy-Six

"Maggie, are you sure we're not lost?" Willy sat on a rock in the bed of a dry creek.

"Of course not. We just climb over the ridge and follow the trail to Placerville."

"Doesn't feel like it's that easy."

"Everything looks different in the dark."

"Let's just stay the night and go on in the morning when we can see."

"Stay here? Willy, what if Many Clouds and Andy are in trouble? We can't just do nothing."

"Nothing? Of course not. It's only… I'm starving."

She laid a comforting hand on his shoulder. "Okay, I'm a bit hungry myself. You remember that big apple tree behind the Hangtown Saloon? We'll go through town and grab a few of those. Ought to keep us till we get home. Come on."

"Wait," he whispered.

"For what?"

"Don't you hear it?" Then she did, a crashing and snorting through the underbrush. She ran through possibilities in her head. If it were human, their current hiding place would probably serve them well. An animal, though, would sniff them out. Only one creature she could think of would travel in such an incautious manner, especially at night. Deer would be bedded down. Mountain lions would creep as silently as possible. Even a wild dog would take some care not to attract attention.

When the boar emerged from the chaparral, it seemed as startled to encounter them as they were to see it, though doubtless not nearly as frightened. It snorted and jumped, its red eyes like coals burning in the darkness. Willy leaped in the air, yelling "No."

They'd been taught to create as much commotion and make themselves as big as possible to counter a mountain lion attack. Hoping the same measures might work for the boar, Maggie followed her brother's cue, throwing a couple of handy rocks in the process. There was a brief standoff, though it didn't seem so brief to the two of them. Then the animal took off up the hillside.

"Nice going, Willy."

"Close call, but we made it. Let's go steal some apples."

Seventy-Seven

It was only a small boulder, hardly worthy of the name, and it shouldn't have been sitting in the roadway. Andy's headlights picked it up just before he drove smack into it, tumbling the passengers into one another and banging his own forehead on the steering wheel. After gathering assurances that no one was injured, he asked Many Clouds to retrieve the kerosene lantern he kept in the toolbox strapped to the running board on the vehicle's passenger side. He'd taken a few wrenches from the box, tucked them in around the back and front seats, and replaced them with the money bag. Not exactly a bank vault, but as long as they didn't leave it unattended, he figured it was safe until they could find a better place. Amelia held the lantern while Many Clouds struck the match that lit it.

She found Andy kneeling by the driver's side front wheel. It had taken him no time at all to discern that the tire was flat. Exasperating, but fixable with the repair kit in the tool box. But when he brought the light closer to the car's underside, he saw that the situation was much more complicated.

"Axle's bent," he growled. "Maybe a blacksmith can repair it, but I suspect it needs a replacement. In any case, we're back to a pair of horses and our own feet."

It was relatively easy for the three of them to push the car to the roadside, trusting that it would still be there and without further damage when they sent someone to fetch it. The money was a different proposition. He'd not wanted to mention it, figuring that it would make everyone nervous and thus more apt to reveal its existence, however inadvertently. The length of rope

Cooper kept attached to the bay horse's saddle served to tie it down for the time being, even though it was impossible to conceal it. They'd just have to hope for the best. Many Clouds thought wryly what a burden wealth could be.

Thus, it was Many Clouds on one horse, the money tied down in front of her, and Amelia and Andy on the other. Many Clouds had wanted to go on foot, but Andy and Amelia both insisted that her condition rendered that unwise. Many Clouds thought it ridiculous, but allowed herself to be talked into trading off with Amelia. Then they set off for Placerville, a distance Many Clouds estimated at about two miles.

Seventy-Eight

Remington Dillinger galloped up to Andy's and Many Clouds' yard. Emmanuel stepped from behind the front yard oak, rifle ready. He lowered the weapon when he recognized Dillinger, who jumped down from his mount trotted up the slope toward the house. Carolyn and Ling Chu emerged from the front door.

"Where's everybody?" Dillinger asked. "I've got information we need to act on, and I mean right away."

"Apparently, everyone's scattered hither and yon, and none of us knows what the others are doing," Carolyn said.

Ling Chu said, "Driving Miss Carolyn to nuts."

Dillinger handed his horse's reins to Emmanuel, who led the appaloosa toward the small shelter that they called a stable, which was beginning to get crowded.

"Unfortunate. Especially now the sun's down."

"Would you care to enlighten us on this 'situation', as you call it, Mr. Dillinger?" Carolyn said.

By this time, Dillinger had run onto the porch. "Everyone, have a seat. This will take a few minutes." His audience gathered. Dillinger continued. "I did what you suggested, Carolyn. Stuck with Jacob Russell, and boy did it pay off."

"How so?" She leaned forward in her seat, almost as if she were zipping down a trail on a fast horse.

"Well, he didn't let much out while we were in the Hangtown except what I told you in the note, that he'd met Gentry. Not important in itself, but then he let slip that Gentry had told him was working on a big project that would surprise everyone and bring new prosperity to everyone in the area."

"And the project? What is it?"

A voice from the gloom interrupted them. "See? I told you we'd make it, and here we are."

"Maggie?" Carolyn said, running toward the road. "Is that you?"

"And me, too," Willy said.

There was an interlude of hugs and exclamations of relief. Then Carolyn spoke again. "Where are Andy and Many Clouds?"

"If they aren't here, we don't know," Willy said.

Maggie added, "We were trying to help Many Clouds track down some information about the crooks, then we were supposed to meet her at Gentry's saloon, but she didn't come, so we decided best thing was to come back here."

"That was a good decision. Come on inside. I'm sure you're exhausted and hungry," Carolyn said.

"Mostly hungry," Willy rubbed his stomach.

"That figures," Maggie imitated her little brother's gesture.

"Then there's no time to waste." And she ushered them toward the house.

* * *

Once the children's plates were loaded, Remington called everyone back out to the porch.

"Let's get back on track here," he spoke with an urgency in his voice. "Now, like I was saying, Gentry told Russell he was working on some big project. And the strange thing about it was, *he* asked *me* if I knew what Gentry was talking about. He said being a businessman himself he might want to get in on it, but that Gentry had clammed up when it came to details."

"Why would he think you knew anything?" Carolyn said, "or that you would tell him if you did?"

"Want to know how much Mr. Remington knew," Ling Chu said.

"Just so, Ling. Russell and I were playing the same game. Each of us trying to extract information from the other."

Carolyn was getting impatient with Remington's circuitous narration. "Remy, we don't need to hear every jot and tittle. It's almost dark. Get on with it."

"All right. Bare bones it is. We finished our drink, and I followed him out of the bar to the train station, on to the train. He got off in Sacramento, and there to meet him was a very pretty lady carrying a ruffled pink parasol and dressed in more ribbons and bows than you'd think it was possible to put on one person. They went to the Beacon Hotel, one of Sacramento's finest, as I'm sure you know. The staff seemed to know them well as Mr. and Mrs. Russell."

"And that's all?" Carolyn asked.

"Nope. I saved the best thing for last. *Two* best things, actually. I recognized the lady, and she is not Mrs. Jacob Russell or Mrs. anybody. Her name, at least her professional name, is Stephanie Dove."

"The famous madam of The Bunkhouse Brothel?" Carolyn smiled and shook her head, casting a glance at Ling Chu, who smiled along with her. "Very titillating, but how does it help us?"

"I did a little homework before I met Jacob Russell. He and Stephanie Dove may pretend to be Mr. and Mrs. Russell at the Beacon Hotel, but there is another Mrs. Russell, a real one, who is a distinguished society matron in San Francisco."

"Does she know?" Carolyn said.

"It doesn't matter whether she knows or not. Even if she does, she surely won't want what's going on to become general knowledge. It would do a lot of damage to her social standing."

"You say two things, Mr. Remington," Ling Chu said.

"Indeed, I did. Who should step forward as our fake Mr. and Mrs. Russell entered the lobby, but a gentleman in a very expensive suit. He and Russell greeted one another like long lost friends. I nearly choked when I heard his name."

"Will you stop this false suspense, Remy?" Carolyn said.

"Yes, yes. I promised. The name is Howard Weitzel."

"Weitzel… Weitzel," Carolyn said.

"President Western Explorations," Ling Chu said.

"So," said Carolyn, "Weitzel to Russell to Gentry. Beautiful work, Remy. Well, we know the major characters in the drama. All we need now is a look at the script."

"Many Clouds and Andy and them ought to be able to help with that part." Remy wore a big smile.

"If they ever get back," Carolyn said. "I know we agreed to wait, but it's way past dark, and I'm getting worried."

"I don't know about this agreement you mentioned, but it seems to me we should be searching in case they're in trouble."

"Search where, though? They could be in Sawtooth Wells, Placerville, or on the road anywhere in between."

"Or maybe someplace else, even," Ling Chu said.

"Got a fresh horse?" Remington said. "My mount's had a tough day."

"No, I'm sorry to say," Carolyn said.

"Never mind. We can make it to the Placerville livery stable. I'll get a new mount there. Off I go, then," he called as he kicked his horse into motion.

Carolyn started to lay a sympathetic hand on Ling Chu's shoulder, then stopped. It was a gesture with too much familiarity. Then she went ahead and did it anyway.

"I guess we're back to waiting, my friend."

"We will do a good job of it," Ling said. "Important as any other."

Seventy-Nine

It was a tired and bedraggled group that straggled down the main street of Placerville under the faint light of a sickle-shaped new moon cradling the evening star. Andy set forth the notion that the women and children would deliver the horses to the livery stable while he went to the saloon for information.

"Why, Andy?" Many Clouds asked.

"I'm not sure. Maybe I'll overhear something, make a scene, stir things up, shine a light on whatever's hiding in the shadows."

"Remember about splitting up?" Many Clouds said.

Andy gaped for a moment like a fish pulled out of the water. He looked toward Amelia, who cocked her head to the right and gave him one of her seldom-used mean looks.

"I know I wanted to get home as soon as possible, but I'm exhausted. So are the horses and everyone else. Let's get a room somewhere and press on to home in the morning."

"All right," he said. "But we might have difficulty finding a place that will accommodate us."

"No, we won't," Many Clouds said. "The Cary House will be perfect."

"The Cary House?" Andy looked hard to make sure she was serious. "All of us? It's the classiest hotel around, and you know they won't take kindly to Amelia, you, and the children."

"Oh, I'll bet they will," Amelia smiled. "After all, we're helping them catch up to modern times."

Andy was speechless for a moment. Then he echoed Amelia's smile. "Well, what are we doing just standing here in the middle of the street, then?"

They hitched the horses outside the stable while Andy headed inside to arrange matters for the livestock and to inquire about repairing the car. He was just about to enter the building when a tall man came trotting out the door, nearly knocking him over.

"Oh, sorry partner," the man apologized and started to hurry on.

"Remington Dillinger," Andy objected. "Wait a minute. What are you doing here?"

"Oh, hey. I was looking for you, Andy. And these folks as well. Come on. We've got a lot to talk about."

"'A lot to talk about.' No one in the history of the world has spoken truer words than those, my not-so-trusty investigator."

Many Clouds stepped forward. "Remington, maybe you'll want to eavesdrop at the Hangtown for few minutes. No telling what you might learn. We'll get ourselves to the Cary House and meet you there as soon as we get settled in."

Remington hesitated, but Many Clouds was in no mood to dither. She assumed Dillinger would do as she asked, grabbed the horses' reins and led them into the stable. It was late, but the stable master was in his office.

The office was a cramped affair with a battered table for a desk. The small, dark proprietor sat in a ladderback oaken chair whose back was missing a couple of slats. A wooden Hercules dynamite box served as a footstool. His eyes flew open, and he tried to spring to his feet at the sight of the crowd of intruders. His feet got tangled up, though, and he sat back down hard.

"Relax, mister—what's your name again?" In actuality, she had never known who he was but thought the "again" might make him think he was the one who had forgotten their previous business. Any advantage was an advantage.

"Slocum. Herbert Slocum." He managed to untangle his legs and rise to his feet. Many Clouds was surprised to find that she could look past him over his head.

"Fine. I'm Many Clouds. We're in a bit of a hurry, so I won't take the time to introduce everyone. We have two horses for you to board overnight."

"That's all right about the introductions. I know you're them Maxwell people. I'm afraid this stable is full up right now."

"I'm sure you'll be able to accommodate us. Just for one night. No stalls necessary, you can just turn the horses loose in a corral, shove some oats and hay their way, and we'll pick them up in the morning."

"I don't know about all that. I have to send out for permission. And you know there's no credit for you like there was once, injun lady."

"No credit is no problem, Mr. Herbert. We'll leave the animals here while you get that permission. And we'll even do some of your work for you. Maggie and Willy, you can help unsaddle the horses and rub them down while we have a little conference. Come on, gang."

She marched toward the horses. The children undid the cinches on the saddles while Many Clouds helped Andy unload the bag of cash and Amelia helped the children take off the saddles and mount them on a wall separating a nearby stall. Amelia and the children got busy with curry brushes and blankets. Sometime during the process, Herbert Slocum disappeared. Andy put his foot on the moneybag and took Many Clouds' hands.

"Well now that you've taken charge, my lovely *injun lady*," he said. "What is our next move?"

"As soon as Slocum gets back, we'll go meet Dillinger at the Cary House, of course."

"Oh, I don't think we need to wait for Herbert Slocum, my lovely. By the time we arrive, there won't be many folks hereabouts who won't know who and where we are."

Eighty

The Cary House had stood in Placerville since gold rush days and enjoyed a reputation as one of the premiere hotels in the Sierra foothills. The Maxwells had rented suites there to monitor the election returns during the election of 1912 two years earlier, and the hotel's bar had set up a tally board that the whole community used as a news center on election night. The word that Andy had won the office of assemblyman from the fifth California district had launched a party that lasted till sunup and beyond.

The subsequent lawsuit that challenged his victory because of his race stalled in the courts, and the new governor, Hiram Johnson, appointed someone else in his place rather than await an official decision. It was a legally dubious move that probably wouldn't have survived a court challenge, but Andy had grown so disgusted with politics by that time that he gave up the fight and decided to take his life in new directions. Except for the one brief drink he'd imbibed waiting to meet Dillinger, this would be his first return to a place that carried many ugly associations.

Many Clouds had never been in the building, having had neither need nor desire. Now, despite her brave front, she quaked a bit inside as they approached the great doors, the polished brass hardware glittering in the gaslight. The expansive windows, painted to announce its name, arched gold-edged gothic with the motto underneath: *Where every guest is legendary.* She'd started all this because she was tired of skulking and waiting. Now she wondered if she'd simply hastened hers and Andy's disgrace. And what right did she have to risk her newborn? Or more correctly, her not-yet-born? Well, the same strength and stubbornness that had carried her through so much would carry her—them—through this as well. Her child would be one tough and daring baby.

She looked over her shoulder and nodded at Andy, who grabbed the handle and swung the door wide for her, just as any gentleman would for his lady. For any lady covered by trail dust, trailed by two scruffy urchins and an older Negro woman. Many Clouds headed for the front desk. Andy, who had been holding the door for three people who happened to follow them in, brought up the rear. The night clerk wore a frock coat and a rather tattered tuxedo shirt. He was obviously taken aback at the entourage facing him.

"Uh… yes?"

"There are five of us. Three rooms, please. One for Mr. Maxwell and myself, one for the children, and one for Mrs. Duprée, whose husband will be joining us presently."

"Mr. Maxwell, is it?" He surveyed the group. Hesitated some more. "I'll have to check."

"No need for that," she said. "I see three keys in a row hanging behind you. I'm sure those will do just fine."

"Well, that's not exactly… It's not customary…"

"Yes, yes, you can see we've been traveling and need to wash up a bit. We'll be much more presentable in no time."

"Lady, I can't just—uh, sir, if you can wait a minute—"

Andy had lifted the countertop gate and headed for the hanging keys Many Clouds had spotted. "Let me give you a hand, son," he said. He grabbed the keys and headed out into the lobby. "Room 209—You take that one, Aunt Amelia. 210 will be fine for you kids. And Many Clouds and I will be right next to you in 211."

"Mr. Maxwell, only married couples can—"

Many Clouds ignored what Josh was going to say. "And we are indeed hungry, as you can imagine. Knowing it's late, you can tell the kitchen we won't be choosy about the menu."

Having distributed the keys, Andy turned back to the clerk. "Now, about the safe."

"Safe?"

"Yes." He hefted the carpet bag containing his withdrawal from Sturges's bank. "We have some valuables we'd like to have locked up. I presume you have a secure facility?"

"Well, yes, but I don't have the authority or the combination." Then his eyes suddenly focused on the front door and a look of relief passed over his face. "Ah, Mr. Billings. Very glad to see you, sir."

Many Clouds turned, expecting to see, perhaps, a rotund gentleman in a top hat. Instead, Billings was in stained coveralls, jangling a key ring like a custodian. "What seems to be the problem, Josh?"

Many Clouds didn't give Josh a chance to answer for himself. "Josh, here, has been very helpful in getting us settled in. We simply need to put some valuables under lock and key and get a bite to eat and we'll be in fine shape."

Billings surveyed the group. "Well, this is certainly an exception to our usual clientele—"

"I tried to explain, sir, but—"

Andy interrupted. "Mr. Billings, if I'm not mistaken, you own the brewery on the Yuba River just west of Auburn?"

"Yes, I do, as you apparently well know."

"And I know as well that when the flood last spring took out your water wheel, Sturges over at the bank refused you a loan to repair it."

"He said it would be a poor investment for the shareholders."

"Yes, and who stepped in?"

"Why, Mrs. Maxwell helped out."

"She didn't just help out. She financed the whole business—recovery and repairs. Without that loan—interest-free, wasn't it? Yes, I thought so—you'd have lost the brewery and a great deal of income. Correct me if I'm wrong, but it seems to me that like the honest man you are, you paid back every penny of that loan. So, do you think it's worth risking a productive business relationship by denying refuge to my family in the dark of night?"

"No, no. Of course not. We'd be glad to make an exception for you and your... group. Josh, I've got some things to attend to in back. Please make sure our guests have whatever they need."

"Yes, sir." Josh, suddenly helpful and accommodating, interjected: "Mr. Maxwell was asking about storing some valuables in the vault."

"Thanks," Andy said, "but we've changed our mind. We won't need the safe after all."

"As you wish, Mr. Maxwell," Billings said. And he disappeared through a door behind the bar.

Andy nodded to Many Clouds, who took charge of ushering Amelia and the children upstairs.

"And you won't forget to notify the kitchen, will you, Josh?" she called.

"Right away, Mrs. Maxwell."

"Mrs. Maxwell." She started to object to the "Mrs. Maxwell" but supposed it was Josh's way of legitimizing renting a room to her and Andy. Their forge-on attitude had evidently forestalled the objections the place usually had against accommodating non-whites, so she decided to put aside her hesitation to sharing a title with Carolyn. She simply said, "Thank you." And everyone headed upstairs.

Eighty-One

Many Clouds felt rather matriarchal presiding over the large table that the Cary House had provided in the dining room, and she had to admit she enjoyed the feeling. Perhaps she was more like Carolyn than she wanted to admit. Or perhaps being in charge automatically gave rise to such emotions. The meal was rather more like breakfast than supper, consisting of a pile of scrambled eggs, a platter of ham, and pitchers of orange juice. Famished as they were, however, no king enjoyed a royal feast more than they enjoyed the late-night fare. Josh had been pressed into table service and helped make sure everyone's plate was as full as desired.

Everything seemed to be proceeding nicely, but it made her nervous for Andy to have the carpet bag under his feet rather than locked away somewhere. His decision to decline the offer of a safe had puzzled and alarmed her at first. However, he was in no mood to trust anybody and was loath to let it out of sight despite his earlier plan to put it in a safe. She couldn't come up with an argument against his decision, but it still left her feeling more vulnerable than she liked. However, the task now was to map out their next steps.

She leaned forward, checked to see that nobody out of their group was in earshot, and spoke softly. "We know a great deal more than we did this morning. It's coal they're after, and they have set up a bunch of proxy landowners to get it, but we still don't know who the 'they' is or how they plan to consolidate all these small parcels into a mining operation. How do we find out?"

"I might be able to help with that." It was Remington Dillinger's voice that interrupted their deliberations before they'd even properly begun. Many Clouds had taken care to sit where she had a clear view of the dining room's main doors, but Dillinger had apparently entered from behind her, and she hadn't seen him come in. She'd have to be more careful. If it had been any number of other people, she might have let out some important information. As it was, she was glad to see him, irritating though he was at times.

"Give us a second, and we'll find you a chair." She exited through swinging doors to the kitchen where she found Josh arranging another platter of ham. It was a small room whose narrow door opened on to an alley. In response to her inquiry, Josh pointed to a delicate looking spindle-backed chair sitting by the doorway. It didn't look quite sturdy enough for Remington, but it would have to do.

"Thanks," Many Clouds said. She picked it up, carried it back into the dining room, and gave it to Remy, who squeezed his way into a place at the table. The chair didn't collapse. She returned to her own seat as Josh entered bearing the second platter of ham.

"Now," Andy said to Dillinger, "if you've got the 'who' of this situation, give." He held up a palm like a panhandler.

But like the raconteur he was, Dillinger couldn't resist playing to a captive audience and building the suspense to its maximum.

"Well, you know that Gentry seems to be an important figure in all this, correct?" Everyone nodded. "And we suspect he wasn't acting alone."

"He has a boss somewhere," Maggie said. It was uncharacteristic of her to remain silent for as long as she had, so it was unsurprising to hear from her.

"You bet he does." Willy spoke with authority and malice, and he stabbed his new knife into the table top.

Many Clouds glanced around to see if anyone on the hotel staff had seen his action. Apparently not. "Put it away, Willy," she whispered angrily.

"Know how you feel, partner," Dillinger said. Willy re-sheathed the knife, but he had a grin on his face.

Amelia spoke next. "Will you get on with telling us something we *don't* know. And where in the world is Cooper, I wonder?"

Dillinger continued his narrative. "So, in the immediate vicinity, we have Gentry." He held up his right index finger. "We have Jacob Russell." He poked forth his second finger. "And we have Howard Weitzel." He waggled the ring finger. "Three men at the center of things. There are other people, of course. Stephanie Dove, for one."

"That whore," Amelia said. "If they've teamed up with her, the operation stinks worse than I thought."

"I'm not sure of her role. She's involved, but she's not at the center of things to the extent the others are."

"Wait a minute," Andy said. "You said these guys are in the vicinity. Isn't Weitzel in New York?"

"Not anymore." Remington smiled. "Earlier today, he was in Sacramento, but ten to one, he'll come in on the next morning train which is day after tomorrow. Then they'll every one of them be meeting right here in Placerville. Perhaps where we're sitting right now."

"Meeting about what?" Amelia asked.

"That, milady, is what we need to find out."

Willy moaned. "Is it going to be more sneaking around and eavesdropping and everything? I'm sick of it."

"Think of yourself as a secret spy," Many Clouds said. "They had hundreds of them during the war. Couldn't have won without them."

"I want to use my new knife," he said. He pulled the knife from its sheath and held it aloft with the clear intention of stabbing the table top again.

"Willy, you're getting too rambunctious with that thing." Carolyn Maxwell strode into the room. Her voice stopped him, and he returned the knife to its sheath.

"Good. Everybody here again," Ling Chu said. He'd entered from behind Many Clouds just as Remington had. Many Clouds was feeling bewildered, thinking the situation was suddenly beyond her control.

"Not quite everybody," Amelia declared. "Cooper's still missing."

"Missing? Not me. Never was." Cooper clomped in from the lobby, dusty and grimy but alive and well. He went straight to Amelia, whom he sought to embrace. She pushed him away.

"Not till you clean up your filthy self, Cooper." After a glance at his crestfallen face, she stood and said, "but I am powerful glad to see you." Then, "Oh, what the heck," and she wrapped herself around him with abandon. Everyone applauded. Then Many Clouds stood as well. She saw that the crowd had grown too large to attempt anything approaching confidentiality in this public space.

"Josh," she called. "We're going to adjourn to Andy's and my room—211. Could you send up some water? We may be there a while."

"Yes, Mrs. Maxwell. Will the other folks be needing rooms?" Carolyn turned toward Josh, then obviously realized he was addressing Many Clouds, not her. Many Clouds decided not to try and explain the complicated situation to Josh. "Ling Chu, am I correct in assuming you will have accommodations among other Chinese here in town?" She knew he would and that he would never consent to stay with the family even if they implored him. They'd tried it before.

"Yes, Many Clouds. That is so."

"And, Carolyn, you will need a room of your own?"

"Let's see how the evening progresses," she said.

"Remington?"

"Not me. I've got other fish to fry."

"So, no more rooms for now, Josh. Thank you." She stretched out her arms as if to gather everyone together and herded them toward the stairs. "Shall we proceed?"

As they started up the stairs, Carolyn found a place beside her. "Well played, my dear. But we will have to talk at some point about who's who around here, won't we?"

Many Clouds smiled, but all the fear and resentments she'd been hoarding poured from her heart like water from a hillside spring. She breathed deep, placed her hand on her baby, knowing a crucial moment was approaching, but the moment was neither here nor now.

Eighty-Two

Many Clouds was happy to have everyone finally together. She thought with their combined information and energy they stood a much better chance of winning whatever battle loomed. However, it had been a long, long day, and weariness began to seep into her bones. It was well into the evening, but the room was hot and close and redolent of sweat and dust. She asked Andy to lead the discussion, but he said she had locked herself into a leadership position and that it would disrupt the group rhythm if she gave it up now.

"I'll take notes," he said, pulling out the reporter's notebook he carried everywhere. And he kissed her. Again, in front of everyone. She was still not comfortable with this public intimacy. But at the same time, she welcomed it. She'd just have to allow the custom to rise like a spring pond with melting snow.

"Okay," she said. "Maybe we should start by listing everything we know, then decide what to do about it. Cooper, you came in late, so maybe you can start by telling us what you found out from the woodchopper."

"The man was a tough nut, but they all crack sooner or later. I'll tell you one thing, you may all think coal's at the center of all this, but that's not the half of it." The room filled with creaks and rustles as people shifted position to improve their line of sight to Cooper. "Not the half of it," he repeated.

Which was when the key fell out of the lock and the door swung open, knocking Maggie against the wall. In strode Sheriff Wilson Hilts. Not a tall man, but broad of shoulder and possessed of greenish eyes that blazed as if he were some creature from the fanciful book *The Wonderful Wizard of Oz*, which had recently taken the country by storm. He filled the doorway for a moment, then shoved his way, gun drawn, into the room to make way for his deputy, Heimholz, whom Andy had met earlier, and three other scrawny, dirty, rough-looking characters who bore the look of somnambulant hangers-on from the Hangtown Saloon.

"We're going to surround you misfits now." He waved his gun barrel as he spoke. "Sizemore." He pointed to a short man with a decided limp, "you take the window. Grinder, that corner." Another man, no taller than Sizemore, headed in the direction Hilts indicated, "and Clamper the other." Clamper sported a dirty brocade vest snugly buttoned over his large belly. The men took stations around the walls, trailing behind them the fog of body odor exuded by the unwashed. Hilts stationed himself in the doorway to make sure no one in the room had a chance to get behind him. The owner Billings was there, too, though he remained in the hallway. Many Clouds couldn't tell whether he had been an instigator of the invasion or if his presence had been coerced. It didn't matter. She was afraid now in a way she hadn't been during any of the recent events. Not during her confrontation with the mayor, not after the murder of her wagon team, not during Maggie's kidnapping. None of that seemed as ominous as this. She clung to Andy's arm, sought to shrink behind him.

"This badge," Hilts said, pointing to the star on his chest, "should speak for itself, but just in case anyone has doubts, I'm sheriff Wilson Hilts. This here beside me is deputy Ivan Heimholz, and these other fellows are my auxiliary special deputies. We received complaints of an unruly and unauthorized assembly and by God, we get here to find that the reports were true. So we're about to make some arrests."

"I assume you have some charges in mind?" Carolyn stood up from her seat on the room's only bed.

"I'll overlook most of the misdemeanors for now, Mrs. Maxwell. But first of all, this squaw needs to learn that miscegenation is a serious matter."

No one in the room needed an education about the extensive and numerous laws prohibiting non-white peoples from participating fully in American life. The discrimination against natives was perhaps worse than for any other group. No federal law existed, but state laws were virtually universal. California was no exception. It's what had kept Andy and Many Clouds from seeking an official blessing to their nuptials. Andy had thought that if they didn't apply for a marriage license, no one would bother them. Apparently not so.

"Take her, boys," the sheriff said.

Andy said nothing but wrapped his arms around Many Clouds in silent defiance of Hilt's order. He simultaneously planted a foot on the gold-filled carpet bag. Remington put his hand on his sidearm. Carolyn extended a restraining arm.

"If you do this," Carolyn asserted, "You'll regret it all your days."

The sheriff hesitated and looked at Carolyn. He smiled. "The kids, too. Wouldn't want them to be without their mama."

Two of the barfly-deputies stepped toward Maggie and Willy. Heimholz sidled in Many Clouds' direction. They moved with a casual swagger, as if they expected their prey to be cowed into submission. Things didn't work out that way. They children had been through enough dangerous situations that they reacted nearly automatically. They dropped to the floor and scrambled under the bed. The deputies leaned down and reached after them, but Willie and Maggie stood up and pushed, tipping the bed on top of one deputy and confusing the other. In the ensuing chaos, they made for the door. They avoided the flailing reach of Hilts, slipped past Billings, who made no attempt to impede their escape, then dashed down the stairs.

"Manzanita patch," Maggie yelled as they crossed the lobby, through the front doors into the night.

In the meantime, Heimholz and Hilts found themselves in a new and entirely unexpected situation. Many Clouds stood in a corner, her knife drawn, and fronted not only by the upended bed, but by Andy, Cooper, Remington, Amelia, and Carolyn. Hilts should have been dismayed, but he wasn't.

"Well, well, isn't this a tidy state of affairs? You're all under arrest. You, squaw, not only for miscegenation but now for threatening a law officer with a deadly weapon. The rest of you for interfering with a duly sworn lawman in performance of his duties." Heimholz looked back and forth between his boss and the defiant group on the other side of the room. "I know what you're thinking, deputy, and I agree we'll have some difficulty transporting everyone from here to the cells. But we don't have to. I'll stand guard outside the door along with Sizemore and Grinder here. Heimholz, we can arrange handcuffs enough for everyone, can't we?"

Heimholz grinned and held up a pair of cuffs that had been attached to his belt. "I have one pair right here and more at the office right down the street. They ought to do the job. So, then. Who wants to be first?"

Remington held out his hands. "Might as well be me. I've always sort of wondered what those felt like."

Heimholz, still grinning, looked to Hilts for confirmation. The sheriff nodded. The deputy held the cuffs high, unlocked them and stepped toward Remington. Once again, things didn't go exactly as he'd planned. Remington was so fast that no one realized what was happening until Heimholz was himself in handcuffs, his arms pinned behind his back. There was a moment of silence and seeming paralysis. Many Clouds broke the stillness. She waved her knife and advanced toward the door. Andy, carpet bag in hand, was right behind her.

"Looks as if we're leaving, Sheriff. If you would please to move aside."

But Hilts wasn't about to give up. He assumed a gunfighter's stance in the doorway, pistol drawn. Andy kicked the bed aside.

"You can't shoot all of us, Hilts. Wouldn't it be better to step out of the doorway?" he said.

"I can't shoot everyone, but I can shoot one and make a considerable mess out of some others. How about I start with you, nigger wench?" He pointed his gun at Amelia.

"Try that, you have to go through me," Cooper said and placed himself between Amelia and the deputy.

"Suit yourself, you black bastard." Heimholz cocked his pistol.

Remington, who had sneaked behind Heimholz during the confusion, shoved the deputy forward, staggering Hilts. His gun fired, and he yelled, "I'm hit."

Remington released his hold on the wounded deputy and tore the gun from the sheriff's hand. "Everybody out," he called. He now had two guns—the sheriff's and his own.

Many Clouds and Andy yelled in unison, "Let's go," as they rushed out the door. Amelia came next, followed by Cooper, who waited till Remington had exited safely, then headed down the stairs.

Many Clouds knew that their escape was but a temporary reprieve. Even with Maggie and Willy gone, there were still six of them. There should be seven, but she didn't see Ling Chu anywhere. They ran pell-mell on to the boardwalk, a disorganized gaggle unsure of what came next. Then right in front of them were Hale Gentry and his thugs, crouching behind his town car, pistols drawn.

"Hands up, everyone," Gentry said. "We need a dose of law and order here."

Eighty-Three

Remington raised both his guns.

Gentry yelled, "Drop those weapons or the squaw gets a bullet." Remington didn't throw the pistols to the ground, but he did lower his hands so that they were pointed toward his feet. Then Gentry yelled, "damn," cried out in pain, dropped his gun, and grabbed his neck. In the next moment his two henchmen did the same. Ling Chu appeared, springing from behind the vehicle and into the passenger seat.

"All go now," he yelled. "Miss Carolyn drive."

No one needed a second prompting. Close behind them, the footsteps of the full Placerville constabulary thundered as they clambered down the stairs to the lobby. The Maxwells jumped into the cars, cramming themselves into whatever space they could find, and Carolyn soon had the car moving at its top speed down Placerville's dusty main street and into the night, the carpet bag of riches on the car floor. They were fugitives now, with a list of offenses against them longer than Many Clouds could imagine. She hugged herself tight, rocked from side to side. She felt a sob rising in her throat, then stifled it and stood high in the back seat of the moving car. Andy grabbed her around the waist. She raised her fists and, in the spirit of the most savage person she'd ever known, poured out a war cry the likes of which hadn't been heard in those parts since her murderous uncle was on his rampage.

* * *

The chase was liberating and exciting, but no one thought they were home free. The immediate problems were obvious. Though the car was faster than a horse over the long haul, a good quarter horse could outrun them for a short distance. And, failing that, it wouldn't be difficult to arrange an ambush somewhere along the road. Furthermore, as Andy had proved already, the roads were full of hazards a horse could navigate easily but which could prove injurious or even fatal to a car trying to move at full speed.

"Where are we going, Ling?" Carolyn yelled.

"You find out," he answered. "Keep driving now."

But Many Clouds thought she knew what Ling Chu had in mind. "Marshal Halstad?" She spoke in as low a voice as possible and still be heard.

"I hope so," he said. He patted her knee and smiled.

On they sped, on the watch both before and behind, fearful that a posse would appear any minute. It wouldn't be long before they reached Sawtooth Wells proper. Then Halstad and safety? Without warning, Ling Chu said, "Stop now." Carolyn obediently braked to a halt.

Ling Chu said. "We walk now to Sawtooth Wells livery stable. Except you, Miss Carolyn. You keep driving."

"By myself? I'll be a sitting duck."

"We all walk. Easy to hide in bushes. They catch you, they don't dare hurt you. Everyone else not so. Money bag under skirt. They no look there. Plus, we can help Marshal Halstad." He jumped from the car. A chorus of objections arose. "No time argue. Everyone out. You here, Miss Carolyn." Carolyn responded to the urgency in his voice. The urge to drive had been mainly for amusement and convenience. Now it was turning out to be for survival.

"Now, Ling?"

"Yes, yes. Go, go," he said. "Everyone else walk fast. Maybe half hour to Sawtooth Wells, I think. Ready to hide all long time if hearing horses or automobile."

Many Clouds had always respected Ling Chu. That respect had now transformed into awe. Apparently feeling that all understood the plan and that he had done what was necessary, he dropped back and allowed the others to string out along the road. Many Clouds tugged at Andy's sleeve, and they joined him at the rear of the pack.

"How did you do it, Ling Chu?" she said.

"How I do what?"

"You know. Disarm Gentry and his men all by yourself?"

He reached into an inside pocket of the long jacket he always wore and pulled out a rolled-up cloth tied with a piece of fabric. "Needles for healing," he said. Ling Chu's use of the ancient Chinese art of acupuncture was legendary in Sawtooth Valley, so both Many Clouds and Andy knew what he was talking about. The use of the bone needles of different lengths and diameters was a complex and difficult business, and Ling Chu was a master.

Andy said, "I guess they come in handy for other purposes as well."

"Handy, yes." He replaced the roll in his jacket.

Many Clouds said. "Stop, Ling."

He obeyed and said, "What wrong?"

"Nothing at all." She cradled his chin in her hand and kissed him on the cheek.

"Not good do that," he said. "We must go." He hurried ahead of them.

"No matter what he says," Andy whispered, "I think it's a fine thing to do." He offered his cheek. Many Clouds planted a kiss there as well. They joined hands as they trotted to catch up with the rest.

Eighty-Four

"Maybe they didn't understand us," Willy said. "I thought at least Many Clouds would understand about the manzanita patch."

There was a whine in his voice, which Maggie knew surfaced only when he was exhausted or afraid. He was probably both at the moment, as was she. She meant to offer comfort, but what she said was, "Or maybe they're all in jail." Willy gave a fierce growl and hacked at the dusty ground with his knife. She laid a staying hand on his wrist. "You're just going to dull the blade so it will do us no good if we have to use it."

"I don't care." He struggled a bit. She tightened her grip. He relaxed, finally, but was almost sobbing now.

Somehow Willy's emotional disintegration strengthened her own resolve. She knelt in front of him and placed her hands on his shoulders. "I know what you're feeling, my dear brother, but we've gotten out of worse scrapes. We'll get out of this one, too."

He looked up into her eyes. Tears traced their way down his dusty cheeks. She thought how badly they both needed baths. It was a ridiculous thought considering how much danger surrounded them. She giggled.

"What are you laughing about?" Willy asked.

"I'm sorry, Willy, I can't explain. I think we've waited long enough. We should probably head back home."

"What if they come and we're not here?"

"We'll leave a message." Maggie pulled out her knife and sliced through her pants, just below the knee. She then sawed out a neat square of denim just a few inches across.

"What are your going to do?"

"Strip the bark off this trunk and carve 'home' on the wood while I hang this up," she said.

"It's too dark," Willy said.

"H-O-M-E," she said. "You can do that with your eyes closed."

While Willy grumbled and carved, she used her own knife to worry a hole in the cloth and hung it on a branch. "Now let's go."

They thought they had little chance of following the fox trail in the dark, so they decided to cross the road and head cross-country. Just as they reached the road, Willy said, "What's that?" They both froze.

"It's a car," Maggie said.

They both jumped back into the manzanita patch.

Maggie said, "We better wait till it passes."

The car was speeding through the night. Its headlights resembled the eyes of a mythical beast. Maggie put a protective arm around her brother, though she was trembling inside as well. The lights flashed by, dust roiling around the vehicle, fuming with gasoline and oil.

"Wait," Willy said. "Wasn't that Gentry's car?"

"Looked like it," Maggie said. "But I swear Grandma Carolyn was driving."

"And did you see Many Clouds?"

"Maybe. I'm not sure. But I think we should change our plans and follow the car."

"In the dark?"

"We can't exactly keep up, but there aren't many places for them to turn off, and if we lose them, we can always go on to the house."

"Is this one of those times?" Willy asked.

"What times?"

"When we have to act like we're grown up even though we aren't?"

"I guess so. Come on along." She grabbed his hand and they jogged off in the direction of the red dots of the car's disappearing lights.

Eighty-Five

So anxious were those who had exited the car to get to Sawtooth Wells and safety that they proceeded at a jog as long as they could. Soon, however, Amelia in her skirts and petticoats began to lag. Cooper, loath to leave her behind, reduced his pace to match hers. Even Many Clouds began to falter a bit.

It was Remington who finally called a halt.

"We need a breather," he said when they were finally gathered together once more. "And I have a suggestion. Gentry and Hilts and a posse are sure to be along any time now. I could stay here and delay them. Maybe enough to make sure you all get to Sawtooth Wells safe and sound. How about it?"

Andy and Many Clouds glanced at one another, each reading the suspicion in the other's eyes. Neither had been a hundred percent sure of Remington's loyalty for some time, but he'd always managed to talk his way past all doubts. He seemed to guess their objections before they spoke them.

"I know I've been a bit of a wild card, but I think I've proved myself. Still and all, if you want me to stick with the group, I'll stay."

Many Clouds hesitated only briefly. Even if Dillinger used this as an opportunity to betray them and join up with their adversaries, any negotiations they'd have to go through with him would take some time. Something they sorely lacked.

Andy said, "I'm not so sure, Remy."

Many Clouds intervened without consulting her fiancé. "Do it, Remy. Leave one of your guns with us and delay those men as long as you can. And thank you. Everyone else this way."

As they walked, she explained her reasoning to Andy. He smiled and nodded. "I understand why you didn't take time to consult, but you had me upset for a minute."

She squeezed his hand and picked up her pace, checking over her shoulder to see how the others were doing. Amelia had lifted her skirts to her knees and tied them in front, the bottom ruffles of her bloomers peeking out from the skirt bottoms. Many Clouds was sure that she was exposing far more undergarment than her normal modesty would have permitted, but they picked up some speed as a result. Amid the sounds of their own heavy breathing and shuffling feet they hurried toward what they hoped would be safety and a chance to rest. They were aching, sweating, and completely out of breath when the dark shadow of the livery stable took shape against the darkness.

"We're going to make it, love," Andy said. He turned to the trailing group. "We're there," he called. "Look." He pointed to the building he and Many Clouds had just sighted.

"Thank the Lord," Amelia groaned and sank to the ground.

"Little early for that, Aunt Amelia," Andy said.

Then the ground began to tremble and the sound of galloping hooves shattered the silence.

Cooper slid his arms under his wife's. "Not free yet, Amelia. Jump up and run."

Eighty-Six

"I can't run no more, Maggie." Willy dropped to the ground.

"Any more," Maggie said. "But at least get out of the road."

Willy rose to his feet and shuffled toward a large ponderosa. Then they heard shouts and felt the ground shake. Their shuffling turned to a sprint, and they were able to duck behind the huge trunk just before a half-dozen or more horsemen galloped past them.

"There's why Andy and Many Clouds couldn't come meet us," Maggie said. "Everyone's chasing them."

"You think we should still head home?" He picked at a hunk of pitch that the tree had squeezed out of its trunk. He broke it off and started chewing on it.

"You know we don't like you to do that, Willy, but never mind. Way I see it now, things have changed. We're not too far from Sawtooth Wells. We might be okay there between Marshal Halstad and Bridget."

"But what if Gentry and the rest of them are waiting for us?"

"And what if they've got someone watching the house and have conked Emmanuel on the head? Sawtooth Wells is closer and we've got people there we can trust. We probably should have headed this way before."

"But we left that message that said 'home.'"

"Home is a long way off right now, and wouldn't we be better off if we could find our folks now that we know they didn't get hurt or tossed in jail?"

"Then let's not wait around." Willy leaped to his feet and trotted toward Sawtooth Wells. Maggie soon caught up with him. Between breaths, Willy said, "I can't believe I'm saying this, but I'm so dirty, stinky, and sweaty I can't wait to get into a warm bath."

"You look like my brother, but for sure you're someone else," Maggie answered.

"Yeah, I'm the one who can run faster than you ever thought." He took off in a sprint. Maggie grinned and kept a steady pace, knowing he'd soon tire and they'd be once more running together.

Eighty-Seven

"I count six," Carolyn said. "What do you two say?" The moon was dim, so shadows and movement were all they could see. She had successfully driven Gentry's automobile all the way to the Sawtooth Wells livery stable, parked it in a stall deep inside, then covered it with a tarpaulin. As it turned out, no one had intercepted them so the group could have all ridden with her. Well, they had no way of knowing that at the time they'd decided to walk.

She'd then posted herself at the hayloft door, a vantage point from which she could keep watch over the quiet of Sawtooth Wells asleep in the night. It had been a long while since she'd spent time amid the sweet and pungent atmosphere of mown hay, and despite the anxiety of the situation, she had enjoyed the respite.

Now that the group had finally arrived, though, she was geared for action. She helped get everyone into the hayloft. The carpetbag safely buried under several hay bales and sacks of grain. It was a safe hiding place until they could get it to the Circle M. Ling Chu was out looking for Halstad. Gentry and his crew had entered town not long after The Maxwells. No one was sure what would happen next.

"I see six as well," Andy said. "Hilts, his deputy, Gentry and his two thugs, and Remington."

"What do you suppose happened to Hilts's so-called auxiliary deputies?" Many Clouds said.

"I'm not surprised they weren't part of this little cavalry. They didn't look much like horsemen to me," Andy said.

"They didn't look like they could stay upright long enough to cross the street," Carolyn said. "But people can surprise you. What about Gentry's thugs?"

"They could be skulking around here, but my best guess is that they're keeping watch at the Cary House in case we circle back."

Four of the six riders had split up and were systematically looking street by street, house by house. Hilts had dismounted and was pounding on the door of Marshal Halstad's office. It was not Halstad's custom to sleep in his office, but he always left word on his door so he could be available. Hilts apparently didn't see or read the message. More likely, he was happy to claim no knowledge of it. He descended the steps and remounted. "They have to be in the livery stable. It would be just like that new owner McPhail to hook up with the Maxwell woman," Hilts told his compatriots.

"And we're here to put a stop to all that," Remington said.

"You said it, Remy. You and the rest surround the place. I'll just go right in the front door."

"Remington." Many Clouds said. "He's been with them all along."

"And we've been paying him to spy on us," Andy said.

"But are we surprised?" Carolyn asked. "We always were suspicious of him."

"Why did he get shot, then, if he's on their side?" Many Clouds asked.

"Mistaken identity? Part of the plot? Who knows?" Carolyn said.

"Neither one," Cooper said. "Woodcutter told me Remy didn't like the smell of things. He wanted out. They wouldn't let him. Shot him when he tried to ride away."

"They?" Many Clouds said.

"Woodcutter didn't know. All he knew was someone had the notion to kill him but got overruled by someone else who thought it was better to have him alive and working both sides." The eastern sky had begun to show some pink, lightening the crests of the dark hills. "But we're out of time to be talking."

As if to affirm Cooper's declaration, Hilts walked his horse to the stable entrance and called, "McPhail. Clyde McPhail. Are you in there?"

Silence.

"We know you've been curled up on your filthy cot. And we know you've got the Maxwells holed up in there. You're harboring fugitives. Come out. Them and you together. Hands high."

"Hilts. What the hell do you think you're doing?" Michael Halstad emerged from the back of the Jensen's Family Café and strode down the street, tucking in his shirt. The whole town knew of Halstad's involvement with Madge Jensen, but it was one of those small town situations that everyone preferred to ignore because of their affection for both parties.

"Hello, Michael." Hilts grinned like a snake oil salesman. "Glad you're here. Tried to rouse you earlier. We pursued some escapees to McPhail's stable. Be glad for your help in rounding them up."

"First of all, 'marshal' is my official title, and I'd prefer you used that rather than my Christian name. Second of all, just who are you after?"

"Carolyn Maxwell for one. She and her Chinaman stole Hale Gentry's automobile, and they were last seen driving it in this direction. She might have gone on to the Circle M, but it's more likely we'll find the car inside."

"Come on down off that horse, please, sheriff. I'd love to hear the rest."

"I'd prefer to remain mounted, Michael, if you don't mind. Never can tell with these people when I might need to take out in a hurry."

"Suit yourself. Who else are you after, and what are what are you planning to charge them with?"

Many Clouds sighted a shadowy figure in skirts slip out of the back of the café and head toward the church.

"Andrew Maxwell and that squaw of his are guilty of miscegenation and a bundle of other more violent offenses. Those little half-breed kids belong on the rancheria in a wikiup instead of living in a house like they were white. And that nigger aunt and uncle of Andrew's have been aiding and abetting through the whole affair. Now, are you going to help arrest them, or do we have to do it ourselves?"

"You have the warrants on you?" Halstad said.

"Come on, Michael. You know we don't need a warrant when we're in hot pursuit."

"Doesn't look to me like you're in hot pursuit. Just sitting in the saddle far as I can see. Now I'd appreciate if you'd just head on out of my town. Come on back when you have the paperwork."

Hilts drew his pistol. "Not your town any more, Michael. Now if you'll just stand down, we'll be going about our lawful business."

Halstad was the most mild-mannered of men, particularly for a marshal. However, Hilts's words brought a flush to his face. He stepped forward, pointed his finger. "You have no authority here no matter how shiny your badge is. Now move on out before I—"

The next series of events happened so quickly they seemed almost simultaneous. Hilts fired, and Halstad dropped. There was a scream. Madge

Jensen emerged from behind her café and ran toward her fallen lover. Another shot. Hilts fell backwards from his horse, which trotted off, dragging his rider, whose foot had gotten entangled in a stirrup. One more shot, and Remington lay face down in the doorway of the livery stable.

"Son of a bitch," Amelia said. Cooper looked at her.

"Yeah, son of a bitch," he said.

"Once said is enough. You don't need to keep on."

"We need to get down there, though." They followed Andy and Many Clouds down the ladder.

Many Clouds, Carolyn, and Andy knelt before Halstad, who had taken a bullet to the neck and bled to death in short order, blood spurting from a severed artery. Hot tears welled up in Many Clouds eyes, and in her blurred vision she saw that both Andy and Carolyn were in a similar state of shock. Madge was sobbing like an abandoned child. Her daughter, Bridget, had arrived and was trying to comfort her, though she herself was too agitated to comfort anyone else.

Bridget had apparently raised the alarm before the gunshots sounded, and a sizeable group of citizens was walking toward the scene. Among them, Many Clouds noted, was Clyde McPhail, the livery stable's owner. He had somehow concealed himself during the shooting, but he appeared now. She didn't hold his hiding against him. He had hosted them at his own peril after all.

The deputy Heimholz had retrieved Hilts's horse and freed his boss's foot. Apparently, the sheriff was not dead, but the stain on his chest proclaimed that his demise was imminent. Hale Gentry stood over Remington Dillinger while Cooper approached, Andy close behind him.

"The man killed the sheriff," Gentry said. "This is what happens to the lawless."

"Lawless. You're one to talk," Cooper said.

"Watch your mouth, nigger," he said.

Cooper ignored him and gently turned Remington over. He had taken a bullet to the abdomen but had survived so far. Cooper removed his bandanna and uncovered a nasty-looking hole just above the man's belly button.

Remington tried to speak, managing to whisper a few words. Cooper put his ear to the man's lips, trying to catch what he said. "Knew this was a dirty business, tried to stop it, but they threatened the kids. Everyone. Watch out for—"

Another shot. This one caught Remington in the forehead. "He was going for a hidden gun," Gentry said.

Cooper stood. "No sucha thing. That was cold-blooded murder."

"Just you and me, nigger, and the court won't allow you to testify against a white man."

Cooper drew back a fist, but Andy caught his arm. "Let's bide our time, Coop. I heard and saw the same things you did."

Gentry smiled at them, a cat licking his lips over an empty bowl of cream, while he reloaded. Carolyn approached, her skirt bloody and dirty from caring for Halstad.

"Hello, Carolyn. Where's my car?" Gentry said.

"Just when I thought you could go no lower, Hale. But you've overstepped this time."

"Overstepped? No, I think you'll find this is not an overstep, but just the first step. Sheriff Heimholz? Don't you think it's time you took command of the situation?"

Heimholz, who had been standing over the body of his boss, snapped his head up, as if he'd been sleepwalking. "Uh, yes. Yes. Boys, you can take these bodies to Placerville to the ice house. We'll bring in the coroner?"

He looked to Gentry for confirmation. Gentry nodded.

As if guided by a single impulse, Many Clouds, Andy, and Carolyn gathered and stood around Halstad's body. Madge was still on her knees and bowed over him, though her sobbing had subsided somewhat. Bridget had a hand on her shoulder.

"We're taking charge of Marshal Halstad's body," Andy said. "The coroner can find him at the Circle M."

Heimholz hesitated, looked to Gentry, who stood mute. "It's kind of irregular, I think. But special circumstances and all. I suppose…" His voice trailed off into uncertainty.

"Maybe you should have them sign a receipt just to keep things on the up and up," Gentry said.

"We're signing nothing," Andy said.

"And send the coroner," Carolyn added. "Alone. None of you are going to touch him."

Heimholz stepped in their direction. Many Clouds stepped toward him, followed closely by Andy and Carolyn. Shortly afterward, a contingent of townsfolk moved forward surrounding the corpse of a man they regarded almost with reverence. Presently, a rotund fellow in a plaid shirt and canvas pants raised his arms, turned his back on Heimholz, and faced the mourners gathered around Halstad. Many Clouds looked at Andy, a question in her eyes.

"Bill Slater. He's the reverend of the town church," he whispered. She nodded.

"Let us pray," Slater said. They all bowed their heads. Even Hale Gentry followed suit, after a pause.

Many Clouds listened to the preacher's words and felt genuine sorrow for Michael Halstad's death. However, what was most on her mind was what had happened to Maggie and Willy. When the prayer was over, she raised her eyes. As if in answer to her concern, she saw her children peeking out from the very hayloft the rest of them had occupied a few minutes earlier. She nudged Andy and signaled him to look upward as well.

He smiled.

Eighty-Eight

Over the years, the Circle M had been through a host of attacks ranging from gun battles to arson. Its founder, Carter Maxwell, Carolyn's father and Andy's grandfather, built the place with the idea that the ranch should be as self-sufficient as possible. He had started construction in 1864, a year when automobiles were not even imagined and five years before the transcontinental railroad had linked the east and west coasts. Materials and skilled labor were hard to come by. Roads were primitive.

In addition to his own sawmill, Carter had constructed an ice house. Each fall, crews ascended to Shingle Lake, lying at an altitude about two thousand feet higher than the ranch house, and sawed out large cubes of ice. When Folsom Prison opened in 1880, Carter was able to employ convicts for that duty, along with many other tasks on the ranch. "Employ" might have been a generous word for how the men were pressed into service, given the political connections Carter had cultivated by that time, but the truth of the matter was never revealed or even spoken of. The solid blocks, enough to last till the following winter, were then hauled back to the yard, piled in the ice house, and insulated by sawdust from the sawmill. A steady stream of settlers populated the valley after the Civil War ended, and they depended on the Circle M mill for their lumber, so the supply of sawdust was abundant. As the population increased and other mills opened, the demand for Circle M lumber decreased, as did the supply of sawdust, but the need for ice didn't diminish. Thus, as he did in so many other matters, Carter Maxwell came up with a novel solution.

Contemplating how many items of warm clothing were manufactured from wool, he overcame his cattleman's natural aversion to sheep and set aside some acreage for raising the animal most cattle ranchers regarded as a scourge. He thus assured himself a steady supply of wool and used it to insulate the ice house. Carolyn had continued her father's practice right down to the present day. And it was in the ice house that they laid Marshal Michael Halstad, swaddled in blankets like a newborn baby.

Once done, a small group who followed them from Sawtooth Wells gathered at the site similar to the manner in which they'd gathered in the street outside the livery stable. Ling Chu had emerged after the gunfight, and, as usual, presented himself in a most uncustomary way. No sooner had a discussion begun about how best to transport Halstad's remains than the chugging of an automobile emerged from the stable. In short order, Ling Chu pulled up alongside the body, and Cooper and Andy and Carolyn and Many Clouds lifted it into the car's back seat. Somehow Ling had managed to sneak the carpet bag in beside it. Predictably, Hale Gentry ran up on the scene, objecting loudly.

"Hey, that's my car. You can't take it."

"You'll get it back, Hale, when we're through with it. In the meantime, take a hike and don't bother us."

Surprisingly, the man backed off. "If there's any damage, you'll pay, Carolyn."

"We've already paid more than we could ever owe you, Hale Gentry. Go crawl back in your cave and leave us to mourn a man who is greater than you could imagine."

Eighty-Nine

During the first part of the journey back to the Circle M, Many Clouds wondered if she'd ever feel safe again. Then she decided it didn't matter whether she felt safe or not. Whatever threatened, her sense of security was up to herself, her friends, her family, not to people like Hale Gentry. The attitude inspired a sense of freedom, even elation, for her. She'd certainly been challenged and beleaguered enough over the years. Pursued by a fake preacher and barely escaped from him and his "deacon" with not a stitch on her back. She thought of poor Maggie and her recent travails. They had that ugly memory to share. When she met Maggie and Willy, she'd been lying half-conscious, singed by a wildfire in a dry creek bed. She'd survived all that and more. She was tougher for it. However, her recent years and months with Andy had been sheltered and secure, and she was about to become responsible for a new life as well as her own. She supposed she'd lost the edge that kept her on the lookout for danger. Now, that edge had returned, and despite the dark aura that accompanied it, she welcomed it. And so, she felt, did the new life inside her.

Not that she was in any danger at the moment. Michael Halstad's body was stored in the ice house, the carpet bag of cash wrapped in canvas beneath him. And it was good to be sitting here in the Circle M's expansive dining room as they gathered for an early supper and planning session. They'd spent too much time scattered hither and yon, wondering about one another's whereabouts and safety. Ling Chu managed somehow to put together a meal of cheese, cold beef, apple slices, and potato salad. Perfect antidotes for their ravenous hunger. But as much time as she'd spent at the Circle M, it had never felt exactly like home. She longed for the little house she shared with her new family. She once again scanned the room to make sure Maggie, Willy, and Andy were near.

"Well, fellow fugitives," she said, "let's lift a glass to what's next." Everyone smiled and sipped, Maggie and Willy drinking their apple juice the way the adults drank their wine.

"Now," Andy said, "what *is* next? Cooper tell us what you got out of the woodcutter."

"Like I said, whoever's behind this, they don't care about no coal."

"Then why all the threats? Why buy up all these farms?" Carolyn asked.

Amelia raised her hand like a school girl. Everyone turned her way. "Plain as the nose on my dark freckled face, you all. They buying up land because they want land."

Silence. Everyone shared looks around the table. Carolyn broke the impasse. "Brilliant, Amelia. And, as you said, simple."

"This woman getting too smart for me," Cooper said. "I need some more of that meat. Pass it on over."

"You could say 'please'," Amelia rebuked him.

"Not enough time the way you gaining on me." Cooper smiled as Maggie handed him the platter of beef.

"But what about all those assay reports?" Many Clouds said. She was a bit perturbed that all her efforts to smuggle the paperwork out of city hall had gone for naught. "They meant nothing?"

"Not so," Andy said. He paused, keeping them all waiting while he finished munching on an apple and washing it down with a swallow of dark wine. "They're after something, all right, but not what we thought."

"What do they want, then?" Carolyn asked.

"I don't know exactly, but I suspect their main purpose was to send us looking in the wrong direction."

Many Clouds had a thought, one that struck her powerfully in middle of swallowing. She had to cough and gulp water to regain her equilibrium. When she was finished, though, she was smiling. "We didn't get all the reports. Just that one page. What if there's coal, but not enough to make it worth mining? That might mean Amelia's more than right. They want the land. But if not for mining, why?"

Carolyn spoke while refilling her wine glass. "Maybe they're thinking about mining something else, or maybe they have something else entirely in mind. Andy, you said this man Weitzel who heads up the mining company is from New York, correct?" Andy nodded.

"And he's supposedly arriving in Placerville on tomorrow morning's train from Sacramento," she said. "So the whole plot could be coming to a head before we know it, maybe too late for us to do anything about it."

Ling Chu had entered with a fresh platter of meat. As he placed it on the table, he said, "Not too late. Mr. Gentry help."

"The car," Many Clouds said.

The sound of hoofbeats from the ranch yard interrupted the conversation. Everyone rushed to the veranda to see what was happening. Amelia grabbed Maggie and Willy to keep them inside.

Outside, Carolyn and Andy encountered five mounted men, Gentry in the lead. Carolyn carried a .30-.30 rifle, a weapon she had used and trusted for decades. Andy's .44 double-action revolver was ensconced in a holster on his hip. Two riderless horses followed behind the five, doubtless to tow the car if it had been rendered undriveable. Gentry had come prepared.

"You're trespassing again, Gentry," Carolyn said. "I was careful to miss you the last time. This time I'll be careful not to."

"Well look at this," Gentry said. "A gang of niggers, redskins, and children making out like they could hold out against a real posse. You stole my car. I want it back."

"Last warning." Carolyn levered a cartridge into the chamber and raised the rifle to her shoulder. "Whatever else happens to the rest of us, you're going to go first." It looked as if she'd either have to back down or actually shoot Gentry.

Many Clouds could see she didn't want to do either one. She decided to speak up. She didn't know for sure if it was the right thing to do, but she sensed that Ling Chu would be able to handle the cue she was about to give him. "Ling Chu knows where it is, don't you Ling?"

Ling Chu smiled, and Many Clouds knew she'd hit her target.

"I show you," Ling Chu said. "You follow." He tripped down the front steps with a briskness that belied his age and headed toward the main barn.

Everyone else watched Gentry swing his horse about and trot in Ling Chu's direction. "Come back here you slant-eyed devil," he yelled. He looked as if he were intent on running the older man down. They'd almost reached the barn when Ling Chu suddenly reversed direction, tore off the small black beanie he always wore and swung it flapping toward the horse's eyes. He let loose a banshee wail the likes of which no one had ever heard him utter before. The animal stopped, snorted, and flared away from the new threat. Incongruously, Many Clouds saw something that almost made her laugh out loud. None of them had ever seen Ling Chu bareheaded. Under his beanie, he was bald as a river rock.

But she had no time to savor the humor of the moment. Gentry wasn't thrown from the saddle, but it cost him some time and effort to control his horse. In the meantime, Ling Chu disappeared into the darkness of the barn.

Andy gave Many Clouds a look of concern. They'd both seen Ling Chu drive Gentry's car into the barn. For Gentry to discover the machine would not only give him great satisfaction but slow down their attempts to disrupt whatever Western Exploration had in mind for the next day's meeting in Placerville. Many Clouds smiled and nodded to Andy to reassure him. She didn't know what Ling Chu was doing, but she trusted it would be to their advantage.

By the time Gentry calmed his horse, Ling Chu reappeared from the barn. "Car gone," he said. "Somebody steal it, you bet."

"Where is it, then?" Gentry was angry.

"Don't know. Parked it inside. Now gone. Look for yourself."

They waited a couple of anxious minutes while Gentry rode into the barn. When he reappeared, he said. "I'm asking one more time. Where is it?"

"You heard the man," Andy said. "We don't know."

"It's somewhere on this ranch, and I'm going to find it. Spread out, boys."

"Not so fast," Carolyn said. She'd lowered the rifle when Gentry entered the barn, but she lifted it back up to her shoulder now and pointed the barrel directly at Gentry.

"Come back with the law and a signed search warrant," she said. "Till then, my original warning stands."

Gentry stared a full minute, then apparently decided not to risk her pulling the trigger. "You're only delaying the inevitable, Carolyn," he said.

"The name's Mrs. Maxwell."

"Let's go, men," he said. He slow-walked his horse under the archway and out of the yard.

Ninety

Many Clouds was making sure that Willy and Maggie were comfortable, settled for the night, and ready for the next day. They generally left some clothes at the Circle M to accommodate their frequent visits, but they hadn't visited for a few months and had outgrown the spare garments. Thus, Ling Chu was scrubbing the filthy pants and shirts they'd worn for the last couple of days. The children were dressed for bed in oversized nightgowns culled from Carolyn's wardrobe.

"Hop in now, kids. It's late, and you're up at sunrise, remember."

As they shuffled their way to their separate cots, careful not to trip over their comically long trains, Willy said, "You're a genius, Many Clouds."

"Ha," she said. "You must have been sneaking some of the dinner wine when I wasn't looking."

"No, truly," Maggie said. "You're the one who figured out we couldn't take the car all the way into town like we planned because we'd get ambushed. Putting it in the shearing shed instead of the livery stable barn. That was the genius part."

"I'm not the only one who figured it out. I was just the first one to say it out loud."

"Well, what about taking the back trail instead of the main road into town?"

"That was obvious, but it won't work unless we get our early start."

The normal road into Sawtooth Wells and thence to Placerville took a couple of hours on horseback. The back trail that climbed the slope behind the Circle M and passed just below Shingle Lake before it intersected with the main road added at least another half-hour to the trip, depending on intervening hazards. The trail was subject to interruptions from landslides and washouts thanks to the myriad springs that gushed spontaneously and unpredictably from the hillside. They'd have left before dawn, but this was not a trail to attempt in darkness.

The plan now was that Carolyn would leave mid-morning with Ling Chu, retrieving Gentry's car from the shearing shed and driving down the main road. Andy and Many Clouds would ride horses over the back trail. They were gambling that the pair wouldn't be harmed even if they were hijacked. This was Andy's idea, and Many Clouds had objected that they were splitting their forces once again. In the middle of her argument, though, she had stopped to reconsider. Their enemies would be scattered as well, and the sight of their adversaries apparently delivering themselves into their hands would certainly confuse matters for them. They regretted leaving Marshal Halstad's remains behind but left word with Amelia and Cooper where to locate them in case the coroner came by. He was to be buried in the Maxwell family plot downslope from the ranch house as soon as legal constraints were removed. Andy and Many Clouds wanted to leave Maggie and Willy behind but soon realized the precocious children might follow on their own.

"What if—" Willy yawned before he could finish the sentence.

"What if you went to sleep?" Many Clouds kissed them both. Andy entered the room then, delivered his own good nights, extinguished the kerosene lantern. They left the room. They needed some sleep themselves and tomorrow promised to be a crucial juncture in this fight for home and hearth.

Ninety-One

Many Clouds, Andy, and the children hitched their horses in the secluded grove they customarily used to tie their wagon when they went to town. October was often a warm month in the foothills, but this day was exceptionally so. Their ride from the Circle M had been hazard-free, partly because most of the springs had gone dormant in the third year of one of the region's frequent droughts. They'd run low on water, and all four of them were thirsty. Luckily, the roadside creek still held some pools of water, and Willy and Maggie climbed down the bank to refill the canteens.

"Do you have cash?" Andy asked.

"Why? You're here."

"We've talked about this so often. You're a grownup woman. You have to be prepared. Here."

Reluctantly, she took the bills Andy proffered. Some of her frontier habits died hard. In the woods or on the plains she could be self-sufficient as anyone. But there was a small part of her that still resisted fully joining the white world, illogical though she knew her reluctance to be.

After that, they headed for the Cary House. They made no attempt to hide or sneak but walked boldly down the sidewalk. Many Clouds carried her satchel, filled with the papers she'd lifted from the city hall office. Andy had a rucksack with the various deeds he'd discovered at the county office in Auburn. If Heimholz or anyone else accosted them on their way, they would invite their foe to meet at the hotel where they would reveal new information, which information would come forth only at a later trial if someone threatened to jail them.

"Look, Andy." Many Clouds pointed at Gentry's car parked in front of the Cary House. Carolyn and Ling Chu had arrived.

"So far, so good," Andy said. He grabbed Willy's hand while Many Clouds threw an arm around Maggie's shoulders.

Loud voices greeted them when they entered the lobby, though the voices were not directed at them. Instead, Carolyn was engaged in a heated discussion with Mayor George James.

"Hale Gentry? Sheriff? That would be like making Jack the Ripper the warden of Folsom prison." Andy had seldom heard her screaming the way she was doing now.

"Given the present circumstances, the appointment is within my authority and responsibility. It will stand until an election can be held."

Hale Gentry stood behind the mayor, a smug grin on his face as he pinned a badge to the lapel of his frock coat.

Carolyn threw her hands in the air and turned in frustration, nearly knocking into Andrew as she stomped away.

"Mother, what's happened?"

"It seems Heimholz has disappeared. Speculation is that he couldn't handle the pressure of the new job and took off for parts unknown. I have other suspicions, but there's no time to act on them. You see what the good mayor has done to fill the vacancy. Weitzel and Russell are inside getting ready for a so-called conference, probably designed to commit some fraud or another."

Andy instinctively placed a protective arm around Many Clouds, who stiffened with a mixture of fear and anger. They'd been hoping to expose the skullduggery of the mining interests and uproot the influence of Gentry and his minions. It now seemed that he was more firmly ensconced than ever. Then things got worse.

"You're under arrest," Gentry called while making a come-hither motion with his arm. From out of nowhere, Gentry's thugs and the two "deputies" who had ridden with Hilts the day before appeared and surrounded the Maxwell group. In no time, Andy and Carolyn were in handcuffs. The men had gone after Carolyn and Andy first in teams of two, apparently assuming that Many Clouds and the children would be comparatively easy marks. Their assumption was erroneous.

Many Clouds, Maggie, and Willy sensed the danger immediately. Instead of freezing in fear, they sprang into action. Many Clouds lowered her shoulder and rammed into the kidney of one of the deputies who was handcuffing Andy, then scampered away. Willy levered a kick at the knee of one of Carolyn's captors while Maggie aimed a similar blow at the crotch of the other. In short order, the lawmen and their victims were sprawled on the boardwalk in a comical tangle of limbs and yelling. Carolyn and Andy were in custody, but Many Clouds and the children were suddenly nowhere in sight.

"After them, you fools," Gentry yelled. "We'll handle these prisoners."

Ninety-Two

Many Clouds and the children needed no plan to send them to the grove where the horses were tied. They all took different routes, but they reunited in short order.

"What are we going to do?" Willy's voice had a whine to it, and tears puddled his eyes to an extent Many Clouds had seldom seen. Even Maggie, who was always ready for a fight, had a hangdog look about her.

"We've got to get out of here," she said. "I don't want to go to jail."

"But Andy and Grandma Carolyn are in jail," Willy whined.

"Not for long, but it's up to us to help get them out," Many Clouds said. Amazingly, she was not discouraged at all. She knew exactly what they should do.

"We're not running and we're not going to jail," she said. "Now buck up and follow me." Everything on the street looked normal and calm. The air was warm and dusty, filled with aromas of gasoline and manure as a mix of wagons and automobiles traversed the streets. A few storefronts to the right, the Hangtown Saloon inhaled and exhaled its regular stream of businessmen and bums.

Many Clouds' first stop was the telegraph office. She directed the children to conceal themselves outside while she resumed the same submissive posture she had used to skulk her way into the mayor's office.

The office was small, the counter only a couple of steps inside the door. The clerk was an older man with a handlebar mustache and a pipe in his mouth. The smoke was so strong it burned her eyes. She suspected there was more than tobacco in the mix. He had his feet on his desk and a newspaper in his hands. He lowered it when she entered, then raised it back up when he saw who had come in.

"This is a telegraph office, squaw. Wrong place for the likes of you."

"Please, sir. Telegram please?"

He sighed, stood, and shoved a yellow form across the counter. "Don't know what good this'll do you since you got to be able to write."

"I know. Will try my best."

"Need cash, too," he added.

She nodded, started printing. She used her left hand instead of her accustomed right to make her printing appear as semi-literate as possible.

TO PINKERTON MAN SACRAMNTO REMY DIE STOP HELP HANGTON PLEZ STOP

She passed the form back to the clerk, who read it with a rueful smile as he shook his head. "You want to send this to the Pinkerton Detective Agency in Sacramento?"

Many Clouds nodded vigorously and smiled as if overjoyed that she'd managed to communicate.

"I think you're wasting your money. This makes no sense."

"But I must send right away. How much?"

"Well, it's your money, but I wouldn't expect an answer."

"No answer. Just please send?"

She paid, then waited the few minutes it took him to activate his key and click away. The telegram finished, the clerk picked up his newspaper and resumed his indolent slouch behind the desk without another word to her. All she could do now was hope her message bore fruit.

Next, instead of heading away from the hotel where all their adversaries had gathered, she steered the children right back in the direction of their conflict, explaining as she went. The children followed reluctantly, but they were forced to keep up with her hurried stride if only to hear what she was saying.

"When I went back to get that spare chair yesterday, I saw there's a back entrance to the dining room through the kitchen. We're going to join this conference."

As they approached the hotel, Many Clouds stayed the children with a gesture and slowly approached the kitchen door. Again, she was amazed that all appeared quiet and ordinary. Across the street in front of the Hangtown Saloon, a ragged Indian held his battered cavalry hat out for money. Whether he'd earned the hat as an army scout or simply recovered it from some discard pile she didn't know, but he made a pitiable sight that wrenched her heart. There was plenty of misery lurking beneath this calm.

Sticking close to the building, they filtered into the alley. The main door to the kitchen was open. Only an unlatched screen door barred the way. Pressing close, she saw two women working at tall tables and two or three others bustling around. She pulled the screen door open enough to squeeze through while at the same time beckoning the children closer. Then the door squeaked. She and the children froze.

"Act as if we belong," Many Clouds whispered. They resumed their hurried way, and sure enough, none of the workers in the kitchen challenged them as they trouped through. Instead, cooks and waitstaff concentrated on preparing the noon meal as if the intruders weren't there. From her own experience, Many Clouds was certain they knew it was dangerous to get involved in matters outside the scope of their employers' instructions. She stopped as they approached the entrance to the dining room.

"*Perdóneme*," came a voice behind them. Two women, both of them short and solid-looking, carried trays of drinks past them and through the swinging doors into the dining room. Housekeeping was commonly thought of as lightweight labor. However, Many Clouds knew different, and the robust appearance of these two waitresses was testimony against the widespread misconception.

The voice of Jacob Russell suddenly filled the room, booming as if he were addressing a crowd of thousands instead of the small group gathered around the table in a hotel dining room. While he held forth, everybody would be focused on him. A good time to make an entrance.

A bar ran half the length of the dining room on the opposite side from where the men were seated. Many Clouds figured it would be a perfect place to conceal themselves until the right moment. They made it to cover without incident, and she was able to peek across the bar to assess the situation.

Her eye fell automatically on a dapper fellow, short and slight of build, with erect carriage and impeccable attire. His brocade waistcoat and carefully arranged cravat gave him an air of authority that belied his stature. Weitzel for sure. At his side sat another frock-coated fellow Many Clouds didn't know but who looked vaguely familiar. She couldn't place him, but something about him disturbed her. She shoved her misgivings aside as unimportant compared to what was about to transpire. Then there was the mayor. Since the table was round, none of the men was, properly speaking, at the head of the session, but Jacob Russell was clearly in charge, glad-handing everyone, directing them where to sit. His sycophant, Miles, made sure there were enough chairs and that they were arranged just as Russell wanted them. She supposed that Gentry and the other fake lawmen were at the jail house.

"Well, now that the little family drama is over," Russell declared, "we can get down to business, eh, Mr. Weitzel?" Weitzel nodded. "Yes indeed. Now, we've told you about the rich coal deposits in the area, but I don't believe you've had the opportunity to see the latest scientific reports. Miles?"

Miles rose and began passing out folders containing multiple sheets of paper. Russell continued speaking while the distribution continued. "We've secured mineral rights to much of the land referred to in the assays. All we need is a few more square miles, and Western Explorations will be able to begin delivering massive amounts of coal to Sacramento and beyond."

Weitzel spoke next. "Even a superficial glance shows that these assays are impressive. Of course, I'll want to see for myself, which is why I came all the way from New York. Paper counts for a great deal, but there's no substitute for an on-site inspection."

Many Clouds gulped, took a breath, and stepped forward. "Mr. Russell, did you say there are coal deposits all around us?"

Russell raised both arms, as if he were being held up. "Whoa, now. What are you doing here? Miles, run and get Gentry. This squaw is a fugitive. She needs to be arrested." Miles jumped to his feet, but Weitzel intervened before Russell's minion could start for the jail.

"It's all right for now, Jacob. I don't like doing business in a cloud of suspicion and mistrust of the kind that's been swirling around us this afternoon. The project Western Explorations is engaged in here is legitimate, and the more people know about it the easier it will be."

"But—" Russell spluttered to a stop. Weitzel was smiling, not only at Russell but at Many Clouds. He seemed to truly want this to be a harmonious process.

"Okay. Somewhat irregular," Russell said, "but okay." They all sat down except Many Clouds.

"Now," Weitzel said. "You—what's your name, if I may?"

"I'm called Many Clouds, sir, an Arapaho from Wind River country."

"Wind River. In Wyoming, isn't it? Beautiful country from what I understand."

"Yes, sir."

"Have to get there some day."

"You would be welcome, sir," she said. She was not certain of the truth of her words, but her instincts told her Weitzel could be trusted. She felt an odd kinship with this man and decided to risk even more than she already had. "Perhaps you'd like to meet my children—stepchildren, really. Come on out, Maggie and Willy."

The two children came out from behind the bar but did not cross the room. They looked wary, like prairie dogs ready to pop back in their burrows.

"Nice to meet you," Weitzel said. Many Clouds had been afraid he would object to having children in such an adult atmosphere, but he seemed sincere about his greeting. At the same time, he obviously wanted to get to the business at hand. "Now, young lady, you had some question about the assay reports?"

"Yes." She breathed deeply. If she failed at this part, everything would be spoiled. "I wonder if we are looking at the same report." She reached into her satchel, retrieved a paper, lifted it high, and set in front of Weitzel. "Perhaps you would like to examine this, Mr. Weitzel." She laid the paper on the table in front of him. "I'm not a mining engineer, but it seems to tell a different story."

Ninety-Three

Russell reached for the document Many Clouds had handed Weitzel. "There's no need to bother yourself with this, sir. It's doubtless no more than a fraudulent distraction."

Weitzel held up his hand to stop Russell. "Give us a few minutes, if you will. I'd like to confer with Mr. Ripley here."

Russell's lips froze into a straight line. "I certainly have no objection to a bona fide engineer delving into things. I simply thought to save some time after your long journey."

An aura of suspense hung over the room. The kitchen crew was distributing mugs as well as pitchers of lemonade and water. Aromas of ham, beef, and coffee floated in from the kitchen as the crew prepared the hotel's noon meal. As individuals poured out their beverages, Many Clouds inched forward so they could assess the responses of Weitzel and Ripley. From her new vantage point, she could see that Ripley carried a sidearm heretofore concealed by his frock coat. As far as she could see, Weitzel was unarmed. However, it was Ripley's gun that concerned her. It was a pearl-handled six-shooter that appeared identical to the one she had torn from the holster of the paisley-scarfed man in front of her house when he'd intruded on their family creekside picnic. It took no more than another surreptitious glance or two to confirm that Ripley was the man in the wagon. The beard was gone. His hair was cut shorter, and he wore a plain string tie rather than the paisley cravat that had first drawn the eye, but he had the same pointed chin and high brow. The same man. Apparently, her trust in Weitzel had been misplaced.

She suddenly felt as if she was stumbling through an unfamiliar house in the dark. She turned her attention back to the papers they'd been discussing.

The report that Many Clouds had purloined showed evidence of coal deposits but nowhere near in the quantity that Russell claimed. What the man's game was, she didn't know, but she suspected it would be revealed shortly. Ripley and Weitzel talked in low voices. It was impossible to understand the words, but they obviously spoke with concern, puzzlement, and even anger. Finally, Weitzel called to Russell.

"Jacob, there's a significant contradiction between these two reports. Can you explain?" Weitzel pushed Many Clouds' document forward, side-by-side with another assay report. Russell made a show of examining both reports closely. Then he chuckled.

"This is a shameless attempt to bamboozle Western Explorations and all the citizens of this valley, Mr. Weitzel. We had a burglary at one of our offices at city hall recently, and this preliminary assay report was one of the missing articles. I won't accuse Miss Clouds of the crime, but she's somehow, doubtless innocently, come into possession of one of the main items."

"Well, Jacob, that will be something for local law enforcement, such as it is at the moment, to straighten out. In the meantime, we have the significant discrepancies between the two documents to explain."

"Your confusion is perfectly understandable, sir. But, as I said, the report that Miss—should I say 'Clouds'?—has presented is preliminary. The report we presented today is the true and complete one. As you and Mr. Ripley can see, the updated version shows vastly more coal than the earlier one."

For a moment time seemed to stand still. Ripley pursed his lips, looking doubtful, she thought. Or was he trying to figure a way out of a guilty trap? How she wished Andy was here. She would have to present the next part of their argument without him and his evidence. She thought of demanding that he be released so they could present a united front, but feared it would start another argument that might erode, even wash away, the fragile good will she had built with Weitzel. Nothing to do but forge ahead on her own.

"There's something else, sir. Andy. Andrew Maxwell, one of the people Hale Gentry arrested, has the proof. His mother, Carolyn, was arrested along with him. They are the largest landholders in the area."

"I've heard the name," Weitzel said. "Go on."

"As I said, Andy has the papers if Gentry hasn't already destroyed them, but I can try to describe what he discovered. Mr. Russell and others have told you that they can offer Western Explorations enough acreage to do whatever mining you want. Is that not correct?"

"Yes, of course."

"Andy explained that in order to mine for the coal you'd need mineral rights on whatever land you used. Is that correct?"

"Yes, yes," Weitzel said.

The man was getting impatient. The mayor was twisting in his seat. Maybe her explanations were too simple-minded.

"I'm sorry I'm not making this very clear. Andy would do much better. But what's most important, I think, is that Mr. Russell has spent money to help people acquire deeds to many small farms whose owners were aging or simply tired of farm work. The farms are located between here and Sawtooth Wells and beyond. His name doesn't appear on the paperwork, but he owns the companies that bought the land.

"Andy suspects that he did not use his own money, but somehow gained access to Western Explorations' funds. With this acreage, it appears that you will have most of the land you need. However, there are two things wrong. The deeds are in the name of individuals who have no interest in the land for themselves. Mr. Russell's companies loaned them the money, and if they default on the loan, which they are sure to do because they are poor people, the land reverts to the lender. To Mr. Russell, that is. Second, the deeds grant no mineral rights. Those would have to be negotiated separately between Western Explorations and Mr. Russell's companies once the land reverts to them when the loans go unpaid."

"You're suggesting quite a twisted arrangement here, young lady. If I understand it correctly, these so-called landowners would walk away with the loan money, almost like a bribe, leaving Jacob Russell holding the deed so he could resell the property to us, extorting a higher price that included the mineral rights? And that he used our own money to do it?"

During her whole discourse, Many Clouds had been sidling closer to Weitzel and Ripley. "I'm not an expert, sir, but if I understand what Andy told me, that's correct."

Mayor James George rose. His tone was cold, his face taut with irritation. "Gentlemen. Lady. This conversation has gone beyond my area of expertise or influence. If you need me, you can find me in my office in City Hall." He tossed down half a glass of lemonade and strode out the door. Russell started to say something to him but turned to Weitzel instead.

"Mr. Weitzel," he said, his voice syrupy and his face contorted into an indulgent smile. "Can we go somewhere more businesslike? This Many Clouds person is no doubt doing the best she can, but she's only muddied the waters. Given a few minutes without interruption, I can make everything clear."

Weitzel got to his feet. "Jacob, with all due respect, unless you can disprove what she says, this entire project seems riddled with misrepresentation."

"Well, I'm not a lawyer. I'm presenting to you the situation as I believed it. I assume our attorneys in Sacramento can clarify anything that is necessary. Why don't we have some lunch and go out and scout the land so you can verify with your own two eyes what riches we're sitting on?"

"You know what I'd prefer?" Weitzel said. "I want to talk to this Andrew Maxwell face-to-face."

"Not advisable, sir. He and his mother are a dangerous pair. Murderers. Of lawmen, no less."

"A regular Jesse James and Belle Star, are they? We'll visit them in jail, then. No risk in that, is there?"

For a few seconds, Russell looked like a fish gasping on a riverbank, his jaws working but no sound emerging. Finally he found his voice. "If you insist, we can arrange a meeting, but the jail is rather small to accommodate us all. Miles, would you run to the jail and ask Sheriff Gentry to bring the prisoners here? Cuffed, chained, and under guard, of course."

Weitzel added an additional condition. "Mr. Ripley will accompany your man Miles, Jacob. I'd like to have any documents that might verify Many Clouds' accusations."

Many Clouds felt hopeful for the first time since their struggle and arrest. Andy and Carolyn would be out of jail. Of course, out of jail did not mean out of trouble. Chains would be a problem but easier to deal with than a jail cell.

All eyes followed Miles, Russell, and Ripley as they left. All eyes, that is, except Many Clouds,' whose attention turned to Maggie and Willy. They were poised to leap over the bar and join the fray, but Many Clouds motioned them to duck out of sight. First, she didn't want them in danger. Second, though, if worse came to worst, their ingenuity might be important—even essential—in whatever action followed.

Ninety-Four

No one sat down while they waited. The atmosphere was still and tense. Many Clouds stole glances at Russell, who seemed absorbed in examining a mounted deer head which had once sported its dozen-pointed antlers in the wild but now was mere decoration in a hotel. The mood was broken by the sudden entrance of the blonde woman, all ruffles and curls, she and the children had seen with Russell a couple of days earlier.

"Jakey—er—Mr. Russell," she exclaimed. "Here you are."

"Marilyn. Not here," Russell was clearly off balance, nearly sputtering.

"I know you said that, but this can't wait. Can we go in private some place?"

Russell steered her behind the bar where Many Clouds and the children had lately concealed themselves. Everyone watched the couple as they carried on an intense and furtive conversation. Finally, the clank and jingle of irons heralded the approach of the prisoners. They all heard what Russell said next, even though he tried to keep his voice low.

"Out through the kitchen, Marilyn. This is nothing we can't handle."

"Why can't I stay? I'm always on the outside with you."

"Soon. Soon. Now go." He gave her a firm push to propel her toward the kitchen, but she looked over her shoulder as she moved out of the room. Many Clouds would have loved to pursue her and find out what was going on, but Andy and Carolyn entered, their chains clanking and jingling, as she exited.

Their entrance took even Weitzel aback. His eyes widened and he stepped aside to make way for the entourage. Many Clouds gasped and ran toward Andy, the left side of his face was the color of a ripe plum. One of Gentry's thugs blocked her path and shoved her backwards. She stumbled but managed to avoid falling.

"There will be no physical contact with the prisoners," Gentry announced. He directed the so-called deputies to seat Carolyn and Andy at the table and to chain them to the chairs. One deputy stood behind each of them. Gentry took a seat at the table and motioned to Weitzel.

"We're ready for your interrogation, Mr. Weitzel."

"I'm not interrogating anyone. I simply want a clarifying conversation. By the way, are those manacles necessary?"

"In the interests of justice and the safety of the community, I'm afraid so," Gentry said.

Weitzel looked doubtful but went directly to the subject at hand. "First of all, Mr. Maxwell, Miss Clouds told us of certain deeds you'd discovered. Mr. Ripley, our mining engineer, and I would like to take a look at them."

Ripley said, "There appears to be a problem, sir. Sheriff Gentry tells me the deeds were somehow destroyed in the fracas of the arrest."

"No 'somehow' about it," Carolyn said. "These apes tore them to bits at Gentry's orders. We saw them do it."

Weitzel's lips tightened. He leaned on the table his eyes focused on Andy. "They are public documents, and I imagine the Placer County office can make copies for us. Many Clouds has accused Mr. Russell of a rather outlandish scheme to acquire land so he can make money selling us the mineral rights we need to mine. Does that sound accurate?"

Russell objected. "This is useless sir. Anything out of this man's mouth is bound to be a lie."

Weitzel raised a silencing hand in Russell's direction without taking his eyes off Andy.

"That encapsulates it, sir, yes," Andy said. "Of course, none of the deeds is in Russell's name. The small landowners are all proxies, but the loans they used to buy the property—those all came from Russell, if only indirectly. One doesn't have to investigate very far to find that he's on the board of directors of every bank and company that arranged the loans. I do have a question for you, though."

"You're not the one to be asking questions, Maxwell," Russell said.

"Please, Jacob. Go ahead, Andy," Weitzel said.

"Did you grant Jacob Russell access to the funds deposited in Sturges's bank?"

"Why, yes. He was the only man authorized to use those funds for the purpose of carrying out the exploration and analysis of resources necessary for the project. Until Ripley arrived last week, that is. He took over from Jacob as the Western Explorations agent at that time."

"Mr. Weitzel," Russell said, "this is ridiculous. Now he's suggesting that Mr. Ripley and I colluded in this fictional swindle. Why would I go through such a fancy charade? If I wanted the land, I could afford to buy it outright."

Carolyn spoke up now. "Andy and I had that same question, and we'd like to thank Mr. Gentry for our respite in jail. It gave us time to consider. Here's what we think. First of all, if you look hard, you'll find that Russell's cash on hand isn't as abundant as he pretends."

Andy went on. "I checked into Russell's finances while I was exploring the deeds I talked about. He owns very little real estate either here or in Sacramento. That which he does own is heavily mortgaged. So, no, he could not afford to pay cash for big lots of land. He had to use Western Exploration money, or money from somewhere, because he had little cash of his own."

"This is preposterous. Pure slander if you'll—"

Carolyn continued as if he hadn't spoken. "His strategy, Mr. Weitzel, is much bigger than coal, at least bigger than the meager deposits you'll find around here. When my father established the Circle M, he built it on the springs at the base of Sawtooth Peaks, springs that are the source of all the water in the valley. He didn't seek to own the whole valley. He wanted neighbors and a community so the whole area could prosper. However, he did want to make sure its resources were protected. Thus, he placed options on certain key tracts that give the Maxwells first right of refusal on any purchase."

"Key tracts?" Weitzel asked. "What does that mean?"

Many Clouds had a sudden inspiration and spoke up for the first time in some minutes. "Water," she said.

Everyone turned toward her. "Now I'm even more confused," Weitzel said.

Many Clouds was for a moment stymied by the sudden attention but saw that this was no time to hold back. "The key tracts would have Granite Creek or other water flowing through them."

"Many Clouds is right on target," Andy said. "Whoever owns water rights to Sawtooth Valley can charge whatever they want for the water and, to use an expression appropriate to the moment, virtually handcuff every other landowner in the valley. It's no less than a scheme to own essential land in Sawtooth Valley and to control the rest by controlling the water."

Weitzel spoke next. "Given these accusations, I'm inclined to scrap this whole project. What do you think, Ripley?" He gave Ripley a sidelong glance as he spoke. There was suspicion there now, Many Clouds was glad to note.

"Understandable conclusion, sir. However, we've already poured in significant resources, and there's not another train out until tomorrow afternoon. I ought to have a firm answer about this situation for you by then."

"Twenty-four hours? Fair enough. Jacob, I guess I'm finally ready to take you up on that lunch and guided tour."

Russell's smile was not forced but relieved. "I think I can guarantee that your mind will be at ease by the time we finish."

The deputies were unlocking the part of Carolyn and Andy's restraints that held them to the table. Many Clouds refused to hold back any longer but rushed toward Andy with her arms wide, ready to embrace him. Just before she reached him however, the deputy turned and put out a stiff arm. She slapped it away and dodged her way to her fiancé. She gently kissed his bruised cheek and whispered, "Sent a telegram to Pinkerton about Remy."

"Brave woman. Believe me about carrying money now?"

Their exchange was barely finished before the deputy yanked her away and stepped between them.

"I believe you about everything, Andy." She turned toward Carolyn, amazed to see a broad smile on her future mother-in-law's face. "Why so cheerful, Carolyn?"

"Because," she said, "this is the end of Hale Gentry. You're finished, Gentry, and I've never been more happy about anything in my life."

"Get them out of here," Gentry said.

The rattling of chains and dragging feet were the last sounds as the jailhouse procession exited the building. It looked a dismal sight, but Many Clouds wore a smile as broad as Carolyn's as she watched the doors swing shut behind them. The kitchen staff entered with platters and bowls of soup and sandwiches. Whatever the conflicts, the Maxwells would be well-fed.

Ninety-Five

Much as she wanted to track down Russell's Marilyn, Many Clouds knew the jailbreak came first. She had no trouble deciding where she'd start the fire she planned as a distraction. Maggie showed the way to the building where Gentry and his crew had held her prisoner. Gentry had an office on the top floor, so he'd care enough about the place to get personally involved in its defense.

They returned to the grove where the wagon stood and waited for twilight. Gentry, as the new sheriff, had stayed in town and left others to run his saloon, so his car was parked in front of the jail. He'd sent both his fake deputies to supper. It was a sign of his arrogance to leave himself as the only guard on his prisoners. The car carried a spare can of gasoline strapped to the running board. She'd use that to set the fire. Serve him right.

She and the children had a jolly, if scary, time gathering kindling and placing it just so. They cleared an area to help prevent the blaze from spreading. They had no wish to burn down the town, only to draw everyone's attention elsewhere while they freed Carolyn and Andy. It seemed a shame to destroy the tangy smell of pine twigs and needles with the poisonous odor of gas, but there was no help for it. Once all was prepared, it took only one match set the blaze, then they all ran to the back of the jail to wait for the alarm. It didn't take long before Gentry spotted the smoke and dashed out the jail door, yelling in an attempt to recruit a team to fight it.

"Keys," Many Clouds called as she and Maggie and Willy slipped into the jail when Gentry exited. The place smelled of granite and red clay, a cold, dead odor.

"Peg on the wall," Carolyn answered.

Carolyn and Andy were the only prisoners in the small, four-celled jail. Willy begged the fun of opening the cell doors.

"We have horses close by," Many Clouds said as they gathered in preparation for their exit. "If the kids ride double we can make it to the house before they even know we're gone."

"Ha," Carolyn said. "We're not going to the house. We're not running anywhere. We're going back to reclaim our rooms at the Cary House."

A deep voice sounded from the jail doorway. "I don't think so. I think you're going back in those cells, and the squaw and half-breeds with you." The limping deputy, Sizemore, was waving a revolver the size of an Arapaho war club at them.

Everyone froze. Andy stepped forward, putting himself between the deputy and his family. He held out his hand. "Give me the keys, Willy," he said, never taking his eyes off the deputy. Willy was hesitant to move, but he stepped over and handed Andy the big ring that held a collection of skeleton keys. Andy held the keys out toward Sizemore.

"Put 'em on the floor, then push 'em over with your foot."

The deputy was a bit smarter than Andy anticipated. He'd been planning to toss the keys high over the man's head, then attack when he shifted his attention. Forced to come up with a variation, he made as if to obey the deputy's order, then caught the ring with a toe and flipped them past him toward the door.

"Nice try, Maxwell, but it ain't gonna work." He backed toward the keys, keeping his eyes and pistol leveled toward at the group.

Many Clouds had had enough of the game. Gambling that Sizemore didn't have the authority or the guts to shoot anyone, she strode past him and toward the door. Her move galvanized the whole group. They swarmed past the lawman, some to his left, some to his right. He waggled his gun one way, then the other, clearly confused. He never fired a shot as they stepped through the door.

"Nice going, Many Clouds," Carolyn said.

Many Clouds hooked her arm through Carolyn's. "Onward to Cary House," she said.

Ninety-Six

Gentry chose not to disturb their overnight at the hotel. That worried them into wondering what he might be up to. But when morning arrived, they decided that pancakes and bacon came first. Ling Chu emerged from wherever he'd been staying. They all exchanged greetings, then entered the dining room together. They'd barely started on their meal, though, when Jacob Russell, Miles, and Weitzel marched in. Neither Gentry nor his deputies were with them. Nor was Ripley. Puzzling.

"Mind if we join you?" Russell announced rather than asked. Miles commenced to arrange chairs and another table to accommodate themselves. He ordered more food as well.

Once settled, Russell smiled and scanned the group. "Quite a daring escapade you all pulled off yesterday. Admirable, really."

Andy nodded. Carolyn and Many Clouds traded glances. None of them spoke. A waitress appeared bearing a pot of hot coffee and mugs. Another laid two platters on the table. One of bacon, another of pancakes.

"Scrambled eggs coming up," the lady with the coffee said.

"Thank you, Minerva," Russell said with a smile.

When they had returned to the kitchen, he leaned forward. "We had an interesting tour of the countryside yesterday afternoon, didn't we Howard?" He didn't wait for an answer. "Our conversation raised some questions that need documental verification, which is why Mr. Ripley is not here. He's on his way to Auburn to collect the paperwork that was missing. Once we have that, we're sure there will be no objection to proceeding with Western Exploration's project, will there, Howard?"

"We shall see, Jacob. Many Clouds, can you pass me that bottle of syrup, please?"

Many Clouds did so, and she delivered it with a question. "Mr. Weitzel, you said Mr. Ripley arrived here from New York only yesterday?"

Weitzel had been about to pour syrup on his pancakes, but stopped, the bottle suspended. "That's correct, though he did leave New York a week or so earlier in order to take care of some family business in St. Louis."

"So you didn't direct him to adopt a disguise and to try intimidating our family into selling our land?"

Weitzel resumed pouring his syrup. "I had you figured for a level-headed young woman, Many Clouds, but you're raising doubts about that. Despite yesterday's assertions to the contrary, Western Explorations had no presence in this area until day before yesterday."

"But you did have a financial presence, did you not?" Andy said.

"Why, yes, we wired funds to the local bank here. Help me out with the name of the owner, Jacob."

"Meyer Sturges."

"Yes. We made the funds in Sturges's bank available to Jacob, here, to manage the tasks of exploration and assay to determine if there were minerals enough to justify a full operation."

"However, Mr. Weitzel," Andy said, "Many Clouds and I can testify that Ripley was here well before yesterday. As could my lawyer, Harry Barker, were he not murdered. We didn't recognize Ripley at first when he came in with you, but it's him all right. He grew a Van Dyke beard, sported a paisley cravat, and parked his wagon across from our house for long periods of time. He tried to serve me with what he said was some kind of warrant, and he threatened Many Clouds and the children. He and Russell were together engaged in the scheme we described yesterday, using your name and money, offering landowners inflated prices in order to secure their holdings."

Weitzel shook his head and laid down the fork he was using to bring a bite of pancake to his mouth. Beside him, Russell was starting on a second helping, nibbling on a piece of bacon with one hand while he speared a forkful of pancakes with the other.

"It would be strange if both Andy and I made the same mistake about his identity," Many Clouds said.

Without seeming to cross-examine him, Many Clouds didn't know how to point out that Ripley's earlier departure from New York left plenty of time for Ripley to play the paisley cravat part and still meet Weitzel in Sacramento.

Carolyn stood suddenly. "Well, well, look who's here."

Gentry and his deputies had entered the room. All the Maxwells stood to greet them. "Going to try taking us back to the hoosegow again, Hale?" Carolyn said. "I wouldn't recommend it."

"Your time will come," Gentry answered. "There will be no repeat of yesterday's travesty." He sent forth what he meant to be a menacing look directed at each of the escapees. Neither of them cowered under his gaze. In fact, Carolyn stuck out her tongue as if it were a schoolyard encounter.

Gentry shook his head. "Very mature, Carolyn."

"Mali Illi quji malum agit," she said.

Gentry flinched for a second at the Latin, which he certainly didn't understand. He did, however, understand the sarcasm in Carolyn's tone. "You can be as flippant as you like, but I am now the law in this jurisdiction.

"To translate Mother's Latin for you, Gentry, it's 'Evil comes to him who evil does.'"

Gentry ignored the jibe. "Getting back to the subject at hand, Maxwell. You and your minions have three murders to answer for. Sheriff Hilts, Marshal Halstad, and Remington Dillinger. Justice will be served, and Placerville will shortly live up to its previous name."

"Four," Andy said

"What?"

"Four murders. Maybe five unless you've solved the killing of our lawyer, Harry Barker, without our hearing of it."

"How about a sixth?" Many Clouds said. "No one knows what happened to deputy Heimholz."

"But we're not the ones who will answer for any of them," Andy said.

Gentry shot a poisonous look at Andy, then cast the same look on all the Maxwell contingent as he continued. "Just be aware that every move you make will be under scrutiny, and none of you is to leave Placerville—or Hangtown—without my express written permission."

He turned, motioned to his sidekicks, and headed for the door. They didn't get far. As they crossed the lobby, three stern men in dark business suits, high collars, and string ties entered from the street. They wore identical bowler hats, which they didn't bother to remove when they entered. They were all well over six-feet tall with shoulders wide enough to invite speculation they'd have to turn sideways to get through a normal doorway.

They backed Gentry and his deputies into the dining room as they proceeded. The tallest of them, a man with a jagged scar across his right cheek, raised high a small leather wallet which held a gold badge.

"I'm deputy U.S. Marshal Martin Finlayson. Marshal Silas Morgenstern will be stationed at the door to the lobby, Marshal Clement Nestor will guard the door to the kitchen." Each of the men displayed a badge of his own as Finlayson called his name. "Those who are seated will remain so. Those who are standing will be seated at the table to my right."

Instead of following orders, Gentry stepped toward Finlayson, his hand outstretched. "Greetings. I'm Sheriff Hale Gentry, marshal. Very pleased to make your acquaintance."

Finlayson did not accept the offer of a handshake.

"Was I unclear about my orders, sir?" the marshal asked.

"Well, no, but I thought that as sheriff, I—"

"Then you will please take a seat as I directed."

Finlayson's air of authority stifled not only Gentry but quieted everyone else in the room as well. He pulled a piece of yellow onionskin paper from an inside coat pocket. He stepped to Many Clouds. "Did you telegraph this unsigned message?"

Many Clouds looked at the telegram she'd directed to the Pinkerton Agency. Why did the marshal have it? She hesitated a moment. She was apprehensive, tried to see if she was falling into some trap, but in the end saw no reason to deny it.

"Yes, sir. But how did you know it was me?"

"The clerk said an Indian woman sent it. You're the only one such I see here. And the 'Remy' in the message refers to Deputy Marshal Remington Dillinger?"

"Remy was a marshal?" she asked.

"That's right," Finlayson confirmed.

Andy said, "He told us he was a Pinkerton agent."

"That was his cover story in case his identity as an undercover investigator was questioned too heavily. He said you all were too smart and persistent to allow him to hide behind a false identity for long. It appears he was right."

Jacob Russell scooped the last piece of his pancake into his mouth and wiped a dribble of syrup from his chin. He scanned the room. Many Clouds surmised that he was pretending to look for more breakfast while he plotted a way out.

"In any case," Finlayson continued, "you deserve our profound thanks. We had been communicating with Remy through the Pinkerton people in Sacramento, and they notified us the second they received this message. We'd lost contact with him, you see, and without this we'd have wasted valuable time and energy trying to find out what happened to him."

At that point, a fourth man, dressed the same as the other marshals, entered the room. "Train is on time, sir. Should be here in fifteen minutes."

"Excellent, Admunsen. Have the agents report here. Tell them they'll have, let's see," he pointed to Russell, Gentry, and his deputies, "one, two, three, four prisoners."

Gentry and Russell leaped to their feet.

"Prisoners? Us?" Russell yelled. "Those are the criminals." He pointed at the Maxwells.

"I don't think so," Finlayson said. "We had a busy evening interviewing the good citizens of Sawtooth Wells, which was where Remington told us he was headed before he quit communicating. The eyewitnesses were in remarkable agreement about what went on in the streets of that little town. Including who administered the coup de grace to poor Remington, who, I remind you—he jabbed a forefinger in Gentry's direction—was a federal officer."

"If by witnesses you're talking about that black scoundrel uncle of Andrew Maxwell's, his testimony will be inadmissible."

"I saw and heard the same thing Cooper did," Andy said.

"You? You're half-black yourself."

"But I'm not," Carolyn said.

"You weren't anywhere near us," Gentry said.

"Close enough," she smiled. "Amazing how sound carries after sundown."

At that point, Marilyn Barker made one of her dramatic entrances. In this case, however, her curls hung straight, covered only by a dust cap, and her dress was a sack-like garment of plain gingham.

"Jakey, you can't just keep disappearing. How do you expect me to get through all this if I never know where you are?"

She ran to Russell's side, looked up to him. He nodded toward the marshals. She looked astonished and fearful as she beheld her audience, then pressed closer to Russell.

Andy said, "Marshal Finlayson, allow me to introduce Mrs. Marilyn Barker, wife of that murdered barrister I mentioned earlier. His death is tied into all this. I suggest that when you interview these people, you ask them and Mrs. Barker about that killing. As Mr. Barker's widow, she inherits land and funds that would belong to Russell should they marry. Many Clouds and I have reason to believe that they killed him to claim it all. And one more thing, if I may. The body of the Sawtooth Wells Marshal is resting at our ranch, The Circle M. We had planned to bury him in our family plot. However, we understand that, given the legal complications, that may not be possible.

"In any case, we'd be grateful if you would take our request under advisement."

"I'm not accustomed to taking investigation orders from civilians, but in this case, I'll make an exception," Finlayson said. He signaled to his men to secure the prisoners. Never had the Maxwells—particularly Carolyn—beheld a more welcome sight than that of Hale Gentry in manacles. There were ways to go—evidence, testimony, trials. It all could last for months. But there was no doubt that Gentry's short career as a lawman was over.

As if to herald a brighter future, a steam whistle sounded, followed by the chug and rattle of the morning westbound train as it pulled into the Placerville station.

Many Clouds found herself in Andy's embrace with no memory of how she'd arrived there, nor did she care. She clung to him as tightly as she could. She thought for a moment of the child, decided the baby just better get used to being hugged within an inch of its life, and squeezed tighter still.

"Enough of this," Carolyn called. "We have a wedding to plan for, and, Andy, you have a concluding article to write for *The Elevator*. Your readers will be waiting."

Andy, without loosening his grip on Many Clouds, said in an annoyed near-whine, "Mother, would you please—"

Many Clouds put a finger to his lips. "A wedding, yes, and don't forget the Thanksgiving."

He smiled at her then kissed her. Right there in public. What a change, Many Clouds thought. These heretofore embarrassing public kisses were becoming commonplace. Altogether, a very good thing. A very good thing indeed.

ABOUT THE AUTHOR

Carl Brush has been writing since he could write, which is quite a long time now. *Scandal in Sawtooth Valley* is the third of a trilogy of historical thrillers set in and around Sawtooth Valley. The others— *The Maxwell Vendetta* and *The Second Vendetta*—provide not only tale-telling excitement but acquaint readers with the characters and events that precede the story of *Scandal in Sawtooth Valley*.

Another trilogy—*Bonita* and *Bonita's Quest* ('*Nita*, the third volume, is in the works)—takes us back to pre-gold rush San Francisco where a young girl discovers a family betrayal and sets out to solve the mystery of her heritage.

Finally, Carl jumped from California to Texas to co-author with the late Bob Stewart *The Yellow Rose, A Novel of the Texas Revolution*, in which we follow the 1836 exploits and (supposed) romance of Sam Houston and the original Yellow Rose of Texas, one Emily West, in their fight to establish the Republic of Texas, which eventually become the 28th state of the union.

You can find Carl living in Oakland, California, near where most of his stories are set. He enjoys the blessings of nearby children and grandchildren.

Historical Figures In
Swindle In Sawtooth Valley

Ambrose Bierce—A noted author who wrote for the *San Francisco Examiner*. He wrote a column called "The Tattler," and penned the classic *The Devil's Dictionary*.

Delilah Beasley—A prominent journalist and writer for a number of bay area newspapers as well as the author of classic works on Negro history, especially *Slavery in California* (1918) and *Negro Trail-Blazers of California (1919)*. She was a widely-respected fighter for Negro rights who had her works published even by established figures like William Knowland. I found no mention of a relationship between her and Joseph Francis (see below), but it would have been odd if they hadn't known one another.

Joseph Francis—Publisher of *The Elevator*, one of several minority publications of the late-nineteenth and early twentieth century. *The Elevator* did not last until the year that the events of *Swindle in Sawtooth Valley* transpire (1914), but as far as I know, Francis was still around.

www.ingramcontent.com/pod-product-compliance
Lightning Source LLC
LaVergne TN
LVHW040135080526
838202LV00042B/2915